SALACIOUS SOCIALITES

A COZY CORGI MYSTERY

MILDRED ABBOTT

SALACIOUS SOCIALITES

Mildred Abbott

for

Alastair & Winifred
and
Winston & Phineas

Cover, Logo, Chapter Heading Designer: A.J. Corza - SeeingStatic.com

Main Editor: Desi Chapman

2nd Editors: Ann Attwood & Anita Ford

3rd Editor: Corrine Harris

Recipe provided by: Cloudy Kitchen - CloudyKitchen.com

Visit Mildred's Webpage: MildredAbbott.com

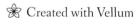 Created with Vellum

Watson paced from the fireplace, trudged across the living room, sniffed at the base of the front door, and then exhaled in a mighty puff of annoyance. After a full-body shake, sending loose hairs scattering like a snowstorm, he headed back my way. Pausing just long enough to look over his shoulder through the window into the darkness of early evening, he let out a whine, then refocused on me and finished his path to where I sat in the overstuffed armchair. He allowed the briefest of scratches between his pointy ears before ducking his head and returning to curl up with his stuffed animals on the hearth.

"What has gotten into you this evening?" I studied my little grump in concern, not that I expected a reply.

Indeed, he didn't even look my way, just continued to stare through the window before letting out a heavy sigh and closing his eyes.

That had been at least the third rotation of his little path, and it was becoming unnerving. A tap on my cellphone resting next to the mug of hot chocolate on the side table revealed it to be barely after seven. "Leo's only been gone for half an hour. The bird club just started." I leaned forward, infusing promise into my tone, not that Watson paid any attention. "He'll be back in a couple of hours with Mexican food."

Nope, not a grunt, glance, or grimace.

I was tempted to say his favorite word—*treat*—but then I would have to get up and retrieve one, and I'd just gotten settled. At least, I would have if my *corgi* would settle down. His nervous energy was seeping into me. Just the weather, I imagined, or Leo being out in it.

Though March was historically the snowiest month in the Colorado mountains, we'd gotten a total of two and half inches of snow the entire time. April, however, had more than made up for it. Barely a week in, and it was snowstorm after snowstorm. The one scheduled to begin in the middle of the night was slated to be the biggest of the year, possibly growing into full-blown-blizzard status, but we were prepared with plenty of food, firewood, candles, and books. We could be snowed in for a week, and it would almost be like a secluded mountain vacation others paid a fortune for.

Still... Watson wasn't typically the kind to get nervous about weather, not even thunderstorms. Maybe this one was going to be different. Another glance out the window suggested he might be right. Technically, sunset was still about twenty minutes away, but it was as dark as midnight, the gathering storm clouds blocking out the moon and stars.

That time, I did more than tap the screen and picked up the phone, getting ready to call Leo, suggest he come home. I went so far as to unlock it, open my speed-dial favorites, and hover my thumb over his name before letting out an annoyed breath that sounded very much like Watson. I was being ridiculous—he was the park ranger, not me, and even if the blizzard did start several hours ahead of schedule, if Leo thought it was necessary, he'd end the meeting of the Feathered Friends Brigade early and tell everyone to head home.

I traded my phone for my hot chocolate, cupping it between my hands and letting the warmth soothe, and then stared at Watson, who now seemed captured by sleep, finally. We were both being ridiculous. Leo wasn't one to take silly risks; I could trust him on that. Plus, I didn't want to interrupt.

After his promotion and job switches with the forest service, occasionally leading Myrtle's bird club was one of the few throwbacks to some of the favorite parts of being a regular park ranger. Though the howling winds suggested otherwise, hummingbirds started to return to Estes Park in April, and the ornithological group had decided to make the jewel-toned flyers their theme for the next three months, starting with Leo's lecture this evening. He was scheduled to take them on a hummingbird "hunt" at the first of their May meetings.

By the crackling fire, Watson sighed in his dreaming, shifting slightly on the stone hearth, then settled once more. Whatever had gotten into him seemed to have passed.

I eased at that realization, glanced toward the dark window, which remained unchanged, and then picked up my new Stephen King novel from the arm of the chair. Things had been stressful the last few months, with ghosts from my past moving into town, and the reminder my dirty ex-cop ex-boyfriend—not that he'd ever had that official status—had decided to make my life his little plaything. As a result, I'd retreated to my literary comfort zone—cozy mysteries, romances, even *Chicken Soup for the Soul* during one particularly stressful evening. But as March died, making way for April showers—or blizzards, it seemed—I recaptured a state of equilibrium, finally. It was safe to wade back into traditional and darker mysteries. I figured my sudden craving for a King novel suggested I felt safe enough to experience literary stress instead of the real thing.

I cracked open the novel, that fresh new-book smell offering an equal amount of pleasure as the hot chocolate. Every part of reading was delicious, even the soft sound of skin against paper as I turned the pages. I read the dedication, turned a couple more pages, but didn't even make it through the first sentence before my love of books distracted me from my *current* book.

My love of books.

I closed the cover, staring at it, then looked over at the collection of novels lining my bookcase. At least eighty percent of those were mysteries. Though I loved every genre, mysteries, far and away, were my version of Watson's *treats*.

My love of mysteries.

That was it. The light that turned on in my brain was bright enough to suggest the sun had decided to arrive unexpectedly and pour through the window. For months now, I'd been feeling the urge to branch out, to add another layer to my life other than simply owning a bookshop and solving the occasional, or frequent, murder in town. I'd been trying to come up with a way to combine my past, blending my years as a professor and time as a mystery publisher into a new adventure, classes helping writers wade through getting a book contract, or diving into the self-publishing world. Maybe becoming an editor or starting a review blog. The possibilities were endless, but none of them felt right—they each seemed more like a *job*, something that would grow wearisome after the new wore off. My love of books, however, would never grow wearisome, never wear off.

The idea arrived, completely realized within that mental spotlight, presented almost like a gift with a beautiful mustard-colored bow. All I had to do was tug at the ribbon and it sprang forth, fully formed.

Mystery conferences.

A gathering of mystery-novel lovers, a celebration of the genre—a chance for readers and authors to meet. And then the next layer was revealed, workshops for aspiring mystery authors, working through storytelling, editing, publishing, everything. It wasn't a new concept, it wasn't even something that didn't already exist; however, the conferences I'd attended, while enjoyable, had either been too serious or too unfocused. I wanted the perfect blend, a celebration *and* furthering of the art.

Excitement blossomed and peace settled simultaneously. Yes. This was something I wanted to do, the icing on top of an already spectacular cake. Almost before I realized, I stood and found myself in front of the bookcase, staring at the beloved covers, already thinking of different classes, workshops, and themes around different authors, tropes, and mystery traditions.

Watson whimpered in sleep once more, pulling my attention, if not my focus, toward him. Not sleep, I realized, as he lifted his head and looked at the door once more.

"Soon, buddy." Still speaking to him, I turned back to the rows of mystery novels. "Daddy will be back soon with dinner." Like I was an insatiably hungry corgi, my stomach rumbled at the thought. Hot Mexican food would be perfect on such a cold night, and with Leo getting it to-go, there was no chance Marcus Gonzalez was going to take the opportunity for an unwelcomed photoshoot.

From my periphery, I saw Watson stand. His body stiffened, then lowered. A quiet rumbling growl emanated from his chest.

All thoughts of conferences faded at that sound,

as did the bright, happy spotlight of future plans and possibilities. Everything narrowed back to the black window across the room. A solitary snowflake drifted past, but nothing else was visible. "Watson?"

He didn't look my way. Instead, he headed slowly across the hardwood floor toward the door, that rumbling growl never pausing.

I rushed past the overstuffed armchair at such a speed I knocked the Stephen King book off the arm. Its loud collision to the floor added to Watson's warning, cutting through the previously silent evening. Even in the moment, my brain ridiculously scoffed at the notion of reading a horror novel—what in the world had I been thinking? But that concern was shoved aside as I raced past Watson to the entry table and pulled open the drawer.

Being a detective's daughter, I knew the proper care and protocol with firearms. However, given the state of things, after a brief discussion with Leo, we'd decided to bend every rule there was and not only leave that handgun unsecured, but loaded. We didn't have children in the house, and while Watson occasionally went on an exploring binge, looking for treats that might miraculously appear, he'd never reach that height.

The weight of the gun in my hand didn't offer

much comfort; instead, it only made my sparking nerves light further. We'd hoped we wouldn't ever need it, that sometime in the near future we'd take the bullets out and put it back in its proper, locked place.

I paused a second, considering. I'd overreacted multiple times in the past couple of months, maybe I was doing so again.

Watson reached the door. He didn't snuffle at the base, only took a sentinel position, hackles raised, fangs bared, growl worthy of a Doberman.

Through the sound of the wind, I heard the crunch of tires outside.

I wasn't overreacting. Even so, I left the safety on; however, I kept my thumb on it, ready.

The crunch of tires stopped, the soft purr of an engine remained.

Maybe I *was* overreacting. This wasn't Branson. This wasn't some assassin. They'd hardly drive up to the front door.

Watson's growl didn't waver.

A car door shut. Someone was headed our way.

I tore my gaze from the door to the side table beside the overstuffed armchair. My cell was right where I'd left it, next to the hot chocolate.

I must have stared at it longer than I realized as a

knock sounded on the front door. I jumped, then was suddenly grateful I'd left the safety on.

"Ms. Page?" A male voice I didn't recognize spoke from the other side. "Oh, sorry. Ms. Page-Lopez?" Another knock.

Watson's growl transferred to a bark, then to a snarl.

I took a couple of steps toward the phone, keeping the gun raised, thumb on the safety.

Another knock. "Winifred, I need to speak to you, please." Though I still didn't recognize the voice, I realized it was familiar. Whoever it was whispered something unintelligible, nothing more than a murmur, almost sounded soothing.

Watson's growl paused, and his head cocked, ears twitching. He took a step forward, pressed his nose to the bottom of the door and sniffed. His nub of a tail wagged slowly, twice. Paused. Then again.

Maybe we'd both overreacted.

"Ms. Page-Lopez." The man spoke louder, a refined, almost aristocratic clip to my name. Not aggressive, but... annoyed? That specific combination identified the visitor a heartbeat before he did. "It's Mason, Ms. Beaker's... er... Ms. Apple's butler. I apologize for arriving so late and unannounced."

Mason. Ethel's butler? That was a first, and ominous.

Watson sniffed again. That time his tail wag didn't cease.

Mason *and* Granny Smith, it seemed. *He'd brought the cat?*

"One second." My voice trembled despite my best effort. As I rushed across the room, I lowered the gun and snatched up my cell before returning to the door. "Sorry for my rudeness, but... what do you need, Mason?"

Watson whimpered and looked up at me as if asking what I was waiting for.

Even from the other side of the door, the butler's familiar patience-thin sigh drifted through. "You are ever *you*, are you not?"

"Mason..." There, my trembling had stopped, traded for annoyance. "What can I do for you?" Though my blood still buzzed, I realized my fear had given way to irritation. It was so like Ethel's butler to show up on my doorstep and still somehow insult *me* for having a lack of class.

"Apparently opening the door like a civilized person is too much to ask for." His bored droll was so familiar I didn't even need to see him to picture his thin face slack but lips tight in a disapproving line. "My mistress has asked me to make a delivery."

"A delivery?" I snorted out a laugh, anger sparking. "Oh yes, I'm sure Ethel is sending me gifts."

"It's not a fruit basket, Winifred. It's papers, Ms. Page-Lopez. I'll leave them out here," Mason snarled, my rudeness finally breaking his decorum. There was a soft plop outside the door. "You can get them at your leisure. You're being sued."

Sued? I balked. *Sued?* Ethel was suing me? Fury flared, burning away all nerves. "What in the world for?" Mason didn't answer, not that I gave him a chance. "Because of the choices her son made? What she and Eustace did to cover up—" I flung the door open and gaped down at the thick manila envelope that fell across the threshold.

Mason had been walking away, but he turned before reaching the first step down from the porch. "My mistress was unaware of the things her deceased husband chose to do to protect their son... to protect Mister Jonathan, *which* you already know."

It was my turn to snarl. "Are you kidding me? With how many people died... she's going to sue..." My brain didn't work any better than my tongue, synapses starting to fire, then shooting off a different direction.

"I am simply dropping off the papers." Mason stood there, darkness at his back, the black satin of his lapels glistening from the porch light. All tall, thin, and condemning. In his arms, the large cat hissed at me in her ever-so-pleasant way, fangs flashing.

Watson trotted forward a couple of paces, looking up at her with a whimper, his little tail wagging.

Both the cat and the butler looked down at him. Granny Smith's tail flicked in greeting, and the briefest and smallest of smiles flashed on Mason's lips.

The gangly butler looked so ridiculous in his formal attire, holding the large cat like a baby, out in the night right before a blizzard to do his *mistress's* bidding. Granny Smith's flicking tail pulled my attention away from Mason's face—it was the only part of the ancient cat still fluffy. The change in her was rather shocking in the short time since I'd last seen her, patches of bald skin now greatly outnumbering what little sparse fur remained.

"She has to be cold." I hadn't meant to speak.

He glared at me. "I hadn't *planned* on taking up residence on your porch, Ms. Page-Lopez."

"She's not doing well. Poor thing." Looking at her was painful, though she didn't seem to mind at the moment. I almost thought she was smiling down at Watson.

"No." All irritation left Mason, pain entering his voice. "We..." He cleared his throat. "Dr. Sallee feels it's time. We had an appointment scheduled tomorrow, but..."

"Oh, I'm sorry." I couldn't say I had any fond feelings for the feline, other than the connection she and Watson shared, but I knew she'd had a long, hard fight with kidney disease. And now, with the storm, it looked like she would have a few more days before she could rest. "I really am, Mason. I know—"

Mason's eyes widened, and I glanced down to realize I'd lifted my hand as I had spoken, the one holding the gun.

"Oh, I'm sorry. I'd thought..." I took a step back and quickly put the gun on the table behind me. As I refocused on Mason and Granny Smith, my gaze traveled over the manila envelope between us. There was no writing, no name, nothing, though it bulged with its contents. Anger washed through me again. "Exactly how many things is Ethel suing me for?"

Mason didn't lower himself to reply. Instead, he simply stared at me in that inane and judgmental way as he shifted the old cat in his arms. At the motion, he withdrew his own gun— which he'd apparently tucked behind Granny Smith—and pointed it at me. "Unfortunately, you are not getting sued. You are, however, coming with me."

With my back to the table where I'd placed my firearm, my instinct was to slam the door shut in his face. I even gripped the edge to do so, but froze. Watson, who began to growl at the sight of the gun and the return of tension in the air, was still at Mason's feet.

"Mason, what are you doing? What is this?" Stall... the only thing I could do was stall. "I know Ethel can't stand the ground I walk on, but—"

"Drop the phone." Mason shifted the aim of the gun from my chest to my left hand, then back to my chest. "Drop it right where it is."

My phone?

My phone! I'd forgotten. Stupidly, I looked down to find my cell still clutched in my hand. Could I unlock the screen and hit Leo's name fast enough? No. But I could throw it, hit Mason's gun hand, or his face, or the cat.

"Don't pull one of your typical stunts, Winifred." Mason's tone returned to boredom, as if this was no greater chore than warming up Ethel's bathwater or whatever he did for her. "There's no use in calling your husband. He's our insurance policy to your compliance."

"Insurance policy to..." His meaning clarified, and horror washed over me, then just as quickly, disbelief. "You don't have Leo, he's at—"

"No, he isn't," Mason interrupted, tsking, even as he shot a warning glare toward Watson, who was still growling. "Unfortunately, Mr. Page-Lopez never made it to the bird club." He glanced back up, hurrying on to clarify. "He's safe. Not a hair out of place, but you'll need to drop the phone and come with us to keep it that way."

Probably apprehended in between Chipmunk Mountain and Ethel's. Or maybe—I gave myself a mental shake, it didn't matter. The how of any of it didn't matter.

"The phone, Ms. Page-Lopez. *Drop it.*" Another gesture downward, then back up. "And please show me your pockets."

I dropped it, what else was there to do? Either the wind picked up, or my blood was rushing through my ears, blocking out sound.

"Pockets."

I read his lips more than heard the words and started to reach into the pockets of my broomstick skirt, then glanced down again, feeling the flannel. "No po—" My throat constricted, but I pushed past it. "My nightgown doesn't have pockets."

He cocked an eyebrow, then glanced down toward my slippered feet. "What about what you're wearing underneath."

I lifted my nightgown high enough for him to see my bare knees.

Watson continued to growl, looking back and forth between us. Though he might not recognize the danger of a gun, he could feel it, but I also saw his confusion. He'd attacked before when someone had tried to assault me, hurt me. But this was different, less clear. Even if he would do so on command, which I doubted, it wasn't anything we'd practiced. I wouldn't do it, not when he might get shot or kicked.

"Very well." Mason took a couple of steps backward. For a second, my hope flared, thinking he'd stumble down the porch steps, but he managed them without even a glitch, then gestured with the gun from me to the sleek black SUV. "After you."

I tried to think, tried to force options into my brain, make my mind go into overdrive and see all the possibilities, play out different scenarios—but none of that happened. Only the rushing in my ears and the fear for Leo.

"As you stated, Ms. Page-Lopez, Granny Smith is cold. I am done being patient." He transferred the gun toward Watson, whose growl increased. "I'm sorry. I truly don't want to, but I will."

"Okay!" I practically shouted it, then crossed the threshold. "Okay! There! You don't. Don't." Leaving the gun and the cell phone behind, I hurried across the porch and sank down to Watson. His confused chocolate gaze looked up at me, then back at Mason, his growl never ceasing. "Go on in. I'll be back. Go on in." I gave him a nudge toward the cabin door, but of course he didn't move. He was corgi stubborn at the best of times, and the idea of him willingly leaving my side in this moment was laughable. I'd have to pick him up and—

"He comes too." Was that regret in Mason's voice? If so, it vanished. "My mistress had specific instructions, Watson is to accompany us."

Perhaps it should have been obvious, considering I was at gunpoint, but it was at that moment I realized there weren't different endings to the evening. Ethel hated Watson just as much as she hated me—

whatever this was would end in revenge, in elimination. Of us both.

That realization told me all I needed to make a quick decision. If a bullet was in store anyway, then I would go out fighting, *now*. I didn't even make it all the way to standing before I remembered Leo and my impulse died. I had to get to him, play whatever game this was, and then we'd fight it together.

Mason must have been able to see my surrender. "Please pick him up and bring him in the car." Still moving backward, Mason reached the car and opened the rear door, then took a few steps away.

I did as commanded. Watson thrashed, not because he hated being carried, which he did, but trying to lunge at Mason as we passed, even earning a hiss from Granny Smith.

I placed Watson on the seat, then feeling like I was entering a hearse, followed him in.

"You'll see zip ties beside you, or possibly under Watson at this point." Mason angled so he could see past me into the interior. "One is already a circle for you, loop one of the others through it and then around your wrist.

"Mason..." Zip ties? Somehow that brought it home even more than the gun. They really were going to kill us. "Mason, you can't actually—"

"Now!" His monosyllabic yell sent Watson into another fit of rage, and even Granny Smith reared back, hissing at him. The gun pointing at me shook.

I did as he asked, retrieving the zip ties, sliding one hand through the circle and then fastening it together awkwardly with the other, rather like a watch.

"Now the other. Loop it through and fasten it."

I didn't need further explanation, and I didn't try to offer an alternative. This one took much longer, but finally I was wearing a pair of plastic handcuffs. When he told me to pull on the ends tighter with my teeth, I had no choice but to comply, and they both bit into my wrists.

"Lie on the floor." At my surprised glance, he deigned to explain. "I'm not having you choke me from the back seat or try to kick. No games. If you're on the floor, I'll hear you attempt to get up—and I'll point out that my gun is loaded."

The ridiculous feeling of attempting to sprawl across the floorboard only heightened my fear. It wasn't exactly a large space, and I wasn't exactly a small woman. Instant and uncomfortable claustrophobia swept over me as I managed to wedge myself on my side, needing to spread out over both the footwells.

Watson sat on the seat, looking down at me, clearly thinking I'd lost my mind.

Mason shut the door as gently as if he were getting ready to head to a red-carpet event. A second later, he was in the driver's seat, whispering soothingly to Granny Smith, and cranked the heat.

He didn't offer any further instructions, no more warnings, didn't even whisper to the cat. He just drove.

There would have been no point to any of it anyway. I wasn't going to fight back, not with Leo somewhere probably at gunpoint from Ethel, or...

Oh, of course. *Branson.*

It showed just how off guard Mason had caught me, and how afraid I'd been that I'd not realized until then. This wasn't Ethel, or at least not only. This was Branson. Although that surprised me. I hadn't felt the end arrive. I'd predicted just the opposite, actually, that Branson had a lot more of his little game to play before he grew tired of it. Apparently, I'd been wrong.

Oddly, that realization soothed a little. Branson was scarier than Ethel could ever dream of being, but I had a greater chance of manipulating him, or convincing him, than I ever would with Ethel.

Watson quit growling during the drive and lay

on the seat right above my head, whimpering and offering comforting licks over my cheek.

I lost track of how far we went, or how long it took, the panic of claustrophobia rising, then falling, making way for the panic of what Leo, Watson, and I were going to face at the end of this drive, wondering how crazed Branson had become—only to be swept away to the confining walls of claustrophobia again. With my nerves and the blazing heat, I began to sweat.

That horrendous pattern continued until Watson suddenly sat up, eyes wide, ears perked, and then he smiled, almost. The car made a turn, and he propped himself up, staring out the side window, and began to pant in expectation. It only lasted a heartbeat or two before he glanced back at me and some of that excitement died, the reality of the moment returning to him. With a disappointed grunt, he plunked back down onto the seat and took his place beside me once more, that time resting his muzzle on the top of my head.

Ethel's. We really were at Ethel's. I recognized that reaction—the spark that almost always flared when we approached Ethel's mansion, and Watson's never-ending hope that she would once more throw expensive sausages from her porch in a rage, offering him one of the best impromptu feasts of his life.

The car came to a stop. Mason exited, then opened the passenger door, and Watson began to growl again. "Please sit up, Ms. Page-Lopez, and then follow me." His dignified, haughty tone was securely back in place.

That request ended up being easier said than done. I was never the most graceful—even when not handcuffed with plastic restraints and lying sideways wedged into a tight spot—and somehow, even in the middle of it all, embarrassment flared for a moment at the truly humiliating display required to get myself to a seated position and then to scoot out of the car.

Mason didn't offer any criticism or commentary, and in that he was very different from his *mistress*. "Watson, too, he'll need to jump."

"No." I started to argue that he should stay where he was, but knew it was pointless and switched to the other argument. "Let me try to pick him up. His legs are too short, his back too long. A jump from this high could hurt him."

Mason simply nodded, gun in one hand, Granny Smith looking thoroughly exhausted cradled in his other arm.

Watson grunted in displeasure but didn't put up the smallest ounce of a fight. He even seemed to help me as I shoved my forearms under his middle, then held him awkwardly to my chest—I thought he'd been heavy the normal way! I'd planned on carrying him like that, but couldn't, not with his weight, not with the awkward position of my arms and the cut of the zip ties on my wrists. Nearly dropping him, I lowered quickly to the ground, but he managed to leap free before I collapsed and had to repeat the process of trying to remain upright again. It was at a much lower distance than the car, however, and he hit the driveway with little more than a grunt.

"After you." Mason gestured toward Ethel's mansion.

I glanced around; there was no one in sight—not that I'd expected there to be—only a couple other shadowy cars in the driveway. On the trip over, the snow had begun to fall in earnest, but I hadn't even noticed it as I'd gotten Watson out of the car. The mansion was dark, no glow from the windows, all the shutters had been closed and secured. I saw no chance for escape, not that I'd have tried, even if there had been. "Come on, buddy."

With the threat of mountain lions, Watson was never off-leash, never free to wander any farther than from the front door to the car—often not even then. But at that moment, I prayed he'd take off, run. Disappear into the woods, go to the next mansion just out of view. No mountain lion was more dangerous than Branson Wexler. He didn't run, though, merely trotted right beside me, so close his fur was in constant contact with the hem of my nightgown. Together we walked up the steps of Ethel's porch, which we'd done so many times before.

"Go on in, it's unlocked." Mason spoke behind us just as I'd started to slow.

Even with my hands bound together the door was easy to open. And for the first time, I stepped into Ethel's home. I didn't notice the details of the giant chandelier over our heads, the color or pattern of the wallpaper, or if the furniture was modern or antique. Wasn't even aware if the floor was wood or marble or carpet. The only thing I saw along the entryway was that every visible door was closed. A glance up the sweeping flight of steps revealed nothing there either. No Leo. No Branson. No Ethel.

The door shut behind us, and Mason let out what sounded like a relieved breath, the first hint he'd even been the slightest bit worried all evening. Somehow, that sound was a crushing weight—confirmation that if there'd been a chance for this to go any other way, I had missed it.

"If you will, Ms. Page-Lopez, please continue through this vestibule and turn to your right. We'll go down that hallway and stop at the double doors on the righthand side." Mason's words were back to clipped robot perfection—free of emotion and personality.

Maybe my fear should have increased as Watson and I went farther into the belly of the beast, but instead, I couldn't keep my feet from speeding up. Ready for answers, ready to see Leo.

Sconces on the wall were the only light, and again every visible doorway was closed. But I followed directions, turning down the hall before stopping in front of a wide set of dark mahogany double doors. Watson sniffed where the light shone through at the base. I'd expected him to bark in joy at Leo's scent. When he only whimpered, the icy fingers that had been running up and down my spine encircled my heart.

"Very good." Mason moved nearer, close enough that Granny Smith hissed at me over my shoulder. He gripped the little brass handle and pulled, sliding the right door back into the wall. "After you. Please take the empty seat."

I had not allowed myself to contemplate what state Leo might be in when we finally saw him, but though I didn't discover him bloody or bruised, the scene which spread before me somehow scared me worse. We were in a gorgeous dining room, the kind my antique-dealing uncles would have loved. Dark rich colors of crimson, plum, and gold. Three chandeliers hung glistening over a long dark wooden table. At the head, at the far side of the room, sat Ethel Beaker. If I hadn't been so horrified, I might have laughed—she was exactly as she always was. Hard face perfectly painted, hair pulled back in a severe manner, both details managing to add years, to make the woman look older, which certainly had never been her intention. A slinky, glittering silver gown glistened from beneath the weight of a massive fur coat covered in scores of foxtails each the same color as Watson's auburn fur but ending in little white puffs at the tips. In one hand she held a silver pistol, and with the other, she lifted a glass of wine, the same color as the walls. "Our guest of honor, welcome. For once, I can say it's a pleasure to see you."

The gun didn't cause a flicker of fear. I was too horrified, too disturbed, too... no description could capture what I felt at the rest of the scene. There were seven other chairs around the long narrow table, three on either side, each occupied by people, their arms secured to the armrests with the same zip ties as around my own wrists, heads covered in brown fabric sacks. The only empty chair sat at the opposite end of Ethel.

"Please take a seat." Ethel actually sounded like a proper host as she gestured toward the chair with a gun. "We can't start without you."

Watson growled. Maybe he had been the whole time, but I only noticed as Ethel glared down at him, the gun angling his way. "Mason." She snapped at him in a tone she typically reserved for me. "Sit that heinous cat down and secure the mongrel. If he moves another inch toward me, this will end now."

"No!" One of the other guests, directly to the right of the empty chair burst out, then seemed to catch herself. Head covered or not, I wouldn't have needed her voice to know Delilah Johnson—her long red hair flowing out from under the bag, and her fifties-pinup-girl body unlike anyone else's in town.

Ethel had swung the gun toward Delilah, but when Delilah gave no further protest, I thought I caught a smile before Ethel retrained the weapon on Watson.

"Watson, no," I whispered desperately to him,

trying to take in the other forms under the hoods. I didn't see Leo's body, couldn't *feel* his presence in the room. Either way, I dragged my attention away, looking down at Watson, pleading. "Be still, buddy. Be still."

"No funny business, I trust?" Mason must have deposited Granny Smith somewhere, as he'd arrived by my side, lifting one of his thin eyebrows. He didn't wait for confirmation, not that he needed any, before leaning down and gripping the extra skin at the back of Watson's neck.

Watson snarled, craned back, fangs bared, ready to bite.

"No!" I'd never screamed at Watson like that, and when he flinched, I did it again. "No. Stop."

Betrayal clear in his brown eyes, he looked up at me with worry and fear. But it was worth it—he was subdued enough to be led over to the side of the room and didn't try to bite Mason. The butler placed his gun on a marble-top table, then used his free hand to secure Watson with a chain around his neck.

From what I could tell, it wasn't tight, at least no more than his normal collar. Unlike Ethel—if she'd been the one doing it—Mason didn't tug or yank or try to assert any power or pain for Watson. He simply walked back across the room and collected Granny Smith.

Watson attempted to come back to me but only made it a couple of steps before he was pulled up short, then looked back in confusion. The chain had been secured to the antique marble-top table, traditional Victorian carving over the legs and the rim. A heavy bronze lamp sat in the middle of it, shimmering with a beautiful stained glass shade of dragonflies.

"I'm sorry, sweetheart," I whispered, feeling my heart breaking as I prayed he could read the sincerity in my voice or in my eyes.

"Join us, Winifred." Ethel's host tone remained, though it now had a lilt of laughter. She was enjoying every moment of this.

Forcing myself to look away from Watson, not wanting to draw any more attention to him, I finished the distance to the empty chair and sat, looking around the table as I did so. Five of the other "guests" were clearly women, though I didn't recognize any of them, save for the one in the middle of the left side—with her rotund body and gingham dress, Anna Hanson was every bit as recognizable as Delilah Johnson. That was little more than an awareness on my part, however, as I narrowed in on the male form directly across from Anna, sitting to the right of Delilah. Large and muscular, but not Leo. Not Branson, either.

"Winifred." Ethel pulled my attention to her. "Can I trust you to behave? I can secure you to your chair like the others, but I'll only do that as a last resort, as you're already bound. Before I do that, if you even breathe wrong, this nasty little town will have one less horrid corgi. Do I make myself clear?"

I tried to speak, couldn't, but managed to nod.

She smiled. "Good."

"Mason..." Ethel tilted her wineglass toward the center of the table, then took another long, slow sip.

Either each step was planned, or after their many years together, the butler required no further direction. Still holding Granny Smith to his chest—who appeared to be sleeping—he stepped behind Delilah's chair and lifted his free hand to her head. For a horrible moment the image of him slicing her neck flashed through my mind, but as he pulled the sack away, I realized he had no weapon. I had to get ahold of myself. As dramatic and horrible as this was, overreacting would only make it worse. I might have already missed chances to get free, to find Leo, to end this. I needed to stay sharp, aware, grounded in reality to find whatever might come next.

Delilah's gaze met mine instantly. Her face was free of makeup, so there were no streams of mascara down her cheeks. However, even if that hadn't been the case, I didn't think there had been any tears. No fear showed in her eyes, fury leaving no room for anything else. In her glance, I saw an echo of what I'd just been feeling. She was *ready*—when the moment presented, Delilah Johnson would be ready. I got no more confirmation than that as she turned to glare at Ethel. There was no gag over her mouth, and she surprised me by not speaking, by not cursing the woman out, not threatening. She only glared and tilted her chin, in a very Ethel sort of way, actually.

With no further production, Mason sidestepped, moving to the next chair, to the man, and pulled off the hood just as easily, revealing Chief Marlon Dunmore. Unlike Delilah, there wasn't fury in his eyes, just fear, worry, and maybe... submission, like he'd already lost. He wasn't gagged either, but a deep bruise bloomed fresh and dark over his cheek, a little cut in the center of it. Maybe I'd missed part of the show, the demonstration ensuring gags weren't needed.

Before I could travel down that path any further, Mason had moved to the third captive, seated to Ethel's left. Unlike the recognition of Delilah, Anna, and the chief, I wasn't exactly sure who I expected, but the unfamiliar brunette revealed came as a shock. Her demeanor fell somewhere between the other two. No tears on her part either, and though she looked resigned, her anger was clear. She did the opposite of Delilah, glaring at Ethel as soon as her face was uncovered and then turned that hate-filled stare on me. Only then did I recognize Mary Smith, more from her blatant feelings about me than any defining features. Something about her presence felt off, which was odd. All of this was off. But... *Mary Smith?* The owner of Bottles, Brushes, and Brie? She'd only been in town a few months. She—

I wasn't allowed to ponder her any longer as Mason crossed behind Ethel's chair, moved to the other side of the table, and removed another hood, this one revealing someone just as unexpected as Mary Smith. Thanks to the older woman's shoe-polish-black beehive of curls, and enough strings of pearls around her neck to look strangling, I recognized Vivian LaRue instantly. The owner of the jewelry shop downtown wasn't her typical picture of perfection. Those black curls had worked loose, some completely free of her updo, maybe from the fabric sack, or in the struggle to get here. Mascara ran down her paper-thin cheeks, and she offered no glare toward Ethel, me, or anyone, only stared at the exquisite place setting in front of her, though I didn't think she saw any of it.

Anna was next. Her makeup had streamed as well with dried tears, and her poufy white hair was flattened in places. Her gaze found me instantly. "Oh, Fred! You've got to—"

The bang of the gun sounded like a cannon in the narrow room, reverberating off the tall ceilings and making my ears ring instantly. Anna and Vivian screamed, the entire table jumped, Watson barked and began to howl; Granny Smith woke with a hiss and snarled toward Ethel. Plaster dust drifted down onto the table, then a second later a large chunk fell with another crash, knocking over one of the candelabras, causing a couple more screams.

"We've already had this discussion, Anna Hanson. I will not have it again." Ethel lowered her gun and aimed at Anna. "And as much as I despise our guest of honor, wearing a *flannel* nightgown to a soiree—" She spared me a revolted sneer before returning to Anna. "—there's not been a solitary moment ever hearing you speak that I have not wanted to shut you up. So, please, give me a reason to end your part of the game a little early."

Anna whimpered, her whole body trembling, but she managed a nod. Unlike Vivian, she didn't stare at her place setting, or at the plaster in front of her but looked toward me. She was terrified, pleading, but every bit as ready as Delilah.

The expression in her eyes resembled that of a soldier waiting orders. Somehow, though I hadn't recognized it in that moment, Delilah's had been the same. They were expecting *me* to get us out of this, expecting me to know what to do.

I had no idea.

"Mason." Ethel's voice had returned to normal when she nodded toward the butler, who had remained behind Anna's chair, staring up at the ceiling. Perhaps he was thinking of the mess he'd have to clean later. Although, that washed away as I realized the ludicrousness of the notion. Whatever was going on, Ethel and Mason surely weren't planning on getting away with this. Or at least not staying in town.

This couldn't be real. It didn't *feel* real.

At her command, Mason moved behind the final chair and pulled free the final hood. Carla Beaker's blond bob, always sleek and sharp was a tangled, tousled mess, and a bruise had blossomed on her cheek as well, the same side as the chief's. Terror and wrath filled her green eyes; dried tears were evident on her as well. She spared me a glance before turning her glare on Ethel. She was ready, too, but Carla wasn't waiting for my directives. Somehow, that provided a modicum of relief.

Somewhere in the unveiling of the other *guests*, Watson had stopped howling and barking after the gunshot, but his continued low whimper, scattered with that deep-chest growl, filled the otherwise-silent space.

Thankfully, Ethel didn't seem to notice, instead looking at me. "As you may have figured out, our other players have already been informed of the rules, which are few. Only comprised of staying where you are and don't speak, or..." She wriggled the silver gun.

Players? Ethel's term threw me off, but only for a second. She'd also referred to it all being a game. With a sinking feeling that was both realization and dread, I looked in front of my own place setting and discovered a name tag on a little pyramid of thick ivory paper. Instead of Winifred, *Mrs. Peacock* blazed back at me in crimson calligraphy. Though I couldn't see any other names, a quick glance around revealed name tags in front of each person, except for Ethel.

"Clue..." My realization escaped in a whisper,

and I looked up across the table at Ethel. "You're using us to play *Clue*?"

Ethel swung the gun my way. "What did I *just* say about the rules?" She shrugged, making some of the foxtails dance, answering me anyway. "But... in a manner of speaking, yes. Though the stakes are a little higher than in the board game." Her gaze flicked over my shoulder, narrowed, and then glanced at Mason once more. "You took longer than expected with her."

Mason merely nodded as he stroked the cat and came to stand at Ethel's right side. "Apologies, mistress."

At my right, Delilah shuddered as if repulsed, but stayed silent.

Ethel didn't seem to notice, returning her focus to me. "Unfortunately, we won't have as much time together as I thought. We've got a plane to catch, so my part of the game ends early." She tsked and shook her head my way, diamond drop earrings sparkling. "You always love to mess up the best-laid plans, don't you?"

"*Mrs. White?*" Carla spoke suddenly. At her right, both Anna and Vivian flinched, probably expecting Ethel's gun to pivot back to their side of the table. "Even in this, you made me the *maid*?"

Ethel kept the gun trained where it was, and as she spoke to her daughter-in-law, actually sounded pleased at the interruption. "Unfortunately, dear, there wasn't a character involving trailer trash. So, the maid had to do."

"Trailer trash." Carla breathed out a sardonic laugh. Part of me was almost impressed she knew the game well enough to remember who Mrs. White, to recognize Ethel's insult, and clearly enough to burn away some of Carla's fear as she leaned forward, putting a little strain on her binds. "Even after everything, Jonathan's secrets, what Eustace did to cover them up, you still have the delusion that *I* wasn't good enough for the Beaker blood."

"*Beaker* blood?" Ethel laughed then. Despite the insanity of this moment, she didn't sound crazed or unhinged, but fully in control and still enjoying herself. "Is *that* what you thought I was checking for? I've never been concerned about Beaker blood, or Apple, for that matter." She took a long sip of wine, lowered the glass back to the table, picked up a napkin and dabbed her lips, indulging in the moment, despite whatever lateness she was worried about. She loved a stage nearly as much as my uncle, Percival. "That was cash, you classless trollop.

Nothing more. No matter the label, I have always been a *Roberts*."

"Maverick's a *Beaker*, though, isn't he?" Carla's defiant tone increased, as did the strain where her arms were bound when she tried to stand. "He is half Jonathan, half Beaker. And half me, half a *White*. Trailer trash though we may be." She laughed. "I guess Mrs. White is accurate after all."

"Shut up!" The fury was so strong, at first I thought it was Ethel, that her voice had changed. It wasn't until Ethel looked to her left and cocked an eyebrow at Mary Smith that I caught on. The woman didn't seem to notice, but kept her brown gaze fixed on Carla as she spoke through clenched teeth. "Shut up and play by the rules. You're going to get us all killed."

Carla didn't bother looking at the woman, maybe didn't even notice, keeping her glare only on Ethel. "My son has more White blood in him than any of yours. He's more me than you."

"I'll get that out of him." Ethel's tone stayed regal, elegant, deadly. "And yes, Maverick is half Jonathan, but the Beaker name doesn't matter to my son either. It doesn't matter what name was slapped on him—same as me—he's a *Roberts*. Just like I am. Just like Maverick is."

Mason had gone pale, looked shaken. He moved the hand that had been stroking Granny Smith and placed it on Ethel's arm, which at some point had pivoted the gun back at Carla. "It's... getting late. We should go, Ethel."

The socialite flinched at the use of her name. I didn't think I'd ever heard Mason call her that. But it worked. Cold resolve replaced her anger, and Ethel relaxed, holding the gun at the ready, not aimed at Carla or myself.

Carla collapsed back in her chair, suddenly spent; she didn't seem near tears, but the fight had gone out of her.

"Now..." Ethel smiled, fully back in control, speaking as her gaze slowly traveled around the table, letting her disdain of each of us shine. "Though we may have to cut this portion shorter than intended, rest assured, you still get to play the game." Rising, she sidestepped to her right, standing beside Vivian LaRue, who began to tremble afresh. However, instead of speaking or pointing the gun at the jeweler, Ethel glanced over at Mason.

He gave a little twitch, clearly having missed his cue, and then he pushed in her chair, with a nod of apology.

Granny Smith hissed at the motion, and across

the room Watson growled, though I wasn't sure if it was in her defense or in challenge.

Thankfully, Ethel seemed to have forgotten Watson was in the room or existed at all as she returned to us, speaking as she walked slowly around the table toward me, Mason following a few steps behind. "As in all games, there's a time limit, which is *actually* the only thing you're playing against now, not me. Your opponent is the clock." She paused as she pulled up parallel to me, then lowered her voice slightly. "Spoiler alert, Winifred, you don't win this one. *I* do."

Without waiting for a response, she continued, keeping her gun pointed toward the table and turning to face us elegantly as she walked, able to stride backward in high heels better than I could forward on the best of days. As Mason walked around her to slide the pocket door open once more, Ethel raised her voice again as she reached the doorway. "You'll have thirty minutes." She chuckled. "And yes, I agree, that's hardly fair, an hour would probably be more sporting. But... I don't care." She took a final step back. "Think of me, won't you? Though I wish I could watch as you all go up in flames, I *will* be thinking of you, rest assured. But then..." She continued speaking as Mason began to slide the door closed. "You'll be burned away from my memory, nothing more than ash. Finally."

They were gone. The door closed with a little click. A second later, a whirring sounded as something heavy slid into place, locking us in.

FOUR

Ethel's heels clicked for a few moments in the heavy silence—only five or six times—then faded quickly as she disappeared down the hall. Then nothing other than the whistle of the wind, which must have been picking up outside, then Watson's whimper.

He pulled me back to the moment, pulled us all back. I looked over at Watson, at his pleading, worried, angry eyes, and stood. I'd forgotten I could.

The others remained where they were, all looking at me as I turned back to them.

"Knife, Fred." Delilah nodded at the place setting in front of her, long auburn hair falling over her face at the motion. "Use the knife."

Her words broke the spell, and the others repeated the mantra, urging me to hurry up. Someone whimpered, another began to cry.

Of course. Even as I reached for it, yanking my left hand along, the place settings baffled me. Each of us had a knife—a shimmering, glistening steak knife on the left of each of our plates. Pointy, sharp. They couldn't be real; she wouldn't have given us knives. The weight of it in my fingers confirmed that she had.

Had I missed *that* chance as well? Weapon right in front of my face... Ethel's glistening silver gun suggested otherwise; the knife wouldn't have stood a chance. Before I got lost to that pondering, however, I turned to Delilah, managing to point the knife awkwardly toward her closest wrist. There wasn't a way to do this without cutting her, the zip tie already biting into her skin. "Here." Changing directions, I pressed our hands together, the handle between our palms, and waited until her fingers curled around it. "Hold it steady. We'll try to cut mine."

She gave a quick nod, twisted her fist slightly, letting out a hiss as the zip tie cut deeper, but managed to hold it up like a spike.

Without waiting, I slipped the middle link of my zip ties over the blade, pulled back and began to saw. "Did any of you see Leo? Did she say anything about where she's keeping him..." As I spoke, I realized that's probably how they got everyone here. "Where they're keeping everyone they took from us?"

Anna gasped across the table. "They have Leo,

too?" Her eyes went wide in fresh fear. "He was going to the Feathered Friends Brigade, same as Carl." Her voice shot up, fresh panic washing over her. "Do they have Carl? Do you think she took Carl?"

"It doesn't matter." Carla bit the words out, sounding remarkably like her mother-in-law. "Didn't you hear her? We have *half* an hour. We have to focus on getting out of here."

"But if they have Carl, then—"

"Shut up, Anna." Carla flashed toward her, almost looked like she was going to bite the other woman. "Ethel just said they're getting ready to get on a plane. And they *won't* be taking Carl, they'll be taking *my son*. And if you lose your mind so we can't get out of here and end up exploding, I'll kill you myself."

"Explode?" Vivian whimpered on the other side of Anna. She'd been the one to begin to cry again. "She didn't say anything about—"

"Good grief," Mary snarled across the table, in the same space as Carla, it seemed. "She said we were going to be *burned* from her memory, nothing more than *ash*. What do you *think* that means? Idiot." She looked toward me, calm, cold fury in her eyes. "Hurry it up, Winifred. You're the only one of us not stuck to a chair, so quit worrying about your husband and act like an intelligent adult."

I didn't bother responding to Mary Smith, nor had I stopped the sawing motion, my growing panic only increasing my speed.

"There!" Delilah cried out in success as my zip tie split in two, and the steak knife flew from her fist at the sudden break in pressure and across the table, making Anna screech as it skittered her way, stopping against the large chunk of plaster.

With the middle link gone, I had full use of my hands, the zip ties cutting into my wrists acting as nothing more than overly tight bracelets. Not bothering to reach across the table and grab the original knife, I snagged the one by Delilah's plate, bent down, and was able to easily slide the flat portion between her skin and the plastic. It was only a matter of a moment before her left hand was free, then her right—Anna giving a little cheer of excitement with each milestone.

Without discussion, Delilah grabbed the knife in front of the chief, beginning to work on him as I ran back around the table to free Carla. By the time I'd cut through Anna's right binding, Delilah and Marlon had freed both Mary and Vivian. I passed the knife to Carla. "Here, get Anna's left hand, please." Without waiting for a response, I hurried across the room, crashing down by Watson on my knees.

It was nothing more than simply sliding my fingers between Watson's neck and the chain, making it spread out slightly, for Watson to rear backward and pull his head free. As it had looked, Mason hadn't been cruel, only used the chain as a choke collar, nothing that hurt him. Watson sprang up, lunging against my chest, making me lose my balance and crash back onto my rump.

"Good boy, buddy. Good boy." I indulged for a second, meeting his embrace by wrapping my arms around him and burying my face in the back of his neck for a moment. "I love you. You're okay. You're okay." And with that, I released him, stood, and wiped tears I'd not realized Watson had triggered from my cheeks, then turned back to the group. Only Vivian remained at the table, frozen in fear. The rest had already spread out.

Delilah addressed Carla. "You're familiar with this house, do you know of any—"

"Hardly." Somehow, even in the midst of panic, Carla Beaker managed her typical snarling tone. "In case you hadn't noticed, my mother-in-law and I aren't exactly best friends. She didn't invite me over for tea."

"Check the windows." As I spoke, I snagged the stained glass lamp that had been above Watson. It was heavier than I'd anticipated, and I had to use my second hand before I accidentally dropped it. With a tug, the plug came free, and the light went off, as I hurried toward the closest window. The dining room was on the corner of the house, it seemed, as two walls were lined with windows—two on the one that had been behind Ethel, three on the side that ran along next to Watson.

"It won't work," Marlon, sounding thoroughly defeated, mumbled even as he strode to another window and pulled open the curtains. "She wouldn't have made it that easy."

I agreed with him, but we had to try. I was already at another set and followed Marlon's lead, steadying the lamp on my hip with one hand and yanking the heavy curtain open with my other— nothing but darkness on the other side of the glass. For a moment I thought the blizzard had arrived, causing a blackout. "I noticed the shutters were closed, no light coming from inside, but maybe we can break through them." A momentary scan revealed the window wasn't the type that would open; I glanced down to make sure Watson wasn't directly below, and then swung the lamp like a baseball bat.

With a howl, Watson skittered back as both the window and the stained glass shade shattered. Even the wood mullions between the panes fell away, leaving the inside of the shutters accessible through the large hole. From across the room, more glass shattered, but I didn't look their way. With a sinking feeling, already knowing what I'd find, I reached into the hole, pressed my palm against the shutters and pushed. Not a budge, not a wiggle, and at the cold pressure against my palm, I realized that though they had looked like traditional wood from the outside, it was nothing more than an illusion. They were metal, solid steel; we might as well have been inside a bank vault. Nevertheless, just like before, I had to try. I used the heavy base of the lamp as a bat one more time and swung it with every ounce of my strength against the metal. It clanged with a horrible sound, but the only movement was the reverberation up the bones of my arms and into my shoulders. Nothing else.

I turned and saw Marlon at the other broken window—he only nodded, confirming what he'd already predicted.

The others hadn't waited around, save for Vivian, who still might as well have been tied to her chair, the only sign of life an occasional whimper. Mary and Carla were at a second set of pocket doors in the center of the wall on the opposite side of the room. Mary tugged at the seam, while Carla kicked. Delilah and Anna were at the other the doorway I'd walked through, the one Ethel, Mason, and the cat had exited. They were having no more luck. Anna played Mary's role, trying to sink her nails between the seam and yank.

Delilah had taken a cue from me, grabbed a bronze statue and was beating at the panels. Splinters of wood sprayed out like fireworks with every impact, and my heart lurched in hope. It seemed hers did as well when she sped up, as Anna got out of the way, swinging the heavy bronze with more strength than I imagined she knew she possessed. No sooner had the wood fallen away than the next swing issued a resounding gong of metal, exactly like the windows.

"No..." Anna whimpered, and without thinking, putting a hand up to touch the door in between swings—not that it mattered, Delilah had already let the statue fall to the floor. As I had done, Anna spread her palm out and turned to face us. "It's metal. Iron or something. It's not wood all the way through."

Vivian let out a sob and collapsed onto the table, head tucking into the crook of her arm.

Metal shutters, wooden doors with cores of iron. I glanced around the room, searching, taking it all in. Other than the door Delilah had shattered, the windows Marlon and I had ruined, and the plaster ceiling Ethel had destroyed above the table, everything was perfect. Rich, decadent, glistening golds, shimmering crystal, dark textured wallpaper, brocade fabrics. It looked like a Victorian dollhouse or like we'd traveled back in time or landed in a Sherlock Holmes movie. Or... I landed on the ivory paper pyramid name tags in front of each place setting... Or a game of Clue, just like Ethel had said.

Letting out a breath, I went to one knee, needing Watson, the soothing clarity he often provided. He was there, of course, right at my ankles, and I sank my fingers deep into his fur. Stretching out, he licked my other hand as I continued to stroke him.

"The remodel..." Carla turned from the door where she and Mary had given up and met my gaze. "Ethel's been planning this. I have no reason to be certain, but I am—those shutters weren't steel traps before, and these pocket doors were just old wood."

"We're in a game, like she said." I nodded my agreement. "Clue. Although... the doors weren't locked in that game. You just had to roll the dice."

"Dice!" Anna clasped her hands. "Maybe there's dice. Or some form of them. Ethel wanted us to play the game, so come on, let's play it."

Mary let out a groan, rolled her eyes at Anna, but offered no more commentary.

"No imagination, as always, Mary Smith. Exactly what I'd expect from you." Anna had despised the Smith family from the second they moved into town, but she didn't allow any more time to scorn before hurrying over to an antique sideboard and yanking out the drawers, apparently searching for dice.

"I agree." The chief looked between Carla and me, and though he nodded, he sounded just as defeated as Vivian. "I'd say it's designed as a game. But she said so herself, it's not one we can win. It only *looks* like a game, but it's nothing more than a trap. She fixed it, just like the games at a carnival. There will be no way to win."

"Well, what choice do we have?" Anger filled Delilah's tone as she spoke. While she addressed Marlon, she moved slowly in a circle, taking in every detail of the room. "Unless we've got an axe or a chainsaw, we can't burst through the walls—and who knows, they probably have steel in them as well. So, maybe there is a way out of this game, and we just..." She froze, face paling. "The time limit. Ethel said we only have thirty minutes." She whipped toward the elaborate grandfather clock. "What time was that? Do we know how much is left?"

"It's been a little over ten minutes." Panic laced Dunmore's voice, and his hand trembled as he pulled a butterscotch from his pocket and began to unwrap it. "I looked when they walked out. We've only got less than twenty left."

"Then let's not spend it arguing. Let's figure things out. I hate the woman—" Carla spoke as she strode toward the table. "—but one thing about Ethel Beaker, she *always* got her way. So if she wanted a game, a game is what she got." She picked up the name tag in front of Mary's chair, glanced at it and flinched. "Professor Plum." She looked toward Mary, then me. "Wasn't he a man? Maybe I'm being too literal, but... Ethel is literal. Do you think the character names mean some-thing?" She touched her chest. "Mine did, without a doubt."

"I was Reverend Green," Anna called out from behind a settee in the corner—she'd lowered herself to hands and knees in her search. "I think he was a man, too."

"I was Mrs. Peacock." Giving Watson a final pat and standing once more, I looked at the table. "I can't see how the names help, though. It didn't in the game, you just had to figure out who the murderer was. One of the names was hidden in a little envelope with the weapon and the room."

"And we already *know* who the murderer is." Delilah, surprisingly, had joined Anna in the search, lifting up the edges of framed portraits on the wall, then pulling out an arrangement of flowers, dumping them on the floor and looking inside the vase. "I was Miss Scarlet, for what that's worth."

A character designed for Delilah Johnson, if there ever had been. Though I couldn't see how it mattered, I moved to Vivian, completely shut down, and picked up her name tag. "Colonel Mustard, another man. That's strange..." I glanced toward the chief. "That should have been your character—closest to a police officer. Who did you get? The only one left is..." I pulled the blank and then realized my mistake. "No, there were only six characters. There's no one left."

"I was Mr. Boddy." He shrugged. "I don't

remember him being in the game, but that doesn't take much deduction to the meaning."

Mr. Boddy. "He wasn't *in* the game, but the center of it. He was the murder you were supposed to solve. The victim. The whole point was to solve who killed Mr. Boddy, with what weapon, and what room." I held his gaze. "Ethel did say she had to cut her part of the game short."

He let out a puff of breath. "I was supposed to die."

Mary cocked her head, seeming captured for once. "Well, that doesn't make sense. You were right here with the rest of us. What was she going to do, take you into another room and kill you and we'd have to figure out where and how?"

"Maybe one of us is involved..." Vivian spoke for the first time in a while, lifting her head to look around the room with fear-filled eyes. "Ethel wasn't going to be the murderer, one of you was going to be. One of you is in on it." She started to stand, but then didn't seem to have the strength. "Maybe you still are."

"Good grief, crazy woman. In case you didn't miss it, Ethel is the murderer, and we are *all* going to be Mr. Boddy." Carla dismissed her with an irritated flick of her hand and looked at me. "You're right, the characters don't matter. This is all a waste of time, all a distraction."

"Here!" Anna cried out from where she stood beside another marble top table, its thin drawer pulled open. A second later, she lifted a large glistening wrench into the air, and looked to me as well. "A wrench. That's one of the weapons in the game, right?"

"A wrench?" Mary had lost interest again, only disgusted skepticism remained. "Some handyman just left it in the drawer. Or not. Who cares? Even if it is part of the game, what does it matter? Can you beat through iron with it?"

Delilah crossed the space toward Anna, inspecting the wrench, and then studying the room again. "Maybe it opens something. Designed to be the key out."

"Maybe." Carla brightened, latching on to that. "Come on." She nudged the chief with her elbow. "Help us look. Time is ticking."

I started to say that wasn't what the wrench was for in the game—it was nothing more than a murder weapon—but decided not to waste time. What would it hurt? Maybe they'd discover something else, or perhaps I was wrong. But instead of helping, I looked at the room with new eyes.

Mary was wrong, the wrench was definitely part of the game. It was larger than normal, and I had never seen a wrench glisten or sparkle like it, nor in that exact shade of silver. Ethel's gun flicked through my mind; it had sparkled in that same way. At the memory, I adjusted my thought. Not just a gun, a *revolver*. Another one of the weapons.

A quick scan through childhood memories and a couple of different manuscripts from the publishing house flashed through my brain. Just like the number of characters, there were six weapons. Revolver, wrench, knife. *Knife!* Sure enough, there it was, sparkling in front of Ethel's seat, the extra-large steak knife positioned in its normal spot left of the plate. That left the rope, lead pipe, and... I settled on the overturned candelabra on the table—a candlestick. I discarded that quickly, not that it mattered. The candelabra was brass, not silver, not like a piece of the game. And again, not that it mattered.

But maybe it did.

We had the characters; we had the weapons. We didn't have dice, but what else *did* we have? The dining room... Maybe this was exactly how Ethel had always had it decorated, though I somehow doubted it. She'd always been more high-end modern. Her slinky sparkly dresses hinted nothing Victorian or antique. She hadn't designed this dining room for her taste but for the game.

I brought the game board to mind, trying to picture the dining room, then looked at the two walls of windows. We were in a corner of her mansion. I wasn't certain, but I thought the dining room on the board game was somewhere in the middle. So that was different. Maybe my theory wouldn't work, but one of my favorite parts of the game as a kid had been what was hidden in the four corner rooms of the game board.

Feeling like I might be losing my mind, I hurried toward the corner between the two walls of windows. There was another marble-top table with two antique upholstered chairs on either side. "Marlon, help me, please."

Though he narrowed his eyes in confusion, he didn't ask for clarification, but hurried my way.

"Help me move this table." I gripped one side as he gripped the other and we shuffled it to the wood floor on the edge of the carpet from which it had sat. Watson stayed right by my feet, nearly making me trip. A second later, Marlon moved one of the chairs, and I moved the other.

The rest of the women, save for Vivian, had abandoned their searches and gathered around us. I shooed them away. "Move over a bit, please." After they did, I lifted the corner of the oriental rug, then pulled it backward.

I had made it about a yard before Anna gasped. "Is that a—"

"Trapdoor!" Delilah beamed at me. "Just like in the game. Good job, Fred!"

The trapdoor had a recessed brass handle, allowing the rug to lie flat. Without waiting I slipped my fingers around the thin bar, bringing it vertical, then giving a mighty pull. A startled squeak escaped me as I stumbled backward, nearly fell—would have if I hadn't retained my grip. "Okay... that came up a lot easier than I expected, opened almost as smoothly as a refrigerator."

Watson scurried around me, poking his head into the hole, sniffing.

"A refrigerator isn't exactly a bad comparison." Delilah, though standing and not sniffing, peered into the hole from the opposite side of Watson. "A light came on when you opened the door."

"I'm not going down there." For the first time, Vivian had left the table—I'd not even felt her close to me. She shook her head as she looked in again, then straightened, ridiculously smoothing some of the black curls in her updo. "I'm not doing it."

"Well, *I* am." Mary, without a moment's hesitation, quite literally jumped, her elbow smacking Watson's nose with her sudden movement. She didn't notice his growl as she landed with a grunt.

My depth perception of the tunnel must have been off from my angle, as I'd thought it was deeper. When Mary straightened, the bottom of her rib cage was even with the surface of the floor. She gave a quick glance around. "Like you said, Carla, time's ticking." With that, she ducked lower and disappeared.

Vivian, still shaking her head, took another step back as if we might hog-tie and throw her in.

Her movement was barely more than an awareness from the corner of my eye as the rest of us exchanged quick looks. "She's not wrong."

Carla nodded her agreement with me and motioned toward the grandfather clock. "We've got less than fifteen minutes."

"Maybe not even that." A whine entered Anna's voice. "She might have been lying. Maybe it was half that amount of time and the whole place is going to explode any—"

"No." Carla scowled. "Of that much, I'm certain. Ethel will enjoy knowing that our stress and fear is ticking up with every minute. She'd want to milk that. I guarantee she'll be looking at her diamond wristwatch the moment thirty minutes hits. Probably counting down right now, loving knowing that we are getting more afraid with every second." With that, she followed Mary's example and disappeared, though she called out back to us, "It's a little tighter than I thought."

It was only at that moment the current reality truly sank in. A tunnel. Under this mansion, and tighter than Carla thought. Panic gripped my throat. It didn't matter if it had been roomy, this was a situation from my nightmares. Tunnels, caves, anything small enclosed... I tried to push my claustrophobia aside, managed somewhat.

Delilah had already lowered herself and disappeared for a second, then popped back up, worry and —pity, possibly, in her eyes. "She wasn't kidding, you can't stand. You'll have to crawl." Her gaze flicked to me and then the chief. "I think the three of us will fit. I *think*..." Then over at Anna. "I'm sorry, you won't."

Anna whimpered. Somehow, though her fear increased, she almost looked a little relieved. "Oh..."

"We'll come back. There's gotta be a way to open those doors from the other side." Delilah nodded to

Anna as if making a solemn vow, swept her hair over one shoulder to get it out of her face, and then disappeared as well.

"After you." The chief held a hand toward the trapdoor, a motion of chivalry. "I can bring up the rear."

I started to sit on the edge to slide in as Delilah had done, and then a visual of what I was about to do flashed in my mind, increasing my panic but also clarifying the reality, and I glanced down on my nightgown. Crawling on that would be a nightmare. "Actually, you go ahead, please. I'll bring up the rear."

He only hesitated for a second, then glanced to Anna as well. "We'll be back."

After he lowered himself and cleared the space, I slid the rest of the way in, slippered feet hitting the smooth dirt floor. From this position, Watson was at my chest, and he whimpered, for once waiting for me to pick him up and bring him along.

I started to, then wondered what was in the tunnel. Probably dramatic to consider traps or bats or a million other things, but if it was only big enough for me to crawl, I couldn't help him if something bad happened.

"Hurry, Fred." Anna had knelt beside the hole

and wiped a tear. Somehow, she managed a little smile as she met my eyes. "If you get out and there's not enough time, you get free. It's okay."

Even in my panic of the claustrophobic tunnel, of the trauma of the past... however long it had been... and my ever-increasing fear for Leo, Anna Hanson managed to cut through it all by saying the most un-Anna-like thing I could possibly imagine. She wasn't exactly the type to kick a person out of the way to escape a burning building, but... the notion wasn't exactly out of the realm of possibilities. "We'll be back." I smiled at her, refocused on Watson who just leaned forward and licked my face—a demand, not affection. I sank my fingers into the fur on either side of his muzzle and pressed a quick kiss to his nose. "You stay, I'll be back." I gave him a gentle nudge. "Stay with Anna, she'll take care of you."

She whimpered, in gratitude, maybe in hope now there was no doubt that we would return, or at least that I would.

He resisted for a second, and then with a grunt, finished the last couple of paces toward Anna and allowed himself to be wrapped in her arms.

My gaze slid over Vivian, who'd taken her collapsed spot back at the table—only then realizing we hadn't made any promises to her. Well... whatever. We were already coming back for Anna and Watson; she could figure that out. Then, taking a deep breath and trying to shut off my brain, I lowered to my knees and ducked my head into the tunnel. It was well lit, thankfully, and reinforced here and there with wood planks, kind of like images I'd seen of coal mines, all four sides smooth dirt.

Several yards away, the chief's backside shuffled along as he crawled—and that was the mental image that had flashed through my mind, what his view would have been if I'd gone first. In that vein, wishing I'd worn more than underwear under my nightgown, I hiked it up around my waist, then made a quick knot to keep it out of the way of my knees where it wouldn't cause me to stumble. I only made it a few paces before I changed my plan. Though the sides were smooth, there were small pebbles in the dirt, instantly pressing in and cutting my knees. Yanking the knot loose, I repositioned the nightgown so the flannel was once more under my knees. It slowed me down, but I figured less than ripping my knees to shreds with every movement.

"Fred!" Delilah's voice echoed from somewhere ahead. "Are you in here?"

"Ye—" My voice cut off, and anger at myself

flared—this was not the time to panic. It was just a tunnel, just a tight space. I wasn't alone. Time was ticking; Leo was waiting. We were all waiting. "Yes. I'm here."

"I've come to a crossroads," Delilah called back again, speaking so fast her words were hard to understand between her speed and the echo of the small space. "Straight ahead, left, or right. Do you think it matters? Do you remember the board game?"

"Just pick one, Delilah." The chief spoke before I had the chance. "Tell us which way you go, then we'll pick the other two."

Not a bad plan, and it didn't slip my notice that neither Carla nor Mary had hesitated or waited to communicate. Even so, I tried to think of the Clue board. Fuzzy memories attempted to clarify—the small yellow squares between all the rooms, the secret passages. There was a dining room, library, billiard room... that was all I could remember, and couldn't recall the placement of even those. "I agree with Marlon." Yeah... audible, but my voice shook. Did it ever. "I don't think it matters. But I don't remember."

"'Kay." Delilah's disappointment was clear in that one syllable, and then she pressed on. "I'll go straight."

"I'm almost to you." The chief called out again, no tremble in his voice, all business. "I'll go right. Fred, you go left."

Left. I nodded. At least I thought I did.

"Fred?" The chief yelled back again, his voice a little clearer, making me think he'd twisted, trying to see me. "You okay?"

No. Not even a little bit. None of us were okay. "Yeah." Still shaky. "Left. Got it."

Then there was silence, of voices at least, only leaving the scuffling sound of knees and fabric over dirt, grunts here and there. After several fumbling lurches, I gave up trying to keep my slippers on and left them where they lay.

I tried to clear my mind, not think about the time limit, not think about Leo, not think about Clue, and definitely not think about the walls closing in— which, they were. Also, some sort of machine had to be sucking the oxygen out as well. The first few paces, I hadn't felt the top of the tunnel along my back. It had been big enough I imagined petite women, like Carla and Mary, could have almost walked in an apelike, hunched-over fashion. The farther I went, though, the less that was true. I could feel it on the top of my spine, brushing against my shoulders, occasionally one of the wooden support beams banged against my hip.

A weird haunting sound issued, soft, echoing, zombielike.

"You've got this, Fred." Anna's voice was already fading behind me before I placed it as hers, much less interpreted the meaning. "We know you'll do it."

Watson's whimper followed, maybe in panic and fear, or irritation that I'd left him. But the sound felt like encouragement and a reprimand, a *hurry up*.

Only then did I realize the horrible zombielike keening nearly drowning them out was me.

I paused, long enough to take a couple of breaths, then surged forward, only slowing as the stupid flannel nightgown tugged and jerked me back every once in a while.

It felt like hours but was probably less than three or four minutes until I reached the fork in the tunnel Delilah had mentioned. Now I was there, I realized I hadn't needed them to announce their direction. The tunnel was lit well enough I could see Delilah straight ahead, crawling like me, and a look to the right revealed the chief, doing the same, but closer.

I took a left and picked up my speed. Another couple of minutes passed—maybe two or three hours

—before I saw the end of the tunnel and Carla on her knees, pressing against the top.

She paused, must have heard me coming, and ducked her head to look my way. "Fred. Good." Her voice was breathless. And though it didn't shake, I could hear fear that matched my own. "Hurry, I can't get this. You're stronger."

Never in a million years would I have dreamed Carla Beaker's presence would be exactly the balm and encouragement I needed. The panic and claustrophobia and fear didn't disappear exactly, but they faded. Following her direction, I increased my speed, though that only made me jerk to a stop a little more frequently as my nightgown continued to act as a trap.

Finally there, I squeezed in next to her.

"I think it must be like in the dining room, something's on top of it." Carla shoved on the underside of the trapdoor to demonstrate. It moved, just a bit.

I wedged in closer, managing to shift to a more squat-like position, claustrophobia truly taking over then as Carla and I pressed together, a tangle of body and limbs. With a few grunts from both of us, I managed to get both my hands on the underside of the trapdoor and shoved.

It moved a little more, and somehow the feel of it

communicated Carla was right. Something was on top; it wasn't locked.

I met her gaze, shadowy in the dim light. "Together, count of three?"

She nodded. I counted to three, and we both shoved with all our might.

It moved more, a few more centimeters, and as it clanged back down, it was accompanied by a thud and a vibration. "We moved whatever was blocking it. Let's keep going."

She hadn't really needed to be told, and we didn't count again but built up a quick shoving rhythm. Each thrust upward caused another thud, another vibration, then finally a crash.

Carla let out a sob of relief.

The trapdoor still didn't swing open, but we'd pushed it open enough I could slip my hand through. A quick touch revealed what I suspected. "It's under another rug. Let's just change to a steady push."

We did, and with much groaning and sweating, after a couple of seconds, we managed to slide the trapdoor up several more inches. Another thud sounded, softer, barely audible—whatever had been on top, clearly had slid the rest of the way off—and then it opened, corners of the rug traveling upward with it, and a rush of fresh air greeted us.

I can't remember who got out first, nor if we helped each other stand or crawled out of the hole, or if we somehow teleported in our panic. One minute we were standing straight again, and the next we were on the hardwood floor, looking around.

I got the sense we were in the room exactly opposite from where we'd been captive, as the two walls of windows were now to the front, like before, but the other to the right. The room was mostly dark, the chandelier above dimmed to barely more than a glow.

An ornate armchair lay on its side by the trapdoor—clearly what we'd knocked over—a pool table sat in the middle of the room, and on the far side, scaffolding went up to the ceiling.

I didn't take in any more than that as Carla and I moved as one, neither needing to communicate to know what to do.

As we raced toward the side opposite the windows, where another set of pocket doors were closed, a crash reverberated, partially through the tunnel, partially from somewhere else in the house. Probably another piece of furniture falling over, another trapdoor opened.

Carla reached the pocket doors a couple of steps ahead of me. She gripped the handle of the one on the right and gave a dramatic pull. As before, when I had yanked open the trapdoor, Carla nearly lost her balance as the door flung open with such ease it slid back into the wall with a bang and then bounced back, almost closing again.

I caught her, steadying, and then we looked at each other in surprise. "Not locked."

Carla only nodded, then shook her head. "I don't know if that means it's a trap or that we caught a break."

"I don't think we have time to figure it out." I pushed the door the rest of the way open; a glance revealed another chandelier and the sweeping staircase. The scene to the right clarified where we were. "The front door!" My body reacted on instinct even though logic knew what I'd find. The door didn't budge, handle didn't turn—it was as solid as a wall.

"Fred?" Anna's voice sounded, panicked and excited. "Fred, hurry!"

Leaving the front door, I joined Carla as we approached the pocket doors across the hall from where we'd just exited. "We're here, Anna." I thumped my palm against the wood in greeting, in comfort, I didn't know.

Watson barked from the other side. Then I heard his claws clattering over the hardwood, and he began to pound—doubtlessly rearing up on his hind legs and beating against the pocket doors with his forepaws.

Despite his heft and strength, the pocket doors didn't so much as wiggle.

Carla and I went to work in tandem, running our hands over the doorframe, the handles, the seam in-between. Nothing.

"I don't think they're real." Moving nearer, trying to see through at the seam where I was digging my nails. "It must be a solid wall made to look like a door or not meant to open."

Carla took a couple of steps back, staring at it in dismay, then glancing toward the front door. From her expression, I thought she was getting ready to say we had to leave the others, find another way out. She only partially did so, gesturing back down the hall Mason had led me through what felt like years ago. "Well, we know the other ones open. You go figure them out, and I'll work on the front door or try to find another way. Is that all right?" She cocked an eyebrow, asking my permission for the first time ever. "Divide and conquer?"

"Yeah. Good idea." I squeezed her shoulder, then I hurried past the staircase, took the same right into the hall I had before, and came to stop in front of the pocket doors.

This one was obvious, not that it helped so much. Parallel two-by-fours crossed the expanse. I thought they were planks, but as I touched them, their cool surface revealed them as smooth metal—steel, iron, whatever—the ends of each fitting seamlessly into the molding of the doorframe. Pushing and yanking and pulling did nothing. There was no key, no way to move them. Except... there had to be.

"Fred." The chief hurried beside me. "Perfect. Let me..." He made a squatting motion, pressing the meat of his palms underneath the ridge at the top plank and pushed up, like he was getting ready to shove a weight bar over his head. Nothing happened, nothing at all other than him grunting in pain and one of his hands clutching at his back. With another grunt, he took a second to inspect, realizing what I had. "Oh... they don't lift. They go into the wall."

Anna and Watson were on the other side now, moving toward our sound, and Watson began his assault on his side of the door once more.

I took a couple of steps back, inspecting. "There's a way, obviously. Ethel and Mason came through here, and you can't tell me they secured these manually. There has to be a latch that lets you pull them into..." The memory returned of them slamming the door shut and then that slight whirring sound. "No... it's mechanical. Automatic. They had to push a button or a lever or... *something*." I hurried forward once more, running my hands over the molding of the doorframe, picturing Ethel and Mason as they'd locked us in. There had to be something easy, effortless, and at the right height and... the tips of my fingers slid into a small space between the molding and the wall. "Here." I pushed it in a little farther, and without even realizing I had found it, depressed a button. The whirring sound repeated, the two parallel bars began to slide back into the wall.

Finally, something relatively simple.

"I couldn't get out the trapdoor I found." Delilah arrived, sounding winded. "I had to double back and got out one of yours. Then I..." Her words trailed away as she reached us and witnessed the final few inches of the bars disappearing.

I didn't waitS I'd already gripped the small brass handles that matched the ones in the billiard room and pulled. I nearly cried when it didn't budge, only slipped free from my grip. "Locked." Not simple after all. "Of course." That had been the sound before the whirring, the click of a lock.

Watson was barking in a fury now. Anna whispered pleading sounds; if they were actual words, I couldn't make them out.

"Here..." The chief stepped up, nudging me aside; lowering to one knee, he dug a hand into his pocket. "They got my cell phone, but not these." A yellow candy fell to the floor as he withdrew what appeared to be a small pocketknife.

It was only a second before I recognized what the tool was, and thanks to Leo, even knew how to use it. Without pausing to explain, Marlon got to work on the lock.

Apparently, the lock was simple and normal—anything else possibly overkill combined with the metal beams. In a matter of moments, with another click the doors opened, and Watson sprang into my arms while Anna threw herself at Marlon, blubbering relief and joy.

Across the room, Vivian still sat at the table. From the look of her, the fresh dark paths over her cheeks, she'd cried again, but the tears were gone. She simply stared ashen-faced and wide-eyed, shaking her head. "You're too late. Too late."

Sweeping Watson into my arms, I stood and hurried back into the dining room, the others at my side. As one, we turned to look where Vivian was staring.

The grandfather clock, of course.

"How much more time?" Delilah gripped the chief's right arm, enclosing him as Anna was latched around his left.

He shook his head, his expression matching Vivian's. "None." He sagged, even as Watson looked to my face beaming in joy, all hope banished from Marlon's. "Absolutely none. It should be in the next few seconds, and there's no way to—"

Anna screamed, and I think I did as well, as the grandfather clock began to chime.

One loud chime reverberated through the room. In actuality, the volume was low enough that at any other time it would have simply faded into the background, but in that moment, it was a bomb exploding.

Watson grunted in pain—I glanced down to where he was cradled in my arms and realized I was squeezing him to me in a death grip. After loosening just a touch, he shot me an annoyed glance but didn't try to get down.

It was such an everyday expression from him that it helped reality sink back in. The clock had chimed—no explosion, no bomb.

"We're okay..." Vivian broke the silence, adding to it by standing, the legs of her chair scraping across the floor. "Ethel was lying. Or it didn't work, or—"

"Or my timing's off." The chief had taken a step back with the chime, as if the explosion was going to reverberate from the grandfather clock, but now I moved a little closer. "I think it was eight o'clock exactly when they locked us in, but... I don't remember any chiming then. I might've been wrong, perhaps it was later than that."

"So, the explosion could still happen any second..." Anna whimpered, stumbled sideways, and then sank into one of the armchairs by the window I'd shattered.

Had the grandfather clock chimed when they left? Or at all while we were around the table? I couldn't remember. The click of the door, the whirring sound of the beam sliding into place on the other side were clear in my mind, but chimes? Even in the moment, Marlon's reading the time out loud had me looking at the grandfather clock, making sure he was right. It was now eight thirty; that was *it*? I had been in my living room a little after seven, pondering the future by the fire before Ethel's butler had shown up with his gun. We'd been in this house for an *hour or less*? It felt like years. It was only eight thirty... The Feathered Friends Brigade still had another half hour of their meeting and...

"Leo..." I flinched, accidentally squeezing Watson again. "Maybe we still have a few more minutes. Let's find Leo, and everyone else they took."

"Who else did they take? Why do you think they have Leo?" Delilah looked at me quizzically, then shook her head. "Never mind, there's no time."

"*Exactly.*" Carla was already striding toward the door. "Let's find a way out of here. If that happens and we haven't exploded, *then* we look for Leo."

"Do you think they have Carl?" Anna whimpered, still in the chair.

"Quit worrying about Carl." Vivian strode across the room, shooting a glare toward Anna. "Let's get out of here, we don't know how much time we have left." The change in the elderly jeweler was astonishing—she'd been nothing but defeated the entire time but now looked like she was Indiana Jones and ready to face the lost Temple of Doom. "Buck up, woman."

Even given the gravity of the situation, Delilah, the chief, and I all gaped at Vivian LaRue as she tilted her chin heavenward and strode out the door and into the mansion.

"If they have Leo, then they probably have Carl." Vivian might not have existed, as far as Anna was concerned, her worried gaze trained back on me. "Maybe Winston and Phineas, too."

"Mason didn't tell you they had Carl when he picked you up?"

Anna shook her head at me, a deep blush spreading over her cheeks, and her gaze dropped to the ground. "Ethel picked me up. Invited me over and said that she... I thought that she..." That was clear enough—flattery was what Ethel had lured Anna Hanson with.

"Maybe they don't have Leo." Hope sprang. "Maybe it was just a way to get me here like—"

"Perhaps." Marlon let out a heavy, shaky breath. "Mason told me they had Campbell; that's how..." He shook his head as well, but met my gaze with something like hope his eyes. "If you're right, then—"

"Not to sound completely hard-hearted, but Carla and Vivian weren't wrong." Delilah snapped her fingers, pulling us back. "We've already wasted another minute." She glanced toward the grandfather clock, eyes narrowed in suspicion. "Maybe we're off on the timing, maybe whatever explosive device they set up isn't going to work, or maybe they lied...." She looked back at us. "Either way, let's get out of here."

"A phone." Anna shoved herself to a standing position again. "Ethel took my cell, but maybe there's a landline. We can call Carl, the police."

Delilah was halfway out the door but turned back to us, narrowed in on Marlon. "Why aren't the police here? No one noticed we're gone? *Seven* of us have been taken, including the chief of police. Surely someone—"

"It's barely been an hour." I gestured to the clock, then jerked my hand back as if that would trigger an explosion. "Hardly long enough—"

"Right," she interrupted with a hard nod and turned back around. "Well, come on."

The second hand clicked with a scream two more times in the silence following Delilah's wake. Then a third, and the three of us sprang into action.

"Holler if you find anything. I'll do the same, of course." Marlon left the dining room following Delilah's path.

"I'll look for a phone, call for help." Anna's tone lifted at the end, words quavering.

"Good idea." I tried to offer her an encouraging smile. "I'll join the others to look for a way out."

We walked out of the dining room together, Anna turning left back down the hall toward the entry, the same as the others. I started to, then noticed on the opposite wall was a matching set of pocket doors in the exact same location as these. I walked toward them, reached for the handle. Watson wriggled with the shift and pressure on his side.

"Here, buddy." I lowered him quickly to the ground. "Stay with me, right by me."

He did, but gave a mighty shake, releasing an explosion of corgi hair.

Without waiting any longer, I gripped the small brass handle and pulled, expecting it to be locked. It wasn't. Pulling it easily back into the wall, I stepped in.

The room was dark; I could only make the shadow of things from the light filtering in from behind me. Feeling beside the doorframe, I found a switch, flicked it, and bright light popped on, making me jump, thinking I'd triggered the explosion. I hadn't.

The kitchen.

The Clue board flashed through my mind. Had there been a kitchen? I thought so. Ridiculous. Like it mattered. This was a real house, of course there would be a kitchen. A glance around didn't reveal much of anything—no landline phone, no Leo tied up and captive. The window to the right over a massive pounded-copper sink with a farmhouse lip, was black behind the glass, doubtlessly covered with the exact same false shutters trapping us in. Beside the sink sat a massive set of knives in their butcher block holder. I considered grabbing one, then rejected it. Ethel and Mason weren't here, they'd had a plane to catch, and with six other people roaming a dark house, there was a high chance of being startled and that ending badly. Another quick scan told me there was nothing in this space, not even a corner for a trapdoor, unless it was hidden underneath the cabinets. Although maybe... none of the cabinets had doors, they were all open, so—

I shut that off. A trapdoor didn't matter, they only went to other rooms, and we'd already been through those tunnels.

I patted my thigh as I turned around, going back into the hallway. "Come on, buddy."

Watson hadn't needed the directive, he was sticking close enough to be a tripping hazard.

As we hurried toward the main hall, some of my nerves started to slow, clearing my mind. I didn't think they had Leo or Campbell. Or even Carl, for that matter. Just threats to get us here. Maybe I was wrong, maybe I just wanted to believe that, but it *felt* right, given that they'd used other methods to trap Anna, probably had with the others as well.

They'd probably been lying about the explosion, too. Nothing more than a scare tactic and... I paused in the hallway at that thought, instantly realizing the error of that thinking. This wasn't just a scare tactic.

They kidnapped us, held us at gunpoint, secured us with the zip ties, both the chief and Carla had clearly been struck... This wasn't just a game, not just a scare tactic. We weren't supposed to survive this.

My nerves returned. That explosion could still happen any minute. Any second.

Carla emerged from a doorway down the opposite hall and shook her head. "Nothing in there, literally *nothing*. Not even furniture. The windows were blocked, just like in the other rooms." She gestured toward a small pocket door as she hurried toward us. "And that's just a tiny powder room—"

"Same for the windows in the kitchen."

Before I could continue, Anna emerged to my left, from the room Carla and I found at the end of the tunnel—the billiard room, I suppose. "No phones, no—"

"*Of course* there're no phones, you imbecile." Mary Smith joined us in the hallway from the other side. "What would the point be of that? They didn't trap us here just to call for help."

"We weren't supposed to get out of that dining room before it exploded." Shocking me, Carla came to Anna's defense. "So maybe there are phones."

"Are you so sure of that?" Mary sneered but didn't slow as she marched past us, heading toward the front door. "An explosion could still happen, maybe a fake time limit was just part of the game. It would make sense... looks like a lot of work for only thirty minutes of fun, don't you think?" As she passed Anna, Mary gave her a wide berth. She didn't pound on the back of the front door with her fists, but ran her fingertips around the molding, looking for switches, hidden triggers, probably.

Not bothering being insulted, Anna turned her wide eyes toward us. "Maybe she's right." Hope returned suddenly. "Maybe if we figure it out within the real time limit, we can..."

"No. If this really was a game, and if it's still happening, we're not meant to survive it." While my words sparked fresh panic in Anna's expression, somehow they calmed me again. "I think..." I spared a quick second to judge the veracity of what I was about to say and found it settling. "I think something's gone wrong. While I agree with Mary that it's a lot of work for thirty minutes, I think we were supposed to be dead by now."

"Definitely." Carla nodded her agreement but began moving again back to where Mary had come from. "But that doesn't mean it won't still happen. And regardless, they're on their way out of town, *with* my son. So, whether there's an explosion or not, the clock is still ticking."

I started to reassure her, say that I thought they'd been lying about having hostages, then remembered the brief exchange between Carla and Ethel about Maverick.

The stairs squeaked above us, drawing all our attention back toward the front door, toward the base of the steps. A moment later, Vivian came into view and gave a little flinch as she found all of us staring at her. She adjusted the strap of her black alligator skin purse over her shoulder, then shook her head. "I don't see an escape upstairs. All the windows are covered, and there're—"

"You thought there'd be escape *upstairs?*" Mary gave her trademark sneer as she passed once more, clearly giving up on the front door.

"Guys!" Delilah's voice called from the rear of the house, toward the direction Carla had been headed. "I found a locked door. All the others I tried opened, so I bet this means something."

Without waiting or discussing, all of us hurried that way, Watson speeding up to a slight jog to stay beside my bare feet. We rushed through the darkness, past the room Mary had exited, through another set of double doors, which were open to a long narrow room. I didn't spare it a glance, hurrying through toward the open doors on the opposite side. A massive mirror filled most of the wall on the other side of the doorway, showing our ghostly reflections back to us, making it feel like we were going to collide with our shadow selves and tumble into a dark and twisted wonderland.

Instead, as we entered the hallway, Delilah called from our left, "Over here."

Carla reached her a couple of seconds before Watson and me, but made room.

Delilah had kneeled in front of a single door. Large and ornate, it was one of the few non-pocket doors I'd seen. That probably meant something as well.

Unlike the dining room, there were no parallel bars securing it in place, though that didn't mean there weren't on the other side.

I reached for the handle, not that I expected to find it unlocked and Delilah to have been wrong; it was merely instinct. Locked, of course, but gave that slight wiggle, like a regular door, like a regular lock. "I think it can be picked." I considered the thick door, then thumped my fist against it. "Maybe broken down if need be. It has a different sound than the ones with the metal center."

"On my way." Marlon's voice sounded from the dark of the opposite end of the hall. He'd come out of another room and thumbed over his shoulder as he ran past the giant mirror. "Ethel's office, I guess. Though not all that modern, not even a computer. Still, I thought maybe I could find..." He didn't finish the thought as he neared, Delilah and I both getting out of his way as he dug into his pocket once more and went down on one knee the way Delilah had been. A moment later, he had his tools shoved into the little lock. It was a matter of a second or two before it sprang free with a loud click.

All of us, every single one, including Watson, jumped at the soft sound, still expecting an explosion.

After that glitch of community freezing, we returned to life—Marlon stood with a groan, the hand holding the tools flying behind him to press against his back while his other turned the handle. The door swung open, and he stepped through.

Watson and I entered behind him just as he let out a soft curse.

We were in the library, shelves of books covering the walls from floor to ceiling. Like before, a chandelier glowed softly, almost romantically; however, the scene on the far-right side was anything but romantic. In front of an ornate antique sofa, rather like the one in the Cozy Corgi's mystery room, lay Ethel Beaker, the foxtails of her fur coat seeming to melt into the massive bearskin rug covering the sitting area.

For a heartbeat, it looked like she'd stopped for an awkward nap or spread out for an artfully dramatic photo shoot, save for the pool of blood under her head soaking into the furs. A large silver candlestick lay partially on the rug, partially on the hardwood floor, glistening in the soft light.

It took a moment to pull my gaze away from Ethel—not until Watson padded a few steps in front of us, growling. Instead of looking at Ethel, he peered up. Following his gaze, a pair of shiny black shoes glistened a few feet above the floor over in the corner, directly above an overturned chair. Mason, still looking picture perfect in his butler's tuxedo, hung from the rafters, the silver rope glistening just like the candlestick.

SEVEN

We stood as one, captured in place and utterly shocked. Only Watson had moved, taking a few more small paces, his growl lowering as he sniffed. Then he stopped abruptly, cocked his head, and looked behind him, behind us. Without a moment's hesitation he spun and trotted quickly across the room, past our little group and to the corner.

He might have been the only thing that could make me tear my gaze from Ethel and Mason. As he passed, I nearly reached out to stop him, except that I'd looked over toward the angle of his trajectory. Granny Smith was curled up under an upholstered chair, trembling. She mewled softly at Watson's approach, seemed to calm when he reached her, and sniffed questioningly. He lay down beside her, and the ancient cat visibly and instantly calmed. She took a few slower breaths, finally ending with a sigh as they curled up together.

A sudden racking sob pulled my attention away from the animals. I turned back just in time to see Carla crash to the floor on her knees, covering her face as she began to cry.

Delilah looked at me with wide eyes over Carla's back, as shocked as I was at her reaction.

"Oh, there, there." Anna reached out and patted the back of Carla shoulder. "I'm sorry for your loss, Carla, but I'm sure Ethel didn't suff—" She cringed. "Well…"

Carla's sob broke into a crack of crazed laughter as she whirled to look up at Anna. "You think I'm crying for *Ethel*? Hardly. That's the best sight I've ever seen in my life!" Another laugh, which also broke, returning to a sob. "Maverick. They don't have him. They didn't get away. He's… he's safe."

Mary Smith stared at Carla, horrified, as if repulsed by such a display. Vivian, however, finally found her humanity and sank down beside Carla, wrapping an arm over her back, then pulling her close. "Yes, dear. Your baby is safe. I'm sure he's safe." A few tears rolled down her cheeks. It showed the stress of the evening that it was only then the face of Julian LaRue flashed through my mind—he'd been killed the previous year. He hadn't been a baby, far from it, and rather horrible, truth be told. However, neither of those things mattered to Vivian. She'd lost her son, *her* baby.

Anna and Delilah let out twin sounds of comprehension along with expressions of pity but then refocused on the bodies. The chief had moved closer, studying the butler. "I... I think it's too late. Even if we got him down, he—"

"Who cares?" Mary sneered once more. "He was trying to kill us. I don't care if he has another five minutes of life in him. Let him hang."

"Good Lord, woman." Anna grimaced at her. "Have some class."

Mary simply scoffed.

"I can't say I entirely disagree with Mary on that one." Delilah looked toward the chief, then to me. "What do you think? Clearly this wasn't part of their plan. So... is the explosion late, or not happening?"

I studied them. The butler first. Mason's body was completely still, not even the slightest bit of swing or sway. It had happened a while ago, I figured. Then the socialite. Ethel... there were no clues to how long she'd been there, but it only made sense it would have been at the same time more or less. "Not happening, I think. I would say this explains a thirty-minute delay that never happened." Another thought hit me as I scanned the library and then back to the door before walking to it and examining the handle. "This is the kind that could have been locked from the inside *before* the door was closed, so it doesn't mean Ethel or Mason locked it when they entered."

Anna caught on the quickest, eyes going wide in fear as she looked around. "Meaning whoever killed them could still be inside? Wandering around the halls with us, waiting to kill us one by one." Her voice had started to rise in panic, then dipped as another realization hit her and she practically stumbled back. "Or... one of you."

"Lord, we're back to *that*?" Mary snarled again. "You're as bad as Vivian!" She gestured toward the scene. "It's pretty obvious, don't you think? The two had an argument, probably about the proper way to fold napkins or something. Having had enough, Mason whacked Ethel on the head, something we've all wanted to do, I'm certain. And then..." Her voice trailed as she looked over at Mason before finishing weakly, "And he... hung himself out of... grief or guilt or something."

It was the easiest explanation, the obvious one.

Two dead bodies in a locked room, the window covered with the same enclosing shutters as the rest of the house. I looked toward the chief, who still seemed to be debating if he should get Mason down or keep the scene intact. "Maybe you weren't Mr. Boddy after all."

He pulled his attention away from Mason and met my gaze. "Then we have the candlestick *and* rope in the library. We just have to figure out who."

"Great, we're back to thinking it's one of us?"

Delilah ignored Mary's repeated question, looking to me as well. "You think Branson, don't you?"

I was almost embarrassed to admit it, but I shrugged. "Yes. And... *yes*, I know I always think Branson."

"Well, who wouldn't?" Wiping her eyes, Carla stood, offering a hand down to Vivian as she spoke. "Are we really supposed to think Ethel Beaker, who has the imagination capacity of one of her rancid fur coats, came up with all of this? Turning her mansion into a Clue game?" She gestured toward me once Vivian stood. "It's about you, obviously. Everything set up for you. Branson's been obsessed with you for years and..." Horror washed over her. "Maverick!

You don't think Branson would take Maverick and—"

"No." I didn't have to fake that at all. "I don't. Like you said, if this is Branson, which surely it is, then it's about me. There'd be no reason for him to take your son."

"Then why am *I* here?" Vivian spoke up with a little croak. "I didn't know Branson. No more than saying hi on the street every once in a while, same as with the others on the police force. Beyond that, no offense, but I don't mean anything to *you*." She gestured toward me.

She wasn't wrong, and at her point, I glanced toward Mary, then Marlon. The chief made a little more sense as far as connections with me than Mary, but not much. "Maybe I'm wrong. Maybe this isn't Branson."

"Can we figure this out later?" Mary sounded a little less sarcastic than normal, just a touch. "Actually, *you* figure this out later. For now, let's get out of here. Whether it's going to explode or not, I am *done*." She flung her hand out toward Ethel and Mason. "If nothing else, let's get out of this room."

"Not a bad idea." Chief Dunmore nodded his agreement. "There's only one door in or out, the windows are covered, so we're wasting time. And the less we're in here, the less we'll disturb the scene."

As he headed to leave, my gaze flicked to Watson and Granny Smith under the chair in the corner. She seemed to be sleeping peacefully, her head resting on Watson's flank. For his part, Watson stayed where he was, offering comfort, but his chocolate gaze stayed on me. I tried to offer him a smile and then returned to Ethel and Mason. As gruesome as their deaths were, it had to mean something.

"What are you thinking?" Anna touched my arm. "I *know* that look. You're figuring something out."

"No, I'm not. If I'm..." I shook my head but didn't look at her, studying the bodies for a few more seconds and then the room. "Why were Ethel and Mason in here? Whether they actually set a bomb or not, with what they've just done to all of us, they had to get out of town quickly. I believed Ethel when she said they had a plane to catch."

"With Maverick," Carla threw in, coldly.

"I imagine, yes." Still analyzing the room, I went ahead with my theory, crazy though it might sound. "Even if Branson is involved, why would they have met him in *here* before they left?" I glanced at Carla, finally. "Do you know how to get to the garage? Actually, there's not a helicopter pad on the roof or something that we don't know about, is there? Ethel wouldn't have meant that kind of flight?"

Carla managed a little laugh. "I don't think so, but I wouldn't have predicted any of this either. As far as the garage—" She gestured to the left, through the wall in the direction I supposed the garage lay. "—it was the first place I tried after getting out of the dining room. It's locked up tight." She spared a small glance toward Delilah. "You said this room was the only one locked, but it wasn't. I just didn't think it meant anything other than they blocked our escape route, although it wasn't really locked. It's got what looks like the inside of one of those shutters covering the entire door. Like a safe."

Pretty much what I'd figured. Once more I scanned the library. Like the dining room, it echoed what might've been on the *Titanic*, stepping back in time. Exquisite. Gorgeous dark shelving, leather and fabric-bound books filling every space, even a little rolling ladder attached at one side. Stained glass lamps, upholstered Victorian chairs, brass and crystal fixtures—so perfect I would have expected the trapdoor from the dining room to lead here, they matched.

They matched.

"If this is like a game board, I think the dining room was where we started, and this library is where we were... or *are* supposed to finish." I cringed, realizing how that sounded, and began to spare an apologetic grimace toward Ethel and Mason, then realized I didn't care and continued. "Not finished like *them*, but an actual end to the game, maybe a revealing of the clues we'd gathered, giving our deductions and best guesses. Then... a way out. I think that's why they were here. They were leaving, they just... didn't get the chance."

"A trapdoor." The chief and Delilah spoke at the same time, but neither seemed to notice as they too looked around the room with fresh eyes.

Anna hurried over to the corner but stopped, clearly not wanting to disturb the animals. "Do you think..."

"No. There won't be another tunnel." If I were Branson... designing a game for me, for Winifred Page-Lopez—or Winifred Page, as I was sure he thought of me—what would I do? That was so obvious it barely deserved the question. "There's a secret lever on one of these books. I'm willing to bet anything if we remove the right one or push it in, or... something, one of the bookshelves will slide away."

No one scoffed, no one laughed. A glance

around revealed a few looks of surprise, but most were nodding as if they too thought it was obvious, given the situation. Only then did I realize Mary Smith had left the room after all.

"Okay, let's rip every book from the shelf, if that's what it takes." The chief cringed at the bodies, clearly deciding there was no other choice but to disturb the scene. "Let's try to at least give a decent circumference to the dead, save what clues we can."

"Yeah, no problem. Wasn't planning on cuddling up with either one of them." Delilah crossed the room and began pulling books from the shelves, letting them fall to the floor.

From the corner, Granny Smith hissed angrily, and Watson let out a plaintive whimper.

Delilah whipped toward the sound, attack in her eyes, but her gaze softened the instant she saw Watson. "Oh, I forgot about you, handsome boy."

"He and Granny Smith bonded a couple months ago. I think he's comforting her, she's probably scared. Either way, I know she doesn't feel good." Mason on my porch—in what was really just a matter of minutes before—flashed through my mind, and it felt like years. "I think Dr. Sallee was originally supposed to end her suffering tomorrow."

Delilah gave a nod and returned to the books,

that time setting them down more gently, no more crashes.

The others joined in, some taking books off the shelves, others pressing against them like they might have a button, others flipping through the pages looking for a key.

I stayed where I was, still inspecting the room, feeling like this was a puzzle I could figure out, that it was designed for me to figure out. The notion made me a little sick to my stomach, but I pushed past it.

I watched the others for a few seconds, glanced back at Watson and Granny Smith, then the bookshelves themselves, the crown molding above, the brocade wallpaper, and then back to Ethel. More specifically, to the sofa behind Ethel. Hadn't I thought it looked like the one in my mystery room? It did—different fabric, but close enough. I wasn't sure how that helped. It wasn't against the wall, maybe there was a trapdoor beneath it, under the bear rug? But I didn't think so.

Then I saw it—over to the left, behind the sofa, next to one of the bookcases. A tall antique pedestal lamp with an ornate Portobello shade, exactly like in the bookshop. At least, I assumed. The light was off so I couldn't be sure about the color. Either way, that was it. I crossed the library, taking the long way around the bodies and stopped at the lamp. For just a second, I hesitated, thinking if I pulled one of the tasseled strings it might be the trigger that caused the bomb. I didn't think so, what would his point have been in that?

So, I pulled it.

A lightbulb illuminated, and sure enough, the deep purple of the Portobello shade matched the one I had spent countless hours reading beneath perfectly.

Turning on the light had been the right call, as it was mere seconds, as I turned to look at the books covering the shelves directly behind the lamp, before something glittering on one of the spines caught my eye.

I gasped at the recognition; I couldn't help it. Nor could I make myself reach out and touch it.

There, shoved into the spine of Erica Spindler's *The Detective's Daughter*—what else?—was a small, glossy enameled pin. One I'd only seen for a matter of moments but was seared into my nightmares. The metal corgi had the same deep orange coloring of Watson, even the same white over its chest. The pin had emerald-green eyes instead of Watson's brown, the only other difference was sprays of little rhinestones here and there. The last time I'd seen it…

I twisted, looking up at Mason hanging from the rafters, almost expecting to find his body morphed into Angus Witt with a knitted mustard-hued scarf around his neck. Mason was still Mason, just a butler, not a knitter or a higher-up in the Irons family. He hadn't miraculously donned a scarf.

I returned to the pin, thinking maybe it too was a figment of imagination—but it wasn't. It looked just as it had when Branson had left it for me the previous year, attached to the old knitter's scarf, as a little gift.

"Here." I had to make myself speak, and I wasn't sure if I was loud enough for anyone else to hear. Waves of revulsion rolled over me at the sight of it. Not just the memory of Angus... even more so, I could almost see Branson's expression as I stood in front of the corgi pin. I had figured it out, and in so doing, acknowledged that he knew me, that I knew him. That on some level we knew how the other operated.

Turning away from it wouldn't change the facts, nor would it help us get free, so I reached out, pressed my thumb against the corgi and pushed. Nothing happened, no whirring, not a click, nothing creaked as it opened.

The second try was accompanied by all of those

noises when I pulled the book free from the shelf. That portion of the bookcase popped forward as if a hinge had been sprung. I gripped the edge, fingers curling around the back, and pulled it open like a gate, revealing a set of concrete stairs down into the darkness.

EIGHT

"You've *got* to be kidding me." Delilah spoke over my shoulder, sounding thoroughly irritated. "This is ridiculous. It just doesn't end."

Her frustration helped wipe away any remaining bit of fear and made me laugh as I stared down into the darkness, considering. "I think this is the end. Actually—" I patted the thick edge of the bookcase. "—*this* was the end, I bet, and will lead to the way out."

"Ah!" Carla cried out from behind, making me look over my shoulder. She stood in the opposite corner from Watson and Granny Smith—who bared fangs in a silent hiss at Carla's outburst—and held up a glistening silver gun. "It was behind this planter. It's Ethel's, same one she used at the table tonight." She squared her shoulders. "Just in case there's another little surprise for us down there, the tables have turned." Doubt flitted across her face, and she inspected the gun, after a moment figuring out how to open the chamber. A satisfied nod revealed it was indeed still loaded.

Marlon sighed. "Well, I doubt we could have gotten much more information from the gun anyway. We all saw Ethel use it. So..." He threw up his hands in surrender. "We've disrupted the whole crime scene, why stop now?"

"That's the least of my concerns." Anna managed to disagree without sounding overly dismissive. "Whatever it takes to get out of here, get home to my Carl and my boys."

"I agree." I wasn't sure if I'd ever meant anything more.

"Me too." Delilah gestured down the steps, then glanced at Ethel. "If there was a candle attached to that murder weapon, I'd pick it up, light it, and wouldn't think twice about fingerprints or whatnot. As there isn't, let's get going."

I couldn't say I'd go that far, but it was beside the point. Though I couldn't see any, I still ran my hand along the inside of the tunnel wall—no light switch or button. "Let's do it." I took a couple of steps into the shadows, then glanced behind me. "Carla, do you wanna come next since you have the gun? Or if you don't want to use it, you can give it to—"

"Are you nuts?" Laughter threaded through her words as she moved up beside Delilah. "I'll use this in a heartbeat."

Figured. As we made our way down the steps, I had a momentary out-of-body experience, floating above us. The view was almost funny. Though mostly a different cast of players, my little group often called ourselves the Scooby Gang. Descending into the darkness, clustered in a rough line with me leading the way, feeling the walls for guidance, we really did look like Fred, Daphne, Velma, and Shaggy tiptoeing through a mystery. At the thought, I realized our *Scooby* wasn't with us. That was fine, Watson could stay with Granny Smith. Plus, while I didn't think there was any trap at the bottom of the stairs, I couldn't be sure.

I didn't count, but there were only around fourteen or fifteen steps until we reached the end. The air had grown slightly cooler, and the wall under my hand came to an abrupt end announcing our arrival. "One second."

From behind, someone grunted; Anna apologized—she'd probably bumped into them. And wouldn't that have made a spectacular picture, Anna knocking us all over like bowling pins into whatever waited for us? Slipping my hand around the corner, I felt against the adjacent wall. Almost instantly, anti-climactic or not, I found the light switch and flicked it.

Bright overhead fluorescents filled the space and wiped away all danger, as it revealed a long garage containing enough space for four or five cars. There was only one present—a glossy black extended sedan, kind of like a miniature limo, and at the end, a garage door.

Without waiting for the rest to reach the bottom or give a second's consideration, I hit the button I found by the light switch. After the silence of the mansion, the garage door moving up—even though it was modern and smooth—made me flinch.

The rest were around me then. A blizzard, at least the beginning of one, raged outside the garage. As the frigid wind rushed in, bringing with it snow and ice, Anna began to cry. "It's over." She choked out a sob as she hurried across the space. "It's over!"

Vivian joined her, letting out a choked little cry of her own.

Carla hurried along after them, but instead of going all the way to the end of the garage, she stopped at the driver's side door of the little limo and threw it open.

"Wait!" Marlon called out, the panic in his voice at odds with what the rest of us were feeling.

Anna and Vivian turned back. Carla didn't, instead ducking inside the car. Delilah and I turned as well, finding the police chief on the far side of the garage.

He held up a hand. "Hold on. Found the bomb."

Anna yelped, though it wasn't necessary; she couldn't see what I did. Though my heartbeat sped up at the sight of just how close we'd come, I knew we were safe. The bomb wasn't technically a bomb. Just a... I don't know, I didn't have a word for it—a small box with a timer that was clearly supposed to ignite a little flame, maybe just a spark, I wasn't sure. The red numbers on the narrow digital display blinked thirty minutes, double-zero seconds—almost like a microwave waiting for someone to hit the Start button. Above the device was the main gas line to the house, which had clearly been tampered with.

"Amateur." Delilah stepped up beside me and let out a shaky breath. "But effective."

"Yeah." I nodded my agreement and called out to the chief, who was inspecting the gas line. "It's closed, right?"

"Yes." He confirmed without looking my way, still testing the gas line, then lowered his hand behind the square device, did something, probably with the wiring, and the red thirty minutes went black. Maybe he'd just unplugged it.

"They really were going to blow us up." I glanced back up the stairs to the library, not that I could see Ethel and Mason. "They really were." I'd known that, as I'd thought many times there was no way they were going to do everything they had done to us and let us live, but still... The confirmation was equally as chilling as the frigid wind rushing inside. It confirmed the other thing I'd already known. "Something went wrong."

"*You think?*" Delilah snorted out a laugh. "Ethel definitely didn't plan on a candlestick to the head."

Carla let out a cry from inside the limo, a strangled gasp for air.

I hurried toward the car, and other footfalls joined me, but I didn't check who, as I pulled up to the open driver's door. Carla was bent over, head on the steering wheel, a phone to her ear as she sobbed. "He's okay? You're sure he's okay? He's *with* you?" There was just a little bit of a pause before she nodded at whatever the answer was. "Let me talk to him."

"We finally have a phone, and you don't call someone to get us out of here?" Mary Smith was back, though I'd not heard her join. "You've got to be—"

"Shut up." Anna glared at her, and for once Mary said nothing back.

"Hi, baby." Carla's tears streamed fresh. "No, I'm okay. I'm sorry, I'm not trying to scare you. Mom is okay." She cleared her throat, and then her voice, though tight, sounded much more normal as she started again. "You keep having fun with Auntie Donna and Elphie, all right? I'll pick you up soon." Another nod, an attempt to speak, failed, and then success. "I love you, too." She hung up the phone, literally, as it had a cradle in the center console, and sank back against the seat, tears streaming as she let out a long sigh, which sounded like she'd been holding her breath the entire time. "Thank God."

As a group, we indulged Carla for another few seconds, and then Marlon stepped forward and bent down, speaking urgently. "Mind if I use that? I'm going to call dispatch."

It was over. Finally.

A few minutes later, Detective Susan Green, and probably half, if not all, of the Estes Park police force was headed our way, and the rest of us used the phone. Neither Leo nor Carl answered. Anna and I both nearly slipped into panic—even though Carl had technically never been under threat—but Marlon had confirmed Campbell was fine, that he was on his way, too. The hostage thing had been nothing more than a lie, suggesting the bird club was still meeting. How that was even possible, I had no idea.

As Delilah took the phone after me, I realized, or remembered, I supposed, that Watson was still in the library. I debated for a moment, not wanting to make him wait in the cold garage, or more specifically not make Granny Smith, as there was no way I was going to separate them. I also didn't relish the idea of returning to the library and waiting there with Ethel and Mason. However, that's what I chose.

I walked back up the steps, barely registering the warmth, and even though I knew we were safe, my heart rate increased as I reentered the library. I tried not to look at the bodies, but I didn't succeed. Having seen the evidence of what they'd planned, a fresh wave of anger leaped over me, followed by vindication—whether that was the moral high ground or not. I didn't know exactly what had gone wrong, and in that moment, I didn't care. I was just glad that it had

—both because it kept us from dying in a ball of fire, and... because they got what they deserved.

Ridiculously, I promised myself I'd never think of Ethel Beaker again as I turned from her and crossed the rest of the room. Kneeling beside the chair, I reached under and stroked Watson. "Hey, sweet boy. It's over. We're safe."

He still didn't budge, though he lifted his head and licked my hand. Something in the depths of his brown eyes told me the second before I realized Granny Smith hadn't hissed or flashed her fangs toward my hand.

"Oh, buddy..." Sure enough, as I stroked Granny Smith's side, it was clear she wouldn't have to pay a visit to Dr. Sallee the next day, that she was finally at rest. "I'm sorry, sweet boy. I know you cared for her." I transferred my stroking back to Watson. He merely let his head fall against Granny Smith once more as he let out a long, gentle sigh, then closed his eyes.

NINE

Watson left Granny Smith's side only once—when Leo walked up the steps from the garage. As *I* hadn't left *Watson's* side, the two of us saw Leo at the same time. I must have sprouted wings, as one moment I was sitting cross-legged on the floor by the animals and the next crashing into Leo, nearly knocking him backward. There might have been words, I'm sure there were, from both of us, but I remember none of them—only the strength of his arms around me, the feel of the stubble on his jaw as I tucked my head into his neck, the warmth of his body. Fear had left fully as those red numbers by the gas line had disappeared, but it wasn't until I was in his embrace that I finally found my breath.

At some point, we broke apart, if for no other reason than Watson's frantic pawing on our thighs threatened to rip us to shreds. Leo sank to both knees and offered Watson the same embrace he'd given me.

A moment later I joined, and for once, as Watson was squished between us, he didn't complain or wriggle free. By the time we separated, however, his tongue was certainly desert dry as he hadn't stopped licking either of us the entire time.

Once released, he padded back over to the corner, looked at us expectantly, and then curled back up with Granny Smith. Through interviews with Detective Green and Officer Cabot—and as expected, nearly the entire force of the Estes Park Police Department—Watson refused to budge. He didn't mourn, didn't whimper, he didn't even look distressed. Simply remained on guard duty. For what had become a new state of existence, I had no clue how much time had passed when we were finally told we could leave. Still, Watson refused.

It was Susan, staring at her Officer Fleabag with pride at him being a good soldier, a protector and defender, who came up with the perfect solution. Not long after, Dr. Sallee entered the library, halted at the sight of Ethel and Mason, and then shook it off, heading toward Watson and the rest of us crowded in the corner.

Watson sniffed the vet's hand as he ruffled the fur between Watson's ears and then stroked Granny Smith's back.

Dr. Sallee issued a long sigh and patted the cat's rump as if she could still feel him. "I'm happy for you, Granny Smith. No more visits to my office, no more injections, no more of me. You left this world safe in the embrace of the best dog I've ever met. Now... you go join your master Colin over that Rainbow Bridge. I have no doubt he's been waiting for you." Another pat, then he angled to meet Watson's gaze. "I've got her now, buddy. Granny Smith is safe. I'll take care of her and love her and send her on to her daddy. Okay?"

Watson studied the vet, cocked his head for a second, then rested his muzzle on Granny Smith's neck for a moment. He gave a little chuff, angled back to nudge her whiskers with his nose, then stood. After trotting halfway across the library and pausing to sniff the bloody candlestick, Watson looked back at Leo and me, annoyance flashing in his eyes.

Witnessing him saying goodbye to his friend had been the first thing that had almost made me cry that evening, but at the sight of his ever-present disapproval, I burst out with a laugh. "Apparently, His Majesty has decided that it's time to go, and we, *of course*, are running behind schedule."

Once Leo and I stood up, Watson scurried the rest of the way to the secret passage behind the bookcase, he didn't bother looking back to make sure we were following but lumbered down the steps and out of view. As we joined him walking from the garage to Leo's Jeep, he frolicked puppy-like in the blizzard, even pausing beside the tires to roll on his back and do his version of a snow angel in the quickly thickening fluff. He was probably just trying to shake off the events of the evening, not actually make a snow angel, but I could swear when he allowed Leo to lift him into the Jeep, I saw the imprint of wings left behind in his chunky loaf-shaped form in the snow.

Tears finally came as we got back to the cabin and reached the front door. I had no memory of leaving it open, but snow had piled up over the threshold. On the other side of the mound, a corner of the thick manila envelope with the supposed papers serving me the announcement of Ethel's lawsuit spilled out —discolored and damp as they soaked up the snow. It was finding the gun on the narrow entryway table that brought me up short and cracked the dam of tears.

The police questioning at the scene had lasted at least twice as long as the time in Ethel's mansion, but those hours had flown compared to the century it had felt like during the twisted game of Clue. But there, staring at the cell phone and gun, the open door, it felt like moments, *only moments* since Mason and Granny Smith had arrived on our porch.

Leo paused long enough to shut the door behind us before taking me in his arms again. Sometime later, the tears slowed, and I found myself on the sofa in front of the ashes remaining in the fireplace, still in Leo's arms, Watson smashed between us again. The tears eventually slowed, then stopped, as did the shaking.

When we finally separated, Leo's cheeks were tear-streaked, his eyes red and puffy, and his voice thick. "I'll never forgive myself, standing there lecturing about hummingbirds, planning our photo-hunting expeditions, and even playing bird trivia with Myrtle's group, all while you were in the fight for your life. I didn't know." Anger flashed in his honey-brown gaze, but quickly faded away to shame. "I would have thought... I would have sworn that I would have *felt* it, you know? Something in my gut, or blood, or... I don't know, some whisper that I was about to lose you."

"Leo." I reached across the short distance, taking his face in both of my hands. "There's no way you could have known. Don't do this to yourself. You can't expect—"

"And to think you called..." He shook his head and choked out a dark laugh. "I was standing there at Habanero's, waiting for our food when you called. I looked at the screen, didn't recognize the number, and slipped it back into my pocket. I didn't even feel it then, didn't feel *you* then." I tried to interject, but he didn't give me a chance as he issued another horrid laugh. "It was Marcus who told me, of all people. He handed me our bag of food and asked if I hadn't heard of you nearly being killed at Ethel's house. Someone had just called him and—"

"Oh, Leo." I sighed; I couldn't even imagine.

"I thought he was joking, being his normal dramatic self, but..." He shook his head again and seemed to be speaking to himself. "I'd called your cell on the way from the meeting to Habanero's, seeing if you wanted me to pick up ice cream, but when you didn't answer, I just thought you were reading, or possibly had fallen asleep. I never dreamed that—"

"Who would?" I gave a laugh of my own and then gestured toward the now-melted pile of snow certainly ruining that spot in the hardwood floor, not that I cared in the slightest. "Who would ever even consider any of this? It's absolutely crazy. If I hadn't lived it, I'd say it wasn't real, that it had just been a stunt, some horrible *Candid Camera* prank."

"I should have seen it coming. It doesn't matter if it's crazy." Anger was back, both the fire in his eyes and in the gravel in his voice. "*Branson* is crazy. This is him. We have to predict the crazy."

Watson whimpered, looking up in concern at the change in Leo.

"Yes, it was Branson. I'm certain." I patted Watson in comfort as I spoke. "But... there's only so much crazy you can actually predict. That's kind of how that goes."

"I'm going to kill him." Once more Leo seemed to be speaking to himself, then met my gaze. "I'm going to kill him. Do whatever it takes so he *never* can touch you again."

Did I experience fear at that? A little. Shock or revulsion that my husband would say such a thing? No, not a bit. Did I think he wasn't serious or simply caught up in the moment? No, he meant it just as much as he had our wedding vows.

I simply slipped my hand into his and held his gaze. "We're going to do whatever it takes to end this. Whenever it is, we'll get our chance. I'm fine with jail, as long as that door is locked and the key thrown away. But..." He'd started to shake his head in disagreement, and I leaned forward, cutting him off. "*But*, if killing Branson is how this goes, then that's how it goes. It's like Paulie has said, at the end of this, it's going to be him or us." Perhaps that notion should have filled me with fear more than ever, considering the night I'd just been through. It didn't. Over the years, I'd learned to trust my gut. Sure, it could waffle at times, at others even be mistaken. That wasn't the case in that moment. My gut wasn't waffling, and it wasn't mistaken; my surety could be heard as I spoke. "We *win* this, Leo. Branson doesn't. You and me? We have a long and happy life ahead." I grinned down at Watson for a moment. "All three of us." Then I looked back to Leo. "I know it. I can *feel* it."

He studied my gaze, and whether he felt it too or simply trusted that Winifred gut, it didn't matter. He gave a nod, the corner of his lips curving to a slight smile, then he exhaled, settling into the truth of it all. "That's good enough for me."

For me, too. "Now..." I squeezed his hands again before releasing them. "I'm exhausted, and I don't wanna think about Ethel, Branson, or anything resembling Clue, at least for the rest of the evening. But... don't think I didn't notice you mention that you managed to pick up our Habanero's order?

Please tell me you didn't leave it behind in your rush to get to Ethel's."

He laughed, a loud burst of a thing, partially crazed itself, before softening to a chuckle. "That entire trip is a blur, but I bet I tossed it into the back seat when I jumped into the Jeep. If so, I'm sure it's a jumbled mess. Not to mention, it's been in the car for hours."

I shrugged. "It's a blizzard, nature's freezer. I'm sure it's fine. And even if it's not, food poisoning is hardly the scariest thing I've faced this evening. I want cheese, meat, tortillas, and as much green chili as I can possibly get." My stomach growled at the thought. "I don't suppose you stopped between Habanero's and Ethel's to pick up ice cream?"

Another laugh exploded. "Oh yes. I also dropped off laundry, picked up the mail, and did an extra-long session in the tanning booth after hearing that my wife had been held hostage and nearly murdered." He grinned and lifted one hand from Watson to gesture toward the kitchen. "I'm pretty sure there's still at least half of that tub of pumpkin spice I bought last week left."

"That'll do." I narrowed my eyes on him. "Wait... you use a tanning booth?"

That time his laugh was barely more than a snort.

Chuckling, I sucked in a happy breath at the next thought. "Oh, I'm going to sleep in tomorrow, like *really* sleep in, and then drink dirty chais until Katie's espresso machine breaks."

"Sounds like a plan." Leo stood, then looked down at Watson. "Before we get the Mexican food, and even before we clean up that pile of snow, what do you say about a..."

Watson sprang up, eyes wide and giving his anticipatory whimper.

"*Treat?*"

Watson howled in delight, sprang from the couch and managed a never-ending trail of circles around Leo's feet all the way into the kitchen.

Sleep in, I did. All of us, actually. Leo took the morning off with the option of the whole day if needed, and Watson was still soundly slumbering on his dog bed as we woke, snoring away, all four miniature legs splayed in the air. He finally roused when the first pot of coffee finished brewing, although I think it was the smell of eggs and sausages that Leo had cooked up. I'd had the notion of the three of us walking the path Watson and I normally took through the woods to the clearing every morning before work, but the snow, which hadn't finished falling, had other ideas.

Before long, and not surprising Leo or myself, I began to get antsy. Of course, I couldn't keep the events of the night before from spinning through my mind, both in memory and trying to puzzle out certain aspects. Doing so in the house would make me go stir-crazy. Shortly before noon, we each got in our vehicles—Leo in the Jeep, Watson and me in the Mini Cooper—and headed into town. Despite the blizzard, with snow tires, my little go-kart was a powerhouse in the winter. Though a little deeper than typical, as long as I followed the path Leo's Jeep blazed before us, there wasn't so much as a slip or a slide.

To my pleasant surprise, once we reached the main roads, the streets were thoroughly plowed—not crystal clear, but easily maneuverable. The town had plenty of warning about this snowstorm, and the mayor had promised the extra plows she'd spent a small fortune on were going to make a difference. She'd been right.

After we passed the intersection of Elkhorn and Moraine Avenues, I turned into the parking lot behind the Cozy Corgi and Leo continued on, a wave from his rearview window, toward Chipmunk Mountain.

Walking over the little bridge from the parking lot to the back path that led to the Cozy Corgi was akin to winning the lottery. Not only had the blizzard turned the already gorgeous mountain town into a fairy-tale winter wonderland, but there were a couple of moments only a few hours before that getting to return to the everyday ins and outs of my life was anything but guaranteed. It seemed Watson felt the same. We might have walked, but we also might have been floating on an extra-large cloud nine all the way into the bookstore.

With an ear-splitting bark of joy that suggested he had leaped up a few more cloud levels to number thirteen, Watson scrambled away from me and completely bowled Ben over.

Amid a cloud of corgi hair thick enough to compete with the blizzard outside, Ben grinned up at me, never ceasing in his stroking of Watson. "I think I might need to give up trying to get my book of Coyote published. I should just start writing stories about you two. You get into bigger scrapes than I could ever dream up. Although, no one would believe them."

"Oh, please, don't do that." I laughed and shook my head. "Living it once was enough. I definitely don't want to read about it. In fact, I..." A scene from the night before flashed in my mind.

"You okay?" Ben paused in his adoration of Watson. "Sorry, of course you're not. That's a stupid question."

He started to stand, but I waved him down. "No. I mean, yes. I'm completely fine. Just had a little memory from yesterday." I hurried on as he winced.

"About books, actually. It's a good thing." I almost shared my idea of some sort of mystery writing conference, but I wasn't ready to. All of that had been washed away, naturally, in everything that had followed. I glanced around the bookshop, lingering as I peered into the mystery room, at the antique sofa so close to the one behind Ethel's lifeless body and then lifted my gaze to stare at the near twin of the purple Portobello lamp.

For a heartbeat, I had the impulse to have Ben help me get the furniture out of there, carry them right down the street through the blizzard to Victorian Antlers and tell my uncles they needed to take them back. The impulse didn't fade necessarily, but I knew enough to slow down before making such a rash decision. That little alcove in front of the river rock fireplace had been one of my favorite places in the entire world. I wanted to sit with it before I allowed Ethel to ruin my special place. I also realized I wanted to consider the conference idea again as well. Did I *really* want to add *another* aspect to what I'd always considered a perfect life? I wasn't sure, but it wasn't like there was a hurry to figure it out.

"Are you sure you're okay?" Ben was still studying me but had returned to petting Watson and spoke around getting his face bathed in corgi kisses.

"Thanks to the snow, we've barely had anyone after breakfast rush. You don't have to be here, you can take it easy."

I hadn't noticed if the parking lot was full or empty, hadn't been paying any attention. "I want to be here, and even if it was the height of tourist season, it's not like you can't handle it yourself. You've had to many times, but..." I gestured above our heads.

"Dirty chai time?" He cocked his right eyebrow, the little scar through it pale against the deep tan of his skin.

"Well past. You have no idea." Though he was a little out of the way from the steps, I crossed to Ben and squeezed his hand, not wanting to take more of his attention than that away from Watson. "Maybe a cliché coming from a woman who had a brush with death, but I realized that I probably don't say it enough. So... I love you, Ben Pacheco. I'm glad you're in my life, maybe not as demonstrably as Watson, but still mighty glad."

"I love you, too." He smiled back, eyes clear and sincere, and then we focused on Watson. "And you too, Watson, you big fluffball. I love you, too."

Watson had just started to calm, but at his name from Ben's lips, his joy sparked again. His whole body returned to wriggling and his tongue to an obscene amount of licking.

Katie screamed, quite literally, as I reached the top of the steps and entered the bakery, scrambling around the marble countertop and rushed the entire length of the space, arms high overhead, brown spirals that had reached her shoulders flying behind her, then plowed into me with such strength my breath was stolen. "I didn't hear you come in! I actually thought you'd be later, maybe after the lunch rush. But I knew sooner or later, your dirty chai addiction would kick in no matter what." Her arms tightened around my neck, not helping the struggle-to-breathe situation. "I promised myself I wasn't going to make you retell the story or relive a minute of it, but it turns out, I lied. I'm going to ask you a billion questions, but don't worry, I'll make you a dirty chai for every question I ask, and I've got these new rolls that will make it worth—"

Chuckling, I managed to pull back ever so slightly and meet her eyes. "It's good to see you too."

"Goodness, I kicked into overdrive, didn't I?" She sighed, then let out a little choked sob and wrapped me into an even tighter hug. "Oh, Fred!"

And that was it, that was all that could happen for several minutes—just an overly tight, soul-healing, somewhat awkward embrace considering our height differences, with my dearest friend in the world.

At long last, Katie finally released me and gestured for me to follow toward the actual bakery and the espresso machine as she spoke over her shoulder. "I swear, if Ethel wasn't dead already, I'd march right over there and beat her to death with a rolling pin." She issued a whole-body flinch, then looked over her other shoulder to the spot where the original little kitchen used to be—which now housed shelves of Cozy Corgi merchandise above Watson's little apartment. "Oh... well, I guess that had already been done up here, *thanks*, Garble sisters. But, for Ethel, it'd be worth a repeat."

I didn't disagree with her, nor did I bother saying so, instead giving Katie's assistant baker a hug as well.

"Glad you're safe, Fred." He grinned his self-conscious smile, the scar over his lip reminiscent of the one his twin had through his eyebrow. "To celebrate, I'll get you one of Katie's and my new rolls— it'll be one more reason to be glad to be alive."

"I have no doubt." I patted Nick's cheek, making him blush, and then continued on, taking my seat at the bakery counter beside the espresso machine. At my back, the blizzard continued outside the wall of windows, covering the charming shops up and down Elkhorn Avenue, adding yet another layer of snow. It was only then that I looked around the bakery and realized Ben hadn't been exaggerating in the slightest. Granted, it was in between breakfast and the lunch rush, and school was in session, but I'd expected at least some customers. Actually, a ton of them, each starving for every ounce of gossip they could get of what happened at the Beaker mansion. Blizzard or not, I was willing to bet all of that was going to change as soon as the noon hour arrived, which was nearly there.

"Here we go." Katie slid the first dirty chai toward me and leaned her elbows on her side of the counter. "I want every detail, of course, but you don't actually have to share any of them now, or at all. I'm just grateful you took the time to talk to me as you drove home last night. I don't know if I would have gotten any sleep for being worried. I hate that you were going through all that and I was just home with Joe. Who knows, we might have been having dinner or going over wedding plans while you had a gun to you—"

"None of that." Before I could even take a sip, I reached across and grabbed her arm. "Absolutely *none* of that. Had the same conversation with Leo last night. No one needs to feel guilty. Nobody did anything wrong, and as much as we love each other, we're not magical creatures who have crystal balls or telepathy." On the way back from Ethel's, I had called my mom and Katie, giving them each the world's briefest update that no matter what they heard had transpired, I was fine and would give them all the details later, possibly much later. "However..." I pulled my grip back and tapped the side of the steaming mug. "You *do* need to feel guilty if you keep me from this little bit of heaven for even another moment."

She snorted out a little laugh and gave a "get on with it" gesture.

I didn't need to be told twice; I cupped the mug in both hands, took a long inhale that washed a warm and spicy wave of comfort all through me, then took a sip. The snow outside might not be close to melting, but I did, thoroughly. I might as well have been a puddle all over the bakery floor.

The same experience as when Watson and I had entered returned—the awareness of these little moments I'd nearly lost. I'd been wrong with what I said to Katie, we *did* have magic, our lives were full

ELEVEN

I knew I was okay, and I knew I'd continue to be okay. However, though part of me wanted to pretend otherwise, it was a certainty I would probably experience flashes from the night before for the rest of my life—sometimes fear, sometimes anger, sometimes just yanked back in time unintentionally reliving aspects of what we'd experienced. The first example occurred when I stepped into Susan's tiny office.

Watson didn't experience a second of that. Though he'd been annoyed to leave Ben, as soon as we'd gotten out of the car and started toward the police station, his mood flipped on a dime—he not only frolicked over the snow-plowed sidewalks but barreled full steam ahead, pulling me along behind him. He didn't stop as we entered, passed the front desk, not even when we walked through Susan's door. As we did so, I finally dropped his leash, my hand in danger of being yanked off my arm. He plowed the remaining distance and leaped at Susan, who'd turned in perfect timing in her swivel chair to look our way.

"Whoa, Fleabag!" Despite the weight of her heavily muscled body, Watson managed to nearly knock Susan back.

It didn't go any further, as even with his enthusiasm, those tiny corgi legs have limitations. His top half had made it onto Susan's lap, his bottom half hung off the chair, between her knees, his hind legs scrambling for purchase so he could spring up and lick her face.

Not so many months ago this sort of behavior would have caused Susan to drive him to Dr. Sallee and demand he be euthanized. Things had changed to the point she wrapped those bulging arms around his back and pulled him up fully onto her chest to give him the type of hug Katie had trapped me in at the bakery. The scene erased the flashback from the night before, and I stared in utter shock as Susan dipped her head into Watson's fur and seemed to simply rest there, maybe even seek comfort.

For his part, Watson nudged at her, trying to shove his muzzle in the space between them so he could lick her face, while his little nub of a tail never stopped its frantic, happy wagging.

Proving equally as shocking, when Susan finally lifted her head and met my gaze, there was no embarrassment or shame, nor did she offer any excuse for this atypical demonstrative display. As she straightened, then released the hug, she patted Watson's back before lowering him to the ground. "You made the department proud last night, Officer Fleabag. Very proud." The patting continued, but now on his head between his ears. "We stand by our fallen comrades, never leave them behind."

Susan wasn't exactly an animal person, and I was certain she despised Granny Smith in life, but it seemed the scene in the corner of the library the night before—or in the early hours of that morning, rather—had done a number on her. As it would with anyone with a soul. Studying her, I realized Susan's affection toward Watson wasn't the only abnormality. Her short, tight ponytail was gone, leaving her brown hair free and wild around her square face. No, that was the wrong description... more tangled and matted, as if she'd been running her hands through it in frustration for hours. Her eyes told the same story —bloodshot, puffy with dark, painfully heavy-looking bags underneath them. Not from tears; Susan hadn't been body snatched, after all.

"You got no sleep last night, did you?"

She didn't bother to deny it or claim it was no big deal, instead gesturing at the boards behind her. "Not a wink. There was work to do."

The boards had been what had given me pause as soon as we'd stepped in. She'd added a new board not long before, mimicking the ones of Eve Dallas in Susan's favorite cop series, and now a couple more had been rolled in. On the opposite side of the wall large sheets of poster board had been taped up and scribbled over with notes. She really hadn't slept— her notes and observations were thorough, and seeing it all in black-and-white, her endless night of work made my throat tighten.

"Are you okay?" Susan asked the question that was going to be everyone's mantra for who knew how long, but I couldn't answer. "Sorry, I should have thought, given you some warning."

The fact that Susan Green apologized should have been enough to break the spell, but it wasn't. Seven of the poster boards were designated to each one of us, a name at the top and our character below. Naturally I lingered on mine the longest—Winifred Page-Lopez above Mrs. Peacock. Below that there were a few scribbled details: older, handsome woman, maintains dignity throughout.

Then, Delilah Johnson as Miss Scarlet: alluring

femme fatale, cunning, seductive. Anna Hansen as Reverend Green. Mary Smith as Professor Plum. Vivian LaRue as Colonel Mustard. Carla Beaker as Mrs. White. Chief Dunmore as Mr. Boddy. Each person's character had descriptions, like Delilah's and mine. Ethel and Mason each had their own poster board, as did Watson and Granny Smith, though none of them had any character names or traits. Looking away from them revealed two poster boards side by side, one listing the names of the rooms found in the board game, the other a list of rooms in Ethel's mansion. Further on, there was a list of all the silver weapons and where each had been found.

"Are you okay?"

Susan's repeated question finally pulled me back to the moment, at least partially. That time, I changed my answer. "No. I don't think so." My gaze returned to the poster with my name and my label of Mrs. Peacock. I let out a shaky breath and continued the admission. "Seeing this, it's like I'm still in the game." I finally looked at Susan, meeting her gaze. "Our lives treated as nothing more than a ridiculous live action game of Clue." That wasn't entirely true, the gameplay had been nothing like the actual game. We might have had our names and there might have been weapons, and the rooms might have looked like they did if the game had come to life, but we'd been locked in the dining room waiting for an explosion. "The game fell apart... or something. There was nobody trying to figure out who murdered a Mr. Boddy, with what, and where."

"She stole the game from Branson, like we said last night." Susan stated it matter-of-factly and then gestured toward one of the empty seats across from her desk. "Sit. You're wobbling."

I didn't follow her directive but continued to scan the real-life versions of the clue sheets provided in the game. I moved a little closer to Carla's and read some of Susan's notes out loud about the Mrs. White character. "Servant or maid, frazzled, nanny to John—Mr. Boddy's nephew." I looked over to Susan in confusion. "Nanny? I don't remember that detail."

"Wikipedia." She made a sweeping gesture over the character sheets and finished with a shake of her finger toward me. "And yes, I know what they say about Wikipedia, but don't return to your professor days and give me a lecture. I'm using every tool at my disposal. Apparently, that was part of Mrs. White's backstory, or... whatever. I don't know if it even matters. I mean, take Anna, AKA *Reverend Green*, who's supposed to be a hypocritical preacher, or whatever. She's hardly my favorite person, but Anna doesn't claim to be a preacher or is even religious, as far as I know. And your character is described as older. You're over a decade older than me, but that still doesn't make you *old*. And definitely not compared to Ethel."

Other than the few moments the seven of us had shared around the table after being set free, I'd not considered our character names again, not for an instant. But now looking at them all, going over the rooms, the weapons... it was overwhelming, room-spinningly so. Finally, I moved to the chair and sat, feeling wobbly just like Susan had said. I continued to hold the remainder of my dirty chai but placed the bag of Earl Grey buns on the desk—I'd forgotten I'd been holding them, but the top of the bag was crumpled, suggesting I'd been taking out some feelings as I'd inspected the notes.

From underneath Susan's desk, Watson whimpered.

She glanced down and didn't snarl but spoke to him with an apologetic tone. "Sorry, Fleabag. I'm out. But..." She gave him a tired smile, an actual smile. "Officer Cookie Dough for Brains is on his way to Paws right now to get you some more tr... uh... stuff."

There were so many things in that moment that also should have made the room spin, and now another—a roundabout second apology from Susan... to my dog, no less. The fact she had thought ahead and was having treats delivered, and that there was a slight sound of affection as she spoke of her nickname for Officer Cabot. However, I jumped over all of that and even the severity of what we were discussing as I leaned forward and spoke in a whisper, for whatever reason. "You sent Campbell to *Paws*? To *Paulie*?"

Her pale blue eyes, red-rimmed though they were, flashed toward me, and for the first time she sounded like herself. "So? I can send my inferiors to do errands."

I leaned closer, not fooled nor looking away. "I thought you told me to not interfere in their relationship or their breakup, that they'd figure it out on their own."

"That's *not* what I'm doing. It's nothing more than Fleabag deserving his favorite... *things* because of his display of heroism and loyalty last night. That's all." She rolled those bloodshot eyes before her voice both lowered and sped up. "*Besides*, it's been two months. Paulie is being an idiot and a coward, as far as I'm concerned. Campbell might not have been directly involved last night, but his name was used in a roundabout threat. It should be a wakeup call that Paulie's moral high ground or whatever he wants to call it is stupid and a waste of time."

I breathed out a laugh and sat back. "Well, look at you, Cupid."

She glared. "Shut up, Peacock."

Despite everything, I laughed, a real one.

From below the desk, a surrendering sigh issued, and I could practically see Watson sprawl in full disappointment over the floor.

Susan spared a quick smile down at him, and then returned to me, all business. "Whether we're right about Branson designing this game and it somehow being taken from him or not, we need to explore every possibility. Because regardless, there're a bunch of pieces missing." She leveled a stare on me. "I know this won't be easy, but are you okay reliving some of it again? And I'm certain it won't be for the last time."

"Yes, absolutely." I wasn't entirely sure that was true but decided it didn't matter. As always, I wanted answers, truth, facts—wherever they led and whatever they cost. "Where do you want to start?"

"Ah..." In yet another surprise of the morning, Susan shrugged with an overwhelmed cringe. "I don't know. There's so much, and it's all so crazy. But... I say we just pick something at random." No sooner had those words left her lips than she shook her head. "On second thought, let me go over a couple of things with you, *then* we'll go from there. I'm guessing we both may need to sit with all of this for a while, let it untangle in our minds. But if we land on something this morning, then great." She started to spin around toward the board, then saw the Cozy Corgi paper bag. "Please tell me that's food."

I'd forgotten them once again, but it was perfect timing. Placing my chai on her desk, I opened up the bag and held one of the Earl Grey buns out to her, took one for myself, and instantly tore off a piece for Watson. "Katie has outdone herself yet again. And to top it off, we'll have a little sugar rush, which is needed."

Susan snagged the one I offered, took a huge bite, and then groaned, her eyes rolling in the back of her head. She savored for a matter of seconds before getting back to work, speaking with her mouth full. "I don't know how much exactly all of you spoke as you wandered the mansion, but I doubt too much. And since we split everyone up last night as they gave the stories, I'm betting some of this will be new info to you." She considered just for a second and then shrugged again. "I'm leaving it up to you, within reason, and how much you reveal to others." There was no warning or question about my involvement, as she pointed to a board with Ethel's name on the top, different than her possible character card on the other side of the room. "As we theorized at the time, it's confirmed Ethel and Mason were leaving town, leaving the country, actually. These were things we found either in the car waiting for them in the garage or on their persons." Even as she bit off another piece of the roll, she gestured at each scribbled line with her other hand. "There were three one-way tickets to Greece. Carla was correct, of course—one of them was for Maverick." Susan paused to grimace at me in distaste. "Ethel had a *paternity test* done on her grandson, had it in the pocket of her fur coat. It confirmed he was Jonathan's son, apparently had to make sure blood was truly thicker than water before taking him along for the ride."

"Wow." Despite the exclamation that escaped me, I wasn't truly surprised by that in the slightest. It sounded exactly like something Ethel would do. "She just couldn't help but add insult to injury where Carla is concerned, could she?"

Susan cringed. "In most cases I would say I wouldn't be able to blame her, but if anything would make me feel sorry for Carla Beaker, it's her mother-in-law." She grinned suddenly. "Although... if anyone has reason to celebrate today, it's Carla."

I laughed again, and though it was dark, I didn't feel all that bad about it. "Oh, I'm certain she is. Both that Maverick is safe, obviously, and that Ethel finally got her comeuppance."

"She didn't pretend otherwise when we interviewed her last night. I actually respected that about her, although we'll have to look into Carla. She *definitely* has motive."

I sat up straighter. "No way! Carla didn't have anything to—"

"I know that. Do I look like a moron to you?" Susan finally sounded like herself, snagged another roll from the bag and bit off a large chunk. "There was also paperwork suggesting that some, most, or all of Ethel's fortune had been wired to an unnamed account. We've got other people working on that already, obviously. Whatever the case, it would have worked, at least had a high probability. By the time her mansion exploded and we discovered she was not in the rubble, they'd have been on a plane. Doubtlessly, Greece wasn't their final destination, or those tickets were fake anyway just to throw us off and they had a flight scheduled somewhere else."

She shook her head. "No, good Lord, I'm tired. The tickets were in with the luggage. Those were real, we wouldn't have found those if they'd gotten away. So... Greece was just the first stop before they disappeared."

A knock sounded on the door, causing Watson to bark. Susan and I both winced.

Officer Cookie Dough for Brains himself stepped in after Susan gave the go-ahead. "Here you go." He strode into the room and put the bag sporting the Paws logo onto Susan's desk, then looked at me. "You're doing okay?"

There it was again. "I am. Thank you."

Dejection forgotten, Watson bounced behind Susan's desk, high enough his ears, eyes, and snout appeared at the top of each leap, those chocolate eyes widening as he spotted the source of the crinkling-bag sound.

Without reprimand, Susan retrieved the expensive buffalo jerky, ripped it open, and gave a huge piece to Watson, not even asking for him to sit first. She smiled after him as he disappeared under her desk and began to eat loudly.

Despite the seriousness of the moment, I couldn't help myself—plus, if there'd ever been a reminder to seize the moment, I'd just received it the night before. Turning to Campbell, I cocked an eyebrow and did my best to keep hope and teasing out of my voice. "Thanks for getting the jerky for Watson. How was Paulie?"

Susan, who'd still been grinning after Watson, shot me a glare.

"He's... good." A blush rose to Campbell's cheeks. He'd been fairly even keel throughout their breakup, always seeming certain they would get back together as Paulie's fear of Branson using Campbell as an expendable chess piece dissipated. A little grin played at the corner of his lips, and he shrugged one of his shoulders. "He... had some thoughts about what you and my uncle went through."

I was certain he had. From Campbell's expression, it looked like Susan's meddling might have just done some good.

"Sit. Help." Susan gestured her partner to another chair, and proving she wasn't so tired she'd lost all bits of her personality, got us back on track with a growl. "If we can continue with the matter at hand, *the life-and-death one*, I'd be *ever* so grateful." Her droll tone transitioned to deadly as she gestured to yet another large sheet with all our names written on it. "Like I mentioned before, there are so many details, so many things that it's going to be an exhaustive, possibly unending list for a while. Some of them won't mean anything, but we have to explore them all to figure out which ones do. One of the things that might matter is how each of you got to Ethel's." Once more, even though all the information was written out, Susan went over it verbally. Probably working through it herself in addition to clarifying all of it for me. "You and Vivian LaRue were the only two picked up by the butler. The timing roughly suggests he delivered Vivian to Ethel less than half an hour before he got you. However, there were no shenanigans with the LaRues—Mason went directly to their home and knocked, and Roger answered the door and let him in. According to both of them, Mason claimed Ethel wanted to talk things over with Vivian, wanted to put their tiff... Vivian's word, not mine... behind them and also discuss a business proposition. Roger wasn't worried about the two of them, so relaxed that he fell asleep in front of the TV. It wasn't until Vivian walked into Ethel's house that the masked man took her to the dining room at gunpoint." She let out a little laugh. "That woman. I get that last night was traumatic, but she just kept melting down, literally disappeared after her interview and Officer Lin found her sobbing in a corner of the kitchen. Total mess. Unlike Mary who acted as if it was all an ill-timed annoyance, even talking to the police."

That sounded right on brand for both of them, but Vivian's and Mary's antics weren't what caught my attention. "Masked man? There wasn't a..." Without planning to, I replayed the memory as I had arrived at Ethel's the night before—wondering if there had been someone standing in the shadows or at another doorway. There hadn't been, I was certain, and all the other doorways had been closed. "I didn't see anyone else, it was just Ethel and Mason. Neither of whom were masked. The only ones who wore a mask, or a bag, were the others at the table."

Susan grunted and glanced at Campbell, but he was already scribbling something in his notebook, then continued. "I wondered about that since you never mentioned a masked man, and we'll return to him, but let's stay with this." She returned to the list. "Like I said, you and Vivian were the only two brought in by the butler. Ethel called Anna—Carl was already on his way to the stupid bird club—claiming she wanted to talk to Anna about being part of the city council, and of course, Anna being her idiot self, ate it up. She believed she was finally making it in with the *it* crowd." Susan made a brief gagging sound before returning to professionalism.

"Carla and the chief came on their own as well—Carla because Ethel wanted to speak to her about Maverick's inheritance, and the chief because of the town council as well. Apparently, Ethel called him in a rage about the mayor, making all kinds of threats. When Anna, the chief, and Carla showed up, separately, the gun-toting masked man took them into the dining room. Again, separately."

Made sense, but the chief felt off, although it took me a second to think of why. When I did, I glanced toward Campbell. "Marlon told me that you were the reason he was there last night. That Ethel claimed to have you as hostage and would hurt you, just like they claimed to have Leo."

Campbell nodded, opened his mouth to speak, but Susan barged ahead. "That's true, but it was Ethel who threatened that to the chief, not the butler. Marlon started to put up a defense when the masked man tried to lead him into the dining room, and Ethel told him they had Campbell to get him to comply."

Campbell let out a long sigh, finally speaking again. "Sometimes, I wonder if Paulie is right, if I shouldn't have moved here, and that it might be easier if I left. Not only for Paulie, but for my uncle, too. First, how me coming out affected May and all her choices, then Uncle Marlon having to balance being my boss and me being his nephew with all the things some of the... other officers have done. And now using me as leverage so—"

"No." Susan cut him off, not an ounce of sympathy in her tone. "We're not going down this road again. It's over. Case closed. You're *not* responsible for anyone else's choices, so *knock it off.*" Without missing a beat, she snagged another beef jerky as Watson's head appeared beside her, passed it down, and then returned to the notes on the wall. "The masked man is definitely one of the mysteries, and I've got a theory on that, but there's another detail that seems strange to me involving masks." She stood and walked to the far side of the office, closest to the door and stopped at a poster board with the dining room table drawn almost like map—every seat labeled with who sat where. "If we're thinking about *Ethel* and not Branson, look at the layout from her perspective. She put you at the opposite end, which could be at the head or the foot of the table depending on how you look at it. In a way, giving you a seat of power, almost equal in importance to hers." Susan didn't wait for me to offer any input before continuing. "And here's where I'm definitely reading into things, but I think I'm onto something. If I try to get into Ethel's mind, horrifying as that may be, she put Mary and Vivian on either side, closest to her. Then in the middle, Anna and the chief. On the end, next to either side of you were Delilah and Carla. Knowing how she feels about her daughter-in-law then—"

"She arranged us by favorites..." I snorted out a laugh. "Or level of hate." If I thought about it, I was certain I would have landed on that same realization at some point. "Probably says a lot that she hated me a little more than Carla. Although... between Delilah and Anna, I'm a little surprised—"

"I'm not. They're on the town council together, and the fact that Delilah is everything Ethel never was and always wanted to be is constantly rubbed in her face." Susan dropped that truth bomb but didn't give me a chance to consider it before pointing at the table illustration once more. "One thing was consistent in all of the interviews—you were the only one who didn't have your head covered. According to your retelling last night, everyone else around the table did when you entered. All the others stated as soon as their wrists were bound a bag was placed over their head. Everyone, but *you*."

"Oh..." I blinked. "Yeah. That's true. Mason led me in at gunpoint, and then Ethel took that part over and..." I'd been staring at the illustration, and things clicked together both from memory and from what Susan had said only moments before. "I was at the equal spot in the table to Ethel. The last to arrive, and everyone else's heads were covered..." I had to tear my gaze away from the drawing and looked at Susan. "Part of it was for show. *For me.* Why would...?" That part hurt my brain. "It makes sense if Branson was the one doing this, but if we think Ethel took it over from him, then..."

"Well, like I said, there's a chance we're wrong about Branson being involved, but we're not. There's a higher chance that we're wrong about Ethel stealing this plan from him, maybe..." She tapped the illustration one more time. "That brings me back to the hoods, specifically the masked man who brought some of you in. Now... *who* might be the large man under that mask? One that is Fred connected?"

"Branson? I don't think he would..." My blood chilled and then a second later heated up as anger appeared. "Garrett."

"Yep." Susan gave a single nod. "Your nasty ex-husband-turned-Branson lackey. Maybe he was doing Branson's bidding last night, or maybe he was doing some of his own and teamed up with Ethel."

"Garrett..." I tried to picture it, but everything

was a blur. Would he really do that? Kill me? Maybe. I didn't think he would, on his own accord, or rather because of his own desire to kill me, but coerced due to whatever Branson had over him? Maybe coerced was a little too flattering for Garret, but still... Then another thought hit me. "There're a couple of ways to go with that, but let's say we're right about Branson being involved, and Ethel taking over the Clue game or whatever. Either way, like you said, Garrett could easily be involved. We might not have proof, but I'm still certain he and Charlotte are here on Branson's orders, *and* Garrett played a role in faking Ethel's marriage license to Colin *after* his murder, but... I don't think he's taking orders from her. Or would be foolish enough to team up with her behind Branson's back."

"Not sure about your second point, but..." She pointed at me. "I agree on him not taking orders from her. For one, he seems *much* too alpha-male—" Another gagging sound, this one less for show than before. "—to *lower* himself under a woman's command." She cringed, then went ahead. "I didn't want to lead you here, but... I'd say it's totally like him to play both sides."

That didn't require any consideration; Garrett would definitely do that. "Large, masked man..." I replayed the scene in the library. "Ethel took the game over from Branson; somehow Branson found out, but... too late to stop it or something and gave Garrett his marching orders. Played along to keep up appearances, then set up a murder-suicide scenario, and left."

Susan simply cocked an eyebrow, waiting as I played over it again.

"Something is wrong there, for sure. I already have a billion questions of how that would work, starting with—why would he go along with it at all only to end it that way? If Branson wanted Ethel dead, he could've set up the same murder-suicide scenario without anything else."

"Yep, we've got nothing but speculation, though I'd bet my badge Garrett would play both sides, and as far as Garrett being the masked man..." Susan spared a quick smile toward her partner. "That's where Campbell landed as well, and one of the main reasons I asked you to come over, seeing if you'd arrive there yourself. And you did... more or less, with my help." Another cringe.

"This is assuming it wasn't an actual murder-suicide." I tried to reason that out, as I had several times already when I couldn't keep from thinking of it. "Mason has a change of heart or a sudden moral awakening at the eleventh hour." It was my turn to cringe. "Or... something."

"Definitely possible. Well... maybe not definitely, but still. However, that leaves the masked man just evaporating into the wind." She walked back over and sat behind her desk and began to type as she spoke. "I'm thinking we start with this—as he seems so good at doing, Garrett Griffin played both sides of the coin last night. Continuing on with the game, but making Ethel think he was under her control, but then double-crossed her, probably on Branson's orders, but maybe having his own agenda." Her gaze flicked over to Campbell once more, her fingers never pausing. "Just a theory, but to have reasonable suspicion... how about we bring in the ex-Mr. Winifred for a little questioning?" She grinned. "Maybe a seventy-two-hour vacation at our spa and jail-cell resort?" Then back to me. "I bet we can get to the bottom of this within those seventy-two hours, hopefully enough to lure Branson out of hiding."

Unexpected relief settled over me when Susan decided to not have me present at Garrett's initial questioning—both to make sure everything was completely by the book and to save me as a secret weapon if they couldn't break through his defenses. My secret-weapon status being my superpower of annoyance, according to Susan. I only considered that relief for a few seconds before simply accepting it and letting it be. Why I didn't feel ready to look Garrett in the face, ask him if he'd nearly killed me, didn't matter. That I didn't want to and didn't have to was enough, at least for now.

As we reentered the Cozy Corgi, Watson greeted Ben with almost as much enthusiasm as he had during our first arrival.

I'd planned on going directly to the bakery to get another dirty chai and, probably, another Earl Grey roll; however, the chatter drifting down the steps changed my mind. We were on the tail end of the lunch rush, but if I showed up, it would certainly extend indefinitely as people clamored for a retelling. My anxiety shot up at the thought. "Ben." I paused as I heard a little panic in my voice and started over, getting a grip of myself. "I think I'm actually going to take a bit more of a break, wait until the crowd thins down."

"Don't blame you, and you're not the only one who feels that way." As he stroked Watson, Ben nodded at the front windows. "Anna dropped in about ten minutes ago to see you. I think it was the first time she'd not gone to the bakery. She got a look kind of like the one you have right now, told me to tell you she stopped by, and then went back to Cabin and Hearth."

"Wow, that is a first." And for some reason, knowing that Anna, who loved the center stage and spotlight to the same level as my uncle, Percival, had ducked and run made me feel a little better about my own instinct. And suddenly, almost as equally surprising, I realized I wanted to see her. Going with it, I glanced to Watson. "I'm going to see Anna, do you wanna come or stay?"

Annoyance filled his gaze that I would dare interrupt the lovefest between him and Ben.

"Winston and Phineas?" I should have led with that. "Do you want to see your buddies?"

Annoyance disappeared, and Watson gave a little whimper as he looked in the direction of the upscale log-furniture store, then back at Ben, whimpering once more.

"It's okay. You go." Ben ruffled the fur between Watson's ears. "See your friends. I'll be here when you get back."

That seemed to do the trick. We made it all the way to the door before Watson chuffed, looked at me with a third whimper, then back at Ben.

"It's also fine if you stay." I released his leash, seeing what he would choose, figuring the chances were fifty-fifty.

He galloped back to Ben.

"Looks like he's needing comfort and pets more than play and naps." At the mention of it, I decided a nap didn't sound half bad. Footsteps sounded from the stairs as people wandered down from the bakery, so with a wave goodbye to Watson, I slipped away before I got caught. Traffic was slow along Elkhorn, but I still probably should have gone down to use the crosswalk as I nearly slipped twice jumping over the mounds of plowed snow and a slick spot right in the middle of the street. It was worth it, however, as I made it inside Cabin and Hearth without getting stopped by any other store owners who might be hungry for details.

The typical snarls and barks didn't greet me, and only in that moment did I realize I'd come to look forward to Winston's predictable welcome of fury giving way to recognition and then adoration—and I definitely looked forward to Phineas's exuberant greeting of puppy love.

The absence of the two rescues wasn't the only unexpected thing in Cabin and Hearth. As I took a few steps in and got a full view of the counter, I stopped dead in my tracks. Anna was in her typical spot near the cash register, wearing one of her usual gingham muumuus and leaning forward over the counter, caught in a moment of gossip. That was all normal enough. But her coconspirator gave me pause. Delilah Johnson, wearing her silk Pink Panthers jacket, was so caught up in whatever Anna was saying that she didn't notice my arrival. Whatever Susan's theories about Ethel's feelings toward Delilah, I would have placed good money that Anna's were just as intense in her dislike of "the hussy"—as Anna often called her. She'd never had a good word for the leader of the Pink Panthers, constantly and ridiculously consumed with thinking Delilah was going to try to steal her husband. I couldn't remember ever seeing a kind moment between them.

"Oh, Fred." Anna noticed me first and gestured me closer. "Wonderful. I was just at the Cozy Corgi a little bit ago, hoping you were there. But when you weren't, I called Delilah, and she was sweet enough to come over."

I'd made it halfway to the counter but halted yet again as Anna's hand came to rest on top of Delilah's and then gave a little pat.

For her part, Delilah didn't even seem to notice, or find it odd. "The timing was perfect for me. I'd debated if I wanted to come to work or not, and I was over there pacing, deciding I had chosen wrong. This little chat was exactly what I needed." She smiled over at me. "Even more so now." Before I could respond, she looked back to Anna. "What do you say we lock the door? Have some uninterrupted time. Probably should have done that when I came in."

"Great idea." Anna became a little more herself as she snapped her fingers before gesturing to me again. "Fred, would you take care of that? Then come join us."

At least some things were normal—Anna's issuing of commands offered a grounding sensation. I followed her direction and then walked back. "Where are the boys? I was hoping to see Winston and Phineas." I barely caught myself. "And Carl, of course."

As ever, Anna softened at the mention of her dogs, and through recent events, her husband. She gestured between Delilah and herself. "I sent them on errands. I wanted some time alone with you, and then Delilah came to the rescue. At the end, they're stopping by Taffy Lane to bring me some treats. Would you like me to..." She flinched, and her eyes widened as she glanced toward my feet. "Oh, goodness, I said the T-word, didn't I? Watson, here let me get—" Those eyes narrowed, then looked at me in accusation.

I laughed and finished my way to the counter. "He stayed with Ben. I think Watson's needing a little extra comfort today as well." After my initial surprise wore off, this new reality made sense, and looking back, I could see it start to unfold the night before. Delilah and Anna had each other's backs when it mattered. And somehow, seeing them like this, seeing just the three of us, emotions threatened to overwhelm.

"It's okay." Delilah reached out, put her hand

over mine and slipped her fingers underneath, clearly reading whatever swept over me.

"It is." Anna followed Delilah's lead and took my other hand, then a moment later used her other to grip Delilah's.

We stood there, the three of us holding hands in this little triangle over Cabin and Hearth's counter. For a while, no more words were exchanged; none were needed. Memories tumbled with emotion, smoothed out to white noise, and then spun and repeated again and again. Finally, though I don't know who pulled their hand away first, we broke apart, and each of us had to wipe dampness away from our eyes.

It was Anna, her gaze hard, who got us back on track. "You're gonna solve this, Fred, and we're going to help you, of course."

"Better believe it." Delilah nodded her agreement.

I paused at that, almost feeling like we were picking up where I left off with Susan and Campbell. "Solve what? You're that certain it wasn't a murder-suicide?"

"I don't care if it was or not." Delilah waved that away as if Ethel and Mason dead in the library was nothing more than an annoying fly. "They didn't do this on their own. We all know it's Branson. And we're going to take him down."

"And we're going to do it slowly, painfully. We'll tie him to a chair and torture him." A grin formed over Anna's lips, and she sent Delilah a wink. "What do you think? Show him a video of Fred and Leo's wedding on repeat until he begs for death?"

"That should do it." Delilah chuckled, though her tone suggested she wasn't kidding on what she said next. "After the mental and emotional torture, we move to physical and *end* that sadistic monster."

"Sounds like a plan to me." I gave a chuckle of my own, feeling a little more normal. Then decided it was time to start. "Susan is bringing in Garrett for questioning, maybe already has him."

"See?" Anna nodded in pride. "You're already figuring it out. Delilah and I were just talking about him, and there you are, one step ahead."

"That was all Susan and Campbell, not me. I didn't ever see a masked man, didn't know any of you had until Susan told me a bit ago." I looked back and forth between them. "You think it was Garrett?"

"Who else?" Anna shrugged. "Unless it was Branson himself, but I think he'd want us to see him."

"Yeah, I do, too." I narrowed in on Delilah.

"That's what you think, too? Garrett has gotten huge since our divorce—the masked guy seemed that big to you?"

"I think so." Delilah hesitated, but only for a second. "Truth be told, you could tell me he was ten feet by ten feet, and I'd believe it. I was so mad, and so..." She hesitated longer that time. "So scared."

"There's nothing to be ashamed about in that." Anna sniffed. "You would have been a fool if you hadn't been afraid. A big guy shows up at your house wearing a mask and toting a gun? How are you supposed to feel?"

"That's how it happened?" I didn't give Delilah a chance to reply. "The masked man just showed up at your house?" I hadn't gone over any of those specifics with Susan, but Delilah was smart; unless she expected someone else to be coming over, I couldn't imagine her not looking through her peephole and refusing to answer the door.

"Yeah." She elaborated without needing a prompt. "The snow had just started, and I decided not to take the bassets on a walk, so I just let them out in the backyard. One second, they're doing their business, and the next, Kenickie loses his mind, starts growling and barking. Then Zuko and Putzie jumped in as well, all three of them tearing across the yard toward the corner of the house." She closed her eyes and shuddered. "In the darkness, I didn't even see him for a second, and then I did, all of a sudden. Standing there all in black, gun pointed at me."

"Good Lord." I shuddered along with her. Surprised as I'd been to see a gun emerge from behind Granny Smith, Delilah's experience sounded a hundred times more terrifying. "What did you do?"

"I started to run into the house. I was going to get my gun, but I couldn't even get the door handle open, it slipped. When I finally got it, he was already to me..." Fear had started to creep back into her voice, but it died instantly, anger returning. "Then he pointed the gun at the dogs, told me to stop where I was or he'd... or he'd..."

Anna offered Delilah another pat. "He didn't, though. Your boys are safe."

"They are." Delilah took a breath and shook it off before continuing. "I go back and forth between wishing I'd trained them to be attack dogs, but I'm glad that I didn't. He might have hurt them if they had tried to bite him. But..." She gave another quick nod to Anna. "They didn't, and they're safe. I left the back door open so at least I wasn't worried about them when we were at Ethel's house. They can't get out of the yard, and they had shelter." She took another breath, gave another shake before her tone returned to all business, and she refocused on me. "He didn't say much, one or two words at a time. Told me to follow him, to drop my phone right where it was—I'd been scrolling on Facebook when the dogs started barking—and had me get in his car, where he made me put on zip ties and..."

"Mason had me do the zip ties as well." I reached over and squeezed her hand—there was a lot of that. I wished there was more we could do, but even that helped, somehow. "When did he put the hood on you?"

"When I got in the dining room and sat at the table." Fear and anger combined. "He put the mask on and then held the gun to my head as someone, I don't know who, Ethel or Mason, probably, cut my zip ties and then fixed new ones to the arms of the chair."

"Did you recognize his voice at all? Catch his eye color? How many people were at the table? Were you able to recognize any of them?"

Delilah smiled at my onslaught of questions, then she sighed. "Well, look at that; you just slid into Winifred mode. That's kinda comforting." She chuckled and then answered that onslaught of questions. "I didn't recognize his voice—like I said, he barely said any words, and with those, he altered his tone, went super deep and gravelly. It was clear that wasn't his actual voice, but..." She shrugged. "I didn't recognize it. Although honestly, if it was Garrett and he spoke in his regular voice, I don't think I would recognize his either." She kept going without waiting for a response. "And no, I didn't see his eye color, or hair, nothing. The mask looked like two layers, though I can't be sure. I was in a bit of a panic. Maybe a thin layer, like panty-hose legs or something... at least that's what Detective Green and I came up with. It completely obliterated any features. And he had gloves, so I couldn't see skin or get any hint of age, hairiness, none of that."

What little excitement I'd had, faded.

"Tell me about it." I must've made some sort of expression, as Delilah nodded her agreement before continuing, "I can't say I thought too clearly when I got into the dining room. I was already terrified, and then walking in to see people strapped to chairs with their heads covered was nearly enough to make me think I was losing my mind. But as I try to picture it, I think there were four of us at that time—four *more*, I mean, me being the fifth. I didn't recognize anyone but Anna because of her..." She glanced across the counter, but barely more than a moment. "Because of her dress."

Anna chuckled good-naturedly. "Sure. It was just the dress." She patted her expansive belly, not the slightest bit insulted, then she took over. "I think Delilah is right that there were four. Unless someone came in between her and me, which I'm not entirely sure about." Anger flashed over her face as well. "Ethel had the nerve to greet me at her front door when I showed up. I can't believe I was such a fool to think she actually wanted to..." Anna grimaced and then jumped over it. "That evil crone actually smiled and said how nice it was to see me. Then she shut the door, locked it, and that masked man stepped out from the shadows in the hallway, pointed a gun at me, and told me to do exactly as he said." She looked at Delilah for a moment. "Thank goodness I didn't bring the boys. Unlike your dogs, Winston would have definitely attacked. There would have been bloodshed at least around some ankles, my little hero." Back to me. "I didn't recognize anyone at the table, but there were three, and based on where they were sitting, I think they were Carla, Vivian, and Mary." She snarled. "Mary... I didn't like that woman to start with, and now even less." She pointed a finger at me. "Haven't I told you from the day she walked into town she was no good, the whole family was no good?"

"You did." I almost stopped there, but didn't, needing a little break. "Although, in Mary's defense you did think they were involved in cheese trafficking."

"Well, after her behavior last night, *nothing* would surprise me. Cheese trafficking would be the least of it." Anna snorted. "Mark my words."

I laughed, but the distraction faded. "And they didn't threaten either of you with hurting someone, other than your dogs, Delilah? They didn't claim to have anyone hostage?"

They both shook their heads, but it was Delilah who spoke. "But they did you... or Mason claimed to have Leo, right? You didn't see the masked man?"

"I didn't." At that moment, a knock sounded on the front door, and disappointment washed over me —I wasn't ready for our private time to be over—but a second later, the wild barking announced it was Carl with the pups. "I'll let them in." Without waiting for confirmation, I hurried over, unlocked the door, and true to form, that barking and snarling went wild. Then, as Winston caught my scent, his fangs disappeared, and his scraggly cream-colored tail began to wag. Beside him, Phineas's whole body vibrated in pleasure at the sight of me, though, this time, he didn't have an accidental piddle on the ground. After a greeting hug from Carl, we were back in and the door was locked. Giving in to pure impulse, I sat on the floor in front of the counter, lapping up every ounce of love Winston and Phineas poured into me, and recounted my version of events from the night before.

Somewhere during my time at Cabin and Hearth, my mom sent a text message—a massive group thing including *every* single member of our family, dictating, not requesting, our presence at her and Barry's house for dinner that evening. Though she didn't spell it out in so many words, it was obvious my close call the night before was the reason. For just a second, as I paused on the sidewalk outside of Cabin and Hearth, I considered asking her to change her plans, feeling that need to take a nap creep over me again. However, by the time I'd seen it, over half the family had already confirmed that they would attend, and... tired or not, being surrounded by my family would be just as healing and cathartic as endless kisses from Winston and Phineas.

I started to head back, the Cozy Corgi lunch rush was definitely over, but then had an impulse I'd never experienced before. Probably prompted by the time I'd just shared with Anna and Delilah. Not feeling the need to inspect or second-guess, I pulled out my phone and searched for Carla Beaker's number, not entirely sure if I had it. Though surely, after all this time... I did, and just as surprisingly, Carla answered on the second ring.

"Hey." Making the surprises never cease, she didn't sound annoyed and even went a step further. "Are you okay?" She laughed, something dark and quiet. "Sorry, everywhere I go today people are asking me that question; didn't mean to do it to you."

"That's all right. Actually, that's why I called you. I think."

"You think?" Her next laugh was a little brighter, but she didn't seem to take offense. "I'm... okay, for lack of a better term. One minute completely shaken up, and the next better than ever, actually." There was a murmur I couldn't make out that was clarified with Carla's next comment. "No, I'm not going to watch how I say it. I'm not about to pretend that I'm going to grieve that... well..."

I had a feeling she was getting ready to say that the evil mother-in-law of hers had been murdered but seemed to have changed her mind.

Before I could think of what to say next, she both surprised and clarified, probably why she hadn't finished her thought about Ethel. "You know what, why don't you come up. Maverick and I are at Donna's."

"Oh yes!" Donna called out, that time clearer than her muttered reprimand a moment before. "We have the cutest little boy who ever lived, the cutest puppy who ever lived, and the best ice cream to ever exist."

Carla grunted. "You catch all that?"

"Sure did, and... I'll be right up." Figuring there was no reason to check in at the Cozy Corgi or bother Watson, I headed directly up Elkhorn toward the new apothecary, moving quickly enough I hoped it suggested I didn't want to stop for conversation or questions. Unlike Cabin and Hearth, Doc's Apothecary and Soda Shoppe not only was locked but had a Closed sign hanging in the window.

Donna hurried over the second I knocked and waved at the glass. She flicked the dead bolt and then, like magic, I found myself yanked down into her arms, the hug almost as strangling tight as Katie's earlier that morning. "I was planning on coming to see you later this afternoon, but didn't want to intrude, as I'm sure you're getting a lot of that. I'm just so glad you're okay." She released me, took a step back and included Carla. "To think I just got you both in my life, Fred again and you for the first time, and then nearly lost you. It's more than I even want to—"

"If you start crying again, Maverick and I are leaving." Carla smirked. "And I'm taking that teddy bear of a dog with us." I'd never seen her so bright, at least in comparison to Carla on any other day. Actually, bright probably wasn't the right word, maybe... light. Like she'd been set free, or a burden taken off her shoulders. She also looked tired, pale, and more than a little shellshocked. I knew the feeling.

"Hi there!" A sweet voice drew my attention over to the left—Maverick, Carla's three-year-old son, sat on the floor, playing with a couple of large cartoon character erasers that he'd snagged from the middle of Donna's shop where she held unusual office supplies. He waved one at me, then patted the dog's head beside him with the eraser shaped like a seahorse. "This is Elba."

"Yes, it is." Donna sent him an adoring grin, then a wink to me. "Elphaba, Elphie, or... Elba, as Maverick says. I always thought when I had a Bernese mountain dog the two of us would be best friends, but she's clearly chosen Maverick over me. Not that I can blame her."

Donna had gotten the puppy the month before,

and she'd already grown a noticeable degree, her large paws even bigger—she would be massive in a few more months. But now, she lay there, still the calmest puppy I'd ever seen, simply letting Maverick gently bop her on the head with the eraser, before twisting to lick his foot.

Maybe it was desperation to find beauty after such a close brush with death, but the toddler and the puppy made such an adorable picture I was brought up short. Though I never would have predicted any grandson of Ethel Beaker's having any amount of lovely softness, that's exactly what little Maverick Espresso Beaker was—huge green eyes that matched Carla's, full rosy cheeks, and deep chocolate curls framing his angelic face. Next to the fluff ball of the large Bernese puppy, they might as well have been an ad for antidepressants. That notion washed away in the next second as Carla's fear and then the relief when she spoke to Maverick on the phone in the garage the night before came back. It wasn't like I hadn't understood, but this sweet little boy sitting there without a care in the world made it even more poignant. Then, what I never dreamed would have been possible, I had to hold back the impulse to hurry to Carla and hug her, try to heal some of the fears she'd experienced the night before.

Instead, I just looked away from the adorable picture and into Carla's green eyes. "With as terrified and angry as I was last night, I can't imagine what you were experiencing."

"I didn't know a person could feel that way, or that much and survive." Carla gave her son a glance, cleared her throat, and adjusted her tone, clearly not wanting to cause worry. "And I know that it's not socially appropriate to say, and I will use coded language for now in front of little ears, but..." She held my gaze as she spoke, and I got the sense she was wanting to judge my reaction. "I would go through it ten times over to get the same result. I didn't expect to be free of *her* for decades. In truth, I thought she might live forever. Now I'm free. *We're* free." She gestured subtly to Maverick. "And she can't poison him, not like she did everyone close to her."

Donna didn't reprimand Carla that time. Neither did I. "I'm glad for you. That's probably not socially appropriate to say either, but I am. And..." I gestured over my shoulder down Elkhorn. "I have to tell you, I appreciate your strength last night. I was just down with Anna and Delilah, and I can't help but feel like we all survived a war together."

"We did, of a sort; a battle anyway." She cringed,

for the first time looking like the more unpleasant version of herself I was used to. "Now don't get me wrong, doesn't mean we're all going to turn into best friends. Delilah Johnson's got the moral equivalent of Jezebel, and Anna Hanson is about as stupid as she is annoying. And you..." She flicked her fingers my way and a little laugh entered her voice. "I'm certain you'll be just as insufferably obnoxious as you always are. But if I'm ever in a pickle where I have my back against the wall again, I want you three with me."

Donna sniffed and clutched at the base of her throat as if Carla had just recited a sonnet about true friendship.

"None of that," Carla snarled at her, but there was a lilt to her voice. "And didn't you yell something about ice cream to Fred over the phone a few minutes ago?"

"Ice cream!" Maverick proved he'd not been lost in his own world as he cheered, then threw his arms around the thick neck of the puppy. Good Lord, they couldn't be cuter.

"That I did." Donna practically bounced behind the retro ice-cream-parlor counter as she spoke. "You want the chai flavor, Fred?"

A few minutes later, Maverick was wandering around the shop, strawberry ice cream cone dripping on the floor as Elphie followed along behind him, cleaning up the melted splotches. We three women sat at one of the high-tops, each with a ridiculously large malt.

Carla cut to the chase after her first scoop of ice cream. "Did you call to warn me about Branson?" She almost grinned. "Because, let me tell you, I don't need any more warnings at this point. I was already clear on him after he killed Simone, but now?"

"No, I actually truly was just calling to make sure you were alright." I didn't bother with asking if she really thought it was Branson or had other theories. She hadn't ever gotten any more proof than the rest of us that her mother-in-law had pulled strings with Branson to fake a wedding license with the recently murdered billionaire fiancé, but she'd been just as clear on it as the rest of us nonetheless.

Ended up, she didn't give me a chance to clarify further than that before she shot another quick glance at Maverick, then leaned closer and lowered her voice. "I know how this goes. You've definitely talked to Susan today, so what's the latest?"

I almost told her, opened my mouth to do so, and then remembered that Donna was Garrett's sister-in-law. I trusted her, but she wasn't convinced her sister Charlotte and Garrett were here for nefarious reasons, and I wasn't entirely sure how she'd take the news that Susan was bringing in Garrett for questioning and a hold. In fact, she obviously hadn't gotten a call from Charlotte saying that exact thing; it made me wonder if Susan had hit a snag. Either way, I jumped over it. "I did speak to Susan, yes. And *yes*, everyone is convinced Branson is part of this, either directly or that he *was*, and Ethel took it over."

"Well *duh*, there's no question about that on either part." Carla's typical annoyance had caused her volume to increase, and she adjusted with another glance toward her son. "Both of those things are obvious. All you had to do was take one look at the house and know Ethel was forced to decorate it like that, and it's just as painfully obvious looking at the guest list. Branson wouldn't have included me. He doesn't care about me in the slightest. And it's not like he would have used me for leverage against Ethel. She didn't care about me either. The only reason I was at that table is because Ethel wanted me dead."

"And the character names." Donna looked back and forth between Carla and me like at a tennis match, making her teal-streaked black ponytail dance behind her head. "I know Carla's matched what

Ethel thought of her, the maid and everything, but the rest of the characters didn't really add up with who was there, right?"

I was glad Carla had Donna, that she'd been able to confide so much to her already. To my knowledge, she hadn't had a close friend since Simone Pryce, and Branson had ended that brutally. "Pretty much, and that was where Susan landed on the guests as well—although she looked at it from the placement around the table as opposed to the character names. People who Ethel hated the most were the farthest away. So... whatever Mary and Vivian did was much less offensive than what I did, but still bad enough to get them killed, it seems."

"Huh." Carla paused, and I figured she was picturing the setup at the table once more, then she nodded slowly. "I hadn't put that together, but it makes complete sense. I think Susan is right." Her green gaze traveled back to me. "I wouldn't have predicted Ethel hated you more than she hated me, though." Then she let out a breath of a laugh. "Couldn't even give me the honor of being the one she hated the most, could she? I wasn't even good enough for that."

Twisted logic, but she had a point. I could see Donna getting ready to offer comfort, but I wanted to keep going, so I changed direction. "Go back to what you said about Ethel's house, I had that same thought last night. I figured Ethel's style was more modern and sleeker, like what was most on-trend on Fifth Avenue or..." I shrugged. "Hollywood, I don't know, wherever the most expensive trendsetters are."

"Totally. That's exactly what she was." Carla answered my shrug with one of her own. "And like I've said a billion times, it's not like she invited me over, especially recently, but I had been in her home several times over the years, of course. The layout was the same, mostly, from what I remember, but otherwise, I truly wouldn't have known I was in the same house. There was nothing resembling anything I'd seen before, and absolutely nothing that Ethel would have chosen, except the chandeliers and the overabundance of gold." She laughed. "Not that I ever would have had reason to find out, but I can also guarantee there weren't lead-lined pocket doors or whatever they were, or safe-like shutters, or a book-case that opened to the garage. That's all new."

"Really new, right?" Donna paused with that spoonful of malt right above the lip of the tall glass, her nearly black eyes continuing the tennis match between the two of us. "I mean, didn't you say you thought she'd run out of money? These improvements wouldn't have been anything she could've been doing, it sounds expensive."

"She could have with Colin's money, what she got after his death. Although I don't know how long that would have taken to transfer to her." I made a mental note to ask Susan, although I wasn't certain it mattered. "Either way, if Branson was the one organizing the remodel—"

"Then he would have paid for it." Donna's tone changed, and she glanced around her apothecary. "He would have had the money to make it a rush job, I assume."

"And hired people who would do it quietly." Carla jumped back in. "I haven't heard anything about Ethel remodeling or work crews at her house. Have you?" She waited the briefest moment for me to shake my head. "Then they were silent and nearly invisible, because otherwise tongues would have been wagging—Estes Park loves its gossip. And especially after her fiancé... excuse me, *husband*—" She gave an exaggerated eyeroll. "—died and Ethel starts tearing through his money to update her mansion before his body is even cold? Yeah, tongues would've been wagging."

I hadn't thought of that aspect, and again wasn't

certain it mattered. "So probably no one local, not Grizzly Construction at least."

Carla snorted out a laugh at the notion of Grizzly Construction pulling something like that off. They'd done the first part of Katie's bakery remodel, and she'd had to finish with another crew.

Donna was still studying her shop, and though I was tempted to stay on track, I couldn't quite let it go. I reached over and touched her forearm. "What are you thinking? Is there some connection between the remodel of Doc's and Ethel's you're seeing?"

She gave a little flinch, and her cheeks darkened. Donna started to shake her head no, but then stopped, though her ponytail kept going. "I don't know. It's just that... with everything that's been going on since I've been in town, everything you've been talking about, Fred. And now this..." Another sigh, then a cringe, and when she spoke, it looked like the words cost her. "Granted, my shop isn't anything like what it sounds like Ethel's mansion was turned into, but even I noticed the construction went really quick. We opened a few months before I originally predicted."

Carla and I exchanged a glance, but I was the one who pushed. "What are you thinking? That..." Maybe I was pushing too hard. Donna had been completely unwilling to consider Charlotte offering her little sister all her business dreams on a platter having any connection to someone like Branson Wexler. "That maybe Charlotte's money isn't all from investing what she made from the publishing company like she said?"

Donna's lips thinned, tightened, and then she finished her headshake. "No, I'm not. I can't believe Charlotte would be involved with someone like that, but... I'll admit some things don't quite add up. Still, *surely* it's not about dirty money."

"It's always about money, and when it is, it's always dirty." Carla took a long sip of her malt through the straw and then continued. "I didn't understand that when I married Jonathan. I know Ethel, along with half the town, thought poor little trailer-trash Carla White was marrying Jonathan Beaker for no other reason than to get rich quick, but I wasn't. He was so different after he got back from college, quieter, hurting, that I just..." It looked like she about gagged at the memory of all that had been revealed about her husband over the last month or so, and she finished by returning to her malt.

"The money." I hadn't gone in that direction yet, and I sat up a little straighter. "Ethel's money, er... Colin's money, actually. If Branson helped Ethel with that marriage license to get Colin's fortune, like we think he did—and *he did*—then there's no way he didn't take some, most, or maybe even all of it for himself, and throw in this whole 'redesign your mansion' stipulation as well." That time I looked toward Maverick, who was now actively offering his ice cream cone to the puppy. Letting that go, I returned to Carla. "I know it's not even been twenty-four hours yet, but depending on what has gone down over the last few weeks, and who knows what's gone on with paperwork and the twists and turns with Colin's fortune, *you* might get some of that money. Branson could come knocking on your door."

Fear flooded Carla for a second, and she looked at Maverick before she shook her head. "No. Ethel had it set to go to Jonathan upon her death, at least as far as I know. And after all that happened with him being taken into custody last month, Ethel made it very clear she was going to make it where if something happens to Jonathan, it all goes directly to Maverick, *not* me. I don't know if she managed to pull that off or not before last night. With how fast she did everything else, I'd imagine so."

I debated for a heartbeat how much to share with Carla, especially with Donna next to us, what she might say to her sister, but then decided to take that chance. If Susan knew, Branson already knew as well. "The police found paperwork in the trunk of the car that showed Ethel had transferred money overseas. I don't know how much or to where, or how easy it will be to get or recover, but if Branson had all of it, she wouldn't have done that. Whether he knows that she had more or not, I can't say, obviously."

Carla waved it away. "You're probably right, and looking back, that actually makes a little sense with the past couple of weeks. I mean, that *is* why I went to her house last night, she said she wanted to talk about Maverick's inheritance. At the end of the day, I really don't care about the money, but... I would like my son provided for." She let out a dark laugh. "And you know what, I'm thinking it, so why not just say it? I wouldn't turn down a little myself. I'm more than entitled after the decades of putting up with that woman."

"That's right." I'd forgotten about the excuse Ethel had used to get Carla over the night before. Another memory from my conversation with Susan returned, and I continued with my overshare. "Did you know Ethel did a paternity test on Maverick? I'm assuming to make sure Jonathan was really his father."

Donna cringed in sympathy but not surprise, clueing me in that Carla had indeed been aware.

"Oh, wait. You did." For whatever reason, Donna's reaction also reminded me of what had been said at the table the night before. Carla and Ethel had alluded to the paternity test, to the Beaker blood. "Ethel brought that up right before she left."

Carla snarled. "Yes. Just when I thought she couldn't add any more insult to injury. She tried that right after Maverick was born, and Jonathan refused to do it, of course, but a couple of weeks ago, she demanded I sign for her to get a paternity test. I guess she couldn't pull the right strings for Garrett and Branson to do that part for her." She looked over at her son, her tone softening. "Making sure Maverick shared her blood before she stole him away after she murdered his mother." She straightened and looked back at me, a new light in her eyes. "You know what, I *am* going to try to get that money. Even if I have to wrestle it from Branson, if for no other reason than to make sure Ethel spends all of eternity rolling in her grave. Who knows, I might give half of it to PETA just for spite of all her stupid fur coats."

Donna and I both laughed, but I kept going. "Funny that you should bring up her fur coat. She had the results of the paternity test right there in her pocket last night. Did you know she'd gotten them back?"

"No." Carla grew thoughtful. "I wonder if that's what triggered her little over-the-top exit last night—she got confirmation that Maverick was Jonathan's, so it was time to take her money, her grandson, and run. So stupid. She didn't love him, not really. Not even sure she ever loved Jonathan. They were just more possessions—things that were *hers*, you know?" She spared one more glance at her son, confirming Maverick was out of earshot, and then repeated the sentiment she had before. "I don't care if it was Branson. I'm going to send him a thank-you letter whenever this is all said and done. In this, at least, he did me a favor. Did the world a favor."

I stayed at Doc's Apothecary and Soda Shoppe for nearly another hour. Only a quarter of that, however, was focused on the night before, confirming that Carla had also experienced the masked man and that she hadn't recognized his voice either. The rest? I gave in to comfort—finished the delicious malt with pleasure, enjoyed being in Donna's presence again after so many years, and took solace in the gentlest puppy I'd ever met and the most cherubic child who ever existed. I even, though I never dreamed it possible, enjoyed Carla. Maybe *enjoyed* wasn't the correct word, but we'd already been pitted on the same side on a few occasions, whether we wanted to be or not. Just like with Delilah and Anna, Carla was now Mrs. White to my Mrs. Peacock; there would be no coming back from that. Strangely, that was more than fine with me.

After leaving Doc's, I paused when I got to the

intersection of Moraine and Elkhorn. I'd been planning on simply returning to the Cozy Corgi but instead looked left, through the whipping snow, up Elkhorn. I'd already spoken to three of the other players from the night before. Brushes, Bottles, and Brie was there on the other side of the street, and just a little farther up, Aspen Gold. Maybe Mary and Vivian could tell me of their experiences with the masked man, see if they noticed some detail that would shed a new light to things. I even took a step that direction before the thought of Mary Smith doused me with a bucket of pure exhaustion. I didn't have it in me, and I wasn't going to beat myself up about that, not on a day that I really wanted nothing more than to stay curled up in bed, napping and reading.

And *that* thought clarified what I was going to do. Spinning on my heels, I returned to my original direction and strode back to the Cozy Corgi—there was a dirty chai and an Earl Grey roll, a crackling fireplace, and a good book waiting for me. There was also a corgi who might or might not cuddle with me as I read. As much as I loved mysteries, there wasn't one there. Book, fireplace, chai, dog, yeah... that won over Mary Smith and Vivian LaRue any day of the week.

Watson emerged from his little apartment under the Cozy Corgi merchandise as I entered the bakery, which was once again nearly empty. He stuck his head through the little flap and eyed me with accusation—sure, he'd chosen not to go to Cabin and Hearth with me, but he hadn't been given the option of Doc's and seeing Donna, one of his all-time favorite humans. A little guilt whispered to me at that, but I cast it aside. Watson, as far as I knew, wasn't clairvoyant; he hadn't known where I was.

I squatted partially and held out a hand. "Hey there, did you have a good time with Ben and naps?" There, made it sound like I'd done him a favor.

Unimpressed, he started to withdraw back into his apartment, then froze, glistening nose twitching, and I realized too late that he did, in fact, have his own sort of canine clairvoyance. Before I could rush down the steps and wash all traces off my body—not that it would do any good as I didn't have a change of clothes—Watson darted my way, sniffing my skirt, my outstretched hand. He sneezed and sniffed again, then took a couple of lumbering steps back before meeting my gaze, just as much murder behind his chocolate eyes as Branson Wexler had ever experienced. Not only was there Anna, Delilah, Winston, and Phineas, but *Donna*, Elphie, and Maverick—the only child I'd ever seen Watson enjoy. *And*, doubtlessly, the smell of waffle cones. I figured at least Carla's scent didn't play into his betrayal.

"Buddy, I'm sorry." I reached out to pat his head, but he yanked it away. "I didn't plan it; I'll make sure you get to visit Donna with me next time."

Hope flashed in his eyes like I'd just said the word *treat*.

"Sorry." I repeated the sentiment and considered turning right back around and heading down there again, but the promise of dirty chai and words by the fireplace was too tempting. "Later, okay?"

No, definitely not okay. He spun, paused at the entrance to his apartment, and gave a soap opera-worthy glare over his shoulder before he disappeared inside. We humans might have been irrevocably changed by experiences in the Beaker mansion the night before, but my temperamental corgi? Not so much.

After a brief exchange with Katie, where I risked making her just as unhappy as Watson—I promised to give her details *later*. Proving she didn't have the vengeance of a corgi, Katie agreed to make my dirty chai, with two extra shots, and warm up an Earl Grey roll, even without the payment of story time. Several minutes later, I was in my version of heaven in front of the fire on the antique sofa and underneath the purple Portobello lamp.

Once more, the sofa and the lamp triggered that flash of Ethel's body in front of the similar pair, but I pushed past it. This had been my favorite spot for years; I wouldn't let Ethel take that from me. I hadn't let Branson ruin it when he'd held Leo and me there at gunpoint, so I'd get past it this time as well. Before sitting, I glanced around the mystery room. The Stephen King book I'd started the other night was still at home, but it wasn't what I was in the mood for, anyway. Suddenly, I realized *mystery* wasn't what I was in the mood for. When what I craved hit me, I gave in to the impulse—going over to the kids' section and pulling out a copy of *The Secret Garden*, one of my childhood favorites. With that, I settled in, fire crackling, chai steaming, and the snow outside the windows finally beginning to slow.

Before long, even before Mary Lennox discovered that hidden doorway, I knew I wouldn't have to change anything in the mystery room. I felt just as safe and protected as I always had in my little haven. True, it would have been ultimate perfection if Watson had joined and napped by me as I read, but even that, his corgi moodiness, was soothing.

That cozy sense of safety lasted all the way until

a couple of pages after Mary Lennox finally got into the garden before it came to an abrupt halt as someone cleared their throat in the doorway.

I nearly dropped the book at the sight of Charlotte Mills—Lord, Charlotte *Griffin*—standing there, backlit by the bright sun pouring in from the front windows, giving a deceptive halo around her thick fall of chestnut hair.

"Sorry." Charlotte's expression was unreadable in her nearly silhouetted form, but her tone sounded genuine. "I know you don't want to see me, and I know it probably feels like I'm invading your space."

I nearly laughed, nearly told her that, yes, she was invading my space, nearly threw *The Secret Garden* right between her eyes. Instead, I didn't move, didn't speak.

Over her shoulder, Ben came into view. Although I couldn't read his expression, either, I was certain he was checking to make sure I was all right. I couldn't provide him an answer.

Charlotte let out of breath and then continued into the mystery room, paused, looked around and sat *on my sofa,* on the opposite end, within arm's reach.

Anger surpassed what I'd felt the night before, though certainly it was connected, probably what I hadn't been able to tap into until that moment. I shook with it, *burned* with it, so much so that it stole my ability for speech.

The growl in the opposite doorway, the one with the stairs up to the bakery behind it, verbalized my anger for me. I hadn't heard him come down, but Watson strode in, ears lowered, fangs bared. As smooth as a Clydesdale, he leapt up onto his ottoman, using it as a pathway, as he bounded over the space between and landed in the middle of the sofa. He took his place with his back toward me, his snarling and fangs flashing at Charlotte.

She popped up like she'd been burned and took a couple of steps away.

I placed my hand on Watson's back. "Good boy."

Charlotte had moved at an angle where she was no longer silhouetted; at that time, I could read her expression, one that threw kerosene on the flames of my anger. She had the audacity to look shocked, insulted, and then hurt. Ben had moved into the doorway in which she'd entered. She looked at him, then back at us. "I didn't come here to kill you, Winifred."

"Really?" I couldn't help myself, not that I tried. "Sorry, I'm afraid I'm going to need you to be more specific. You mean you didn't come here *today* to kill me? Because that's definitely the ultimate result of you coming to Estes Park."

"When did you get so dramatic?" My childhood best friend added to her level of audacity by sounding disgusted, superior.

"When did *you* get so—" I caught myself, shook my head, and took a breath. I wasn't going to worry about my manners where Charlotte was concerned, but I also wouldn't allow myself to be lowered to some sniping *Real Housewives of Estes Park* scenario. Closing *The Secret Garden*, I placed it on my lap, and kept my other hand on Watson's back before looking to Ben. "Thank you." I almost told him he was fine to leave, then changed my mind. "I'd appreciate you hanging out with us, if you don't mind."

"I don't mind at all." Twisting, he leaned against the doorframe, the sunshine now giving his long, unbraided black hair a much more deserved halo than Charlotte had earned.

Charlotte let out a disbelieving breath, sounding insulted once more and then looked to her right, the doorway Watson had entered. Katie stood there, arms crossed, taking the opposite sentinel of Ben.

"Figured something was up when Watson came out of his apartment snarling." She'd been addressing me but twisted ever so slightly to look at Charlotte. "I'm not one to care about what people think, but I must admit I'm impressed with you, Charlotte. How you can walk anywhere with your head held high —*let alone* in here of all places—and act like you don't deserve to be run out of Estes Park with flaming pitchforks, I have no idea."

Charlotte's temper—typically more even-keeled than mine—flared in that moment, and knowing her like I did, I could see it took every ounce of willpower to hold it at bay. Finally, she refocused on me, still having that expression of betrayal, and shook her head. "Never mind. This was a mistake." Only then did I notice the sheen of tears in her familiar brown eyes.

Tears! Whether real or fake, they sparked my own temper. Actually, no, that was already blazing; they sparked my curiosity, which was always dangerous. "You came all this way—" I wasn't entirely sure if I meant the distance of a block down Elkhorn, or the drive across Kansas from the Midwest. "Don't waste the trip. What do you want?"

"Nothing you'll give. Like I said, this was a mistake." She turned and headed toward the door, and to her surprise, mine too, Ben slid over, blocking the path. She hesitated, then lifted her beautiful chin, stood like that for a second, then, instead of giving him some retort, looked back at me. "*You* accused *me* of doing business with thugs, and here I am surrounded with—"

"It's called friendship, Charlotte. Something we *both* know is a concept you can't grasp." Okay... so maybe a little *Real Housewives of Estes Park*. "Now, *what* do you want?"

Watson had stopped growling, but he sat at attention, ears back.

She debated, then gave in. "For the third time, a wasted trip, but if you must know, I wanted you to help clear Garrett's name."

I balked. If I'd been holding the mug of chai, I probably would have dropped it. And if it hadn't been for Katie's and Ben's similar reactions, I might have thought I'd misheard. As it was, disbelief rang in my voice, alongside an astounded laugh. "You can't be serious."

"I know you've got your reasons to think what you do, but Garrett had nothing to do with what happened to you last night. And... I'm sorry for what you experienced." Charlotte sounded sincere, like she meant it—which didn't mean anything. "But Garrett would never do that to you, nor would I."

I didn't bother with arguing that point, Katie's

snort did it for me. Instead, I tried to put the pieces together—I'd thought she meant clear his name in general, being involved with Branson, or some big-picture item. Then I realized she'd only spoken about the night before and understanding dawned. "Oh. I guess Garrett's been taken into custody. Were you with him when Susan picked him up?"

The front door of the bookshop opened, but I didn't look to see who it was, though they headed our way.

"He didn't have anything to do with it, I swear." Charlotte didn't answer my question directly. "Detective Green won't listen to us. Garrett and I were together at the house all last night. She thinks he's some masked man, but he wasn't. He was with me, I swear it."

"Do you really think any of us would consider you a reliable alibi?" None of this made sense, which made me think there was some larger plot behind it, had to be.

"Yes." She met my gaze, held it. "You know me, Fred. You can tell when I'm lying. And I swear it. I swear to you, Garrett was with me. He had nothing to do with this."

"You're wrong." Sadness, maybe regret, stole some of my anger, and though I attempted to keep it out of my voice, I failed. "I can't tell when you're lying—that's been proven to an embarrassing and painful degree. As far as I'm concerned, for my own safety and sanity, I have to assume if you're speaking, you're lying."

Hurt, genuine it seemed, flashed in her eyes. "I thought you were better than this. That you wouldn't let past hurts and mistakes get in the way of truth. Setting my husband up to take the fall for what happened to you isn't going to change anything."

"Did Branson order you to do this?" The figure who'd paused beside Ben in the doorway stepped fully in, taking form, and Paulie—without his corgis at his side—addressed Charlotte head-on. There wasn't anger in his tone, and there might have even been the quaver of fear. "That's the only explanation that you'd come here and think Winifred would try to clear Garrett's name. You're Branson's tool, nothing more or less than that." He stood straighter, and though thin, he filled himself out, trying to look bigger. It didn't radiate as threatening, but it didn't come off weak either. "But that's the thing. You're not just facing Winifred, you're facing *all* of us. Your presence here threatens all of our lives, but even if it didn't—" He gestured toward me. "—we'd still stand against you, for her."

"I know who you are, Paulie." Charlotte didn't back down from him, not at all. "You're the last one to preach. If the stories are true, *you* were Branson's little pet. Running around town doing his bidding."

"Exactly." Paulie didn't flinch, didn't falter. "Which is why I know without a doubt what's happening. So, right back at you, lady. I know who *you* are as well."

"You don't really believe what you're saying, that's obvious." Charlotte's voice was calm, but there was a bite of steel in it, an edge I might have missed if I didn't know her so well. "If you truly thought I was here because of Branson Wexler, then you wouldn't speak to me that way. You'd think it unsafe. You'd be afraid Branson himself would take it as a threat or a challenge if he heard about it."

"You're not even trying to deny it anymore, are you?" I stared at her in disbelief, genuine disbelief. "You're *literally* threatening Paulie with Branson right in front of all of us."

"No, I'm not." She gave a scornful laugh and rolled her eyes. "You're not the same woman I used to know. You've gone off the deep end, drowning in conspiracy theories and seeing monsters in every shadow."

Before I could respond, Paulie sidestepped,

putting himself in Charlotte's line of vision once more. "When you give this little report to your boss, feel free to tell Branson that I'm not afraid of him anymore." His voice quivered, belying his claim, although, in a way, proving it all at the same time. "You can also tell him that we're going to take him down, make him pay."

"And *you*, right along with him." Katie joined Paulie, moving to stand shoulder to shoulder with him.

Charlotte stared at them in disgust and then looked between their shoulders at me. "Whoever this masked man is, if he even exists, I'll prove it wasn't Garrett. And then you'll come to me with an apology."

"All right then." It was all I could manage—the pull between laughing or attacking, and maybe even crying, too strong to figure out which way to go. "Anything else?"

She turned toward the door once more, made a flicking motion for Ben to step aside, which he did, and then started to walk past. "Actually... yes." She turned and looked back at me. "Leave Donna alone." And with that, she turned around again and strode out of the bookshop.

Those last three words threw me off more than

anything else Charlotte had said. Her tone had been different, her... energy—to borrow the term from my mother and stepsisters—had been different. That hadn't been a warning; it had been a plea, one born from fear and worry. And it confirmed everything we already knew.

As soon as the front door of the Cozy Corgi closed, Paulie plopped down on the sofa like all strength had been ripped from his body. Watson chuffed at the disrespect but allowed himself to be patted as Paulie apologized.

The four of us stared at one another, all caught in different levels of disbelief and astonishment at what had just happened. Ben took a seat on the ottoman, and a moment later Katie joined us, reaching out to touch Paulie's knee. "Are you all right?"

Paulie shook his head, but when he spoke, there was no quaver in his voice. "I heard about last night, of course." He looked at me then. "I almost came over a hundred times today, wanting to check on you, but... for some reason couldn't make myself. Then I saw *her*... saw Charlotte walk in here, and it... I don't know, it was the final straw. It's just so..."

"Ridiculous," Ben finished for Paulie at the exact time Katie snorted out, "Obvious."

I gave a little laugh at the two of them. "Yes, *both* of those things."

"I have to admit," Paulie charged ahead, not distracted. "As much as I feared the things Branson would do, last night and what you went through was even more... I don't know the word, so whatever it is... but *more* than I could have predicted."

"I thought of you several times while it was all going down. How you said it will be Branson or us. I've agreed with you, but even more so now." I wasn't certain how much Paulie had heard, so I clarified. "Last night wasn't entirely Branson, however. I'm not sure of the details, but we think Ethel stole it from him or something. Which means, we didn't experience what Branson actually had planned. I have a feeling that though it wouldn't have ended in a big explosion, it might have been worse."

"Yeah, Campbell told me." Paulie looked at Ben, Katie, and me in turn and then began to stroke Watson again as he spoke. "I have a theory on that. Not that it matters, at this point, but I think Branson probably would have tried to pit us against one another in his little Clue game. In one way or another."

"In a *Hunger Games* sort of situation—" I chuckled. "—to put it in literary terms." I hummed my skepticism. "Maybe, but that's hard for me to picture. With as much authenticity to the Clue game that I saw in the mansion, I think Branson would have stayed to the rules somehow, though I'm not clear how it would have all played out. And like you said, I'm also not sure it matters at this point."

"I was right about it being Branson or us at the end of all this." Paulie jumped over my thoughts on the Clue game. "But *you* were right, you *and* Campbell, about not letting him steal our lives from us in the meantime." Still stroking Watson, Paulie looked to where he and Charlotte had been standing only moments before. "I let him do that to me years ago, I can't believe I let him do it again."

Ben reached down, placed a hand on Paulie's shoulder, as Katie had his knee. "So, don't let him do that anymore."

"No." Paulie nodded. "I won't. Never again."

A few hours later found Mom and Barry's home ready to burst at the seams. That would have been true enough when all the members of my stepsisters' families were present, as they numbered eight in total, but Demetrius had come along with Gary and Percival, and I'd invited Katie and Joe. Realizing I'd have to relive the night in Ethel's mansion, I decided I might as well do it all at once. Plus, Katie and Joe were family, so they belonged.

So, in front of sixteen people crowded in Mom's living room, and one corgi in pure bliss wedged between Barry's and Leo's affection, I retold every minute detail of what it had been like to be Mrs. Peacock.

Knowing this would be the case, Mom hadn't bothered with making a formal sit-down dinner, instead opting for trays of sandwiches—of both meat and vegetarian variety, breads from the Cozy Corgi

Bakery, cheese, appropriately enough from Mary Smith's shop—a large tray of vegetables with creamy artichoke dip, and an unending pot of vegetable stew —which was perfect for the freezing weather that had been left, along with drifts of powdery white up to our knees, by the blizzard.

Though I'd been over the details with Susan, Campbell, and Leo, it was a different experience telling it from start to finish to my family. Mom had given strict orders to everyone there'd be no interruptions, to save all questions until the end—like I was a guest speaker at a university. Surprisingly, though there had been plenty of gasps from Zelda, Verona, and Percival, the family had followed Mom's directive. Somewhere during the telling, it stopped being personal, some of the emotion fading away and turning it into an experience—rather like what had happened on the steps down to Ethel's garage the night before, but instead of having an out-of-body experience watching my family gathered in the living room, I was an observer of the memory, traveling through the tunnels and from room to room. It was grounding and somehow brought up more questions that I'd not been able to access at the time.

"And then," Katie piped up the second I'd come to the end of my tale, leaning forward so her spirals hung around her face as she addressed the rest of the family, "Charlotte had the nerve to show up at the bookshop and ask for Fred's help! For Garrett!"

"*What?*" As if that had been the most shocking revelation of all, Percival let out his greatest shriek yet—or maybe he was making up for the fact Katie had gotten to speak before him. "You're kidding!" He whipped toward me. "I like a woman who flies in the face of expectation and convention, but... that's truly next-level gall."

"That doesn't make any sense, more than it is shocking." Mom spoke—she alone hadn't had a bite to eat the entire time, only sat with her hands folded in her lap, knuckles white with strain. "Nor does it sound like Charlotte." She hurried ahead when a couple of sounds of disgust burst forth. "No, I'm aware that she's not the same little girl that grew up coming over to our house to visit Fred. But regardless of how she's changed and the choices she's made, Charlotte is not stupid." Mom looked at me, sounding the perfect blend of concerned mother and ex-cop's wife. "That was a message, she wasn't trying to be subtle."

"I agree." I'd thought it at the time, but in the hours that had passed, I'd grown more certain. "There isn't the slightest chance Charlotte wanted my help or expected me to give it. I'm not entirely sure what the message is, but—"

"It's just more of the game." Demetrius spoke from where he sat next to his doppelganger of a great-uncle, Gary. "Although whether it's meant to throw you off or just taunt you is debatable."

"Clearly." Gary nodded his agreement and cast a look at his nephew that was both sad and hopeful.

"You haven't heard from him? From Branson, I mean?" Leo paused in his patting of Watson and didn't seem to notice, as he instantly received a corgi nose nudging his elbow.

Gary glanced at Leo, and in that small flicker of his ever-kind dark gaze, I caught the slightest edge of offense, insult, and worry. It was only a second before he turned that gaze to Demetrius, revealing he was fearing the same thing as Leo, despite his best efforts.

Demetrius showed no insult at Leo's obvious challenge, only gave a shrug of his muscled shoulders. "No, it's been a couple of months. Not since everything happened with August and Colin."

"Has anyone else noticed that? That the last two or three months have been nothing but Colin Apple and drama with the Beakers? Since January actually, when everything went down with Colin's nephew and the vet's niece." Zelda twisted her long brunette hair and looked toward her twin. "Verona and I were talking about that today. At first, we thought it probably had something to do with the relationship of Mercury and the moon's rotations, but from everything we can tell, they're not responsible for—"

"*Mom*," Britney hissed a reprimand, sounding like the embarrassed teenager she was, though she instantly rallied at both Zelda and Verona's hurt expressions. "Sorry. I suppose we should all look at every possibility." She glanced my way and hurried onward. "Charlotte comes into Doc's every once in a while. She never stays long, but she goes out of her way to be nice to me. It feels genuine. If I didn't know better, I'd be fooled by her."

"Even complimented my spectacled jasper." Ocean spoke up as he pulled a stone of striated gray and pink from his pocket—the two cousins worked at Donna's shop on evenings and weekends. "Like I'd ever care about *her* opinion."

"Brecciated jasper, Ocean, not spectacled. It's not wearing glasses." Verona offered her son a long-suffering sigh before offering an explanation. "*Brecciated* jasper helps with willpower, endurance, strength, organization, and energy. I thought it would help him with his first job."

"It hasn't helped yet." Britney sneered teasingly at Ocean. "You misplace the ice-cream scoop every time Stephanie Song comes in, organization and willpower both out the window. And let's not talk about the lack of ducks you've sold for the drama club's fundraiser."

Verona scowled at Zelda, as if her twin was responsible for this mockery of crystals and gems.

Ocean only waggled his eyebrows at his cousin, then turned my way. "You know who *never* comes in? Garrett." His grin turned wicked. "Not that I blame him, since he was almost poisoned by a malt, but I wish he would. Maybe the second time would be a charm."

"Ocean!" Noah, who'd seemed lost to his own thoughts, as normal, reprimanded his son in a very atypically serious manner. "We do not joke about murdering people, even if they deserve it."

Ocean rolled his eyes, and Joe snickered. As most of the family turned to look at him, a blush bloomed over his near-giant's face, and he lowered his bowlful of stew. "Sorry, it just strikes me every once in a while what lives we lead, talking about murder and mayhem as if it's commonplace. Which... I guess it is." He shot a wink at Ocean. "I agree with you, Garrett does deserve it, but... I have to take your dad's side. The whole no-killing thing is a pretty good rule. If you don't believe me, just ask my ex-wife. I don't think she's enjoying life behind bars."

"Your ex-wife murdered someone?" Demetrius's voice shot up in genuine surprise.

The blush over Joe's cheeks deepened, but Katie interceded on her fiancé's behalf. "Next time you come down for a pastry, you and I will sit down and go through all the drama. I'm surprised you haven't heard already. I'll fill you in on my serial-killer parents. You're not the only one with a checkered past, Demetrius Follows." She gave him a friendly wink and then looked back to me. "There're lots of bunny trails we could go down, including Charlotte's behavior today, but whether it was a message or a distraction, I can't help but feel it's not overly vital. At least not yet." She held my gaze, studying me. "What does your gut tell you about Garrett? Was he the masked man? Whether he was or not, I'm certain he was involved."

The whole family turned to me as they had at Joe's snicker. *Winifred and her gut*, like it was a magic eight ball that would reveal all answers. Sometimes it did, sometimes not so much. This was one of those times for the latter, and I shook my head. "My gut's not telling me much at this point, other than

screaming *danger, danger, danger*. I think if I'd inter-
acted with this masked man, like a lot of the others, I
might have a better sense—even if he'd disguised his
voice, I think I would recognize Garrett—but
whoever was underneath that mask, I never saw.
Don't know if that means he was in another room of
the house or gone already." I shrugged. "Or... maybe
waiting in the library to stop Ethel and Mason from
killing us."

"That's rather odd, though." Percival spoke
calmly and seriously, which in and of itself was odd.
"Why go through all the trouble of gathering you up,
securing several of you to chairs in the dining room,
and then double-crossing Ethel and Mason?" He
shook his head, then answered his own question.
"Although, if it's Branson we're talking about, just
more games and mind tricks. Maybe it's as simple as
that."

"Probably." For the first time in a while, I pushed
Branson aside and narrowed in on Percival and
Gary. "Whatever the case, and whatever game the
masked man was playing, if he was playing one at all,
and regardless of how the entire thing was set up, last
night was *Ethel's* moment. It didn't end the way she
hoped, obviously, but it was all her. It felt that way
last night, and it's become clearer throughout the day

as we went over who she'd brought to the mansion, how she got them there, and even how she arranged us at the table. I knew she hated Carla, Delilah, Anna, and me, although I didn't quite grasp how deep that went with Delilah and Anna, but I'm confused about Mary and Vivian. I wanted to go talk to them today and just couldn't make myself. Hopefully tomorrow. But do either of you have any thoughts? Did she mention anything during town council meetings?"

Both my uncles snorted out laughs and shared a knowing glance. Giving a little chuckle, Gary motioned toward his husband. "I'll let you handle that, my dear. You do love a spotlight."

"That I do." Percival shimmied his scarecrow shoulders and lifted his chin as if finding his best angle for their camera. "Mary is easy enough. Although, like you suggested, Fred, I'm a little shocked at the level of hate Ethel had for her, but it's been growing. The Smiths have been reclusive."

"Evasive, you mean."

"Yes, actually, that's more accurate." Percival didn't snap at his husband's interruption or correction, instead nodding. "From everything anyone can tell, the Smiths have *money*, based on how they both purchased and remodeled two shops at one time on

Elkhorn. Also, the home they bought, while not grand like Ethel's, isn't exactly a dump. From all indicators, they should be players in the upper echelon of Estes Park social society, in which Ethel was the queen, or at least saw herself that way. Mary ignored every attempt from Ethel to form a friendship."

"*Friendship?*" Gary snorted out a second interruption but didn't stop there. "Ethel didn't have friendships, she had pawns and other chess pieces to move around. Everyone in town was just another piece in her game to rule Estes." He cringed. "I wouldn't have guessed the game was Clue, more Monopoly or... I don't know, is there a game version of *Valley of the Dolls?* Regardless, Mary chose not to play, even worse, didn't bother with as much as a response to any of Ethel's attempts. Acted as if Ethel didn't exist or matter."

"That's how Mary has treated everyone in town." Joe spoke up then. "Actually, her husband and son as well. They don't take part in anything with other store owners. Other than opening their shop, they might as well be ghosts."

"True." Percival stole the spotlight back, returning to me. "If anything, Winifred, I might have suggested Ethel hated Mary even more than you.

Being ignored and looked over is far more insulting than having the status of arch nemesis."

"I didn't see Ethel as an arch nemesis." I considered that for a moment... I wouldn't have assigned Ethel such a label, but I suppose it wasn't too far off. "However, I can see what you mean. And from Ethel's personality, that makes sense. Did she ever bring up Bottles, Brushes, and Brie in town council? Try to get them closed down?"

"No. But then again, she wouldn't have. Ethel only brought things up in town council that she knew she could win. If she was ever going to do that, she'd have a firm plan in place." After Percival explained, he glanced at Gary once more. "As far as Vivian... they used to be thick as thieves ages ago, but as with anyone close to Ethel, that shattered spectacularly. Ethel found her annoying, desperate, and crass, but worthy of murder?" Before Gary had a chance to respond, Percival sat even straighter, gave a little flourish of a squawk, and whipped back toward me. "Actually, now that I'm saying it out loud, I'm rather offended that *I* wasn't at that table. Surely, I ranked higher than mousy Mary Smith and shoe-polish Vivian LaRue." He gave a hiss reminiscent of Granny Smith. "All I can say is Ethel better be thankful *I* wasn't waiting for her in that library after such a snub."

Katie snickered. "Oh yes, you would have shown her—much more than a candlestick to the head."

That earned her a sneer. "I would have done it with more flair, darling. More pizzazz. Maybe strangled her with a sleeve of her flea-ridden fur coat."

"Do you mind if we *don't* talk about different ways to murder people in front of the kids?" Noah spoke up again, sounding a little dreamy even in his reprimand.

"Oh really?" Percival whipped his way without missing a beat. "And *whose* shop almost blew up half the town?"

"Percival!" Mom used her reprimanding mother voice on her older brother. "Really. Let's not turn on each other."

Through it all, Demetrius had been looking back and forth, eyes wide with amazement as if watching a rather unbelievable reality television show—very similar to the expressions both Leo and Joe had worn as they'd joined the family in turn. I couldn't quite make out what he thought of all of us, I knew our family dynamics were very different from what both he and Gary had grown up with as Follows. He seemed a little amused, a little perplexed, and fairly uncomfortable.

"I'm just glad you're okay." Britney spoke up, sounding every bit the peacekeeper she'd started to become recently. "I can't imagine being trapped in that house, secret passages, dead bodies, locked doors."

"If you knew you weren't going to die, it would sound fun." Britney's little sister, Christina, grinned over at me. "It really had trapdoors and tunnels like in the Clue game?"

"It did." Even at the memory, a momentary claustrophobia swept over me. "Just... just like the game."

"Maybe we can sneak in there, play a real-life version." Leaf grinned at his cousin, excited secrecy lacing his words.

"Oh yeah, that's gonna work." His older brother shoved him on the shoulder. "You don't plan on sneaking away *in front* of Mom and Dad, doofus."

"Ocean," Verona snarled at her eldest. "Don't call your brother names." She turned that snarl onto her youngest. "And seriously, Leaf, if you even *think* about doing that, there will be no electronics for a month."

Leo had been oddly quiet the whole evening,

although, maybe it wasn't odd. He seemed heavy, worried. Similar to myself. Even the way he stroked Watson felt more for comfort than for Watson's enjoyment. He'd looked up at me suddenly when Christina had mentioned the tunnels, and whatever he was thinking had solidified. "What about the corgi pin? I'd forgotten, it was just another bizarre, horrifying detail among many, but if it's the same one that was on Angus's scarf and not a duplicate, then how did that get out of police custody?" He didn't wait for an answer, though his low voice grew heavier, quieter. "Maybe the masked man is someone on the force. Officer Babcock wouldn't surprise me at all." He gave a little flinch. "Or Dunmore. I don't want to think that, but... we know he has secrets, that Rhonda had dirt on him before she was murdered. You saw the photos."

"Leo..." Zelda reached over and touched his knee as she shook her head—some of those details hadn't been discussed in front of the younger kids for fear they'd say something at school.

"Oh, sorry." Leo cringed, then looked at me. "It's something we should consider."

I chilled at the thought, both that the chief was involved and at the memory of the pin. It had been enough that it was a reminder of Branson, a message from him in and of itself. In the torrent of things to consider, how it had gotten there hadn't yet whispered. I had a feeling Susan had overlooked it as well, as I couldn't recall it on the sheets of paper covering her office. "That could make sense. I don't want to think it, but it could. If Branson found out about what Marlon is keeping secret and decided to use it against him, or threaten his wife in jail, or Campbell..." I replayed moments with the chief from the night before and shook my head. "We've got to consider it, but unless he's the best actor in the world, which I've never gotten that impression before, he was scared last night. Just like the rest of us. He thought he was going to die."

"Well..." Demetrius spoke up again, offering another shrug of those wide shoulders. "From my experience with Branson, and even more so after hearing you all talk about him, it sounds like something he would do, right? Using someone, forcing them to do things and then discarding them when they're not useful anymore? Isn't that what you said he would probably do to me?"

In the couple of months since Demetrius had been caught being here at Branson's behest, he rarely referenced it directly. The whole room stilled as he spoke, and after a moment, Gary put a reassuring hand on his nephew's back.

"So your vote is yes, that the chief is involved?" I met his gaze—not challenging necessarily, but inspecting. As I did, something in my gut whispered. Maybe not my gut, maybe just fear in the back of my mind, but I couldn't quite grasp what it said.

"Yeah, makes sense to me." Another shrug as Demetrius glanced around the room, then back at me. "You've got pictures of the chief doing something, even though we don't know what it is yet. He had access to the pin in lockup or wherever they kept it." When Zelda groaned at the renewed details she'd tried to keep from the kids, he offered a fourth shrug, this one in apology, though he returned to me. "You said yourself, it sounds like things didn't go exactly as they had originally been planned last night, right? Maybe being left with the rest of you was the only surprise for the chief."

Gary let out a long breath. "That's something to consider. I hate to think that about Marlon. He's a good man, but..." Gary shrugged in an identical way to his great-nephew. "We've seen good people do horrible things when they feel trapped in a corner."

Someone else spoke, maybe a few people, but it all became buzzing in my ears, as I stared at

Demetrius and Gary. I tried to unthink the thought, tried to argue with it, tried to cast it off as ridiculous, but couldn't.

"Fred." Mom's voice cut through the fuzz; I got the impression she'd said my name a couple of times. "Are you okay?"

Coming back to the moment, I found Watson at my feet, looking at me with concern. A glance toward Leo revealed a matching expression over his face as well, but he was looking back and forth between me and Demetrius in a way that suggested he was beginning to understand. "Yes, Mom. Sorry." I forced a smile her way and then bent down and pulled Watson into my lap, more for a distraction than anything, as he instantly began to squirm—he'd wanted to offer comfort, but this was more than he'd bargained for. Afraid my suspicion had already been caught, I threw out another topic, the first one that came to my mind. "Another thing we're exploring is the character names, if they mean something. They definitely did for Carla and Delilah, but the rest of us... I'm not so sure."

"That's right." Percival swallowed it hook, line, and sinker, grinning at the rest of the room. "Anna as Reverend Green, can you imagine? She wasn't flattered by that label, let me tell you. Although, other than Miss Scarlet, is there a desirable character in that game?"

The others began to toss theories, becoming a buzz once more. I allowed myself one more passing glance over Demetrius and Gary before landing on Leo and having a silent conversation. Gary Follows, even in his senior citizen years, had the build and bulk of an ex-football player, still large and muscled. Though decades younger, his great-nephew seemed nearly a carbon copy—just as handsome, just as muscular, even though he never played football. Other than age, the only real difference was that Demetrius was quite a bit shorter. However, that wouldn't keep anyone from describing him as large. *Especially* in a moment of fear. *Especially* when a man with Demetrius's physique wore a mask and held a gun.

The following morning, I called Susan on my way downtown. I swung by the Cozy Corgi long enough to pick up a dirty chai for me, an Americano for Susan, and a bag of Earl Grey rolls and a couple of breakfast empanadas. Watson had just enough opportunity to fawn over Ben before leaving in time to avoid the breakfast rush for the second day in a row.

As before, Watson's annoyance at leaving Ben so soon lessened as we parked in front of the police station. However, it wasn't merely excitement over seeing his favorite detective—judging by the drool, a clear and passionate expectation of more buffalo jerky played a role. Clutching the container of drinks and the pastry bag tight, I kept up with his eager pace and managed the briefest of hellos to dispatch as we hurried through the entrance and down the hall to Susan's office.

She'd left the door open, and—whether hearing Watson's clamoring paws or simply due to being that good of a detective—hollered for us to come in before I knocked on the doorframe. Unlike the day before, she swiveled in her chair just as Watson was preparing to leap into her lap, and held out her hand. "Stop right there, Fleabag."

He did, skidding to a halt and issuing a pitiful whimper.

"Nope." Susan shook both her hand and her finger at him. "Yesterday was a fluke. A deserved one, but nonetheless, today, we're getting back to officer training. And officers, fleabags and otherwise, do *not* hug, embrace, sit in each other's laps. Or drool." She scowled as if she tasted something sour. "Looks like I've already missed the opportunity on that last one, but so be it. *Now...*" She stuck her hand in the already opened bag on her desk, the sound of crinkling plastic causing Watson to whimper again. The sound died under Susan's deadly glare. "Sit." She held up a piece of jerky.

Watson whimpered once more and looked up at me as I transferred the drinks and the bag from my grip to the desk.

"No." Susan snapped her fingers. "Don't look at

your mom, she's not going to save you." Another snap. "Sit."

With a mighty sigh, Watson sat.

Susan scrunched up her nose in consideration. "I don't appreciate the attitude, but... I also kind of respect it. So... here." She lowered the treat, nearly losing a finger and almost managed to hide the curve of a smile before she pointed under her desk. "Over here. Lay."

She hadn't tried either of those commands on Watson before. For a moment, I thought he was confused, but after Watson gave yet another dramatic sigh, he plodded beneath her desk and out of view. As he received another piece of jerky a moment later, I assumed he'd followed orders.

"Now... *stay.*" She gave him a third piece for good measure, then snagged her own treat from the Cozy Corgi bag, starting with an empanada.

I sat across from her. Despite having serious things to discuss, I couldn't help myself and had to try to claw out information, hoping I might entice Susan to share a little gossip—first time for everything. "I was surprised you told me not to pick up a hot chocolate for Campbell..." At her glare, I adjusted; Watson wasn't the only one she was training. "For *Officer Cabot*, I mean. Is he not here today?"

She scowled, chewed, then spoke with her mouth full. "Coming in late. He texted last night and requested a couple extra hours this morning."

"Really?" I tried to hold back a grin and failed. "That's curious..." I also failed to keep the giddiness out of my tone. I almost sounded like Katie.

"I'm going to start calling you Anna Hanson."

Okay... maybe I sounded a little bit more like Anna than Katie.

"Besides, Campbell coming in late isn't why you called me this morning, nor to deliver breakfast." Susan considered the empanada. "Second breakfast, I suppose."

"No, but..." I almost gave up and got down to it, but then just couldn't, leaning forward and letting a little corgi whine of my own enter my voice. "Oh, come on, Susan. Paulie mentioned yesterday after he told Charlotte what's what, that he wasn't going to let Branson make him stop living his life anymore. That *had* to mean his relationship with Campbell."

Susan glared while she leaned farther and popped the rest of the empanada into her mouth, chewing long enough I nearly gave up on getting a response. Finally, she swallowed, dusted her lips off with her fingers and rolled her eyes. "I told Officer Cookie Dough for Brains he should make Paulie wait, pay him back for acting like a coward for the last two months." She sniffed. "He disobeyed orders." Once more, she almost succeeded in hiding the little curve of the corner of her mouth. She really used to be better at stifling such things.

I sighed, relaxing. "Oh, I'm glad. I know Campbell was certain things would work out, but also know that wasn't fun, and I hated seeing Paulie in such a state."

"Oh, *me too*." Susan pulled an Earl Grey roll out of the bag and making her voice breathy, continued. "I've lain awake worried about their romance night after night after night. Wondering would they, wouldn't they? Practically cried myself to sleep thinking about each of them forlorn and sad and lonely in their little beds. Paulie crying to his disgusting corgis and Campbell telling his woes to that fat hamster of his." Breathlessness left, and she stared at me with half-lidded eyes. "I feel like I can breathe again now that Tweedledee and Tweedledum are back together."

I tried not to laugh, then unable to stop myself, risked death. "That was dramatic. Percival would be proud."

Susan sucked in the first gasp I had ever heard from her, at least in that register. Daggers entered her eyes, but thankfully she didn't lean over the desk and stab me in the jugular, just grabbed the Cozy Corgi bag and pulled it toward her. "The rest of this is mine now."

It was worth it.

A knock sounded on the door I'd closed behind us.

Watson barked from underneath Susan's desk and then scrambled out to take a protective stance at the edge, splitting his defense between the two of us.

Chuckling, Susan grinned down at him without a reprimand, saving that for whoever was behind the door. "Clearly not wanting visitors at the moment. Grab a clue."

I winced involuntarily at the word *clue*, which was ridiculous. I was distracted a second later as the door creaked open, and someone risked being a victim of homicide.

That proved wrong as Chief Dunmore poked his head in. "I'd rather not hear the word *clue* again for my entire life, if you don't mind." He attempted a smile toward Susan but didn't succeed. He looked older, haggard, exhausted. "Sorry to interrupt, but I heard Fred was here." He sent a smile my way, then down at Watson. "And Officer Fleabag."

I was fairly certain he was the only person who could use Susan's nickname for Watson without receiving an earful. As it was, Susan cringed. "Sorry about that, both about my rudeness at your knock and using that word." She spared me a quick glare. "As you may have noticed, Winifred always brings out my pleasant side."

He chuckled, came the rest of the way in, and closed the door behind him. Watson had stopped growling, cocking his head at the crinkling sound coming from the chief's pocket as he withdrew a butterscotch candy. "Oh, sorry, buddy." Marlon chuckled and bent to pat Watson's head. "Didn't mean to get your hopes up." After Watson replied with a grunt and turned around to disappear once more under the desk, the chief refocused on Susan. "Have you had a chance to discuss the security system with Fred yet?"

"No." She looked a little surprised but regrouped quickly. "We hadn't quite got down to business yet."

"Oh, I figured that was why she was here."

"Winifred called me, actually," Susan explained even though the chief hadn't asked directly, and then motioned toward me. "You said you had some thoughts over dinner with your family last night about Demetrius. Maybe you can share with both of us at the same time."

"Demetrius?" The chief's eyes widened. Instead of taking a seat beside me, he crossed his arms and leaned against the wall. "*He* was involved the other night?" Before I could reply, he let out a breath of understanding. "Oh... he received orders. Perhaps Wexler heard about Ethel speeding up the game and ordered him to handle things."

I merely shook my head, intending to say it wasn't why I'd come, but I'd been frozen by the chief's theory. Hearing him mention Demetrius's name highlighted how easily Demetrius had turned the family's focus and suspicions onto the chief. If Demetrius had been the masked man, he could have just as easily set up the scene to look like murder suicide, Branson could've told him how to get into the library—through the secret passage and into the garage. That was obvious enough, even in that moment; the possibility made me nauseous. It was one thing to know he'd been sent here to cause chaos at Branson's whim, but to consider Gary's great-nephew capable of murder? Although, why not? If he'd been the masked man then...

"No. That's not your theory." The chief looked

at me, puzzled. "I can tell. Sorry, I should have let you talk. Go ahead..." He gestured for me to continue.

"Well..." Though I'd come to discuss Demetrius with Susan, I couldn't help but feel like I was betraying Gary by bringing it up with the *chief*, which was ridiculous. I pushed past it easily enough, and as I spoke of my theory, I addressed the chief and Susan equally. "We had family dinner last night, and Demetrius didn't say anything that made me suspicious necessarily, but as I was looking at him... well... he's not as tall as Gary, but he's muscled, very strong, very fit and in shape." I shrugged, now wanting to discard it completely. "I wouldn't describe him as a tall man, but I would a big man, a strong man. Large... well that could be relative, and he might seem even larger than he is to someone who's nervous and being held at gunpoint by a man in a mask."

"Yeah..." Susan nodded as she closed her eyes, clearly trying on the picture for size. "It also works with what the chief just said." Those pale blue eyes opened and looked at me in sort of an apology and sort of a you-gotta-face-facts expression. "We've known since we discovered Branson sent Demetrius here to play both sides of the coin that he could betray us at any moment. We can't trust him, not for a second."

"I know. I don't. I want to, but... I don't." I looked toward the chief. "You saw the masked man, what do you think? Would Demetrius be tall enough to match the figure you saw? He's quite a bit shorter than Garrett."

The chief hummed. "I don't know that he is. I would say Garrett more fits the bill from what I recall, but you're not wrong. Nerves can alter reality sometimes." He gave a disgusted grunt. "And Garrett Griffin isn't crumbling at all in his story, even after a night in lockup. Not that we're even close to releasing him, not yet. I still lean toward him, but... Demetrius could be involved, even if he wasn't the masked man. Maybe?"

I pushed past the possibility of Demetrius; it was too much. "You said there was something about the security cameras or something? There's some sort of video?"

"No." The chief sucked on his hard candy as he shook his head again, gesturing for Susan to take over.

She did. "Going through that place took all day yesterday and well into last night. A couple of shifts of officers did nothing other than photograph, categorize, label, everything. They found wiring and cameras throughout, in every room, and even in the tunnels." She paused for a second, a muscle in her jaw twitching, and then she continued, anger filtering through. "But no one can figure out where it goes. There's no recording device on scene, and our best tech guys, so far haven't been able to find a remote destination, or even tell us if it was recording or not at the time."

"*So far*." The chief sounded as if he was trying to soothe Susan. "They will."

"Branson." Even as I said his name, I felt embarrassed. "I know it's easy to go to him, just like shouting out Jesus to every question asked in Sunday school or something, but *come on*, it *is* Branson. If it was Ethel's security camera, the recordings would be there somewhere in the house or on her devices. Either way, if cameras were in the tunnels, it was part of the Clue game Branson designed, so he could watch it remotely or record it for later enjoyment."

"Yes, of course." The chief nodded again. "We would agree. Branson is our—"

Susan smacked the desk, making Watson bark again, though she didn't offer him any apology. "*Remotely!* Fred, that's it. Obviously we figured it was being sent somewhere, but the way you said it

—*watch it remotely*. Like a show." Grinning, she turned toward the chief. "That could be the explanation for Garrett, or Demetrius, possibly. If Ethel truly did steal this game from Branson and enacted it sooner than he'd planned, *and* if she didn't know about being recorded, then maybe he saw the game begin, you all being brought into the dining room. Realizing what was happening, he sent someone, just like you said, up the secret passage from the garage to stop Ethel and Mason from killing everyone." She snorted out a disgusted laugh. "From killing *Fred*, let's be serious. The only one Branson would have cared about being blown up was Fred. But..." She looked at me then. "It plays with how the night went down."

"Yes, it does. So... that would mean the possibility of someone else *besides* the masked man. *Two* unknown people, not just one." That felt right, or at least like a logical possibility. "Send Garrett or Demetrius or some other person under his control, make it look like Ethel and Mason had a last-minute, deadly argument, and then left just as easily as they'd come." Though I didn't want to feel grateful to Branson for anything, a wave of gratitude washed over me that he might have been watching, might have saved us. Although, if he had, he was nothing more than a spider wrapping a bug in its web and saving it for a future meal.

"It's a new line of questioning for Garrett, in any case." The chief sounded hopeful, though that fell apart a second later as he looked at me gravely. "We'll probably need to bring in Demetrius sooner rather than later. Hopefully not to hold overnight like Garrett, but... I can't promise."

"I understand." Guilt bit at me again, especially when I had the impulse to tell Gary before it happened, so he wouldn't be caught off guard, but I couldn't. I trusted him, I truly did, and I believed he would do what was right, but I didn't want to put him in that situation. Better to hold on to that guilt myself instead of asking him to share it.

"All right then. Well... better too many leads than not enough." The chief nodded toward me, Susan, even bent down and offered a little wave to Watson before he turned to leave.

Demetrius hadn't been the only theory from the night before that I'd wanted to discuss with Susan. Part of me screamed to wait until the chief left and bring it up then, but I gave in to the other impulse, and as I did, I sent a mental apology to Susan, for all the good it would do. "We also wondered if *you* might be the masked man, Chief Dunmore..."

He froze with his hand on the doorknob, his back to us.

Susan straightened and turned my way slowly, pale blue eyes filled with shock. Not anger, not yet.

Dunmore turned to face us. There was no anger in his expression either, no shock, just a tired sadness, some shame. "Did you?" His gaze flicked back and forth between Susan and me. "The *you* involved in that theory would be..."

"Just my family." I hurried on before Susan could get pulled into it and then rushed ahead to clarify once more, bending the truth. "Actually, just Leo and me. But... you're a large man, too, Chief Dunmore."

"Yes, I am." He patted the beginnings of a firm belly. "Not all muscle like when I was younger, but..." The first words of that had sounded like light-hearted humor, but they died quickly enough. When he spoke again, his gaze stayed on the ground, maybe on Watson napping under the desk again. "And what would make you think I'd have anything to do with the events of last night? Especially when I was at that table with you, in the tunnel with you?" His gaze met mine then, a challenge in their depths... but what kind I couldn't label. "Nearly blown up with you?"

I wished I hadn't opened this can of worms, but

now that I had, might as well see it through. "As we've discussed with Demetrius, Branson has a habit of using someone and then discarding them when their usefulness is over. A quality most people like him possess. Perhaps after you helped gather everyone, you made it look like you were one of the victims, as well, thinking that could be your alibi, not realizing Ethel had taken it over from Branson and... and..."

"*And* you just realized the flaw in that comment, didn't you, Winifred?" There was the anger I knew Susan would have. "Those two things don't match. *Ethel* stole the game from Branson, then you can't tell the chief *Branson* was finished using him and decided to blow him up." Susan snarled, a disgusted expression over her face that I hadn't seen in years. "You are better than that, Winifred. I know things are stressful, but that's just sloppy."

I nodded; she was right. Even if there wa another person who Branson called in to stop the explosion when he saw the game had been stolen, it wouldn't implicate Marlon.

"It's fine." The chief smiled, a sad thing. "We've been through a lot these last many months. My family for sure, yours as well, and then that night..." He spared Susan a glance. "You can't understand unless you were there. Crawling through a tunnel, thinking that any minute the world would explode." Back to me. "It's okay."

"I'm sorry. I..." What could I say? As I searched for a way to make it right, the other factor, the certain one, announced itself. I hesitated there as well. I knew Susan was already working on it, she'd discussed it with me a couple times since discovering those photos. She thought she was close to figuring out who the other man was. Again, I only debated for a moment before doing my normal and leaping. "Rhonda Bigler had dirt on you, Chief Dunmore."

He flinched, eyes wide.

"Fred!" Susan leaned forward, growling my name, fury blazing in those pale blue eyes.

Underneath her desk, Watson whimpered at the change, confused.

I pushed on, daring the chief to look away from me. "If Rhonda Bigler found out, then someone else had access to that knowledge as well. Who's using it against you now? Was it Ethel? Is it Branson?"

"Fred!" Susan barked my name that time, slamming her open palm on the desk.

Watson growled, coming to my defense.

With a little flinch, she glanced under the desk, and a very rare moment of shame flashed over her face, but she shook it off with a literal shake of her head. "Sorry, Fleabag." She looked back to me, but she'd lowered her tone, probably for Watson's sake. "Let me handle this. Like I've told you."

The chief flinched again, that time his gaze whipping toward Susan, confusion clear, then his eyes widened with horror and understanding—an expression that answered a question I knew Susan and I both hoped somehow wasn't true, even though we knew it was. "You know?" His whisper was to his detective, not to me.

Susan kept her glare on me a moment longer, then turned slowly to her chief and gave him a nod. "I do. Since Rhonda Bigler's murder. We know that you've been bribing a member of the staff at the correctional facility to sneak luxuries to your wife. There are photos of you meeting in the street at night with a member of the staff."

Okaaayyyy. Susan hadn't shared that specific detail with me—sneaking in luxuries. That's all we'd figured, but apparently, she'd gotten confirmation.

The chief went ghost white, then with a mighty sigh, collapsed in the chair his nephew had used the day before. He sat in silence for several moments, then finally looked to Susan. "Why haven't you said anything?" He threw his arms wide. "Why am I still chief if you know this?"

It was Susan's turn to hesitate, during which, she shot me another glare, then looked back to Marlon. "Because my informant hasn't agreed to go on record yet. Because I wanted things to be airtight before I presented this to... before I confronted you—"

"It's true, I won't deny it. I will confess." He slumped, sinking back into the chair—looking older and not at all like a large man in that moment, more broken, withered, and old, barely hanging on. His hand lifted, covering his eyes to rub at his temples. After a couple of long shaky breaths, he lowered it and sighed. "I'm almost relieved. I never dreamed I'd do anything like this, but when May... when I had to arrest my own wife... When she killed... I..." Another shaky breath, another sigh, then a nod. "I'll resign, right here, before the night is done. I'll call the mayor and—"

"No. You're staying in your position." Susan shocked me, and from the chief's expression, him as well. But she clarified quickly. "At least for now. Whatever happened the other night is big, and it could be our one chance to bring down Branson before something even bigger happens. And if this goes down, if the chief of police is caught in corruption in the middle of this, then all of this is wasted, because you know—" She shot another glare my way. "—*you know* Branson will have a way to use it to wriggle out of anything we could've ultimately pinned on him, or Garrett, or Demetrius, or anybody." She spoke to me through gritted teeth. "We just need to keep our mouths shut for a little while longer. Do you really want to lose the chance of nailing Branson and Garrett because the chief does what—*bribe* someone to sneak his wife extra pillows or candy or wine or whatever? Is that worth losing Branson?"

"No, of course not." I glanced at the chief, realizing he hadn't specified what exactly he was sneaking to his wife. Though I supposed it didn't matter; they didn't have anything to do with the Clue game. But then the other reason I'd wanted to talk to Susan arrived in the form of Watson barely squeezing out from underneath the desk and plopping down beside me. "The corgi pin." I met Susan's eyes again, challenging her. "In all the other details, we forgot about it, but that pin looks identical to the one Branson left me on Angus's scarf. So, unless he has a duplicate, *somehow* it found its way from evidence and police lockup into Ethel's house last night." I softened my tone, just a touch. "I'm sorry, but it looks like until this very moment, the chief didn't realize we knew what we know. Which means, Branson or Ethel, or whoever, had something to hang over Marlon's head get him to do what they commanded. That corgi pin didn't wander out of lockup all on its own."

Susan shook her head, giving a frustrated sort of laugh. "The *chief* is the one who reminded *me* of that this afternoon. *He's* already got officers looking into it, tracking down how it got from police custody, because yes, when the *chief* checked on his own volition, *he* discovered and reported that the pin had indeed disappeared from police custody."

"Detective Green..." Marlon spoke softly at first and then more firmly. "*Detective Green.*"

She finally looked away, toward him.

"Don't let me ruin the relationship you and Winifred have built over the years. I've brought this on myself, by choices I've made, through the dishonor I've brought to the badge. If you two already knew this, how could she *not* be suspicious? Rightly so." He included me in his final few words. "I'm sorry I let you down, both of you."

SEVENTEEN

The breakfast rush had slowed to a trickle by the time I got back to the Cozy Corgi. I must have worn my emotions on my sleeve as not a solitary one of them asked for details about what had happened at Ethel's mansion, offering me instead cringing smiles of sympathy and a wide berth.

After a brief greeting with Ben, Watson retreated to his apartment, probably licking his emotional wounds. I did the same with a dirty chai. The moments in Susan's office after the chief had left had been tense, with enough friction in the air it practically crackled, threatening to make good on the explosion that never arrived the other night. Things hadn't felt like that between Susan and me since my first few months in town when we were pitted against each other due to Branson Wexler. Somehow, after all we'd gone through, this felt worse, so much worse.

"What were you supposed to do? Not bring it up?" Katie leaned against the other side of the bakery counter. She'd listened with wincing sympathy as I'd filled her in, but shifted to best-friend role, taking my side and allowing irritation to enter. "Susan will get over it. If she doesn't, something's wrong with *her*. You felt the moment was right and went for it. You followed your gut instinct."

Grimacing, I looked up at her. "Well, if that isn't proof that my gut isn't infallible, I don't know what is."

"What are you talking about? That's some mighty twisting of reality." Now Katie's irritation seemed directed at me. "You calling the chief on the carpet right there made him confess. Whether it was on Susan's timetable or not—which was already weeks overdue, if you ask me—it's the same difference. *That* was because of you."

Well... part of me lightened at that. Katie wasn't wrong. Some of that brightness dimmed as I realized she wasn't exactly right either. "Sure, he confessed, and was guilty, but not of what I accused him of, not exactly."

"Who cares?" Katie threw up a hand. "Susan shouldn't. She doesn't have to keep digging to find out exactly what the chief did, or convince her source, or whoever, to come forward. The chief already admitted what he was doing."

"True." I acknowledged I was in the middle of a pity party, but it wasn't merely that I was embarrassed or even that I regretted following my impulse. I wished I had slowed down, if for no other reason than to show Susan the respect she deserved. Honor the relationship and trust we'd built; it was hard-fought... and I'd damaged that, regardless of outcome. We could have arrived at that same destination just a little later with a different path that wouldn't have burnt bridges. Although, perhaps they weren't burnt exactly... maybe just missing a board or two that could be replaced.

I'd planned on walking to the next block to speak to Mary and Vivian about the masked man, but instead decided to spend a bit of time reading. Mary had a similar effect on me as Ethel, and I didn't trust my reactions. Maybe after finishing *The Secret Garden* and a couple of chais and Earl Grey rolls by the fire...

"Hey, good to see you. Your normal?" Nick spoke from the other side of the bakery counter, though I didn't look to see who had arrived.

"Yeah, that'd be great. Thank you." The familiar

voice paused for a moment before speaking again. "Oh, actually, Percival wanted me to pick up some of those tea rolls or whatever that was we had last night."

As expected, I found Demetrius, the other muscular man of my suspicion.

Noticing me, he offered an easy, if not somewhat self-conscious smile of greeting and waved. "Hi. You doing okay? You look sad."

That had to be the thousandth time I'd been asked that question in the past day and a half, and once more, the answer was a resounding no. "I'm okay, thanks for asking. Just haven't hit my minimum caffeine requirement for the morning yet." I took a sip of my chai and then decided to inquire how much of a bridge I'd burned with *him* the night before. "How are *you* doing after last night?"

"I..." Demetrius paused, glanced around at the few occupied tables, and then considered Nick before he answered. Clearly knowing the Pacheco twins were part of our little Scooby Gang and had probably been informed about what had been discussed at Mom and Barry's house, he went ahead, lowering his voice. "I'm fine. I'm really not offended or upset about you all wondering if I was involved. I can't blame you. Something would be wrong if you weren't feeling that way."

Katie nodded her agreement, giving me a meaningful look as if Susan should have been saying the exact same thing to me.

"I appreciate that." I wondered if he'd say the same thing whenever Susan, the chief, or... someone... decided to bring him in for questioning. Who knew, they might call or show up any minute in the middle of the bakery.

"Thanks." He reached out and took the pastry bag from Nick, then paid, his muscular arms flexing his dark blue thermal shirt with every twist and turn as he retrieved his wallet.

I couldn't help but study him, picturing Demetrius securing others around Ethel's dining-room table, kidnapping Mary Smith at gunpoint from the back of her shop. Arriving out of the darkness in Delilah's backyard. I could see it, even though Demetrius wasn't as tall as his uncle, or Garrett, or the chief, for that matter. He still unquestionably qualified as a big man.

"You're wondering about me in this very moment, aren't you?" He smiled again and surprised me by coming around my side of the counter, offering a quick smile to Katie and then sitting on a stool, leaving one between us. "Ask me anything."

I seemed to be continuing my absolutely horrendous job of hiding any emotions or thoughts, but what did that matter? I didn't deny but offered a smile of my own. "Okay..."

But what could I ask? What could trip him up? What could prove his innocence? I went through all the sheets of papers and diagrams covering Susan's office, played through flashes of the night in Ethel's mansion, considered quizzing him about Garrett or Charlotte. Nothing seemed to click; there was no question that would catch him off guard if he was guilty. Nothing that would create the same reaction in him the chief had just demonstrated.

Actually... maybe that was the problem. It wasn't a question I needed, not words at all. I played through the scenario quickly, knowing it was a risk and could come to nothing, but... it could be worth it. "You know what, Demetrius, I'd have to get permission from the police, but I've been wanting to go back to Ethel's to see it with fresh eyes, in the light of day. Would you be willing to come with me?"

He blinked, surprised, clearly not expecting that request. After that brief hesitation, which I couldn't determine if it held meaning in and of itself or not, he nodded. "Sure."

"I'm coming, too." Katie didn't miss a beat, nor did she leave room for argument. "Don't ask Susan's permission, just tell her that I'll be there. Or..." She grinned. "Don't mention me at all. I'll just show up."

I didn't consider arguing or asking Katie to stay away—she was one of the smartest people I knew and full of random information, which sometimes proved surprisingly useful. However, I wasn't about to call Susan and ask for permission. I considered the chief, I actually thought he might give it just out of amends, but talk about burning bridges. Instead, I landed on Campbell, who'd still involve Susan without me ruffling her feathers directly. With no more consideration, I picked up my cell. If I was quick enough, maybe I could catch him before he reached the station.

"You're sure Susan doesn't want to kill me?"

Campbell made a questioning hum. "*Well...*" His concerned expression broke a second later. "Just kidding. She's not planning your murder, though it was probably a good idea to have this request come from me."

Paulie waggled his eyebrows after exiting the car and slipping his hand into Campbell's. "Judging from what I heard several feet away, of how Susan sounded on the other end of the phone, she's not *not* hoping someone *else* is planning your murder."

Campbell smirked. "Point taken."

"I always wanted to go in here." Katie joined us at the base of the steps leading up to Ethel's large front porch. "Not exactly the circumstances I would have chosen, but... Ethel's not here, so that part will be more pleasant."

Paulie snorted out a little laugh, but it faded as his gaze traveled to Demetrius. He let out a breath, glanced down to his and Campbell's interlocking fingers, then spoke firmly. "I'm just going to put this out there. In one way I'm not in a place to judge—Branson and Chief Briggs at the time, had control over my life for a long time, put me in the exact same situation as you, Demetrius, more or less. So, I might understand, but that doesn't mean I trust you." His muddy-brown gaze flicked to me, an equal warning there. "None of us should."

"I don't blame you." If Demetrius was insulted he didn't show it and met Paulie clear-eyed, with an open stance. "You'd be fools if you did." He gestured up toward Ethel's mansion. "I think this is part of my test, though I'm sure it won't be the only one."

His directness added a check mark in both the sincere and manipulative columns. It could be either.

"Let's do this." I clapped my hands and refocused on the house. Even though it was now in full daylight from the early morning sun, the memory of it from the other night, being led up the steps at gunpoint, flashed. This was going to be a little more challenging than I'd thought, but maybe that aspect would be a good thing as well. Another thought gave me pause. "The cameras aren't still recording, right? Branson won't be watching us right now?"

"No, we may not be able to tell where the feed goes, but we've jammed all frequencies. No one is watching anything. But remember—" Campbell used his Officer Cabot voice, which wasn't all that different than his friend voice. "—Detective Green wants us all to stay together. Everything has been cleared, but we still aren't supposed to disturb anything."

Her other specification was to leave Watson at the Cozy Corgi. I knew it was simply to keep the crime scene intact, not add more corgi fur, but I couldn't help but wonder if she was punishing me. I also thought it might be a missed opportunity;

though he would doubtlessly be looking for treats, his nose had led us to many important details over the years.

We moved over the sidewalk as one, our shoes crunching through a few icy spots. Most of the snow in the yard had been trampled by countless shoes of police, but it lay thick and untouched over the roof and eaves. Now that the shutters had been opened, the mansion looked welcoming, almost Christmassy. At least it would have, if there'd been candles glowing from within or something, or... you know, if a person could forget the mansion had been a ticking time bomb.

I think the other four were talking as we approached the front door, or it could have just been the cadence of the buzz in my ears and the pounding of my heart. I only realized I was holding my breath as Campbell slid the key into the front door, the lock clicked, and it opened without event. Perhaps I'd been expecting the explosion. I needed to get a hold of myself. Sure, part of me had wanted to come back to the mansion and face it, to see it again outside my memory, but more importantly, I was looking for any sort of clue and studying Demetrius's reactions for some telltale sign. I could do neither if I spent every step reliving the events of two nights before.

As I stepped in, some of the tension eased. This was a completely different experience, to the point I could almost believe it was another house. First and foremost, no butler and angry cat were at my back with a gun, but equally helpful, light poured in from every angle. With the flick of a switch behind me, the elaborate chandelier overhead flared to life.

At my side, Katie let out a breath of wonder.

It was beautiful; I couldn't blame her. Despite being wide with tall ceilings, the hallway had felt tunnel-like before, but in that moment, with all the doorways open and light pouring in, it was grand, spacious. I didn't take in any more than that as I looked through one of those open doors—the one on the right—and found the dining room. I barely spared half a thought that it was open at all. We'd decided that particular door was completely fake, *couldn't* open... Who'd been with me at that point? Delilah? Carla? Without landing on an answer or waiting for Campbell's permission, I found myself inside, unaware of taking the steps.

Though there was evidence of police every-where, very little of that registered as the minutes that felt like hours superimposed over the scene. Walking in from the other side, finding a table of hooded guests with Ethel at the head. The bang of the gun, the crash of plaster knocking over the candelabra. And there, the broken stained glass lamp I'd beat against the window, the fractured dragonfly pieces mixing with clear glass from the window over the hardwood floor. In the far right corner, the carpet was still pulled back, the trapdoor still open to the tunnel.

"I'm not going in there." I only realized I was moving backward when I bumped into Katie, though I didn't look at her. The buzzing in my ears beginning to screech. "I'm *not* going in there."

"You don't have to." Her fingers curved gently around my arm, her voice a barely audible whisper of comfort. "There's not one thing you have to do here. And the second you're ready to leave, even if it's right now, we will."

I didn't speak, just continued to stare at the opening. I watched as Paulie crossed the room and bent down to look, the blood leaving his face. Wordlessly securing his weight on either side of the tunnel, he leaned in so his head disappeared, then a moment later re-emerged and peered around the room from his kneeling position. "It really is like the game. Secret tunnels, ornate Victorian mansion. Kind of like the movie, too."

"Except no Tim Curry." Campbell had moved

farther in as well, directly halfway between Paulie and me. "And not as funny."

"No, not funny at all," Paulie agreed. Still inspecting the space, some of the fear evident in his eyes faded, and when he spoke again, it had given way to anger. "He's sick. This isn't a revelation, but just more proof." That brown gaze traveled to me. "Branson is sick. I'm sorry you had to face this. I think... I think if he had his way, I would have been with you. Been one of the players. I'm sorry I wasn't here for you."

"I'm glad you weren't." I wasn't sure if Paulie was right, though I could see why he would think so after Branson had used him for so long. However, I rather thought Branson was still the center of Paulie's world at times, where Paulie was nothing more than a discarded, forgotten game piece to Branson.

"Okay..." I did my best to shake it off, turned, then left the room. We'd come back there if need be, but I wanted a break. I walked through the doorway we'd just entered, crossed the hall into the billiard room, speaking through it as I did so, though I wasn't certain if I was speaking to myself or the rest of the group. "This tunnel is where Carla and I came up. There was a fork somewhere in the middle—Delilah went straight, the chief went right, and Carla and I went left." At the memory, I realized there had been a fourth person in the tunnels. Mary. She'd actually led. Did I know where she came out? I couldn't recall.

"Huh..." Katie stood by the pool table, hands on her hips as she inspected the room. "I see what you were talking about, that Ethel stole the game from Branson before he was ready." She gestured toward the scaffold. "Not even finished with all the wallpaper in this room." Turning again, she landed on me. "And I also see what you mean about the style. Granted, I didn't know Ethel... didn't know Ethel at all, but she wouldn't have chosen this. Burgundy damask wallpaper? That's not her."

"It's not Branson either." Paulie picked up the eight ball off the pool table. "Although, I don't know if anyone actually knows the *real* Branson, what his style might be. But this is nothing more than a set, a real-life Clue game." He let out a shaky breath. "I wonder what Branson's rules would have been? How he would have made us play this out?"

"There's no sense in wondering. It's over, he didn't get that chance." Campbell stepped up to Paulie, clasped his hand once more. "We're safe, we're all safe. And we're safer together—"

"I know." Paulie cut him off, though it was gentle and apologetic. "I was wrong, I was already clear on that, but all this drives it home. Branson is going to do what he does. And..." He looked at me again. "It's you. This is all for you." A little laugh escaped him, and he leaned back, his hips resting on the edge of the pool table. "It doesn't matter what's important to me, what I love." He pulled Campbell's hand to his chest. "*Who* I love. Branson doesn't even notice. It's all about you."

That hadn't been a revelation to anyone, but clearly Paulie hadn't quite grasped it until that moment. "I'm sorry." I meant that more than almost anything I'd ever said. "If I could change—"

"Don't be sorry." Katie was beside me again. "None of this is your fault either."

"It isn't." Anger flashed from Paulie again, and he stood straight once more. "Don't forget that all this started before you arrived in Estes Park. Branson was controlling me before you were here, before the two of you had even met. None of this is your fault."

The buzzing in my ears faded away, and I started to argue with Paulie, remind him of... But then I couldn't land on the event to remind him, because... he and Katie were right, I *had* forgotten. I couldn't find words or couldn't find my voice, I wasn't certain which, but managed to nod in both thanks and acknowledgement.

After a moment, Campbell spoke up. "I know some of you went upstairs the other night, but I don't think you did, Fred, if I remember my notes." When I shook my head in confirmation, he continued. "That's where you'll see the biggest proof of what we've been saying. The dining room and library appear to be completely finished, but lots of the other rooms down here are only partway. Upstairs is largely untouched, looked like it was next to be completed."

"Maybe he was just going to have the games downstairs."

Campbell shook his head at Katie's theory. "No, there's scaffolding upstairs too, and it appears to be more in the deconstruction phase, other wallpapers taken down. It would have been next."

"Let's see." That sounded wonderful, a chance to get out of the game, out of rooms where I'd been held captive. Without waiting, I left the billiard room, glancing at Demetrius, who was inspecting the tunnel in the corner by the overturned plant. I'd forgotten to keep my attention on him, to look for signs. I'd try to change that if I could. Even at the thought, however, I turned my back to him, continued to the entryway, and headed up the sweeping staircase.

Proof of Campbell's theory was evident the second I arrived at the landing—scaffolding on the far side and strips of cream-and-gold paper already removed from the upper part of the wall. Unlike below, there was no art, very little furniture.

The calm that had begun at the realization in the billiard room solidified as the others joined me on neutral ground. My steps grew more confident, more at ease as I naturally took the lead. As below, all the doorways were open, and light from outside filtered in. Through a doorway on the right, I caught the edge of a fourposter bed and headed toward it.

From the size of the room, the king bed, and the massive marble bathroom visible through another open door, it was clearly the master suite. Nothing had been done in there, from what I could tell—no scaffolding, no Victorian furniture. No furniture at all other than the bed and solitary side table with a lamp. The walls were a pale dusty pink—pretty but dated somehow. I couldn't be sure of that as neither fashion nor interior design was my forte, but it still gave that impression.

Katie spoke up again as she peered into the bathroom. "Maybe things were cleared out getting ready for whatever Branson was going to do in here, or... this is proof of what you've been thinking the last several months, Ethel's struggle with money. We'd wondered about her selling off her possessions, this floor kind of looks like confirmation."

It did. Even the wall of built-in bookcases was empty, and I was certain she hadn't packed whatever had been there and stuffed the boxes in their trunk to be taken on their escape from the country. These bookcases, too—the shade of white and their plain wood framing with overly thick, clunky panels running both horizontally and vertically between the shelves—felt dated, especially framed by the pink walls.

"Whoa..." Demetrius crossed to another open doorway. "She hadn't sold *all* of her possessions."

I followed and peered in beside him. "Now, this is all *Ethel*, and what I expected. No Branson here." The closet was nearly half the size of my entire living room. The walls were the same pale pink, and the shelving the same material and color as the built-ins. But this wasn't empty. A crystal chandelier hung from the ceiling over an island built of the same white wood but with a Carrara marble top. Every conceivable space was filled with clothes—fur coats, sparkling gowns, racks of shoes, scarves, hats, countless accessories. Here and there, however, were small gaps and empty hangers.

"These were in the trunk of the car." Campbell went to some empty hangers in the middle of the fur coats; stickers had been affixed to their satin surfaces with evidence numbers. "This is all she packed. Traveling light."

"Wow," Demetrius breathed again, and whether he was the masked man or not, he wasn't faking his astonishment as he turned in the middle of the closet, clearly seeing it for the first time. "I can't get used to the amount of money some people have." He cringed at where Campbell stood. "And fur coats? Really? Who is she trying to be, Snoop Dogg?"

"No." Katie's disgust at the fur laced her words. "She was Joan Collins in *Dynasty*."

"Who?"

I ignored Demetrius's question and nodded at Katie—leave it to the trivia queen. "That's it, totally it. Sure, Ethel might want the newest and shiniest from Fifth Avenue or whatever, but that's exactly how this feels—*Dynasty*. Dated." I laughed, something I definitely hadn't predicted doing in Ethel's mansion. "How have I not seen it this whole time? She's been living her own version of some soap-opera diva."

"Her *and* Percival." Katie laughed as well. "Although *please* don't tell him I said that."

"No promises. That's too good to pass up." I smiled at her and then crossed to the one section that was completely empty other than some overturned containers. "Looks like she took all of her jewelry. Smart." I picked up a jewelry box, lacking sparkle but containing ivory satin.

"There was quite a bit in the trunk, but not as much as what's indicated here. And it looked like she packed them in a hurry—some of the jewelry had broken, there were pearls all over the floor— suggesting what we already theorized about Ethel initiating this plan quickly, stealing it from Branson," Campbell confirmed. "If you're right about her selling her furnishings, it looks like she got started with selling her jewelry as well."

"Until Colin's money came along." Paulie smirked. "If we're right about Ethel using Branson to fake that marriage license, she paid a price for it."

"That she did." I put the jewelry box back in its place and glanced at the furs. Granted, I didn't know Ethel all that well, and I definitely didn't know the resale value of furs, but I was a little surprised. I would have predicted jewelry being the last thing Ethel would have parted with. But maybe not.

"Um... Campbell?" Katie called from the bedroom. "Did the police document this? I don't see any numbers or tape or anything."

I followed on Campbell's heels, Paulie and Demetrius beside me as we left the closet. The four of us stopped dead at the sight of Katie beside the white built-in bookcases. One of the wide vertical panels between the section of shelves had pulled open like a door, showing shadowy darkness inside.

"No..." Campbell shook his head as he walked toward her. "Not that I know of. A hidden room? Passageway?"

"Passageway." Katie nodded and angled her cell phone, flashlight glowing into the dark. "There're steps going down."

"That's not in the game." I hurried over, joining Campbell and looking in. "Branson took some liberties here." I grinned over, marveling at Katie. "How did you find this?"

She chuckled and a little blush rose to her cheeks. "Well... these panels looked oddly thick, especially considering the era it seems they were built, and I started thinking about Ethel and Joan Collins." Another chuckle and her voice sped up. "Grandma loved soap operas. One of her favorites was *The Bold and the Beautiful,* and that made me think of Adrienne Frantz."

From Katie's pause, it was clear we were supposed to know who that was, but a quick glance at the others revealed they were as clueless as me. "Hon, is this some Google binge you went down recently, 'cause I'm not following."

"No. It's not, actually." As she explained, her voice sped up even more. "I watched this show where Adrienne, she was an actress on *The Bold and the Beautiful,* obviously, was selling her home. This was probably... I don't know, six or seven years ago. Anyway, she sold it for around three and a half million dollars, and she'd bought it for barely *half* a million right before the turn of this century." She paused for a breath and then pushed on again when we just gaped at her. "I guess that's not the point. Anyway, in this house, she had a bookcase that opened to a secret room. It didn't have paneling quite this wide, but it looked pretty much like this. Plain white wood, nothing special. Dated. And... Ethel being a soap opera star, in theory, I just thought..." She shrugged. "You just have to push on the panel, not that hard at all, considering. It popped right open."

"Whoa." Demetrius stared at her wide-eyed and blinked, clearly speechless.

I couldn't help but laugh at his expression, appropriate, given Katie Pizzolato. I threw my arms around her in a quick embrace. "I love you so much, you little weirdo."

"I... don't think this is from Branson." Campbell had pulled out his own phone, using it as a flashlight. "This is older, dusty, not like the tunnels or the passage from the library down to the garage."

"Really?" Rude or not, I wedged myself in, partially nudging Campbell out of the way in my haste. The space truly was narrow. If I squeezed all the way through, I would have had to suck in, and even then, there were no guarantees—also indicating it wasn't built for Branson.

Not offended, from his tone, Campbell placed a warning hand on my shoulder. "Fred, remember that we haven't documented this yet. Don't disturb any evidence, please."

"Okay." Without really thinking what I was agreeing to, I nodded and lifted my hand. "Actually, may I see your phone?" Campbell handed it to me, and I angled it into the passageway—nothing more than a steep narrow staircase. Just the notion of going down it made my skin crawl; it looked even more claustrophobic than the tunnels. Campbell was right, it did look old, tattered cobwebs here and there and dust over the steps. As I angled the flashlight back, something caught my eye. "There're footsteps here, er... footprints. I don't really know how to tell these things, but they look fresh and..." Something glinted. Without thought or remembering the commitment I'd just given Campbell, I sank down, braved the narrow space, and reached in to pull out the little fragment as Campbell groaned.

"What is it?" Paulie leaned forward, nearly bumping into Katie's head as he tried to see.

"I'm not sure. It's..." As I twisted it, Katie aimed the light from her phone, and the half pearls in my wedding ring glinted in the exact same way. Sucking in a breath, I looked up at her. "It's part of a pearl. Crushed or broken from the rough feel of it."

"A pearl." Campbell breathed out and despite himself took the little fragment from me, twisting it to get a better view. "That would seem like a coincidence, since we found pearls scattered all over. Ethel must have used this as she was sneaking out her jewelry. Although why would—"

"I don't think so." Another image from two nights ago flashed in my mind—the hood being pulled off the person seated at Ethel's right-hand side, revealing Vivian LaRue and her nearly claustro-phobic amount of pearls gathered around her throat. "Campbell..." I didn't know what this meant, but it didn't feel like a coincidence. "Do you remember, or do you think it would have been taken down in notes anywhere, if Vivian was wearing her pearls at the end of the night when the police were doing their interviews?"

EIGHTEEN

Proving my relationship with Susan hadn't reverted all the way back to when I first arrived in Estes Park, she didn't look tempted to murder me when she'd arrived at Ethel's mansion. She wasn't gushing or bubbly either, but Susan never was. Simply cold and professional—maybe a little colder than normal...

The ultimate evidence I hadn't ruined our relationship was when she suggested I visit Vivian LaRue on my own and use my ever-powerful annoying kryptonite to crack her. No one could recall if Vivian had been wearing pearls during the interviews or when Roger arrived to take his wife home. However, Susan remembered Vivian disappearing at some point, claiming to be overwhelmed and needing a moment. It had been assumed she'd taken space outside, or in a restroom to cry and pull herself together. Maybe so, but Susan agreed with me—no way it was a coincidence there were pearls scattered all over Ethel's bedroom floor and another crushed in a hidden staircase the very same night one of the Clue victims had worn enough pearls to empty half an ocean.

Upon returning to Elkhorn Avenue, I didn't join Katie as she went back to the Cozy Corgi to get a fortification of a dirty chai, or even to retrieve Watson. I was on a mission. I had a direction, for the first time since being shoved into a twisted real-life board game, and felt like I was on the edge of some answers. That was better than caffeine.

Aspen Gold was on the next block, directly across from Victorian Antlers. To get there, I had to cross in front of both Old Friends, during which I managed not to glance in to see if Charlotte was visible, and Bottles, Brushes, and Brie. I *did* look in those windows, and though I noticed James Smith, Mary was nowhere to be found— however this went with Vivian, I planned on coming back before the day was over and speaking to Mary. After just being in Ethel's house, I thought I could do so without getting too triggered. As it was, I hurried up to the end of the block and stopped before the water wheel at the rich red door that had been lacquered with a coating of gold. Not bothering with a deep breath,

I pushed it open to the sound of a high, clear chime, and stepped in.

My heart sank as Vivian LaRue looked up from behind one of the countless glass cases filled with jewelry. Just like two nights ago, from chin to cleavage, there was nothing more than a tangle of pearls. I might have given up that very instant had her eyes not changed from the typical placid greeting to a potential tourist customer to... fear. At least, that's what it looked like to me, if I wasn't reading into it.

"Oh... Winifred." The quaver in her voice suggested fear as well, although, that didn't mean anything. She'd been terrified, more than any of us, at Ethel's house. Perhaps seeing me sent her back to those moments, feeling that bag pull free to find me as the guest of honor at that horrid table. "There you are, dear." A strange comment, but what truly caught me was her nervous glance toward the back wall, where a heavy gold embroidery curtain hung in front of the doorway to the back rooms.

"Here I am." Why not just go with it? I continued into the pentagon-shaped shop, the black-and-gold vertically striped wallpaper reminded me of jail cell bars, as they always did, although, it also brought to mind the similarly styled paper on Ethel's second floor, which had been in the process of being removed. "I just wanted to check in, see how you're doing?"

"That's kind of you." Once more, she glanced toward that curtain, her worry clear.

"Are you all right?" Perhaps I was interpreting things wrong, maybe the game had renewed, or Branson had showed up. I hurried the rest of my way to her and lowered my voice. "Is there someone in the back? Are you in trouble?"

"What?" She flinched, looking at me in confusion and washing away my spark of fear. "Oh no, no. All is fine." Forcing a smile, she lifted an arthritic hand and patted the pearls covering the base of her throat. "Just a little jumpy is all, after everything. I'm sure you understand."

"Oh, I definitely do." She was lying, at least I thought. Her reaction to me was so different than the others who'd shared that experience with me. The rest of us had a new and powerful bond. Clearly that wasn't there for Vivian. Probably not for Mary, either, but time would tell. That pondering was swept away as I glanced down at her crimson fingernails as she lowered her hand from her throat. Hope shot through me again, excitement.

Vivian LaRue was drowning in pearls as normal, but each of them was encased with little clasps of gold. I had no idea what the term would be, but they reminded me of the setting in rings. Each of the pearls—there had to have been a couple hundred— held those little gold clasps on either end so up close the necklace looked almost more comprised of gold than pearls. This was not the necklace she'd been wearing at Ethel's. Also, not the necklace I'd seen her in before, or thought of as her signature.

"What is it?" Her hand lifted to the necklace again, twisted knuckles looking painful, worry thick in her voice. "Do you like it? I can order you one similar, or we can make one custom, we can even put diamonds between each pearl, if you want…"

I'd been staring. I forced my gaze to lift to meet hers. "Oh no. Thank you." I hesitated for a moment and then decided to dive right in. "These weren't the ones you were wearing the other night at Ethel's, were they?"

Another flinch, another worried glance toward the golden curtain. "Goodness no. I… I got rid of those." Her other hand rose, patted at the shoe-polish-black curls sweeping up over her head. "I couldn't bear to be reminded of that night."

"Got rid of them?" I let my astonishment filter in. "They looked like they cost a fortune."

Anger flashed. "I didn't say I threw them away."

Vivian gave herself a little shake, forced another smile to her painted lips. "I apologize, like I said, I'm just... spread thin right now. Not to be rude." Yet another glance at the curtain. "Could we talk later? Now is not the best time."

"Of course." I smiled as well, then looked pointedly at the curtain, letting my gaze linger before returning to meet Vivian's.

I saw some of that familiar fear in her eyes, not as intense as the other night, not life-and-death, but... not exactly blasé, either. If she wasn't afraid for her life, then Branson hadn't snuck into the jewelry shop. I hadn't interrupted a robbery, so, then... what? That answer was obvious—Roger. Her husband had to be back there, and it seemed Vivian thought I had information she didn't want her husband to know.

Maybe I did. Might as well take a stab at it. I pulled the pearl fragment from the pocket of my broomstick skirt—Susan had allowed me to take it after it had been photographed to the level the thing probably felt like it was a movie star, and with the promise I would bring it back. I held it out to Vivian in the palm of my hand. "I found this a little bit ago, so you see, I know you didn't throw your necklace away. You left it scattered all over Ethel's bedroom."

Even under her makeup, her thin skin went waxen.

I didn't get any telltale signs from Demetrius, but Vivian LaRue was handing them out like Halloween candy, so I ran with it, picking the pearl fragment up with my other hand and twisting it so it gleamed between us. "This one was in the secret stairway behind—"

"The kitchen, yes, I know." She grabbed it with a snarl, then flinched when she realized how loud she'd been, and once more looked toward the curtain.

That time, after a second, the fabric rustled. Roger pulled it back, stepped partway through, With his pallid complexion and thinning slicked-back shoe-polish black hair, he'd never looked more like an aged vampire than he did at that moment, peering out from behind the veil. "Vivian... are you all right? You sound—" Some of that vampiric quality faded when he saw me. "Oh, Winifred. My dear, thank you for helping keep my wife safe the other night. She said you bravely entered the tunnels when—"

"Roger. Don't, please." Vivian's voice had been sharp, but she hit reset quickly, her hand holding the pearl shooting down to the glass case. "Sorry, love. Just any little thing makes me relive it. I... I don't want to think about those tunnels."

"Me neither." I didn't have to fake my reaction to that at all.

"Oh, I'm sorry." Roger nodded an apology to both of us. "Well, Winifred, I know things haven't always been easy between us, but I still want to thank you for—"

"Roger, *please.*" Vivian infused a plaintive whine in her tone that time. "Sorry to interrupt you, but Ms. Page is in a hurry and about to leave. Do you mind giving us a few moments?"

He flinched, and for a heartbeat seemed like he was going to argue, then softened as he looked at his wife in a way that suggested he remembered he'd nearly lost her two nights ago. "Of course, my love."

I didn't bother correcting the name change, only pivoted back to Vivian as the curtain slid closed once more, and crossed my arms over my chest, cocked my eyebrows in a hopefully fairly accurate impression of Detective Susan Green, though probably much less intimidating.

Whether that was the straw that broke the camel's back or not, Vivian snarled at me once more. "*Fine.* Hold on. I'll get them. Better you than the police, I suppose. Though they were mine to begin with, and I deserve them." As she turned, she continued muttering and crossed the store.

Completely thrown off, I let my arms relax at my side as I turned to watch her movements. I had no idea what she was talking about.

She paused at the curtain, listening, then continued to the far side and kneeled in a fashion that looked rather painful behind one of the display cases of jewelry.

I barely hesitated before bending down but caught the glint of the pearl fragment Vivian had left on the glass case. With a quick swipe, I stuffed it in my pocket before bending once more, looking underneath as if peering under bathroom stalls.

Vivian was on her knees, sliding an air-conditioning grate free, pulling something out and then putting the grate back in place. With an audible intake of painful breath, she stood, then glared at me all the way over, forgetting to listen at the curtain. She shoved a black snakeskin purse at me. "Take it. Throw it away, for all I care."

My hands moved on instinct, accepting the purse from her without really considering. The weight was much greater than expected, and I looked down. For a flash, the purse looked familiar, and then I placed it. "You had this as you came down from the steps the other night. When—"

"Yes. We already know that, why do you want to

rub it in?" She remembered the curtain then, and turned back to me. "That Smith woman walked in on me in Ethel's closet the second I grabbed this. Didn't have time to get anything else."

Still not quite putting the picture together, I opened the purse and found the source of the weight, and all the gold and glistening gems sparkling up at me shouted that they should have been obvious. Campbell had said the amount of jewelry in Ethel's trunk didn't match the space that had been emptied in her closet. Now we knew why. One other detail nagged, but it clarified a second later. "You went back up during the interviews, said you needed the bathroom, but filled this purse with Ethel's jewelry."

"*My* jewelry." She snarled in a way that reminded me of Gollum from the Lord of the Rings movies, furthering the impression as she threw out another gnarled hand at the purse. "Nearly got caught again. I don't know who, but I heard them coming up the steps, so, I had to get into that stupid hidden passage, like I was young again. I still don't know how I broke my necklace, caught it on something, maybe my own fingers." She glared at them, as if the gnarled arthritic knuckles had betrayed her. Tears glistened in her eyes as she glared back at me. "Close that."

I did, but still felt frozen in place. This wasn't at all what I'd expected, though maybe I should have. "What do you mean *your* jewelry? You actually went to get them while we were looking for a way out? When we thought we were going to die?"

"What do you think I mean? It's my jewelry, the store's jewelry. And *yes*, I wasn't going to die with them in *her* evil clutches. They belonged with me." She gestured, encompassing Aspen Gold and then wiped a tear from her eye. "Ethel took them all from us, from me. Made me lie to Roger." She cast a head-shake toward that curtain, letting out a breath that hinted at both guilt and pity. "Tourists steal, but not that much."

I was getting large pieces of a puzzle, but they weren't snapping together to form a logical image. Suddenly, worried about Roger emerging myself, I cast a glance toward the curtain, which remained still, as I shuffled through those pieces. Vivian said Ethel *took* the jewelry from her, not *stole* the jewelry. Made Vivian lie. "You used to be friends with Ethel, didn't you?"

"That was a *long* time ago." Venom dripped from her words once more. "What *are* you doing? You got what you came for, now go. Before—"

"Before Roger finds out about the jewelry." Yes,

that part had been obvious, but the pieces had finally clicked together, the picture clarifying. Ethel hadn't stolen the jewelry in secret; she hadn't needed to. Not that I could picture Ethel stealing. No, getting dirt on her friend and blackmailing her for jewelry was much more Ethel's speed. "What did she have on you, Vivian? What secret did she threaten to tell Roger to make you give her all this jewelry?"

"Get out. Now. Leave." Anger and fear danced within Vivian with such passion it looked like warring personalities behind her eyes.

"You knew about the hidden passage, and I never told you it came out in the kitchen." That was a pointless card to play. If she'd gotten into it from the bedroom, *of course* she knew where it ended up. But still.

"Leave, Fred." That time, it was more of a plea than fury.

I couldn't let up. Maybe this led somewhere, maybe it didn't, but I had to know. And even though Vivian had been through an equal amount of trauma as myself that night, I chose to put her through a little more. "Okay, I'll leave. But you know Detective Green will have some questions. Maybe get a warrant. She'll probably have to bring you and Roger down to the station and—"

"No!" Fresh fear flashed, almost equal to what I had seen from her at the table beside Ethel. Tears threatened as well. She shook her head, as if not believing this was happening, then sniffed. "I hate you. No wonder Ethel despised you so much. No wonder she wanted you dead."

Her words forced me to take a step back, feeling like I'd just received a blow.

Vivian was already on the move, still wiping her eyes as she reached the curtain and poked her head through. "Roger, would you come here, dear?"

I had no idea what was about to happen, and I took a couple more steps backward, toward the door. This was a jewelry shop with who knows how much worth in diamonds and gold—they probably had a gun for protection.

Roger joined us once more, hands free of any weapon, genuine concern over his face. "Darling, what is it?" He stroked Vivian's upper arm and glanced toward me, clearly wondering if I was at fault.

"We just... it's a lot, from the other night..." Vivian gestured toward me. "Survivors, you know. Would you mind giving us a few minutes. Just... so we can..."

She didn't finish whatever we had to do, nor did

she need to. Roger acquiesced instantly. "Oh, of course. I'll just go back and make sure that I don't come out until—"

"No, not there." She almost sounded panicked, but she adjusted quickly. "I can actually use a sugar rush, if you'd go to Taffy Lane and get a..." At that point I could read her thoughts. Taffy Lane was just around the corner, behind the water wheel, much too close. She proved me right with her next request. "You know what? Actually, the Cozy Corgi, in honor of Fred. Would you go to the bakery and get us something sweet? I don't care what—cake, brownies, chocolate."

"Yes, of course." If Roger picked up on any of his wife's deceit, he must have attributed it to her fragile state after all that had happened. A few moments later, after getting a jacket, he left the store and headed down to the Cozy Corgi.

As he passed the large square window with the display of jewelry, Vivian moved to the front door and twisted the deadbolt. "I don't know why you're putting me through this, you or Detective Green. That jewelry was mine, and I went through that horrible night just like you did."

She was right, and truth be told, I felt guilt at putting her through more, but I didn't back down, nor did I let her catch a hint of it. "Vivian, what did Ethel have over you? Why did you give her so much jewelry?" As I spoke the questions out loud, I understood. "Oh... you knew of a secret passage to the kitchen. A secret passage from Ethel's *bedroom*." I turned and looked out that square window where Roger had just disappeared. "You had an affair, and Roger never knew."

As quick to tears as she'd been in the mansion, rivers of mascara streamed over Vivian's cheeks, matching the black curls towering over her head. "It was *eons* ago, and only a handful of times."

"Ethel caught you." Puzzle piece after puzzle piece clicked. "You'd use the tunnel behind the bookcase if she came home too soon. But she caught you."

"Why do you need all these details?" Anger was back, and desperation. "What good does it do? I didn't kill her, she tried to kill *me*. Tried to kill *you*." She threw her hand out toward the purse. "And those were mine. She wore it all over town, without a doubt, hoping Roger would notice. I don't know how he never did." Disgust filled her features then. "And now *you*! You do *this*, after she's finally gone. After my torment could end. You're just as bad as she ever was."

Again, every word was like a slap, a punch,

spittle across the face. "Here." I thrust the purse out to her. She just stared at it. "Here!" I yelled the word, hadn't meant to, but shook the purse her direction. "Take it. Take it."

She did.

I turned and practically ran for the door. Twisting the deadbolt, I had it halfway open before I came to my senses, realized I was caught in a moment of panic and trauma and a billion other things that only Ethel Beaker could inspire. Inhaling the deep breath I didn't take when I'd entered Aspen Gold, I turned to face Vivian LaRue once more and found my voice relatively calm. "I'll have to tell Susan about the jewelry, and why. If she needs it, I'll ask her to be discreet."

Vivian only clutched the purse to her chest in a way I didn't think had anything to do with the jewelry. More like a woman who nearly lost her life, had recently lost her only adult son, and now feared ruining her marriage.

"I'm sorry, Vivian." I barely got out the whisper, wasn't even sure if she heard.

Then I turned and walked away, thinking Susan was right about my kryptonite-level superpower.

NINETEEN

By the time I got back to the Cozy Corgi—walking the back way along Fall River to avoid Roger—I'd given myself enough of a pep talk, or reality check, to water down some of my guilt. I didn't have anything to be guilty about; I hadn't done anything. *I hadn't been sneaking around with my friend's husband and got caught. I hadn't blackmailed my backstabbing friend for jewelry for years. I hadn't been keeping secrets from my husband, and I definitely hadn't kidnapped that betraying friend and tried to kill her.* I was neither Vivian LaRue nor Ethel Beaker. The only ones innocent in all of that were me and Roger LaRue, I supposed.

Yes, maybe I'd made an old woman cry after experiencing a trauma only two days before, but... there again... *I hadn't done anything wrong.* That logic might have been circular, but it didn't make it any less true. Either way, I wasn't about to go into

Bottles, Bushes, and Brie in that frame of mind. Mary and I clashed heads at the best of times; I couldn't imagine what would have happened if I'd attempted then. A couple of dirty chais, read a few chapters, and then a fresh start.

As I walked up the steps to the bakery, I decided dirty chai and the mid-morning snack was needed even before calling Susan, but I'd do that before settling down to read. However, the sight that greeted me as I reached the bakery had the power to push even the allure of a dirty chai out of mind. Katie sat at the long booth beside the shelving of Cozy Corgi merchandise, her laptop open in front of her. Katie on a laptop googling something wasn't exactly surprising, but looking down where Delilah Johnson sat on the floor, Watson's head in her lap, and both women laughing uproariously wasn't something that happened every day. Or... ever. True, Katie didn't loathe Delilah Johnson like she used to, but they were slightly above cordial, at best.

Before I had the chance to attempt to make sense of this little scene, Watson noticed me, sprang up, and scurried my way, almost with the enthusiasm he would greet Leo. Only as he hopped up, forepaws on my knees, did I see the fear in his eyes.

"Oh, buddy." I sank down, ruffling behind his

ears with both hands. "What's wrong? I'm okay. Goodness, you look so worried."

He whimpered, twisted to nudge my hand away, which I thought meant he was already over me petting him, but then he preceded to sniff it as if inspecting for treats.

"He's been looking for you." Katie paused in her laughing to cast a sympathetic smile toward him. "I think it threw him off when we left together and I returned on my own."

And if that didn't bring back the guilt. I went the rest of the way to the ground right in the middle of the floor and wrapped him in my arms. We seven human victims hadn't been the only ones stressed and traumatized in Ethel's mansion. Watson had as well, of course. "I'm so sorry, sweetheart. I'm fine. I'm not going anywhere. We're safe."

Watson replied by shoving his muzzle underneath my hair, sniffing my ear, my neck. After a chuff, he reared back, those chocolate eyes looking deep into mine, nearly human. I could almost read the thoughts behind them—to the point where I actually saw when he was convinced that I was okay. The tension left his body, and he chuffed again, though this one was followed by a grunt. With a seal-like twist, he freed himself from my embrace and trotted back the way he'd come. He paused by Delilah, making me think he was going to return to her lap, but instead looked over his shoulder at me, gave another human-worthy look full of disapproval and betrayal, and then disappeared into his little apartment.

All three of us watched the dog-door flap close, and then Delilah and Katie glanced at each other and got lost to laughter again.

After a few seconds, and getting myself up off the floor, I joined them, both at the table and chuckling along. "Apparently, Watson decided I am safe enough he can be angry and offended I left him for so long."

"And if that doesn't say long-term relationship, I don't know what does." Still chuckling, Delilah gripped the edge of the table and stood before sliding into the booth beside Katie and looking at me. "I came over to see you, but Katie said you were heading up to talk to Vivian and Mary. I was going to come back, but then..." A sidelong glance toward my best friend, and they both started giggling again "Well... one thing led to another..."

"It's been a giggle-fest," Nick called out from behind the bakery counter, though didn't lean over to show his face. "You wanna dirty chai or a pastry or anything, Fred?"

A glance at the table revealed Delilah's and Katie's half-empty mugs and two plates with only crumbs remaining. "That would be wonderful, Nick. Thank you!" I refocused on Katie and Delilah. "Now... what in the world? That's not like you two." Before they could answer, I narrowed it on Delilah. "Actually, why did you come to see me? Is everything okay?"

The mirth left Delilah's expression, instantly replaced by heaviness. "I just... I wanted to ask about your gut, actually." When my eyebrows raised, she offered a little smile and continued without more prompting. "About Garrett. What does your gut say about him? You really think he was the masked man?"

"You don't?" Knowing how frustrating having your question answered with a question could be, I elaborated. "I don't really have a gut feeling about Garrett one way or another; I never saw the masked man, remember?" I debated for a second about offering my other theory, then went ahead. It wasn't like Demetrius didn't already know I was considering him. "I've been wondering about Gary's great-nephew, Demetrius.

He's almost as big as Garrett, at least muscular, but in a more natural, less middle-aged man doing lots of steroids sort of way. But he's not nearly as tall."

"The height is part of it." Delilah closed her beautiful blue eyes and shuddered. "I woke up wide-awake from a dreamless sleep last night, at least it felt dreamless. Sat upright in bed, heart racing, I might have even screamed when I woke, I don't know. But I thought I could feel him in the room, as if he might be standing over in the shadows... just like when I looked over and he was there in the yard."

She must have already said this part to Katie as Katie wordlessly reached over and placed a supportive hand over Delilah's.

"No one was there in your room, I take it?" Probably a stupid question, but gooseflesh had broken out on my arms as a shiver had gone down my spine.

"No." She gave another shudder and then a soft laugh. "All three of the boys sleep in the bed with me, and the only thing scaring them in the middle of the night was their mama waking up acting like a crazy person. I think I about gave Putzie a heart attack. But no, if anyone was in there, they would have woken me up, not the other way around."

I couldn't quite put my finger on why Delilah's story scared me like it did. Other than waking up and sensing a stranger in your room, or in your backyard. Then I did. We knew there was a mystery masked man wandering around out there, but he hadn't really felt like an immediate threat, as his role was over now the game had finished. But... perhaps not.

Delilah didn't wait for another question before continuing. "Maybe this is ridiculous, since there was clearly no one in my room, but I could almost see him. And it didn't feel like Garrett." She hurried on. "Maybe that means I'm just remembering how he felt in my yard the other night, and that person didn't *feel* like Garrett, but for whatever reason, I can't quite access that memory. It's all just a blur and panic." She began to speak faster. "And even there, I don't know Garrett, don't know what he feels like, so how could I say the masked man didn't *feel* like Garrett?"

"Maybe your *gut* says it's not Garrett." Katie's hand was still over Delilah's, and she nodded my way. "Kind of like Fred's gut talks to her sometimes."

"Maybe." Delilah acquiesced, clearly not satisfied with that explanation. "Or maybe I'm just worried that it's not Garrett and the real man is still out there and is going to show up again."

Horrible thought. I leaned closer. "When you think about him, picture him, in the room or in your yard... does he feel like someone you know? Can you even access that? Maybe not Garrett or Demetrius, but someone more familiar."

She started to shake her head and then paused. "You know... I hadn't thought of it like that. I'm not sure how to answer that question, but if I flip it..." She narrowed her eyes again, considering. "For some reason, I have the feeling that he knew me, if that makes sense."

"Kind of does. I think." I gave what I hoped was an encouraging smile. "We're going to figure it out. For now, Garrett's still on hold, so I suppose that's something." We sat in silence for a few moments, and then I forced a smile. "Goodness, I feel like I'm a total wet blanket today. First down at—" I gestured to the left, encompassing Aspen Gold, but pushed ahead. "And now here. You two were laughing like you're at a comedy tour or something, but I put a stop to that."

They both smirked and gave stiff laughs again, sharing a quick knowing glance with each other. Katie pulled her hand back and started to explain as Nick delivered the dirty chai and a plateful of pastries for the table. "Campbell mentioned the movie *Clue* at Ethel's this morning, said something about Tim Curry not being there."

I nodded, then realized I wasn't following. "I think I missed a step. And granted, I saw that movie once, years ago. I know it's a cult classic, and I liked it, but it never made my favorites list. I remember it being kinda funny and having a bunch of different endings or something?"

Katie nodded. "The endings are actually part of the point. Just like in the game, depending on how it's played, the characters have different roles. One time Miss Scarlet—" She gestured toward Delilah. "—is the killer, the next time she isn't. The movie plays with that, the characters doing different things, and we were picturing some of you as the movie characters instead of the game characters."

"I think I need more of this." I took a long swig of the dirty chai, which Nick made *almost* as delicious as Katie's. "It may take a few minutes for it to kick in, 'cause I'm still not catching on."

Delilah chuckled. "There's nothing to get, not in the sense of solving anything, just explaining why we were laughing." She kept going without me needing to prompt, tossing her long auburn hair over her shoulders in a sultry manner. "*My* character, Miss Scarlet, pretty much stays the same, no matter if it's game or movie. In the game, I'm the noir vixen type, in the movie, Miss Scarlet is a madam based out of

Washington DC. Not exactly something I would do, but... not exactly something I *wouldn't*, either."

That earned her the slightest side glare from Katie, but she didn't lecture Delilah about that particular aspect of her lifestyle. "Most of them don't fit, just like Mrs. Peacock—in the board game you're that older, grand sort of lady, and in the movie you're a senator's wife who's guilty of taking bribes. Neither fits you at all. Carla, as Mrs. White, is the maid in the game, which makes sense why Ethel would give her that, but in the movie, you're led to believe Mrs. White murdered three of her husbands. Which... it's kind of a stretch, but Ethel definitely would have considered Carla as murdering Jonathan's social standing or whatever."

Some of that was starting to make sense. "So, you're thinking maybe the Clue characters in the movie is how we were assigned, *not* the game."

"No." Delilah offered a sympathetic smile. "You're being too literal. We weren't solving *anything*. We just started talking, and it felt good to not be serious about it. The main one we were picturing was Mason's character, comparing him to Tim Curry, and those two couldn't be more differ-ent." As Delilah spoke, Katie snickered again, issuing the same reaction from Delilah, who spoke through it. "I mean... you can't see Tim Curry without seeing Frank N. Furter from the *Rocky Horror Picture Show*. Then you end up with Mason in his *oh so proper* tux and sporting lipstick, high heels, and fishnet stockings. He would have hated it."

"He might not have, but Ethel would've." Katie elbowed Delilah. "I kind of have a feeling Mason would have looked better in her furs than Ethel did."

I had about as much experience with the *Rocky Horror Picture Show* as I did with the *Clue* movie. Truth be told I wasn't in love with either—comedy wasn't typically my favorite, especially the offbeat, slapstick kind. Maybe that was the problem; I was missing the humor, or maybe missing the point. "But Mason didn't have a character the other night. He was the butler, he was only himself. The game didn't have a butler character at all." I held up my hands. "Sorry, I'm sure I'm still being too literal. I don't mean to be a wet blanket again."

"That *was* the character." Katie nodded at me as if I had gotten the correct response but didn't realize it. "Tim Curry was the butler in the movie, just like Mason was the butler in real life, and the other night, right?"

"In the movie, one of the endings was where you discover Tim Curry was only *pretending* to be the butler but was the actual Mr. Boddy. One of the twists." Delilah grimaced. "Which doesn't really work in this situation, but still. I'm taking laughter where I can get it, and, politically correct or not, Mason in fishnets and lipstick is a mental picture I'm going to hold on to. Especially with poor old Granny Smith in his arms."

Personally, I cringed at that mental picture, probably more because of Granny Smith than anything else. Though even as I tried to wipe out the alternate version of Mason, I replayed the words Delilah had just said. "In one of the versions, the butler was actually Mr. Boddy... the owner of the mansion... the victim."

Katie and Delilah both stilled at the same time, staring at me with similar expressions, though Katie was the one who spoke. "You just thought of something, what is it? Because Mason ended up being a victim as well... or a murderer if he killed Ethel before hanging himself?"

"No, not that part." I held up a hand. "Hold on. It's almost there." It was, I could feel it, like a puzzle piece starting to snap, but which one, *what* was there? If the butler was really the owner of the mansion, then that would mean Mason and Ethel switching roles. That didn't make any sense—Ethel would never be a maid, never lower herself to the status of help or a servant. And Mason? It was like he'd been born to it. All that "my mistress" stuff, waiting on the sidelines ever so proper. Always ready for an order, taking so much pride in his role. Always standing guard at the door to Ethel's mansion when Watson and I would try to speak to her.

It was right there; I could feel it. The answer was there with Mason.

"Katie, do you..." I changed directions, looking at Delilah. "Actually, *you*. You're the local. Do you know how long Mason worked for Ethel?"

Delilah paused to think for a moment, then shrugged. "No idea. I don't remember a time without him. But it's not like I ran in the same circles as the Beakers, especially back in their heyday. I'm a lot younger than them."

"Hold on, let's say goodbye to Tim Curry for a moment." Katie whipped toward her computer screen, giving the mouse pad a firm tap, making me think she just closed Tim Curry's window, and then her fingers began to fly. "This may take a minute."

A picture began to form, one I didn't think required any answers from Google. If Mason had been there for as long as Delilah could remember, that was quite a while. And though I'd only been in town a few years, Ethel's life had changed quite a bit since my arrival. Her husband Eustace had died shortly after I moved to town, in Carla's coffee shop, and then she was alone in that mansion for years until her sudden relationship with Colin. But she hadn't been alone; *Mason* had been by her side.

"Here..." Katie twisted the computer to face me. "This is barely skimming the surface, but this is from *The Chipmunk Chronicles* in 1976. You can see Mason in the background of the picture."

I twisted the computer slightly as the light cast a glare over the screen, and then the article came into view. It described an open-house fundraiser thrown by the Beakers—the same mansion we'd wandered through that morning. To celebrate the completion of their house, the Beakers were throwing a party and charging for admission, the proceeds to benefit charity. The photo showed a young Eustace and Ethel standing in front of their mansion. Eustace looked sour even then, and Ethel, waifish but rather pretty; without the hardness she'd develop later, but bundled in one of her ever-present fur coats. Further back, Mason stood on the porch, wearing a tux, tray in hand.

As I stared at that picture, I knew. In one of those gut feelings, I just knew. "Hold on. Be right back." I jumped, pulled out my cell, and got the number for Aspen Gold as I hurried to Nick. "Do you mind if I borrow your cell phone for a second? Just in case caller ID shows the Cozy Corgi or me."

"Um... sure?" Dusting flour off his hands, Nick pulled his cell out of his pocket and offered it, no qualifications needed.

"Thanks." I dialed the number and held the phone up to my ear, heart pounding so loud I wasn't sure I'd hear if someone answered.

It only took two rings for Vivian to answer. "Aspen Gold, how can we make your life sparkle today?" Maybe I was projecting, but I thought I still caught a quaver in her voice.

"Vivian, this is Winifred. Don't hang up, or I'm calling Susan." Whether I felt guilt over our interaction half an hour before or not, I pulled the same trick. Even so, I didn't give her a chance to hang up. "Was it Eustace or Mason?"

She hesitated, long enough I thought she was gone, but I heard her breathing.

"Be honest." I pushed harder, as I always did. "The more you're honest, the less likely it is I'll have to involve Susan or ask around and get people talking."

"The second." She hissed the words.

"Excuse me?" I caught on then; either Roger was beside her, or Vivian simply couldn't bring herself to say Mason's name.

"The *second*." She hissed it again and hung up the phone.

Ethel had caught her friend in bed with her butler, not her husband. For a heartbeat that seemed like less of an offense than Vivian having an affair with Eustace. Unless... *Ethel* had been in love with Mason.

Yeah... I might not have proof, and I wasn't entirely sure it mattered, but that was it. Ethel had been in love with her butler.

I wandered back to the table with Katie and Delilah like I was meandering through a mountain trail looking at the scenery—but in this case, it was a whole new set of puzzle pieces clattering down around me, adding a completely different layer over what I'd thought I knew. I finally joined them, dazed and far away, though not enough to keep me from reaching for the dirty chai.

"You *did* find out something!" Katie slapped the top of her laptop closed and then leaned forward, looking like I was handing out candy.

"Who did you call?" Delilah peered over her shoulder, back toward the bakery counter, as if the person might be there.

Watson had stuck his head out of his apartment as I returned, pulling my attention his way, probably thinking I was getting ready to abandon him again. His chocolate eyes narrowed as I sat, giving me a clear warning. Apparently satisfied the message had been received, he waddled backward, doggy-door flap closing again.

"Hold on a second..." I sat there, staring through the one-way mirror into Watson's apartment, shuffling puzzle pieces and debating as that buzz began to build in my blood—the one that suggested we were close, so very close. Finally, I turned back to the others. "Well, Ethel had a much different reason for making Vivian part of the game, although I still don't think her label as Colonel Mustard had anything to do with it."

"Really?" Delilah's voice took on an Anna and Percival quality. "I smell scandal."

"Multiple," I confirmed without thinking, then realized I had promised Vivian I'd be as discreet as possible. *Was* that possible? I inspected both Katie and Delilah—I knew all the official members of our unofficial Scooby Gang could be trusted to never pass along a delicious tidbit for other people's titillation. Delilah, however, while she was on the periphery of our Scooby Gang, I wasn't so sure. Although... considering Delilah's perspective on illicit liaisons, I decided to go ahead. Plus, there would be no way to talk about the details in such a way that anyone paying a modicum of attention wouldn't be able to figure them out.

"Well... what are you waiting—" Katie prompted a second before realization dawned behind her eyes, and she glanced at Delilah.

It seemed they were both at the top of their game, as Delilah gave a little flinch. "Oh... you're concerned about me." Proving she was just as quick as any sleuth within the pages in the mystery room, Delilah looked back over her shoulder once more and then returned to me. "You just discovered the reason Ethel had it in for Vivian LaRue. It's obvious it's of a private nature, so you know where my mind is going." She sat a little straighter, challenge and defiance flashing in her deep blue eyes, a remnant of how our relationship had been at the beginning—apparently that was going around today. "An affair, then. Obviously. Vivian played around where she shouldn't? Although the idea of anyone tangling the sheets with Eustace Beaker behind Ethel's back is cringeworthy, for a whole host of reasons."

Katie sucked in a gasp, gaped at Delilah, then me. "Oh..." Then she shuddered. "*Oh...*" Much different that time. "Can we go back to thinking about Mason in fishnets? That visual is much more appealing than Vivian and Eustace. He was horrible.

Don't get me wrong, Ethel wasn't exactly Miss Congeniality while I worked at Black Bear Roaster, but Eustace was deplorable."

I considered leaving it there, but then realized two things. One, it didn't matter who the man was, as far as Vivian was concerned, probably. She still wouldn't want it to be known, so why hide *the who* from Delilah? And two, much more importantly, I didn't want to damage my relationship with her, and Delilah had proven many times to be more than trustworthy. It was with that thought in mind, I met her gaze instead of Katie's and shook my head. "No... not Eustace."

Confusion flickered, and then Delilah let out a gasp. "*No!*"

"What?" Katie looked back and forth between us, instantly irritated at not being the head of the class for once.

"*No!*" Delilah repeated, sounding even more scandalized than the first time. Despite her clear enjoyment, she once more proved trustworthy by glancing around again, then leaning forward and lowering her voice. "Vivian LaRue had an affair with *Mason?*"

"*What!*" Katie practically bounced to her feet. "Really? When? How long ago? How did Ethel find out?" Confusion returned. "Wow. I knew Ethel had a queen-of-the-world complex, but she really must have felt like she owned Mason or something to decide her old friend deserved to die for having an affair with her butler."

I started to correct her, but Delilah handled it for me, patting Katie's hand on the tabletop. "You're cute, Pollyanna. Very cute." When Katie only glared in confusion, beginning to give way to temper, Delilah clarified. "Vivian wasn't the *only* one having an affair with Mason."

Katie let out such an explosive breath of frustration her curls danced. "What's with the vagueness? Just tell me who—" She stilled, comprehension slamming into her. Then she blinked. "Really?" Without waiting for confirmation from Delilah, Katie twisted to me. "*Ethel Beaker* had an affair with *the help*?"

"That's what I'm thinking. Like you said, I know she's Ethel, but would she really feel murderous because someone had an affair with her butler if she didn't have her own feelings toward him?" Out of my depth, I pulled Delilah in. "Sounds like you agree with me, that Ethel's reaction was based on her own romantic feelings, not from protocol or class or something."

"Oh yeah." Delilah was back, catching on to

where I was and then going a million miles ahead. "I don't know how it wasn't painfully obvious the whole time, the two of them in that house all alone after Eustace died. That was bound to pull them together, of course she turned to him. I can't imagine what Mason felt when she went off and got engaged to Colin. I bet he—"

"No," I cut her off, continuing to whisper quickly. "Mason and Vivian's fling was a long time ago, apparently way before Eustace died. I'm guessing decades ago."

And that had the power to fully surprise Delilah to the point it actually took her several seconds to respond. When she did, she gave an appreciative nod. "I've got to say, didn't see that coming. Having an affair with her butler right under the king of the manor's nose? If I didn't hate her so much, I might just be impressed."

Katie spared a disgusted glance but then swiveled back to her computer and opened it once more, her fingers beginning to fly.

I didn't ask what she was doing; whatever it was, I felt certain she'd make a proclamation any moment. Instead, I got back to the bigger picture and used Delilah as a sounding board. "Maybe it doesn't matter, but this changes things for me, at least partly.

Specifically, why we were all there, why Ethel chose us. It wasn't mere petty grievances like we thought."

Delilah cringed as she waffled a hand. "Yes and no. Maybe from your perspective, but not Ethel's. I can promise you *I* never had an affair with anyone Ethel cared about."

"Well, *that's* improbable. The number of men you *haven't—*" Katie had mumbled to herself, and apparently hadn't meant to speak out loud as she froze and turned with slow horror toward Delilah.

She needn't have worried, as Delilah let out a cackle and threw her arms around Katie's shoulders. "Oh, I sooo want to wrap you up, take you home, and put you on my bookcase. You're just so adorable."

Katie grunted, shimmied out of Delilah's embrace, and began typing again.

Still chuckling, Delilah returned to me, continuing. "Ethel hated me, not because of anything I did to her, other than refusing to bow down and worship at her feet or follow all of her commands. She hated who I was, how I lived my life, and that I wouldn't apologize for it. And it wasn't because she had some evangelical moral-high-ground junk."

"No, I agree. Percival thought she was jealous of you."

"Without a doubt, and no wonder I love your

uncle." She left that behind and jumped to her antithesis. "Same for Anna, although completely different. Maybe Anna has some deep, dark secret of what she did to Ethel, but I doubt it. Ethel hated Anna because, just like me, nobody tells Anna Hanson what to do. And Ethel was disgusted by Anna in the opposite way of me—she found her low class, ugly, and fat."

"*Delilah!*" Katie stopped typing and turned again. "That's horrid to say. And remember who you're sitting next to, I'm not exactly a size eight."

"No, you're not, and don't you ever feel bad about it for a second, you gorgeous creature." Delilah bumped Katie on the nose but didn't pause when she sputtered. "Fat isn't a dirty word unless you use it as a dirty word, like Ethel would. Ask Anna, she's not going to pretend she's anything other than that, and she's not apologizing for it, either. I'm merely saying her physical combined with all of her personality aspects added up to Ethel hating her, just like she did me. And I can guarantee you, over the decades with the two of us, Ethel thought of countless ways to murder Anna and myself."

Katie issued a grunt that suggested she was only partially mollified but returned to the computer.

"Okay... let's go with that. It's pretty close to

what we were thinking for you and Anna anyway." I had snagged one of the lemon bars and gestured to myself as I brought it to my plate, leaving a dusting of powdered sugar behind. "Similar is true for me. We all know that she hated me with a passion, so no surprise there. As far as Carla, she made it her life's mission to show the entire world how much she despised her daughter-in-law. So, we've got five players who Ethel truly hated and would enjoy torturing."

"Ah, I see where you're going." Following my lead, Delilah picked up a pastry as well, though she chose one of the Earl Grey rolls. "That leaves the chief and Mary Smith—and *why* Ethel hated them to that same degree."

"Exactly, and I have no idea." I realized that was wrong. "Actually, with Marlon, there's more going on there than we realized, so there may be something. And with him I would guess financial or blackmail or something of the like."

"Okay..." Delilah cocked her head in puzzlement. "Clearly, I've missed a story."

"I'll fill you in. It's all going to be public knowledge soon enough anyway, but stay with me on this. Maybe it doesn't matter, but... if we assume I'm right about Dunmore, then we have a reason for every-body, except for Mary. So—"

"Here!" Katie gave a little cheer, cutting me off and then swiveled the computer so the screen was facing out. "May I present Mason Vasner." She started to explain as Delilah and I turned toward her. "This whole Ethel-and-the-butler romance got me thinking." She pointed at the screen to the original article of the Beaker mansion. "A line in here caught my attention—Eustice bragging on Ethel, saying she was completely in charge of building their home, from the initial blueprints all the way to completion, that he couldn't take any credit for it, as he was busy working or whatever. *Man's* work." She rolled her eyes, but pressed on, the tinge of scandal seeping back in. "Well... if Mason was already their butler, as indicated by this photo, *and* Ethel designed the house, then *she* is the one who put in that secret passage from the kitchen to the bedroom. What if Eustace never knew about it?"

"Ethel, you wily vixen!" Delilah truly did sound impressed, equally as when she nudged Katie's shoulder playfully. "And you too, thinking such thoughts. But I bet you're right. If Ethel and the butler were having a long-term affair, then a secret passage from her bedroom to the kitchen... her domain to his, makes perfect sense. And it's brilliant. While Eustace is out doing *man's work*, as you say, Katie, Ethel and Mason can be up in their little love nest, and if the man of the house comes home suddenly?" She shrugged and simultaneously flipped her long hair over her shoulders again. "Mason just slips into the tunnel and back down to the kitchen. Eustace would never suspect. No crawling out windows, hiding under the bed, or ducking into closets."

"Spoken from someone with experience." Though Katie probably tried to sound repulsed, she didn't quite manage that time.

"No, darling." Delilah waved her off. "All that's for amateurs and the pathetic. *I* only use the front door."

"Before we go into waters that I have *no* desire swimming in—" I smirked at Delilah and then gestured toward Katie. "—what else did you find?"

"Nothing that indicates a proclivity to murder or where this all ended up, but just a fuller picture of Mason. That *might* be helpful, as he clearly fulfilled more than just a butler's role, which was already obvious when he picked up Fred at gunpoint." Katie grimaced. "There's a big gap in Mason's history, and I can't figure out where his path crossed with Ethel's or how he became the Beakers' butler—*or* entered that profession at all. I may just need more time, or maybe it's intentionally erased."

"Hmmm." Delilah rubbed her hands together. "Well... maybe I'll contact my Pink Panther sister who specializes in such things."

"No need to call Beth yet." Katie scowled. "I didn't say I was giving up."

Delilah was right; Katie was adorable—she always wanted to be the first one to know the answer to a question, and doubtlessly didn't want her Google skills questioned, even when compared to a hacker. "You found something in Mason's past that's telling?"

"No, not necessarily. The only telling thing was Ethel designing the house, the rest is just interesting trivia. But..." She waggled her eyebrows. "We all know random trivia sometimes is the key to the whole thing." She pointed to another open window on the computer screen, the picture black-and-white, grainy. "Mason was the youngest of *thirteen* children. Bob and Mary Vasner only had five of those children when this first picture was taken in the forties... so before Mason was born. Anyway, his parents and some of those older siblings traveled in a... circus, although, at the time, it was called a freak show."

"A freak show? Seriously? Why?" Delilah leaned forward, getting a better look at the picture, then flinched. "Oh." She let out a disgusted breath and sat back. "This world can be so cruel."

"It can, I agree."

As Katie confirmed, I followed Delilah's example and leaned forward across the table to get a better view. The picture clarified things instantly. "Oh Lord." A sick feeling washed over me, promptly followed by disgust and anger.

The small family stood in front of a tent in the background. The bars at their back and on either side indicated they were in a cage, though as there were none across the front of the photo, maybe it was just a prop or stage. In any case, a large wooden sign over their heads made things clear enough—*The Living Doll and Leprechaun Family*. Mary Vasner was a little person. Though hard to guess specifics, she seemed to stand probably around four feet tall. She was beautiful and clothed in a baby-doll outfit. The blond curls around her face looked like a wig and had giant bows on either side. Bob Vasner was slightly taller than his wife, and from the disproportional shape of his body, he appeared to have a form of dwarfism. He wore a tattered striped suit, his hair a wild mass around his face, and at his feet, a pot of gold. Two children stood beside Mary, already towering over their parents, while the other two beside Bob appeared to have inherited their father's dwarfism. I couldn't tell what might be the case for the small baby swaddled in Mary's arms. All appeared stoic and sad.

"You're sure this is Mason's family?"

"Yeah." Katie nodded at me and tapped a third window, bringing it to the forefront.

Bob's funeral announcement from an Arkansas newspaper in the mid-sixties. It showed a photo of the entire family, none in costumes, simply outside a family home—this one brighter, happier. From the photo, it appeared only four of the thirteen children had inherited either their father's dwarfism or the short stature of their mother. Mason was easily identifiable even as an early teen despite his thick mop of dark hair. He was the tallest of the siblings and stood straight and strong as if on guard.

We sat there studying the photo. I couldn't decide if this aspect of Mason's history was merely an interesting insight into his family and past or if it somehow played a role in what had occurred at Ethel's mansion.

"I'm just gonna say it..." Delilah gave a warning glance toward Katie as she offered a disclaimer. "And I'm not saying this is my thought or belief, just like with the word *fat*. But this is *Ethel* we're talking about, so think about Mason's family from *her* perspective." She included me into her comments once more. "We don't know about Mason's financial status as a young man yet, but based on this picture, they weren't exactly upper class. That alone would probably have taken Mason out of husband material for Ethel, but *this*? She wouldn't have considered it, no matter how much she might have fallen in love with Mason as he worked for her."

"Agreed. But we don't know when Ethel fell for Mason, maybe it was while he was their butler. Or maybe it was before. If Katie is right about the passage from kitchen to bedroom, which makes sense, it was at least before they moved into this house." I leaned back, suddenly frustrated. "I can't tell if this is a distraction or if it's part of it. Ethel didn't kill Mason, so it's not part of the motive."

Delilah gave a little flinch, started to shake her head, and then spoke up. "I'm sure this is just coincidence, but his mother's name was *Mary*." She pointed toward the computer screen. "We were just wondering what got Mary Smith to the table." She shrugged, finishing without giving a theory.

Katie and I exchanged a glance, neither convinced, though Katie tried it on for size. "Maybe Mary Smith is a relative, a granddaughter or great-granddaughter and named after Mary Vasner." Even as she spoke, she shook her head again, dismissing her own idea. "She was blackmailing Mason and going to expose family history? Or maybe she somehow knows about Mason and Ethel's relationship?"

"Oh..." I cringed. "I can't believe I'm going to say this, but I think I prefer pure coincidence in this case. Just two women randomly named Mary. Otherwise..."

"Yeah, I agree." Delilah looked defeated. "Plus, that family history wouldn't be worthy of blackmail, not today, not for a long time now. You'd have to be a truly wretched person to..." She snorted out a little laugh. "Well... Ethel, wretched person... maybe I'm talking myself into it."

"I doubt it." I let out a long breath, then took an equally long swig of dirty chai, finishing the mug. "I'm going to need another one of these to go. It's time to walk down the street and try to have a discussion that I've been putting off." As I pushed up to stand from the table, Watson poked his head out the doggie door again. "Perfect timing, sir."

He eyed me suspiciously.

"Don't give me that look." I shook my finger playfully at Watson, which only earned me more of a glare. "This time, you're coming with me. Between my annoying personality and your shedding, I bet we can crack Mary Smith like a nut."

The lunch crowd filtered into the bookshop as Watson and I stepped into the bright sun on Elkhorn Avenue. From the way he trotted happily along the sidewalk, several paces ahead of me, I feared he was under the impression we were going to visit Donna at the apothecary. I didn't bother trying to explain, not that I knew how to anyway. Instead, I used the short distance to do a bit of self-talk, try to find an appropriate balance for walking into Bottles, Brushes, and Brie. It was one thing to use my super-power of annoyance, as Susan said, but I also didn't want to get triggered into acting in a manner that would leave me frustrated with myself. Mary Smith didn't spark that indignant fire quite as much as Ethel Beaker, but she wasn't too far off.

Proving my instinct correct, as we crossed to the other side of Elkhorn, in the opposite direction from Donna's, Watson pulled a sit-down strike in the middle of the intersection, staring meaningfully toward Doc's.

"Watson Charles!" I slapped my thigh and gave a little tug. "Do not act like a spoiled little brat. Especially in the middle of the street."

He only glowered.

"Can you imagine what Susan would say if she saw you right now? She'd—"

At Susan's name, Watson hopped back up onto all fours. After a second, though he gave a longing glance toward the apothecary, he followed with a slight spring in his step. Donna might be catnip as far as he was concerned, but Susan wasn't half-bad either.

I felt a little guilty that he'd misunderstood my use of Susan's name, but didn't try to clarify, lest we have another test of wills. We finished crossing the street and headed up the other block, speeding up as we crossed in front of Old Friends. Though still cold, the massive snow drifts from the blizzard were beginning to melt in the noon sunlight, leaving rivers over the shoveled concrete. I only realized the implication of this as we reached the door of Bottles, Brushes, and Brie—I hadn't brought my purse, so I didn't have tissues, paper towels, or otherwise. For a heartbeat I considered using the hem of my skirt on Watson's paws but discarded that quickly. I had some pride, despite what some might suggest. And ultimately, it only added to that annoying superpower, so I went with it.

As we entered the wine-and-cheese side of the exclusive new shop, Watson pulled another sit-down right in the doorway. Accusation blazed in his eyes— there was no Susan Green present, no one offering fancy jerky or calling him Officer Fleabag. There was, however, the front door closing behind us. Adding insult to injury, it bumped into Watson's rump and nudged him farther inside. Watson whipped around, snarling, then realizing it wasn't a person, he turned his glare back onto me.

"I've made it perfectly clear you are not only unwelcome in my shop but stated that you are not even to darken the door." Mary Smith, naturally, stood near the back, adjusting some bottles of wine, and had witnessed the entire scene. "I must confess, the fact Ethel lumped me into the same category as you is one of the most insulting experiences of my life."

"You know, *most* warm-blooded humans feel some sort of connection after surviving a trauma together. What in the world is wrong with you?" Well... that moment of self-talk went up in smoke instantly. I'd like to say this was a record time that things had melted down between Mary and myself, but that probably wasn't true. The temptation to turn around and just walk right back out the door whispered. Instead, I forced myself farther in, dropping Watson's leash as I couldn't handle attitude from both directions. "Listen, I'm sorry. I don't want to bother you, and I'll be honest—I don't want to be in your presence any more than you want to be in mine. We clearly don't bring out the best in each other, but I need to talk to you."

"Right…" Even that tone, *seriously?* It was like she was Ethel's clone. "Because you're Winifred, bookseller and crime fighter. Instead of wearing a cape, you have on another of those god-awful skirts."

For about three seconds, I felt an aneurysm build behind my eye, and then it vanished—or possibly exploded—as I laughed. At the insulted flinch Mary issued, I only laughed harder.

She took a step back, concern over her nondescript features, as if she feared I'd gone rabid and was about to attack.

"This is ridiculous, Mary." Despite my best effort, I couldn't quite stop chuckling. "Why are we doing this? Clearly, we're never going to be friends, but *this?*" I gestured between us. "It's ridiculous."

"What's *ridiculous* is how rude you were upon our arrival in town and have continued in that vein ever since." She moved forward again, fear of rabies apparently dissipating. As she spoke, her husband and son appeared in the arched doorway between this shop and the connecting painting studio. "What's *ridiculous* is that you shove yourself in every drama that happens in town. What's *ridiculous* is—" Her voice had risen in anger, and as it did, Watson trotted up beside me, offense forgotten. But then her words broke off with a crack, though she tried again. "What's ridiculous, is that..." A tremble in her voice sounded, and she looked close to tears. "Is that I was there at all, with you, with all of those stupid people. In that stupid situation. With that stupid, evil woman." I realized she didn't just look close to tears, one had actually rolled down her cheek.

"Mary, dear." Her husband moved farther into the room, heading her way, comfort in his voice. "It's okay. You're safe. Nothing is going to—"

"Stop!" She turned toward him, fury burning away any of the fear she'd displayed. "Not here."

He halted, looked wounded.

"Go, James." Mary gestured out the store. "Take Robert with you. Go pick us up lunch or something."

She shot a warning glare at her son. "Lock the doors when you leave and put up the Closed signs."

"Mary, come on. Let's—"

"James." She growled her husband's name.

Watson growled back.

Her husband deflated, gave a nod, then motioned for their son to follow. For his part, Robert didn't look on the verge of arguing or tempted to comfort his mother, nor even that insulted at the behavior. He simply nodded my way with the smallest of gestures and followed orders. Even in the moment, it was impossible not to both notice and marvel that a man who looked like he just stepped off a movie screen was the offspring of two people who could pass you in the middle of the street without being noticed.

As the two of them left, completing both the tasks Mary had issued on their way, I forgot about the moment at hand, about the Clue game, about what Mary and I had shared. Instead, over a billion other questions tumbled around. There was something strange or maybe just off about the Smith family. I didn't think they trafficked in cheese like Anna had originally suggested, but there was something.

"You ask why I don't like you, Winifred?"

Mary brought my attention back to the moment. I didn't point out that I hadn't asked that question.

"Because of this, right here." She pointed at me and leaned against the case holding the gourmet cheeses. "You stand there, uninvited, unwelcome in my space, and I can see you judging my family, wanting to pry your nose into our lives, into our business, wanting to discover every little secret we have. I don't know if I've ever met another person as entitled and as obnoxious as you."

Perhaps it was being called out on exactly what I had been thinking, but I didn't rise to the bait that time, just shrugged my acknowledgement. "Detective Green calls it my superpower to be annoying, among other things. She's used *obnoxious* as well a time or two."

Mary merely grunted, although it almost sounded amused. Before she gave in to that emotion, however, she crossed her arms over her chest and glared down at Watson. "Your dog is leaving a pool in the middle of our newly refurbished hardwood floors."

"I'm sorry." An inspection revealed it wasn't quite as bad as Mary had stated, and I discovered Watson staring up at me—I thought he was trying to determine if we were in a danger moment or just another one of Mama's dramas. I smiled down at him in reassurance, then back to Mary. "I should have brought a towel or something. I didn't think. Again, I'm sorry." I wasn't going to offer to leave. "I don't wanna take up too much of your time, and despite what my behavior says, I'd also like to give you the space that you want."

"You sure don't act like it." She didn't offer any other comment.

I opted to jump over that to move this along. "The fact is, Mary, while things didn't go the way Ethel had planned, all of us were in that room and slated to be killed two nights ago. I've figured out a reason for absolutely everyone except you." That was only a little stretch of the truth, but I continued with it. "All the major grievances that Ethel had against us are clear, except yours."

"Other than her being an insufferable snob, I had no problem with Ethel Beaker, nor she with me. We avoided each other." When Mary started answering, it took me a second to realize that's what she was doing; I hadn't expected it. "I have absolutely no idea why I was there, which is exactly what I've told the police during their insufferable questioning that night when all I wanted to do was get home to my family. There's nothing else to tell you, not that it's any of your business."

"That's actually where I landed with things. Between you and Ethel, I mean. My only theory is that you didn't give her the respect she thought she deserved, especially from someone new in town, a new business owner in town."

"Great." Mary uncrossed her arms in finality. "Then we're on the same page. Over and done. You can leave now."

What in the world was Mary Smith's story? Even that night in Ethel's mansion she'd avoided us, seemed annoyed, like we were simply getting in her way. She'd explored the mansion on her own instead of trying to figure things out with the group. "Mason's mother's name was Mary."

She blinked. "What?"

"Yeah." I nodded, hope entering at her apparent surprise. "Do you think you might be related to him? That there's some connection to—"

"Who's Mason?" Pure exasperation radiated from Mary, and then dawning entered. "Oh, the butler. No, I'm not related to him. And so what if his mother's name was Mary? I..." She halted, going stony. "There you go again, trying to figure out questions about my personal life, about my family. It's *none* of your business. No, I'm not related to the butler, to the *lady of the house*, to anyone in this town. And for the billionth time, I don't know why I was there. You're luckier than I am that you have a reason. At least when you wake up at night reliving it, you know what you did to deserve..." As she spoke, her anger had shifted to fear, the quaver reentering and the tears threatened to form again.

Even in that moment, Watson started to respond as he so often did to someone in turmoil—taking a few tentative steps forward, ready to offer comfort.

His movement broke Mary's spell, and she shook her head again. "We're done here, I have nothing to give you. And even though I don't want to give you anything, at this point, I would, just to satisfy you and get you out of my shop. But as I don't..." She gestured toward the door. "Feel free to let it hit you on the way out."

Watson had stopped and offered a grunt.

I latched on to that bit of emotion other than the anger I'd seen from her. "But that's it, Mary. When I wake up at night, I know there's someone else involved. Mason is the one who picked me up at gunpoint, and he's dead. But the man who got *you*? The man who got Delilah?" I moved closer to her without even thinking. "*He's* still out there. He could come back."

I figured I'd pushed too far, but judging from the fresh rush of fear in her eyes, apparently not. "They... decided it was your ex-husband. He's in custody."

"Maybe. I'm not so sure." I took another step. "I'd like to be sure so we can both sleep easier, because I'm having flashes too. For me it's the tunnel, feeling the walls close around me, thinking that at any moment it would explode and either fire would come rushing through, or I'd be buried under it all and in an even smaller space."

"The tunnel." She snorted. "*That's* what scared you? That was nothing. Only problem with that was I was barely strong enough to get the door open." She almost sounded embarrassed by that, but she didn't linger, fear and anger blazing in her eyes then, and she stepped toward me. "All of that was a show. It was ridiculous, even in the middle of it. Try being outside your house at night walking back from your... your studio, and then there's a man stepping out of the shadows, completely masked, gun pulled. He just stares at you, you turn and run, try to make it back, try to decide if you go to your studio or to your house, which one's closer" She was caught in that moment now, and a tear rolled down one cheek, then the other. "And then he's on you, grabbing you so hard from behind that he knocks the wind from your chest. You can't scream, you can't call for help. He just covers your mouth and nose with his leather gloves where you can't breathe and drags you back. Back into the dark, through the trees. Back to his car. I thought... I thought he..." She wiped those tears away. "I thought it was something a lot worse than a fancy dinner table and a stupid murder-mystery game." As she'd spoken, Watson had approached her feet again, but she didn't notice. Another tear fell as she looked away, that time speaking to herself. "I *wish* I woke up thinking about the tunnel. I think of trees, the dark, I'll never be able to walk across my yard again without... never hear the snap of twigs in the woods... never smell butterscotch or leather without being right back there." She flashed back to me. "*You* had an old man and a *cat* drive you to a dinner party and a tunnel." She finally glared down at Watson. "You even got to keep your emotional support dog or whatever he is."

"I'm sorry, Mary. That sounds truly horrifying, even more than—"

"I don't want you to be sorry." She sneered. "I just want you to go."

"Okay." Without a doubt, I'd gotten all I could from Mary Smith. And in a way, though it wasn't anything of use, it was more than I'd expected. It was the most real I'd ever seen her. I bent and picked up Watson's leash. "Come on. Come on, buddy."

He continued to look at Mary, and I couldn't tell if he was still wanting to offer comfort or something about her confused him, but it only took a little tug to convince him to follow.

I was a few feet away from the door, visions of what Mary described flashing through my mind, when I paused, disbelieving, then turned back to Mary.

"No. Whatever it is, just *no*." She shook her head, pointed toward the door. "Leave me."

"I will." Even as I asked it, I almost couldn't believe what I'd heard, though I was certain. The puzzle pieces were already snapping into place. "Did you say you smelled butterscotch?"

The debate between asking for forgiveness or requesting permission was short-lived, more of a simple ponderance than actual choice to be made. I'd already attempted to burn one bridge with Susan; I wasn't going to take a match to another one on the same day. I'd anticipated a little more pushback, but there was none. It was *her* call to bring in Campbell as well—the two of them had been having burgers from Penelope's in her office when I'd called, so they were together anyway.

From the way Watson dragged me across the police station, double his speed the last few times we visited—which meant at this point I nearly had to run to keep up—I thought he feared I'd burnt those bridges with his favorite detective as well. However, that theory was debunked the second we stepped into her tiny office, with the smell of greasy-spoon burgers and fresh cut fries thick in the air. Watson whimpered in the most pitiful of tones, trotted to Susan's desk, and the second she looked his way, he sat automatically.

"Well, look at you." She cast a sad smile down at Watson. "Somebody's learning. Following orders without even needing the commands."

"I think this time he might actually be disappointed with buffalo jerky. The smells are even making *my* stomach rumble." We'd missed lunch, although as I'd had pastries with Katie and Delilah less than an hour before—that should have counted.

"No, he won't." Susan reached into a white paper bag, the crinkling sound prompting Watson's whine to shoot up an octave. She pulled out more crinkling paper, yellow this time. When she unfolded it, a large chunk of ground-beef patty emerged. She held it aloft and cocked an eyebrow at Watson. "Okay, Officer Fleabag—*stay*."

His nub of a tail wagged with such ferocity it threatened to put a dent in the floor, but... he stayed. When Susan finally lowered his portion of the burger, Watson didn't give his normal impression of a shark, but daintily took the juicy morsel between his fangs as if he'd learned elegant manners at our so-called dinner at the mansion two nights ago. That refinement ended instantly as he swallowed the hunk of meat with a giant gulp, then belched. Resuming his whimper, he peered up for more.

"Later, Fleabag, later." She turned to me and then gestured to the empty chair across from her desk, next to Campbell. "Have a seat."

She hadn't asked me for proof on the phone, and she didn't then, either. Only looked at Campbell as I sat. "Are you ready?"

Campbell had attempted a smile as I'd squeezed in beside him, but only shook his head at Susan. However, after a moment, head still saying no, he muttered, "Yeah. Just do it."

He didn't ask for proof or clarification either. Maybe things had already been pointing in this direction, or maybe it simply made all the puzzle pieces fit too snugly to be doubted.

Susan picked up her phone—the landline on her desk—hit a button, closed her eyes, and waited. Just when I thought she was going to put the phone back and say no one answered, she sat a little straighter. "Chief, yeah. Mind coming to my office? There's been some details emerge I'd like you to look at."

Somewhere in the exchange, Watson had given

up begging for more burger and had taken shelter under Susan's desk. He'd squeezed out just enough that his head and most of his neck were on my side, and he rested his muzzle on my boot, the rest of his body still sheltered in the little cave and close to Susan's feet.

Chief Dunmore gave a solitary knock before pushing the door open. "I don't have much time, Detective Green. I was just on my way to meet with..." He stopped right inside the door when he saw me, and probably the expression over his nephew's face. I hadn't had any doubt as I had left Bottles, Brushes, and Brie, and apparently neither Susan nor Campbell had any either. But if any of us did, that momentary flash would have cleared it all up—the realization that crossed Marlon's face, followed by the flash of panic, and the thought of turning to run so loud it was audible, then the acceptance as his expression fell and his shoulders slumped. He took another step in, closed the door behind him, then pulled the chair over, placing it right in front of the door and sitting down. Maybe to block others from entering, maybe to keep himself from running. He opened his mouth to speak and then shook his head and gestured with his hand for us to proceed.

We hadn't planned this, not more than just agreeing to do it. Not wasting any time, to my surprise, Susan turned to me. "You want to? Or would you rather me?"

I wasn't sure which would be more respectful to Susan, then figured if she was offering, she might prefer if I handled the ugly part for her. "I can."

As I turned to face the chief, he scooted his hips up, allowing space for his hand to reach into the pocket of his pants. He pulled out a butterscotch, then relaxed back into the chair as he unwrapped it, fingers shaking.

All three of us stared at it.

He'd gotten the golden hard candy into his mouth and had started to stuff the wrapper back into his pocket before feeling our attention. Following our gaze, he inspected the wrapper, which had started to shake more, then looked to me, the question clear in his eyes.

There was no question, if there ever had been, so I didn't word it as such. "Mary Smith smelled butterscotch on your breath when you captured her in the woods outside her house."

The chief stared back down at the wrapper. "Oh." He took a long, deep breath in, then let it out—

it shook just like the golden wrapper—but said nothing else.

Susan gave the smallest clearing of her throat, and Campbell spoke up, his one word clear, steady. "Why?"

The heavy silence settling in the room was broken only by Watson's snores, soft and gentle. Peaceful, though how he managed when the rest of us were wound so tight it felt like the world might shatter, I had no idea.

Finally, with another nod, decision made, yet again, the chief erased any nonexistent molecule of doubt. "They got to the man I was using to make your aunt's life a little easier in prison. Not sure how much they offered him, but more than me, more than I'm able." Marlon looked at Susan next, a plea for forgiveness clear in the tenor of his words. "They were going to kill May, make it look like an accident, or a fight with another inmate, of all things. I..." He didn't meet anyone's eyes as he finished the thought. "I didn't have a choice."

The silence returned, but for less time, and Susan leaned into her anger, her disgust, which I imagined was a whole lot easier than her hurt and betrayal. "So you were going to let *six* other people die, and a dog, for your wife? Your wife who had already killed two people?"

"No. I didn't think they were going to kill anyone." When Susan scoffed and Campbell breathed out a small groan, the chief doubled down. "No, I really didn't. It was just supposed to be a game. I figured some people might be scared, but no one was supposed to die."

The words were true, I thought, but there was something off in the lilt of his voice as he ended the sentiment. "But you didn't think that at the time, did you? Not when it started." I wasn't sure when he'd come to the realization, maybe a day or two before, maybe that night as he picked up Mary and Delilah. I also wasn't sure it mattered. "Did you know they were going to put you in the chair with us?"

"Yes." After a moment, he continued, not waiting for any of us to prompt. "That way no one would suspect it was me. But they never mentioned a bomb or fire or any of that. It was just supposed to be a game."

"You keep saying *they*." Campbell had pulled out his notepad and was scribbling, and though sadness could be heard, his voice still did not quaver. Across from him, behind her desk, Susan stared at Campbell, clearly proud. "Who are *they*? Ethel and

Mason? Garrett Griffin? Branson Wexler? All of them?"

Marlon stared at his nephew, sharing some of Susan's pride, his voice thick with guilt. "I'm sorry, Campbell. I didn't want this for you. We brought you here to make things easier, to show you that you're accepted."

"Yeah." Campbell laughed, dark and hard in a way that didn't sound like himself at all, and he laid down the pen, meeting his uncle's gaze. "But then you and my aunt killed people, so... thanks for the love, but on the whole realm of murder or homophobic family members, I think I choose..." He looked down at his notepad, finishing with a whisper. "Neither. I choose neither."

"*I* didn't kill anybody, Campbell." The chief leaned forward, reached out toward his nephew. When Campbell didn't so much as make a move, the chief lowered his hand and rested the weight of his elbows on his knees. "I really didn't." Apparently giving up on Campbell, he looked toward Susan and me in turn. "It doesn't make me innocent, I'm not saying that, but I've never killed anyone, not even in the line of duty."

"Line of duty." Susan snorted, still sinking into that anger.

"You didn't kill Ethel or Mason?" Maybe I should have left it there, not led the witness or whatever they'd say, but I couldn't help myself, even in that moment, needing to paint the chief in a better light if possible. "You were part of it, part of the planning, part of the game. You could have snuck into the library and tried to make things right—save yourself, save all of us. Then set it up to look like—"

"I wasn't part of the planning or part of the game." He met my gaze, leaving very little room for doubt. "As soon as the door shut in that dining room, Fred, I didn't know any more than you did. And I wasn't part of any of it until about two hours before when they texted me photos of May, telling me what they'd do to her."

"Who's *they*?" Susan interrupted again. "Answer your nephew's question."

Campbell merely lifted his pen, waiting.

"Well..." The chief sat back, and there was a slight click of the butterscotch on his teeth when he spoke next. "It was Ethel who contacted me, but she said it was Branson pulling the strings, controlling everyone, making her do this. Said the threats to May were from Branson." He looked to me. "I... I don't know, now. Clearly Branson was making her do *some* things, but I don't know how much. She'd obviously taken the night into her own hands, but... was getting me involved only her or also Branson? I can't figure it out now. There's been no follow-up from him, so—"

"Why Mary?" Perhaps it didn't matter, maybe it did, but it just didn't make sense, and I needed to know.

The chief let out a whoosh of a breath that was part laugh, part groan and shook his head. "It wasn't supposed to be Mary, but... it was too late."

Susan and I exchanged a glance, and even Campbell looked up from his notepad.

The chief didn't wait for a prompt. "Jennifer was taking a meeting with Mrs. Gunn... er... the next-door neighbor with the Smiths. She'd mentioned it to me earlier in the week, campaign stuff. The Gunns are out in the woods. It seemed the best place, and the timing was perfect with what Ethel wanted."

I didn't know Mrs. Gunn, and as such it took me a second to make the connection to Jennifer Sallee, the vet's wife. "The mayor? Ethel wanted you to get the mayor?"

Susan didn't give him a chance to respond. "I thought the two of them were in cahoots. Isn't... or *wasn't* Ethel helping finance the mayor's political agenda in return for the mayor bringing her on up in society outside of Estes?"

He gave another laugh, this one rather sad and looked at me. "The mayor severed that relationship after her discussion with you last month, Fred." He tsked. "I was proud of her and felt like such a hypocrite the whole time when I knew I was bribing an employee at the jail for May."

Now that *did* make sense, Jennifer Sallee taking away the promise of Ethel's hopes and dreams for spreading her wings outside of our little mountain town. Yeah, I could see Ethel feeling that betrayal was worthy of death. "Then, what happened? Why Mary? You were at the wrong house?"

The chief slumped in his chair. "Do we really have to..." He shook his head and sighed. "Yes, of course we do. And I guess I'd better get used to it." A tear rolled down his cheek, and he wiped it away, seeming to grow heavier with every word. "Like I said, they live out in the boonies pretty much. I was able to park my car behind the houses, go through the woods, it's not very far to the little dirt road running behind the houses. I was going to... good God, just saying it out loud..." A sigh, a shudder, then more. "I was going to snag Jennifer as she left. We'd go the back way, less chance of being seen. I knew her car would still be out front, but that didn't matter, not for how long the game was supposed to last. I was heading toward the back of that house when I looked over and Mary Smith was standing there. I still don't know where she came from, or why she was out at night—she was in the backyard. But she saw me... I didn't have a choice. It's not like I could let her go in and call the police. So..."

"I bet Ethel loved that." Susan was utterly flat-lined as she spoke.

"She... she did not."

The chief didn't elaborate—at the memory, his cheeks flushed. However, in that moment, I didn't care. It still wasn't adding up.

Before I could point that out to the chief, Campbell did it for me, rising to the occasion and doing his job—even as the strain of keeping emotion out of his voice sounded painful. "So, you were contacted a couple of hours before the game was scheduled to begin. Told that Aunt May was in danger if you didn't oblige, and this was possibly Ethel, Mason, Branson, or some combination thereof." He checked his notes, bouncing the tip of his pen down the page as he spoke. "You went to get the mayor at Mrs. Gunn's house but had to take Mary Smith instead. Then what? You delivered her and went and got Delilah Johnson?"

"Yes." Marlon gave a solitary nod and finished

the rest. "And then before the butler brought back Fred, I sat in my seat at the table—everyone already had the sacks over their heads—and allowed Ethel to fasten the zip ties to my wrists, and then we waited."

Watson's breathing transitioned to a snore, sleeping and dreaming through the entire exchange. Oh, to be a dog. My life was wonderful on the whole, but... Watson's was probably better.

The thought barely flickered before I returned to the chief. "You really didn't sneak into the library and kill Ethel and Mason?" It wasn't really a question, I had already been convinced and only gave him the chance to shake his head before continuing, addressing both him and the room at large. "That means we have a fourth person involved. It could still be Garrett, or maybe Branson arrived? Someone else?"

"Or maybe it's exactly what it looks like." Marlon shrugged. "The two of them had a fight, or Mason had second thoughts and couldn't go through with it. Maybe a moment of anger and didn't mean to kill Ethel, then riddled with guilt..." He turned back to Campbell, hope seeping in. "You see, son? I didn't kill anyone, I really didn't. And I did everything I could to save all of us, to get us out of there. I didn't want anyone to die." He gestured toward me. "Ask

Fred, she'll tell you. I helped unlock doors. I searched for—"

"I don't hate you." Campbell sniffed, wiped the back of his hand across his cheek and when he spoke again, the tremble in his voice left. "I don't hate Aunt May either. I'm grateful to both of you for loving me, even if it... wasn't perfect. But I wasn't a kid when I moved here. I'm not a kid now. I was fine before, and I'll be even more okay now. This won't break me, Uncle Marlon, if that's one of the things you're worried about." Though there was very little resemblance between the two men, Campbell leaned forward, taking the posture his uncle had only minutes before, elbows on his knees as he drew closer to Marlon's face. "But I'm a *good* cop, and I will *always* be a good cop. No matter what."

"I..." The chief gave a shrug and a smile. "I hope that's true. I hope life allows that to be true for you."

"It won't matter what life *allows*." Susan stood, moved to the side of her desk and placed a large hand on Campbell's narrow shoulder. "My partner won't crack, Dunmore. No matter what. His soul and his backbone are made of stronger, better stuff."

That they were. Campbell had grown more and more impressive every day, but I saw the chief's point, at least somewhat. And then I thought of

Mary attempting to run away from him, terrified. Entering that dining room with a long table filled with guests with sacks over their heads. Thought of Watson scared under that antique table—and changed my mind.

The orange of Garrett's jumpsuit clashed with the shade of his skin and hue of his chlorine-bleached blondish-green hair in a way that nearly made my eyes water. Rather strange, considering his deeply tanned skin was a different shade of orange. For the third time in two days, I had that flash of an out-of-body experience, or perhaps it was more the past folding into the present—the Garrett Griffin of eighteen years before, handsome in the suit he'd worn at our wedding, flickering over this strange giant of a creature he'd become. I had to literally bite my tongue to keep from asking what flashed in my mind every time I saw him—*What happened to you?*

"Are you really going to make them leave these on?" He held up his hands, his wrists cuffed together. "*You* asked to see *me*, and I'm actually agreeing." Without waiting for a response, he glanced toward the one-way mirror of the interrogation room. "I don't believe no one is watching us, or recording, so even if I wanted to kill you, I wouldn't."

A rumbling from Watson's chest issued from underneath the metal chair where I sat, echoing strangely through the cold room.

"Yeah, I wouldn't even kill *you*, you fat thing." Garrett glared at Watson, then twisted to Officer Jackson. "Take these off, or I'm not talking to her."

Officer Jackson merely looked my way and cocked an eyebrow in question.

The temptation to have Jackson leave the cuffs on whispered—both to get under Garrett's skin and simply for my own enjoyment. However, that was one of the ways I knew we were similar—stoking our tempers only made us dig in our heels more. "It's okay, Brent. He won't hurt me." I lifted my gaze to Garrett's eyes. "That would only make his boss angry."

He groaned. "I thought you were insufferable when we were married." Garrett held his hands up to Officer Jackson, and then shook them vigorously once freed, though I knew he had worn them for no more than the short walk from lockup to the interrogation room. After that little production, he flicked his right hand from Brent to the door. "Okay, little man, run along. We're supposed to have privacy, right?"

Officer Jackson gave no hint of hearing him and looked at me. "I'll be right on the other side."

Garrett shuddered in a trembling, mocking way until the door closed, and then he grew serious, turned back to me, glanced at the observation mirror one more time, and then crossed to the metal table and took a seat. "Isn't this all a little strange, Winifred? You're treated like a cop, allowed to do things that're definitely not legal." He gestured between us. "Your dad would find this a mockery."

"How is this not legal?" I copied him, both his calm tone of voice and his gesture, skipping over Dad entirely—going down that path would burn this down before we'd even begun. "No one forced you to come in here—you were *invited* to speak with me. No one's recording. There's nothing attached, good or bad by us talking. This is merely a visit."

A visit Susan nearly refused. I'd waited in her office when she, Campbell, and the chief left. I wasn't exactly sure where he was at the moment—in a cell, getting questioned, who knew. By the time she'd come back in, alone, I'd called Leo up on Chipmunk Mountain, filled him in on what had transpired in our very busy morning, snagged a piece of jerky for Watson from Susan's drawer, and shuffled through the day's events over and over again. When we'd both agreed that we doubted Garrett was the fourth player, sneaking in and setting up the murder-suicide scenario, Susan concurred, finally. Garrett might not be responsible in this instance, but he would be for things to come. Had been in things in the recent past, even if we didn't have hard proof, yet. If she was going to draw out the seventy-two hours to the last minute, I wanted to take advantage and see what I could pull from him, even if it didn't make sense until later.

"Fine, maybe not *illegal*, but still weird." He leaned back slightly, peering under the table toward Watson. "As is your relationship with that dog." He didn't growl back as Watson gave him a warning, just refocused on me, crossing his arms and resting them on the tabletop. "You weren't even a dog person when we were married." The tiniest of flinches and a slight shift in tone. "Or did I just not notice?"

That question was the first since his arrival in Estes Park in which I'd heard the man I had married all those years ago, at least a hint of him. I answered in kind, allowing time to fold in on itself once more, letting it feel like we were just discussing things over our breakfast table at our tiny house in Kansas City. "I wasn't. You're right, or... maybe I didn't know that I was. Never had a dog growing up, which, looking back, I find rather strange." I dropped one of my hands to my side, and Watson answered with a lick across my knuckles. "It may have been Watson specific, at least at first, but I have to admit, there's rarely a dog I meet I don't fall for anymore. Although—" I chuckled. "—it could just be that my life is inundated with them now."

"I've noticed that." He shrugged one of his massive shoulders. "They're fine, I guess. Most of them around here are too small to count as dogs, but Donna's pup? She's going to grow into a real dog. She's going to be huge."

"She really is. Not to mention calm." I laughed again. "Elphie is the most easygoing dog I think I've ever met, especially for a puppy."

"You haven't seen her around me." He grinned, and once more I saw my ex-husband under the horrible tan, horrible hair, and twisting of steroids. "Elphie is *not* a fan of Garrett Griffin." He even winked. "The two of you should start a club."

"I don't think it would stay only the two of us very long." Somehow, though it was an insult and I'd meant it that way, it also wasn't. Almost like an inside joke.

Which was exactly how he took it. "Oh, I've no doubt." The moment passed, at least mostly, when he leaned forward, his tone morphing back into what I'd become familiar with over the last couple of months. "What are we doing in here, Fred? I'm not stupid, I know Green is just making a point with these seventy-two hours, whatever she wants to say. I also know that regardless of how this conversation ends up, it won't change that fact." He raised his eyebrows, holding my gaze. "I *also* know, I can tell, that you don't believe I had anything to do with what happened at that snob's mansion." Another shoulder shrug. "You might have, I'm not sure, but you don't now."

I didn't confirm. "Charlotte came to see me yesterday." Good Lord, was that only yesterday? "She wanted me to help prove your innocence?"

If I wanted a telltale reaction, I didn't get it. "Did she?" I couldn't even tell if he'd been aware of her visit or not.

"She also confirmed that you two are here at Branson's whim."

He scowled at that. "No, she didn't."

"She *also* confirmed that she's afraid of what

Branson will do to Donna because of my relationship with her."

"Ah." He gave the slightest shake of his head, and I thought neither the sound nor the motion was intentional. "I'm sure you're reading into things, as always." He didn't give me a chance to respond before spreading his hands. "What are we doing right now, Fred? I still don't get it."

"I'm not sure, not entirely." I opted for honesty. "I think I'm feeling a little desperate. Thrown off."

Another small flinch, then once more, the Garrett from so long ago was there, at least the ghost of him. "How could you not? From what I hear, what you and everyone else experienced that night would throw anyone off." That ghost hardened. "Not to mention the effect of being paranoid all the time, constantly thinking your ex is so obsessed with you, that he's *right around the corner*."

Watson growled again at the way Garrett said those last five words, almost like Jack Nicholson during one of his manic episodes in *The Shining*. A taunt, a promise.

"This was a mistake." Laying his hands flat on the table he pushed himself up, the metal chair scraping across the floor. "Like every interaction with you, it's just an exercise in frustration, but that's also confirmation that I made the right choice. Because, *wow*, what if I had stayed trapped to you? I'd have pulled a Mason and strung myself up from the rafters a decade ago."

Oh... that was it. Or at least *maybe* that was it— why I'd needed this. A little realization that didn't amount to much, although maybe it did. The disgust and anger at our past. "I know you weren't happy in our marriage, Garrett. Neither was I, though I didn't quite realize just how true that was until it was over. I had no delusions, and it wasn't just the cheating. You weren't happy, I wasn't happy. Maybe we could have been, if we'd made different choices. I don't know. But we weren't." It took all my effort not to stand and face him eye to eye, to allow him to remain looking down on me. "But I know this—you didn't hate me, not during our marriage, not even at the end, even though I thought you did. Even though you might have felt like it from time to time."

"What is this?" It seemed to be Garrett's question of the moment, not that I could blame him. "Another attempt at closure?"

"You *do* hate me now, at least a large part of you. And I can even sense it growing in Charlotte." I paused just long enough to see if he would respond.

He didn't. "I'm sorry, Garrett. I really am. To you and Charlotte both."

He'd started to scoff, but he must have heard my sincerity, as his sneer went slack, and he stared at me in puzzlement. "Why? You've developed martyr syndrome? Taking responsibility for my cheating, for Charlotte ste—*acquiring* your portion of the publishing company?"

Acquiring. That took an effort in restraint, but I let it pass. "No, of course not." I stood then, felt Watson shuffling to avoid the chair as it scooted back, then repositioning himself between my boots under my skirt. "However things went down in our marriage, and however things went down in Charlotte's and my company, neither of you deserve *this*. I would never wish any of this on either of you."

He paled, almost giving himself a natural skin tone for a second, but he didn't respond. Maybe couldn't.

And this, too, was the confirmation I needed, the reason for this brief exchange. I had already known, we all had from the moment they'd arrived in town, why they were here. Charlotte had admitted it in all but word at the Cozy Corgi the day before. Garrett's expression did the same. In the midst of the insanity that was Branson's designs upon my life, this simply offered more confirmation, further grounding, made it more real.

"I promise you this..." I continued to hold his gaze. It didn't even take all that much effort despite looking at each other longer than we had in years. "I'll help break whatever chains Branson has over the two of you, and I'm sorry he's using you as tools to get at me. It would be smart if the two of you would help us, because whether he had something to do with Ethel and Mason or not, that's *exactly* what he'll do to you and Charlotte when he's done, when you've fulfilled your usefulness. He'll throw you away and never think of you again."

Garrett only stared, more confirmation, not that it was needed. His expression remained placid, but there was something in his eyes—not a cry for help and not a curse, but... something.

I'd almost left it there, but instead placed my hands on the table as he had moments before and leaned nearer to him. "But I also promise this—it doesn't matter to me why or how Branson got you involved, doesn't matter to me if the two of you are scared for your lives. If you help him hurt my friends and family in any way, I'll make it my life's mission to turn the seventy-two hours into seventy-two years."

He swallowed—not in fear, he wasn't intimidated, nor had I expected him to be. After several moments, he shrugged both shoulders that time. "Good luck with that." He crossed the room, kicked on the door, and Officer Jackson answered.

"You really don't think he had anything to do with Ethel and Mason?" Susan had popped into the interrogation room a matter of minutes after Jackson had led Garrett back to his cell. She hadn't even bothered to sit during my short debrief, as there wasn't much to share.

"I don't." I'd settled on the floor, my back against the wall, stroking Watson, who sat between my legs. "Not sure if he and Charlotte are weakening and not meaning to confirm in multiple ways that Branson sent them here, or if they—and maybe Branson—have accepted that there's no sense in trying too hard to fool me."

"Hmm." She grunted, almost sounding impressed. "I'm surprised you didn't suggest they're both silently crying out for your help. The old Fred would have."

I answered with my own grunt, considering.

"That's true, I probably would have. But no. I think if that was to ever happen, things would have to get much, much worse for them." I gave Watson a pat on his rump, and he scurried off my skirt. I stood, earning a glare from Susan at the corgi hair that fell from the crinkled folds of fabric. "How are you? Campbell?"

"The chief has been officially booked." Susan jumped over both questions. "For his involvement at Ethel's *and* for what he's been doing for his wife." She shook her head, and when she spoke again, sounded tired. "I knew Chief Briggs was rotten, could feel it. Just like Wexler. But I didn't with Dunmore. I trusted him, I didn't see it coming."

"I don't think you could have. He's not like Briggs. Marlon's a good man, just one who got in over his head and made bad decisions." Again the thought of Mary's brief run from him flashed in my mind. "*Very* bad decisions."

Susan refrained from further comment and peered down at Watson, who'd trotted over to her and sat without prompting. "Cute, Officer Fleabag, but don't think I didn't notice *someone*—" Her gaze flicked to me briefly. "—got an extra buffalo jerky stick without permission. You're lucky *you're* not in a cell for seventy-two hours."

He only continued to stare up at her in pleading adoration.

She rolled her eyes, then leaned against the wall, letting out a sigh. "Is it just me or have the past couple days flashed by in a matter of hours but also seemed to take *years*. I'm exhausted."

"Me too." I really was, to the point I could almost ask Susan to lock Watson and me up for those seventy-two hours for an uninterrupted three-day nap. "Ethel seems like a lifetime ago, but also like I'm just walking down into that garage and finding that flashing thirty-minute makeshift bomb."

She offered another grunt. "Yeah, I'm sure you're more tired than I am. I can't imagine what that night must have been like." She bent, patted Watson's head, then opened the door to the interrogation room again. "But you two get out of here. I'm going to try to wrap up paperwork, if possible, and call it an early day myself."

Surprising both of us, Watson sprang up and then dashed through the door, letting out a happy bark, leash whipping behind at his escape.

"Great." Susan rolled her eyes. "What does that mean? Someone arrested Ben, Leo, or your stepfather? If I have to put up with Barry Adams this afternoon, I'm calling it an early retirement."

I almost commented about Susan knowing Watson's list of favorite people, but figured I'd cut her a break and not tease in her fragile state of being —at least as fragile as Susan Green was capable.

As we approached the entrance, Watson's other favorite person was kneeling on the ground and greeting him with equal enthusiasm, petting him and releasing a torrent of corgi fur.

Carla Beaker sat on the long bench next to her, glaring daggers at Susan. "You've *got* to be kidding me? You told *Fred* before *me*?" She stood, hands trembling. "Whatever this is, it's no one's business but *mine*."

"Carla..." I halted, completely confused. "I don't know anything. I'm not sure—"

"Fred is here for a different reason." It showed how exhausted Susan truly was that Carla got by with having such a tone. "And I didn't know you were here, either. I'd asked Officer Lin to call you to set up a time."

"Yeah." She gestured down at Donna, who looked uncomfortably caught in the middle. "And told her to tell me to bring some support, that I might need it. You *really* thought I was gonna wait around to find out what that was? I came as soon as I got off the phone with her."

"Oh." Susan let out a long breath, one that was shaky.

Noticing, Carla paled. "It's that bad?" Fear replaced anger. "Just tell me now. Get it over with."

"No." Susan attempted a smile and gestured toward her office. "I'm just tired, but I'll see you now. Why don't you and Donna come on back?" She offered what I thought was meant to be a smile my way. "We'll chat later. Maybe tomorrow. I say let's not even think about anything else for the rest of the day."

Carla followed Susan as Donna got to her feet, giving Watson a pat goodbye and squeezing my arm as she passed. "You doing okay?"

There was that question again. "Yeah, I'm fine." It took all my willpower not to ask what was going on.

Releasing me, she followed the others. True to form, Watson followed right along with her.

"No, buddy." I snagged the end of his leash just in time. "We'll see Donna later."

He whimpered, then gave a pitiful mournful howl before glaring back at me.

Carla paused in the doorway to Susan's office and looked in to where I assumed Susan had already disappeared. "Fred really doesn't know?" I couldn't hear the response, but I was certain of the answer, as I had absolutely no idea. She sighed, looked back to me, then Watson, then Donna. Then me again. There was a softening in her green eyes. "You know what, I have exactly one person in my life who I trust besides my son." She let out a choked laugh. "Not that I ever had many. But somehow, now that Ethel is gone and everything being revealed, it only highlights how alone I've always been. I know we're not friends necessarily, and *Lord knows* you drive me absolutely nuts, but I trust you. And..." She glanced at Donna again, then back to me once more. "Well, it's clearer than ever that you and I are on the same side. So... whatever I'm about to hear, I'd like you to do it with me. Bring the mutt." She didn't wait for my reply, just disappeared into Susan's office.

Donna smiled in a sappy way, like she'd just lived a rom-com moment and hurried back to Watson, assuring him all was fine, then filled me in as much as she dared in a brief whisper. "Officer Lin called a little bit ago. Apparently, there's something from the other night they've uncovered that they think Carla needs to know as soon as possible. They asked her to bring support, and... to not have Maverick with her." She started to head to the office, then glanced back, explaining one more detail. "He's with Nate and Elphie."

I followed Donna and Watson back into Susan's office, which was beginning to feel like a second home. Part of me wanted to turn around and leave, both feeling like I was intruding and unsure if I could handle another bomb drop, but curiosity and affection for Carla Beaker, to a level I never would have imagined, superseded.

Carla and Donna sat across from Susan, occupying where Campbell and I had been less than an hour before, Watson shoved against Donna's legs, of course. I claimed the chair the chief had sat in, hoping whatever was about to be revealed wouldn't be as bad as his betrayal.

For just a moment, Carla gaped, wide-eyed, around Susan's little office, and I could imagine what she was feeling, had experienced it myself at the sight of all the boards and papers laying out each of our stories, the characters Ethel assigned us. She paused on her own sheet, the things written there, some of which weren't overly flattering, and then switched to Susan. "Tell me all at once, whatever it is. I've already been at wit's end, and now this? You call with some vague warning, making me think it's something about my son because you want me to leave him at home. I've never been so—"

"I'm sorry, it wasn't meant to be a warning." Susan's apology stopped Carla in her tracks, and she pushed on before it could continue. "I didn't intend to scare you, but I can understand why I did." She spared a quick glance toward me. "We received some information this morning, the kind I did *not* share with Fred, but I wanted to pass it on to you as soon as possible." She pulled a small pile of papers from the stacks covering her desk. "I asked some colleagues in Denver to take a look at these as they have more experience and expertise in this area than we do." For a moment, she looked like she wasn't sure what to say and then, in pure Susan fashion, charged ahead. "I think you're aware that Ethel did a paternity test on your son?"

"Yes. Forced me to allow it so she wouldn't cut Maverick from his inheritance. As if I would have ever cheated on Jonathan." Carla had slipped into disgust, but it fell away as she sat up straighter. "Why? Was there something bad in there?" She flipped back and forth between panic and anger. "He *is* Jonathan's son. I don't care what that test said. I was faithful, have always been—"

"He's Jonathan's son. And... yours, obviously."

She handed the stack to Carla but didn't pause in her explanation. "Ethel didn't just search for paternity, but had an extensive, *quite* extensive, DNA and genetic testing completed as well."

"Okay..." Worry increased in Carla's tone, along with dread. "I... don't understand." She'd taken the papers and stared at them, all color drained from her face.

Donna had continued petting Watson, but her hand slowed in a way that suggested she might know what was coming.

"One of the things that caught our eye, and one of the things I didn't understand, which is why I contacted professionals before reaching out to you, was one of the findings." Susan gestured across her desk toward the papers Carla held. "Near the top you'll see a section labeled observations. In it, it says that they discovered a mutation in Maverick's TNT gene." Susan wrinkled her nose. "No. No, it's the..." She fluttered her hands. "Whatever it's called doesn't matter."

"TTN," Donna offered up before she'd even read the papers.

"Yes." Susan nodded.

"A mutation?" Carla's voice shot up, and she

looked back and forth between Donna and Susan. "What does that mean? Is he sick?"

"Do you mind?" Donna spared a quick glance toward Susan.

"Please." Susan looked more relieved than I'd ever seen her. "As a pharmacist, I'm sure you understand this a lot more than I do."

Donna gave a little wince. "Not my main area of study, obviously, but I'm familiar." She smiled gently at Carla but didn't waste any more time, taking the papers and giving them a brief look, then nodding. "Okay, that's what I assumed." Back to Carla. "Mutations in the TTN gene indicate a... risk or possibility for cardiomyopathy. It's a very common genetic heart disease."

Carla whimpered and cringed back.

My heart broke for her, she had received blow after blow after blow for the last couple of months—in some ways, for the past couple of decades.

"It's kind of a good thing," Susan broke in. "At least that's what—"

"A *good* thing?" Carla's voice shot up again; it was almost a relief to hear her anger. "How in the world is a heart disease a good thing?"

"That's what they told you?" Donna's question was addressed at Susan, who nodded. She scanned the report for another second and then nodded as well, but this time to Carla. "Like I said, it's a *risk* or a *possibility*. All it means is that Maverick is a higher risk to develop this heart disease at some point."

"How is that a good—"

"*Because...*" Donna reached out and grabbed Carla's wrist. "Now we know. It may never show up, but if it did, it could have done so quietly and not made itself known until it was too late. There are things to do, precautions to take, from diet to tests..." She shook the report she held in her other hand. "This very easily could save Maverick's life. Of course, there are tests that would need to be run *now*, but nothing's come up so far, and he's about the healthiest little guy I've ever seen." She smiled. "Again, this is a *good* thing. Like the gene that lets women know if they're susceptible to breast cancer or not, it can save lives. For all the horrible things Ethel did, she might have saved Maverick's life from a sudden heart attack when he's twenty or forty or who knows. But now... he's a billion times safer than he would have been before this information."

Carla was trembling. At some point, Watson had popped up and laid his head on her lap. I doubt she even noticed when she began to stroke his head.

"You're not just trying to sugarcoat things, make me feel better?"

"No." Donna shook her head and smiled, a genuine bright thing. "I'm really not. Sure, it would be better if there was no mutation at all, but really, this is a very, very good thing."

"I'm sorry to scare you, Carla." Susan apologized for the second time in minutes—the Earth had to have stopped spinning. "I didn't want to tell you this over the phone, and I didn't get the explanation quite as clear as what Donna offered, but it matches what they told us. They said you would need to know so you could help keep your son safe." She smiled. "Ethel, despite her best effort, apparently did something good."

Carla let out a long shaky breath, glanced down into her lap, gave a little flinch of surprise realizing what she was doing, then continued to stroke Watson. "Why would Ethel do that?" She murmured to herself more than anyone else from the way it sounded. "Why was she worried about anything else other than if Maverick was a Beaker or not."

Something rang familiar in those words, but I couldn't place it. Even so, I thought I understood. "Because she and Mason were taking him out of the country to… wherever they were going to end up. It might have been selfish, but Ethel loved him. I imagine it was precautionary, that way they would know how to take care of him, just in case something happened."

"Or make certain he was worthy enough to take with them." Susan, too, had spoken to herself and gave a little flinch, clearly not meaning to say it out loud. For the third time, she apologized to Carla. "Sorry."

"No, you're totally right." Carla barked a laugh, and it was a comfort to hear the growl in her voice. "That's more what it was. Guaranteed."

"Huh." Donna grunted as well, though it was a very different sound, and unintentional.

"What?" Carla whipped back to her, panic flaring again. "What did you find? Is something else wrong?"

"No!" Donna had released Carla, but she grabbed her again, shaking her head. "No, not at all. I'm so sorry. I was just reading and was a little surprised, but absolutely nothing's wrong."

"Well, what is it?" I hadn't heard Carla take that tone with Donna before, but I couldn't blame her.

Proving it really was nothing dangerous, Donna gently pointed to something else on the page. "On the fourth chromosome, they found an abnormality on the FBFR3 gene."

"*Donna!*" Carla's snarl was so vicious that time that Watson ducked out of her lap, scurried across the office, and darted under my skirt—my brave little Superman.

"Sorry." Donna didn't pause for another prompt. "Again, nothing that's wrong, and nothing that will affect Maverick in any way. It's just that they found he's carrying the gene that causes dwarfism, so... there's a possibility that he could pass it on to children or grandchildren, but very remote."

"Dwarfism?" Carla sat back, not horrified, just shocked. "What does that mean? How could that happen? No one in our family—"

"It's not always hereditary, but—"

"He's not a Beaker." I hadn't meant to cut Donna off, but now that I understood why Carla's words a moment before sounded familiar, I turned to her. Not that she gave me a chance to speak.

"Fred! I have already said, he is *Jonathan's* son." She looked every bit as ready to kill me as Ethel had been.

"No, I know. He is." I couldn't help but laugh at the realization. "He *is* Jonathan's son. But he's not a Beaker, neither is Jonathan."

"*What?*" Carla's voice shot up once more, and she looked at me like I was mad. Susan and Donna did as well.

"Don't you remember when you confronted Ethel that night at the table? About the paternity test, about *you* not being good enough for the Beaker blood." It all clicked together, every single bit. As it did, I felt myself calm; it seeped through in my voice. "Ethel said she never cared about the Beaker blood, that she only cared if he was a Roberts, which I assumed was her maiden name."

"It was." Carla nodded, had calmed as well. "Yeah, I remember." She scrunched up her face in confusion. "You're not going to say she somehow found out that *she* wasn't Jonathan's mother. That would be the most ridiculous thing I..." Her eyes widened, and she sucked in her breath. "Oh... not a Beaker. *She* cheated on Eustace. Ethel cheated on Eustace. Jonathan was never a Beaker." She laughed, though it was short before fury blazed in her eyes. "And *she* had the nerve to accuse me constantly of cheating on Jonathan."

"Mason..." Susan barely breathed the butler's name, nodding slowly, and looked at me. "You said Katie found out that Mason's mother was a little person and his father had dwarfism."

Carla looked back and forth between us, gaped at me as I nodded in affirmation to Susan and then breathed it out in shock. "Jonathan was Mason's son?" Another laugh. "The mighty heir to the Beaker fortune was the son of the *butler*?" She threw back her head and really laughed—in a frantic, manic, almost uncomfortable manner until tears streamed. Laughed in a way that suggested all the tension that had been building was starting to escape. "Good grief. I've got to admit that the day Eustace Beaker died was one of the happiest in my life, promptly followed by Ethel's. But I wish they were alive right now so I could see the look on his face. There is *no way* that man knew Jonathan wasn't his son. None at all."

"I don't think Mason knew either." I said it to Carla, but instantly turned to Susan, working through it. "You found the main page of that report in Ethel's pocket in the library. Why would she have had that with her? Everything else was packed, ready to go—all the paperwork, finances, everything else. She didn't throw that test in Carla's face, there was no reason for Ethel to have it on her during her messed-up Clue game." It was all speculation, but I knew I was right. Could feel it like I hadn't felt certainty in days. "How much you wanna bet her little announcement to Carla was the first time Mason had heard that proclamation of Ethel not caring if Maverick was a Beaker? How much you wanna bet he'd seen that report, already had it partially or fully figured out, had it with him and confronted Ethel with it in the library?"

"Hit her with the candlestick in a rage." Susan played it through, nodded even as she spoke. "And then hung himself. Either out of guilt, remorse, or to avoid consequences."

"Or because he'd just killed the woman he loved, whether she betrayed him or not." That was my guess, though I supposed we'd never know.

"That hypocritical, evil..." Carla shuddered, shut her eyes, and then twisted back to Donna. "I don't care who his grandfather was. That gene doesn't pose any danger for Maverick, can't make him sick, or shorten his life?"

"No, sweetheart." Donna shook her head and smiled. "And thanks to that test, he's now safer than he's ever been in his life."

"Thank God." Carla sat back, wiped tears from her eyes, and then breathed out another little laugh. "And actually, with Ethel gone, we're *all* safer than we've ever been in our lives. Even if we didn't realize it."

The mystery-room fireplace crackled as snow began to fall over Estes Park again later that afternoon. For the first time in what felt like years, although unbelievably it was only three days, relaxation fully and completely washed over me. Leo had come down from Chipmunk Mountain after I'd left the police station, and I'd filled him and Katie in on all that had been uncovered and what we believed happened between Mason and Ethel. There was no way to prove it, but I was as certain as I could be. And if we chuckled somewhat indulgently that Susan was going to finish out Garrett's seventy-two-hour hold, just for good measure, I wasn't going to feel guilty about that.

After Leo headed back to Chipmunk Mountain to finish the day, with the promise of picking up Golden Rabbit *and* a couple of pints of Ben and Jerry's on his way home, I'd decided another childhood favorite was in order, since I'd finished *The Secret Garden*.

With the fire heating against the April snow, Watson snoring peacefully on his ottoman, and the light from the purple Portobello lampshade falling over the first chapter of *A Girl of the Limberlost*, I was caught off guard once more by a figure silhouetted in the doorway. For a moment, I thought it was Charlotte, coming to berate me for not getting Garrett free, or to offer some vague threat. But then Jennifer Sallee moved the rest of the way in and motioned to the other side of the antique sofa. "Mind if I sit?"

Watson lifted his head, inspected the mayor through narrowed eyes, then with a groan, returned to his dreams, not the least bit concerned.

"Please do." I swiveled, sliding my feet from where they'd been stretched out, to the floor, and closed the book in my lap. "I assume Detective Green filled you in on everything that's gone on today?"

Jennifer sat, nodding slowly, her long hair swaying slightly. "Yeah..." She let out a breath and looked at me. "I'm ashamed to admit both the level of terror that rushed through me when Susan informed me I was supposed to be one of the players in Ethel's game, and the immense relief that I wasn't." She attempted a smile. "If presented with such a scenario beforehand, I would have sworn I wouldn't have more than batted an eye, that I would have fought the masked man off, broken out of Ethel's mansion, freed everybody."

"There was a time I probably would have thought the same." More than probably. "I've learned the hard way that's much easier said than done. And don't be ashamed that you're glad you missed out on that experience, it's the only sensible reaction."

She nodded again, seemed to get stuck staring at Watson, a million miles away more like.

After giving her several moments, I offered a prompt I'd been given countless times over the last three days. "Are you okay?"

More nodding, and then Jennifer seemed to come back to herself. "It's strange and a rather horrible experience discovering you're not exactly who you thought you were."

I thought she meant Jonathan Beaker not being a Beaker at all and then realized the obvious. "Marlon said you'd severed ties with Ethel, that you decided to not use her money for your political campaign. Sounds to me like you were exactly who you thought you were, in the end."

"It shouldn't have taken seeing myself through your eyes when you confronted me last month to make me wake up." She flipped her hair over her shoulder, almost resembling Delilah. "I'm one of the good ones, at least that's what I told myself. Incorruptible." She chuckled, though there wasn't really any humor in it. "Sorry. I didn't come here for a pity party or whatever I'm doing. I actually came to..." That time her laugh was somewhat more genuine. "Well, to say I was sorry. For letting you down, for letting the town down, and—"

"You didn't." I reached over, grabbed her arm and squeezed, but didn't let go. I figured there was more than one trigger to her crisis. "You also don't need to feel guilty about not being with us in Ethel's mansion, or even for what Mary experienced. None of that was your fault, no matter what choices you made before."

"Maybe not. If I hadn't angered Ethel, maybe she wouldn't have—"

"This was about me, not you." I sighed. "I do my best not to feel guilty about that and fail most of the time. A lot of the drama that's happened in Estes recently is because of me. But as I'm constantly reminded, it's nothing I chose or nothing I caused, but still... none of this was your fault."

"Yours either."

I shrugged. "Like I said, sometimes I agree with that."

"I'm dropping my campaign entirely, I wanted you to know. No more ambitions of being governor of Colorado, or..." A slight blush rose to her cheeks and her voice dipped. "Or fantasies about being the first woman president."

"Oh..." I couldn't help but smile. "You *did* have goals."

"I did. Self-aggrandized, clearly." She sat straighter and began to sound more like herself. "I'm not going to move too rapidly and withdraw from politics in Estes, not yet. But I am considering it. I've proven to not be the woman I thought I was."

"Again, Jennifer, that's not true." With a final squeeze on her arm, I released her and sat back. "Like I said, in the end you did the right thing. And I would imagine, now that you've looked into that darkness, shadow, or temptation, whatever you wanna call it, and are on the other side, you'll recognize when it whispers again. If anything, I'd say you're more equipped to be exactly what we need in all our politicians, whether that's local, state, or even presidential." I winked. "I'd vote for you."

She flinched, looking genuinely surprised, and

when she spoke again, her voice was thick. "Well, I'll have to sit with that for a moment... or several." She cleared her throat and then offered me a smile as well. "And you? I've been knocking on your door to become part of the town council for ages now, and here we are with yet another open seat."

I shuddered. "You realize that prospect is looking worse every day."

"Really?" She leaned closer, offering a scandalized whisper. "I would think it would sound better than ever now. Didn't you hear? Ethel Beaker's seat is available."

I laughed, tried to pull it in to be respectful of the dead, or whatever, and then laughed all the harder. "You know, I *did* hear that."

The mayor continued chuckling, absentmindedly reached out to stroke Watson in his sleep, and received a mighty glare for her affection. After an apology to him and quickly withdrawing her hand, she proved to be ever tenacious. "I still wish you would consider it. You can do a lot of good, not that you don't already."

"Even if I was slightly tempted, I've been playing with the idea of expanding into the book world again, though I'm not sure how. I was thinking mystery conferences and such, but..." Goodness, that idea felt like three years ago instead of three days. "I don't know. At the moment, I just want to enjoy what I have."

"Fair enough." She gave a wink. "But in fair warning, this won't be the last time I ask." She grew serious once more. "However, that isn't why I came by. I just wanted to tell you what I did before... that I'm sorry, and more than anything, thank you for helping me see the slippery slope I was going down. I appreciate it." Before I could tell her no thanks was needed, she stood, started to turn toward the door, then froze. "Oh, Rene wanted me to invite you and Watson to a little ceremony for Granny Smith."

I let out a sigh at the thought of that old, raggedy cat. "Of course Dr. Sallee is taking care of her, just like he promised Watson."

"Yes. He's one of the good ones, that husband of mine. Truly incorruptible." Jennifer sighed softly and looked at Watson as she spoke. "One of us will let you know when, and we'll, of course, adjust our schedule to meet yours. When her ashes come back, we'll spread them over Colin Apple's grave, as he dictated in his will. Colin had his faults, to be sure, but he adored Granny Smith; he and that cat were inseparable. But Rene thought she deserved a proper memorial with the few she seemed to care about."

"I couldn't think of anything more perfect for her, or him." My heart warmed at the thought. "We'll be there."

The rest of the afternoon was a balm for the last few days—Watson's snores, the snow, the fire, the book, more pastries, of course. I didn't experience a solitary flash from Ethel's mansion, didn't consider Garrett or Charlotte, didn't even dwell on future possibilities for the book world. The moment was enough, more than.

After Katie and I locked up, I called Leo as I got into the car, offered to pick up the ice cream so he could come straight home after getting the Chinese food. He took me up on the offer and said he should be home within the hour.

Gripping a grocery bag with pints of Half Baked and Chocolate Therapy in one hand, I used my other to open the passenger door of the Mini Cooper for Watson to hop out. Though it was still well over an hour before sunset, with the clouds and the snow, the evening was dim. Quiet, relaxing, it would be a perfect night to be home with hot Chinese food and then ice cream in front of the fire.

Perhaps it was a testament to how relaxed I'd

been in the mystery room, or how drained Watson and I were from the past several days, that it wasn't until we'd almost reached the porch that Watson growled. For my part, I hadn't noticed or felt anything at all. Even so, from the second the rumble issued from Watson's chest, I knew what was about to happen. Without even thinking, I dropped the bag of ice cream and slipped my hand into my pocket, grabbing my cell.

"Don't do that." Branson accentuated his calm command with the cocking of a gun. "What fun would that be?"

Watson's growl turned into a snarl.

"Oh, come now, Watson. You know your mama is always safe with me." He chuckled. "Sorry, Fred. I know that gets under your skin."

Maybe fear prickled over my skin or trailed down my spine, surely, but I didn't feel it. Instead, frustration and exhaustion settled in equal measure, weighing me down. I should have seen this coming, and I couldn't handle any more. With a sigh, I turned in the direction Watson was glaring and found Branson leaning against the edge of the cabin, nearly concealed in shadow, though some of the evening light glinted off the pistol. "It's also ludicrous to make that claim when you're holding us at gunpoint."

"Valid." He didn't move but gestured slightly with the pistol. "Drop the phone next to the bag, please. And don't try to tap the screen without me noticing, making some random phone call. Such desperation is beneath you, plus, I'll notice, and I'll react."

"Oh, Branson." His name was a sigh on my lips, an unintentional mummer. "Do we *have* to do this? I'm so tired."

He didn't answer for a few seconds, and I got the sense he was debating, maybe changing plans, granting my request. "Sorry, Winifred. I know you've been through a lot. That wasn't my intention."

The laughter that burst from me sounded just as tired as I felt.

"Fair." He didn't sound insulted. "I guess I should say *how it all went down* wasn't my intention. But yes, we have to do this." He stepped out of the shadows, walked toward us slowly, footfalls crunching ever so softly on the snow.

I tightened my grip on Watson's leash; his growl increased. The momentary options flashed through my mind—running, fighting, sitting down and sobbing, or just lying down in the snow and taking a nap. Instead, I followed directions and dropped my cell next to the ice cream. "Now what?"

"We take a drive." Branson continued his path toward me, pausing just out of Watson's reach. "I'm sure you know where."

For a second, I didn't, but then the obvious hit me, and I couldn't hold back a groan. "Seriously?"

"I put a lot of effort into that. I won't let Ethel waste it all."

"Fine." I gave another sigh and took a step toward the porch. "Let me just put Watson inside and—"

"Again, you force me to say I'm sorry." He gestured with the gun to the car. "He goes with us, of course. Watson will get you to behave better than I ever could on my own."

Another option flashed through my mind—dropping the leash, making Watson run. However, he wouldn't. Not unless I did something cruel, which I could never do to him. And even if I did, Watson out in the woods, in the snow, at night. *No...* He was safer with Branson.

Another gesture to the car. "I parked elsewhere, somewhere you don't need to know. For now, you drive." He paused, considering Watson. "If you don't think you can keep him under control as you drive, put him in the trunk."

"He'll be fine." I took a couple of steps toward

the Mini Cooper, having to drag Watson with me, then paused to look back at Branson. "If you so much as touch a hair on Watson's head, I'll drive us over a mountain or into a tree or—"

"That works for me, Fred." The smile softened, a dreaminess entering his expression. "As long as I'm with you."

With that, my exhaustion vanished, drowned under a wave of revulsion.

Watson stayed on my lap as I drove, which between his heft and the slickness starting to cover the streets, made it a very real possibility that I might unintentionally keep that threat of driving over a mountain or into a tree. He didn't squirm too much, thankfully, but I didn't trust him not to attack Branson, or rather... didn't trust Branson's reaction if Watson gave it a try.

In truth, very little of my attention was focused on the road or Watson's uncomfortable position—fear overtook everything. The pounding of my heart blotted out Branson's quiet instructions... if that's what they were. Flashes from three nights before collided with projections of what he might have planned—the tunnels, the dining room, the six weapons, although, those weren't there; the police would have taken them for evidence. Of course, that didn't mean Branson didn't have a spare set.

The rush of blood and adrenaline continued to speed up across town, reaching a fever pitch as we entered the exclusive subdivision overlooking Mary's Lake, and finally came to stop in front of Ethel's sweeping porch steps.

Branson might have given me directions of how to exit the car, to hold Watson's leash, walk up the porch, but I had no recollection. Just a vague memory of those actions, the flash of him ripping down the yellow police tape across the door and then smooth as silk picking a lock with one hand while keeping the gun aimed at me with the other.

As I stepped back inside Ethel's mansion for the third time in so many days, the opposite of what I would have predicted happened. My fear fell away, my blood pressure dropped—not to the place that I could claim to be relaxed, but below the panic level—and my brain began to take over again. It didn't matter what Branson had planned, I only needed to keep him occupied for an hour, maybe a little more. Leo would show up at our house, find my car missing and the ice cream and cell phone in the snow, and he would know. He would call Susan, and they would both realize where I was. It was obvious.

However, Branson might be crazed, but he was still no fool. If he hadn't picked up the ice cream and my cell, it was because he wasn't worried about them. Whatever he had planned wasn't going to take too much time. Some of that panic rushed back, though I tried to hold it at bay—I needed to stay as alert and clear as possible.

"Don't look like that." Branson tsked as he locked the front door and flipped on a switch illuminating the chandelier, then adjusting the brightness so it was a soft glow. "You don't actually think I brought you here to kill you, do you?"

"You said yourself, you didn't wanna waste the game."

He flinched, and disgust edged his words. "Stop it. Immediately! Don't act like you don't know me. Don't act like you don't understand." He didn't notice Watson growling, thankfully. "Don't be stupid. You are *not* stupid. You know the point of the game wasn't to kill you, and that isn't why we're here. So *don't* act like you are afraid of me. It's insulting. To both of us."

The anger radiating contradicted his words. I knew he believed he wouldn't kill me, maybe believed the game hadn't been to kill me, either. But that didn't mean he couldn't surprise himself. "So, what was the point of the game, then?" I could claim asking the question was merely killing time for us to be discovered, but that wouldn't entirely be true. "Or was it a game of terror, where you sit me around the table with those closest to me and kill them one by one?"

He snarled, lip curling over his teeth. "If that pompous butler hadn't killed Ethel, I'd do it myself. Taking my gift for you and twisting it, making you afraid. After all my work, after all that effort." He reached out as if he was going to take my hand, but Watson lunged, growling and snarling. Branson took a couple of skittering steps backward, even that movement graceful.

"Stop, buddy, *stop*." I kneeled instantly, slipping my hand into his collar, clearly the length of the leash was too much. "Please."

He continued to growl but didn't pull against my restraint too hard.

Branson stared at him, taking several slow breaths as if he was counting to ten. "I think we should probably secure Watson somewhere. I don't want to hurt him, but if he tries that again, I can't promise that I won't, either by accident or in temper."

"Fine." That worked for me. A relief. "How about we put him in the car?"

"No." He gestured down the hallway with the

gun. "There's a little half bath; just put him in and close the door."

I remembered, vaguely. I'd done nothing more than poke my head in and then abandon it. Without waiting, I scooped Watson up and hurried down the hall, flicking on the light in the little powder room and pressing a kiss to Watson's head before murmuring apologies as I placed him on the floor and slid another pocket door closed.

He began to bark like mad and pound against the wood panel. I hated to leave Watson in his panic, his fear, but he was safer. And I was more likely to find a way out or something to use against Branson without trying to protect Watson.

"Now..." Branson held out a hand, his tone elegant and stately, like a lord of a manor. "Shall we?"

I stared at his hand like it was a viper, a bomb... or like it was the hand of someone who'd killed countless people and seemed to make it his life's mission to torture me. With a glance at the powder-room door, where I could just make out the flash of Watson's pacing shadow underneath the gap, I slipped my hand into Branson's.

"Allow me to give you the tour, my dear."

The *shall we* and the *my dear* were new. He

hadn't spoken like that before, not like some fancy aristocrat.

He took a step back toward the entrance, then paused, looking at me with apology. "I do realize you've seen everything, but humor me. This moment was stolen after great effort and great cost on my part. I will never forgive that woman."

What Branson had said moments ago returned, now that Watson was safe. "Mason killed Ethel in the library?"

He grinned. "With the *candlestick*." Then he chuckled. "If they were going to ruin this, at least they played out a version of the game themselves."

"Then he hung himself?"

"With the *rope*, in the *library*." He laughed, and it wasn't crazed or wild. It was the same laugh I had heard on our dates, as we sat at the windows at Chipmunk Manor overlooking the lights of Estes—pure enjoyment, almost wholesome-sounding. "It was the butler. How cliché is that?" Another laugh, though it turned dark. "Even that they got wrong. There wasn't a butler in the game."

"So... you *were* watching." Without thinking, I pulled my hand from his, insulted, which was utterly ridiculous. "You watched us in terror as Ethel stole the game from you and nearly killed us all. You just sat back and watched. Did you have popcorn?" Me and my temper.

Again, Branson looked wounded instead of furious. He clasped my hand again, yanked it to his chest. "Never." His fury came then, though not at me. "I don't remember the last time someone attempted to go behind my back, much less achieved it. I did *not* know you were here; I did *not* know that was happening. Not for a couple of hours after it was over. I was in... I was overseas, which is why it took me so long to get back to you, to make things right." He pulled my hand from his chest to his lips, kissing my fingers. "I watched in horror, even though I already knew you were okay, as you fought for your life. Watched in tears your struggle, and how close you came to dying." His grip was iron on my hand, but he flung out his other, gesturing with the gun. "In the place I designed for you. As a gift. She used it to cause you pain, to nearly take you from me."

I'd already known it had been a split-second event that had saved our lives, but it hadn't been clearer than at that moment. The fact that Branson hadn't been watching? He hadn't even known until after? I hadn't expected that, and I wasn't entirely sure why it made a difference. But it did. Even after the revelation that Maverick was Mason's grandson, part of me had still wondered if Branson had met Ethel and her butler in the library and handled things on his own.

"I'm sorry, Winifred. I'm so sorry." He pressed a kiss again to my fingers, then released me and took a step back.

He was sincere. Branson's remorse and even his fear were palpable, and despite having come to terms with his instability—which seemed to be growing more intense every interaction—I couldn't quite add it up, nor could I hold my tongue. "You act like you're devastated to cause me pain, but you continue to torment me, make it your life's mission. You sent Garrett and Charlotte to live here. You called me from Wanda's porch threatening to kill the Twister Sisters..."

"I did not." Anger flashed again. "And that was for you as well. I took Dean and his father out of the picture, for *you*. It was only a matter of time before they came and hunted you down in retribution for ending the Irons family."

Branson had been the one to initiate the midnight massacre, taking out most of the remaining Irons family members. However, I knew what he said about Dean's vendetta was true, but I also knew it was only one of Branson's motives. And *what* was

I doing trying to make sense out of Branson's actions?

"Besides..." Coolness entered his tone again, reflected in his smile. "You're only *assuming* your ex-husband and your ex-best friend are here on my command. Endless accusations on your part, my dear."

Who was he kidding? I didn't think he expected me to doubt Garrett and Charlotte at this point; it was just one of his games. I didn't bother saying so, but as he cocked his head in that mocking way, the light from the chandelier illuminated him more clearly than I'd been able to see all night. Like the last time he'd been in town, sitting in my mystery room, holding Leo and me captive at gunpoint, which was really getting old, he'd been back to his picture-perfect self—tall, dark, and handsome, swept-back hair, understated but expensive clothes, elegant, refined, beautifully sinister. The same was true in that moment, though there was more gray than black at his temples, and between his bright green eyes, something was different about his nose. It took me a moment, and then I recalled. I'd punched him in the woods outside my cabin. Slapped *and* punched, but the second had brought blood. "Your nose is crooked. You didn't get it set." Good God, what was wrong with me? Watson's continued barking seemed to be asking the same thing.

"I did not." He smiled again, his voice shifting to pride. "It's not every woman who would break my nose, and not only because I wouldn't let them get away with it, but who could even manage to try, let alone succeed."

And my skin began to crawl once more.

Apparently, I didn't do a very good job of hiding that, as a wounded expression flickered over his face, followed by anger. "You can pretend to be disgusted by me, Winifred. And *yes*, I know you married little goody two-shoes with the checkered past. But you know *me*. Just like I know *you*." He moved closer, lifted his hand, and gripped my jaw, tempting me to punch him again. "You've proven it over and over again, and you did so that night. Standing in the library, not shaken by Ethel's and Mason's worthless bodies. Your brain working. I could see what you were thinking. You knew I'd made this for you, so you thought to yourself... *What would Branson do for me?* And you knew. You didn't even need a second guess, it was instant. You told the others to find a lever in the books, because that's what I would leave for you. You saw *The Detective's Daughter*. You knew. You discovered my gift, my little corgi pin."

He drew nearer, so close I could feel his breath on my face, smell coffee and chocolate. Close enough I thought he was going to kiss me. "You know me, just like I know you."

Even with his fingers digging into my jaw, I thrust it upward in defiance. "If you try to kiss me right now, I won't just break your nose, I'll shove it through your skull."

"I know you would." He smiled in a way that made me regret my words. "I know you would try." He released me, leaned away, and repositioned the gun.

Had I missed my chance? I'd forgotten the gun; I could have grabbed it. Regret was pointless. *Be ready for next time, look for another option.*

"The minutes are ticking faster than I would like." He used the gun once more, gesturing up the steps. "You've already seen down here. Come upstairs, let me explain my vision."

I only hesitated for a moment, then stepped in front of him and took the steps slowly, one at a time.

"You see, I'd only been planning on this first floor, only the Clue game at the beginning. But then... I wanted to give you more." As he spoke, the steps creaked from behind. "Each of the rooms up here was going to be fashioned after your beloved mystery novels. A game on the first floor, your mysteries on the second. The perfect birthday gift for you."

I froze. *Birthday* gift? That was a little less than two months away, the end of May. Ethel really had stolen this from him. Unable to stop myself, I turned around, anger and disbelief coursing through me. "How is this a *gift*? What is broken in you to make you think this is a gift? Making people I love play a real-life murder-mystery game? Making one of them kill someone else so that there'd be a Mr. Boddy? What would you do? Kill someone else every ten minutes if I didn't guess correctly?"

"No!" he growled again, offense returning. "That was Ethel. *She* spoiled it, poisoned it. This was a *gift*, something you would have loved. Something you've been wanting."

"Something I've been wanting?" The gun was forgotten again. However, I saw my chance. We were three-fifths up the stairs. I could shove him, kick him, knock him down the steps. Dive at him make us both tumble. "The only body I want to see dead is *yours*. Were you going to let someone kill you, and then I would have to figure out who? If so, let's pretend today is my birthday."

Pain swept over his handsome face. "No. Your father was going to be Mr. Boddy, not me."

I'd lifted my hands, getting ready to shove him, but they got stuck. I got stuck. Everything stuck, even my brain. As I tried to reason it out—a million options flashing in half a heartbeat—the back of my mind screamed the reminder that there was no figuring Branson out, and to push him, push him, *push him.* "My father is dead. What were you going to do, desecrate his grave?"

"No, darling. Use him in name only." He gripped both my hands, which were still frozen in midair; I couldn't tell if it was because he knew what I'd intended or simply to accentuate his point. "The gift, Winifred, was that you were going to finally figure out who killed him."

It was probably a good thing Branson had a hold of me, as I might have sunk to the ground right there on the steps like some vapid damsel in distress in a black-and-white Hitchcock film. "What do you mean who killed my father? What other players would you get that would..." Then it clicked, my knees found their strength, and I understood. I still should have shoved him, still should have ripped the gun from his grip and ended everything right then, but instead, I stared into his flashing green eyes. "You said you didn't know who killed my dad."

"I didn't." He smiled, gentle certainty and pride. "But I do now. I know who killed Charles Page, and I was going to offer them to you on a silver platter."

"Who?" I didn't rip my wrists from his grip—if anything, I would have grabbed him. "Who killed Dad?"

Branson smiled, pleased, indulgent. Releasing one of my wrists, he moved his hand to my face, cupping my cheek. "See? A gift you want. A gift you've wanted for a long, long time." His fingers tightened under the bone of my jaw. "A gift Ethel ruined."

"Branson!" I jerked my jaw free, glaring at him. "Who killed Dad?" As the question faded again, so did delusion. I knew who killed my father, in general —the Irons family—and Branson didn't know more than that. Even if he did, this was all a game... a fact that was on full display all around us.

Watson's barks echoed from the powder room. I wasn't sure if they'd increased or gotten lost as I sank into Branson's trap.

"No." Branson's smile continued, and he didn't try to recapture my face, even let go of my other hand. "Not now. It'll be a gift for another time, but one you'll still receive."

"The Irons family killed him, a bust gone wrong." And just like that, I allowed myself to be tripped up again, pulled back in, as he knew I would be. But I didn't have to stay there. "It doesn't matter. Dad is gone, and so is the Irons family. And at some point, you will be too."

He skipped right over that last part. "But those responsible for him *specifically*? Not gone, not imprisoned, not dead."

Fearing my knees would weaken once more, I grabbed the stair rail lest I reach for him. I didn't ask again, but I didn't fight against it either.

"They're out living their lives. This whole time, just living their life while your dad is gone. While you and your mom grieved, while the world kept turning without Charles Page. *They* were eating, drinking, and laughing that they got away with it."

"They... in singular sense..." I tried to ignore, I truly did. "Or... two people? More? And what do you mean *they* were there that night? They pulled the trigger? Or they set him up, and they were why the operation went bad?"

He held my gaze, those green eyes glittering in the light of the chandelier, and then captured my hand once more, hurrying around me and up the steps, almost like a child. "Come on. Let me explain what these rooms would have been. What I was creating for you."

I was swept along the rest of the staircase until we were nearly to the top, and I regained my senses when—real or imagined—Dad's voice whispered in my ear, reminded me who I was. That I was a detective's daughter. *His* daughter. That I was more than that, actually. That I was Winifred Page.

Gripping Branson's hand as tightly as he did mine, I spun on the steps, twisting with all my might. Even if I lost my balance and fell, I'd take him with me.

He'd had one foot lifted, ready to step on the landing, and the force of my spin yanked his other foot off the last step. Branson swung out to the left, feet scrambling and tripping on the steps, his body crashing into the banister. I released my grip at just the right moment, and the momentum threw him over... almost. He managed to grasp the wooden railing and use the force to his advantage, pushing off with such strength, multiple snaps of wood sounded in the silence, though nothing broke. He flung himself backwards. His body crashed into mine, smashing me against the wall. We were momentarily pinned and then he stumbled, his feet slipping on the steps as he tried to right himself.

I pushed as his feet scrambled, and he tumbled backward.

Even in that moment of tangled limbs and stairs and chaos, Branson proved ever lithe and graceful. Shooting out a hand, he managed to grasp another of the spindles—more snapping of wood, but still it didn't break—and stopped his fall. He grunted at the jolt but didn't yell, didn't curse my name, but looked up at me, those green eyes flashing once more— enjoyment, thrill, like I'd given *him* a gift instead of the other way around.

I shot out my foot, kicking him just under his right collarbone with my boot, shoving backward. Even with that, he didn't fall—retaining his grip on that spindle and spinning the opposite way so his back crashed into the railing that time. He was in no danger of tumbling to the floor below, and there was no way for me to get past him, not without Branson grabbing my legs, tripping me, sending me headfirst down the long flight of steps. So, I spun and ran up the last several steps as my mind whirled—where to hide, where to run? Had I seen a weapon, *anything* I could use, when I'd returned the day before with Campbell? Then it hit me—the passage from Ethel's bedroom to the kitchen. Another tunnel. One I didn't even know if I could fit through.

It didn't matter. All those thoughts flashed in the span of two steps, and as I reached the landing, Branson's hand gripped around the ankle of my boot and I fell, crashing hard against the wood landing. From below, Watson's barking and howls went wild, the scratching of his nails on the pocket door adding a frantic beat to Branson's and my heavy breathing.

I kicked with my other foot, the heel of my boot making contact with his forearm and got myself free, scrambled to a standing position before I heard the click of the gun.

There was a small debate—try to run, throw myself down the steps again.

Neither, obviously. This chance was over. Perhaps there would be another one.

With his free hand, Branson smoothed out his clothes, then raked his fingers through his hair as he joined me on the landing. I prepared myself for a slap, possibly to get hit with the pistol, but he didn't look angry, only pleased. Proud. I misinterpreted that expression for a second, thinking he was proud he'd thwarted my escape, but then I realized it was pride *for me*. He was proud of me for my attempt, for my fight.

Everything in me revolted against him.

He issued a long, satisfied sigh and came to a stop less than a foot away. "Don't do that again." He gave a wince of a smile and somehow managed to infuse his threat with the lace of apology. "I told you I didn't want to hurt Watson; that doesn't mean I won't. I've had to give that warning on multiple occasions at this point. It's growing tiresome."

For the first time, I felt tears threaten, but I held them back and changed my perspective. I would not be looking for another chance. I'd hope Leo got home earlier than expected, that he and the cavalry would ride in at any moment. But if not, probably not, then I just needed to live through this. Branson didn't want to kill me now, his game wasn't done. "What's the..." When my voice shook, I took a breath and tried it again, though I couldn't bring myself to smile or even sound interested, my words were steady on the second attempt. "You said the rooms up here were going to be about books, right?"

He studied me, then apparently decided I'd come around to his way of thinking. "Yes. With you in mind. Where would you like to start?" He gestured toward a doorway. "In the first guest room, I would have had Agatha Christie's *Murder on the Orient Express*." Then through another hallway. "Down there, in what Ethel had fashioned as a sort of solarium—" He rolled his eyes. "—Daphne du Maurier's *Rebecca*. I know you love that one." He paused again, maybe waiting to see if I had snatched one of those up, then turned toward Ethel's bedroom. "And here, Sherlock Holmes, of course. I was still debating between *The Hound of the Baskervilles* or *A Study in Scarlet*."

"Sherlock Holmes."

He nodded and showed further approval at my sudden answer. "Of course. Was there really any other choice?"

Like I cared about the themes. Maybe I'd been wrong, maybe there would be another chance. I could grab his gun, go down the secret steps and... I let that go as we walked into the bedroom. It was a stupid fantasy. One that would fail, one that would hurt Watson.

So, what to do instead? There were only two options—try to make this last longer so there was a chance the police would arrive or try to give him the adoration he craved so he would end this portion of the game early.

I wanted to do the second, so badly, but that only

guaranteed another time, another round of this sick game of his. Whereas with the other... chance, even if it was the smallest possible, this might finally end.

"*A Study in Scarlet.*" I moved further into the bedroom—which was exactly as it had been the day before, though part of me had almost expected Branson to have made some changes. "Where Sherlock and Watson made their entrance. And... taken literally, deep red would be beautiful in here, especially combined with the richness of the colors and textures you were using below for the Clue game."

Branson had followed me in and perched his hip on the mattress, resting his back on one of the thick columns of the bed. He held the gun loosely, almost resting it against his leg as he studied me through narrowed eyes.

I paused, unable to read his expression. "Although, I suppose with the other book, a dog theme would be nice. It could—"

"Ah." He laughed. "Killing time. Talking about décor, that's not you. What do you expect, Fred? That Leo will ride his white horse up the steps if you just keep me talking?" He clucked his tongue. "That was a weak attempt, and pointless beside. I *know* what I'm doing. And yes, time is growing short, but there's still a little left."

He was right, definitely not my best attempt. Was there another to make? And then I realized there was, though, it required giving in to him, giving in to my own delusions. "Who were the other players going to be? Does whoever is responsible for Dad's death resemble one of the Clue characters? A vixen like Scarlet? A maid like White, corrupt preacher like Green? Of course, not literal, but..."

"They do." That pride was back as if he'd crafted my personality, my brain, my intelligence, my cunning. Like he was responsible for who I was. "And no, not literally, of course. But yes." He snarled suddenly. "*Not* like what Ethel did. Ridiculous. I don't even know why she bothered using the name tags. Complete waste."

"Who was I going to be?" I moved closer still. I wasn't planning on drawing near enough to steal the gun and shoot him, but I wasn't going to discount it, either. Watson's ever-increasing barking only seemed to urge me onward. "Was I going to be Peacock like Ethel chose for me?"

Confusion flickered. "Weren't you listening? *You* weren't one of the characters. This was a Clue game *for* you." He shook his head in disappointment. "You would have determined which of the characters it was in the envelope, discovered who killed your father, you would be the one rolling the dice, so to speak."

He was wrong on that, which surprised me. The players in the board game *were* the characters. You chose your colored marker that corresponded with one of the suspects. Only you didn't know if the chosen character—and by default if *you*—was responsible for the murder or not. I almost pointed that out, then feared his temper going a different direction if he realized he'd done all that work on a faulty premise. "And up here?" I gestured around the bedroom, out the doorway. "What was supposed to happen up here with the books? Another mystery revealed, or would it still be about my..." Emotion swept over me, unexpected, and I had to push it down. "About my dad?"

"No, not part of the game." He patted the spot beside him on the bed. "Just an experience for you. Getting to live out your favorite novels."

I couldn't make myself cross to him, sit beside him. "Is that why you were overseas? Getting things to fill these rooms? Were you in England, buying things from London that would match Sherlock Holmes?"

"No, not London." He surprised me by answering. "I was gathering one of the players, actually, or at least would have. Ethel pulling this little stunt caused me to come back earlier than expected."

"You were getting one of the *players*?" Despite myself, he'd captured me again, but it didn't require much of a leap to figure that out. "*Irene*. You were in Moscow, getting Irene." The last member of the Irons family—at least the last one not murdered or jailed.

"Yes. I'll give that one to you, Fred, but not confirming if she's the one responsible for... Mr. Boddy." That time the pride in his smile didn't seem self-congratulatory, but all about me. "Even so, I fear once all the players were assembled, you might have figured it out too quickly. All this work would have been for nothing. Perhaps Ethel did me a favor after all."

All this work. Talk about an understatement. He'd gone to Russia to capture someone for this big reveal, some game. "Why me, Branson?" That question was real too, not a bit about killing time even if I tried to claim otherwise. "What makes you do all this because of me... for me?"

He patted the bed again.

I obliged, not even aware I'd moved. "You're free from the Irons family. You're not subservient to them any longer. *You're* the one making the rules. Why are you making your entire life about me?"

He'd opened his mouth as if getting ready to respond, then flinched at my question. Blinking rapidly, insult filled his voice. "My entire life is not about you, Fred."

I laughed, I couldn't help it, didn't try to hold it back and gestured around the room. "You commandeered a woman's home and are creating a Clue game. You've sent people from my past to torment me and—"

"You think that's *all* I'm capable of?" He stood, gun lifting, upper lip snarling. "You think I'm that weak, so inept that this is the only thing I can do? That I'm going around the globe only for *you*? That every waking moment is spent daydreaming about *you*? That I can't walk and chew gum at the same time?"

A different fear settled over me than I'd experienced all night, maybe ever in his presence. "I'm... sorry."

"In case you didn't catch it, I wasn't exactly sitting around staring at the screen waiting to see you walk into this mansion. I didn't get some alert that you'd arrived." The gun was trembling now, though it wasn't pointed at me. He moved closer, spittle flicking against my cheeks as he spoke. "I am building my life, my empire. You are nothing more than one tiny aspect. I am not *obsessed* with you, and you are *not* my equal, however much you want to pretend, and no matter that you are closer than anyone I've met. Do you think me some villain and you my great nemesis who'll take me down one day? You are not. You. Are. Not."

He held my gaze, fire blazing in those green depths. Finally, I nodded. It was all I could manage.

Apparently, it was the right move, as after a second longer, he let out a breath, straightened, and took a step back. "I'm sorry I've given you that impression." He took another step back, shaking his head. "Actually, I can see why you would think that. I've indulged you. Well... that ends now. You'll see exactly where you land and the importance of—" His eyes flashed behind me.

For a second, I didn't realize why, and then I heard it—a whispering creak of old hinges.

Even as he blinked again in confusion, he took another step back, lifted the gun, aimed over my shoulder.

The secret passage. Someone had crept up from the kitchen.

Another creak.

Just as I was getting ready to launch myself off the bed, barrel into Branson's stomach, he fired, the sound deafening in my ears, the rush of the bullet ruffling my hair as it passed.

Then a second shot, not as loud.

Branson spun, gun swooping in another direction. It wasn't until the arc of blood fanned out behind him that I realized he'd been shot. The motion sent him careening into the bedpost, hitting the shoulder where blood seeped from his shirt just above his chest. Even a bullet didn't slow Branson's reflexes; he raised the gun again, aimed to the bedroom door.

I finished the motion I'd started a second ago, launching myself off the mattress, crashing into him. As I made contact, Branson fired his gun again.

At the impact, we both fell from the bed, landing on our sides, Branson grunted, and as his wounded right shoulder hit hard against the floor, the gun skidded from his fingers.

I'd seen this movie, read this book, too many times. The woman rushes after the gun, crawling, and the man gets up, stands over her. I'd hit the ground just as hard as Branson, but I hadn't been shot, I hadn't been wounded, and even if I had, the adrenaline pounded so hard I didn't feel a thing. Instead of lurching toward the gun spinning off toward the bathroom door, I fulfilled the promise I'd made on the steps, and with every ounce of force I had thrust out the heel of my palm, smashing upward against his nose.

A loud crack, another gush of blood, and he screamed.

One hand reached to cover his face, as if to stop

the blood or assess damage, and his other shot out toward my neck.

I shoved his hand aside, bringing my knee up in our laying position, not caring where it made impact. It did, judging from his grunt, but I didn't get to inspect where as a black shoe came down on Branson's shoulder right above the bullet wound and pressed him to the ground.

Another gun came into view, only a foot or two above Branson's head. "Goodness, Wexler. That's gonna leave a mark." Susan didn't pull her foot away. "I think Fred here made it where you're not going to be the pretty boy anymore." She didn't look at me as she spoke, kept all her attention on Branson. "Fred, are you all right? Can you move? If so, please get out of his reach, for crying out loud."

I scrabbled then, no grace, no finesse. Just a tangle of broomstick skirt, boots, hands, hair, and blood over hardwood floor. As soon as my feet found purchase, however, I rushed the couple of yards to where the gun had stopped spinning just inside the bathroom door and snatched it up.

"Don't shoot him." Susan still didn't look at me. "I mean, if he tries to even get a foot off the ground, sure. But no revenge. Not with me in the room."

I aimed the gun at Branson, but there was no temptation to pull the trigger.

"Fred?" Susan still wasn't looking at me, keeping all her attention on Branson. "You good?"

"I'm good." My voice was barely audible over my panting, but I sucked in a breath and tried again. "Not hurt, not going to shoot."

Branson had let out that one scream, but now as he lay on his back cringing as Susan pressed her weight into the bullet wound, he simply kept one hand covering his smashed nose and glared. Not at me, but at Susan.

She smiled down at him. "You know, I've pictured this day for quite a while. Even planned something witty to say... but you're not worth it."

Branson didn't curse, didn't taunt, only glared.

"Cabot? You're not shot, are you?" A little worry entered Susan's voice at that, though she kept her gaze and gun trained on Branson.

"Nope. Right over my head." Campbell had emerged from the secret passage from Mason's domain to Ethel's. He was already walking our way, gun pointed at Branson with one hand as he pulled cuffs free with his other. "Kept low while I pushed open the door."

"You might have cookie dough for brains, but you're no idiot." Susan paused and spared the briefest of glances my way, though it didn't linger even long enough for her to get out her question. "Fred, you wanna keep holding this piece of trash at gunpoint, being my second, while Cabot cuffs him, or would you like to do the honors?"

It wasn't even a temptation. "No, I'll stay right here, be your backup. If I never touch him again, it'll be too soon."

And with that proclamation, Branson finally looked away from Detective Green, twisting ever so slightly to meet my gaze—and in those green depths I saw hurt and pain harden into hate. Even with three guns pointed at him, he still managed to make my blood run colder than it ever had before.

He didn't put up a struggle as Campbell slipped the cuffs onto his wrists, just brought his hands back up to cover his face and remained lying on his back as Susan commanded. "You're staying right there until the other officers get up here. I don't care if you've got a broken nose, a worthless shoulder, and are cuffed—there won't be any shenanigans. Just in case you think there's some way you're going to slip out from our grasp again, you won't."

Even as she spoke, Officer Jackson and Officer Lin entered from the bedroom door, each with their weapons drawn. From somewhere below, more footsteps sounded barely audible above Watson's frantic barking and howling.

"How did you know?"

Susan took a step back, finally releasing her foot off Branson's shoulder, and looked at me. "Leo. Apparently, Wexler here made a fatal flaw and messed with the tram on Chipmunk Mountain, probably trying to buy time by keeping Leo stranded. At least we're assuming that's why it didn't work. Considering all the repairs that happened recently, that thing should be smooth sailing for years. Typically, I'd say it was a little enmeshed and paranoid that Leo's first thought was to call you in a panic. But he was right. When you didn't answer your cell, he called me, and..." She glanced back at Branson and rolled her eyes. "No mystery there. Where else would he have taken you tonight? I mean really, Wexler. If you're gonna be a villain, at least be creative."

I almost laughed, genuinely, at Susan faulting Branson for his creativity in the middle of the house he was designing to be a Clue game.

She glanced back to me. "From the sound of things, I think Officer Fleabag is in need of some assurance that his mama is okay."

"Yes." With that, I lowered the gun and didn't look at Branson, but as I started to rush past Susan, blood trailing down her right arm pulled me up short. Reaching out a shaky hand, I placed it beside her shoulder. "You're shot."

"Grazed. Don't be dramatic." She gave another eye roll. "Almost missed me entirely." Her pale blue eyes met mine again, held my gaze, and she smiled. "Thanks to you."

The moment passed. She returned her attention to Branson and started giving orders to the other officers. I continued on my way, passing my gun to Officer Jackson before I left the bedroom.

I rushed down the steps and released Watson from his little prison. He pawed me frantically, all over my shoulders, barking and nipping and licking, smelling, whimpers going high-pitched as he sniffed the blood on my clothes. That only lasted a second before he seemed to realize it wasn't mine and calmed.

Deciding I didn't want to see Branson come down the steps or being led away, and didn't want to give him the opportunity to see me, I swept Watson into my arms, stepped back into the little half bathroom, pulled the pocket door closed, and sat on the floor with Watson Charles in my lap. I wrapped my arms around him, and the two of us just stayed there safe and secure until it was over.

Two days later, Reverend Green, Miss Scarlet, Professor Plum, Mrs. White, Colonel Mustard, and Mrs. Peacock gathered around a long table in one of the conference rooms of the police station. Not resembling Ethel Beaker at all as she'd stared at each of us with disdain in her dining room, Detective Susan Green looked at each of us in turn—Anna, Delilah, Carla, Mary, Vivian, and myself. She'd already filled us in on Branson's whereabouts. He'd been transferred to a high security prison, waiting, without bond, for trial. We were safe; it was done. Although... really, for the players of that particular game, it had been over the second Ethel and Mason had died, even if it hadn't felt like it.

"The question is, would you like to see it?" Susan gestured toward a large projector screen on the wall behind her. Watson shuffled at her feet to get out of her way, while continuing to stare up at her, a trail of jerky-beseeching drool threatening Susan's slick shoes. "It's up to you. We have the files that show every single minute of that night, every room each of you entered. All of it, even after we showed up. Everything until the following day when we jammed all frequencies cutting off Branson's access."

Susan had informed me the day before that even though Branson had refused to say anything, not even a single word, they had still uncovered a treasure trove of evidence from him—both for this situation and a few other unrelated events. It was certainly not a fraction of what existed out in the world, and definitely small potatoes compared to whatever larger things he'd hidden away behind firewalls, passcodes, and whatever labyrinths he'd created. However, the recorded feed from Ethel's mansion had been delivered to his laptop which had been in his car he'd left parked in the woods about a mile from my cabin.

"In there, obviously, is included the recording of what transpired between Ethel and her butler. You all lived it, so now that we've finished our debrief, it only seems right you have the option to witness as much as you may need to come to grips with what you've experienced." Susan held my gaze for a moment before including the others once more. "You can watch it as a group, on an individual basis, in any combination you'd like. And you can also pick and choose what you'd like to see."

The six of us didn't answer, only looked at one another, questioningly. Or, at least some of us did. Mary glared straight ahead, not looking at anyone, and Vivian kept her gaze in her lap.

I was about to speak when Mary surprised us all. "I don't want to see what we experienced, I was there. But I, for one, want to witness the scene in the library. I want to see Ethel get what she deserved for what she put me through."

"Fine, we can do that." Susan gave a nod and then a quick glance around the table. "Is that what the rest of you want as well?"

"Isn't this going to hurt the case against Branson?" I couldn't help myself. I didn't want there to be a crack anywhere. Branson had confirmed his plans were bigger than me, than the Clue game. Whatever empire he was building needed to be demolished. "Surely showing us this will hurt its viability as evidence, or—"

Susan cut me off, her tone hard. "I don't care. Although, I do think this is well within the realm of legal and appropriate, considering. Ultimately, this doesn't matter, not against Branson. There's plenty of other evidence both for this night and many other things so far. Nor for Dunmore. He's already admitted to it all, he's not going to fight against anything. Branson's behind bars and will stay that way, regardless if you see the recordings or not. You all lived with the trauma; *you all* are what matters."

Well... I couldn't argue with that. Trauma—the word didn't quite capture it. I wasn't sure how close things had come the night before, but I couldn't accept Branson was simply going to taunt promises about my father's murderer and then just pat me on the head before disappearing once more into the night. That look in his eyes... the hate... That might've shown up even if Susan and Campbell hadn't been present.

"I don't." Carla's voice was barely a whisper, a tenor I wasn't used to hearing from her. "I'm sorry. That doesn't mean no one else can, but I... I don't want to see." Her voice grew stronger. She lifted her chin, straightened her shoulders, and flipped back the edges of her straight blond bob out of her face. "I hate my mother-in-law, have for a long time and with very good reason, even more now. But I don't need to see her death, nor do I want that image in my mind. I will just be thankful that she is no longer in my life, and be thankful that, despite her best efforts to be cruel, her actions have ended up helping my son."

"I don't want to see it either." Vivian's tremulous whimper was right on brand, and she still didn't look up.

"Neither do I." The way Delilah said it sounded as if she was adding solidarity to Carla.

Beside her, Anna shook her head as well, though I got the sense she probably would have leaped at the chance if it had been the group consensus.

"Nor do I." Though curious and not all that squeamish—but like Carla, I didn't want that image in my mind. There were enough flashbacks from that night without adding another one. **"**However, is it what we thought?"

"It is." Susan nodded, then raised her eyebrows as she inspected the table waiting for that objection. When none came, she continued. "As with everything, Branson spared no expense, so the image was crystal clear, and the sound was as well. So, we saw and heard it all, like a reality TV show—from your search for escape through the mansion, to what unfolded between Ethel and Mason. As they entered the library and headed toward that trapdoor in the bookcase, Mason pulled out the top page of Maverick's genetic testing." She cast Carla a tight smile but didn't pause. "Apparently, he found it in the paper-work as he packed their luggage that day. We don't know precisely when, if it was hours before the game began or moments before he left to pick up Vivian and felt the ball was already in motion. We can't find that moment on film, but I bet we will. We suspect —" She glanced toward me. "—that if he had any remaining reservations around it, the conversation between Ethel and Carla at the table about Ethel not caring if Maverick was of Beaker blood or not was the final straw, or the final clue, where Mason was concerned. Either way, he confronted her with it, pointed out the clear genetic line shared with his family, not Eustace Beaker's."

Watson's growing impatience flared, and he reared up and pounded Susan's knee with his forepaws.

Proving how caught up in the moment she was, Susan neither redirected nor murdered him, but simply patted Watson's head and continued. "Ethel confessed, told him that Jonathan was his son, but she'd kept it from him the whole time. She tried to brush it off, tell him they needed to keep going, but he grabbed her, pleaded. She took the paper out of his hand, folded it, and put it in her pocket. Told him that, yes, Jonathan was his, *but* pointed out it was only because of her that his son had a lavish life, and that Mason himself had a lavish life, because of the sacrifices *she* had made. Then she demanded they get on with it. As she turned and headed toward the bookcase, he grabbed the candlestick and gave one mighty swing to the side of her head. She fell, the gun flying across the room. From the looks of it, she was dead moments after she hit the floor."

Watson whimpered again, pulling Susan's attention down to where her hand was still stroking him.

She flinched, yanked her hand away, and glared at it as if it had just betrayed her, and then snarled to Watson, "Sit, Fleabag."

He sat but his whimper didn't cease.

"And the butler?" Proving she was more curious than she'd let on, Anna prompted, leaning forward slightly.

"Mason fell to his knees the second Ethel didn't get up, instantly sobbing." Disgust filled Susan's voice. "He ran out of the library and into the study where they'd apparently arranged that silver rope, hurried back into the library, relocked the doors, and... well... you saw. Hung himself. He was dead around the time you all discovered the tunnels."

We all sat in silence, maybe stunned, maybe reliving it.

"I'd still like to see." Mary didn't sound the least bit embarrassed by her request. "Alone. And if you've got one of Dunmore hanging himself in the cell, I'd like to watch that too."

Susan flinched as if a little shocked, which was a rare state for Detective Green. It took her a second to speak, and when she did, her tone was cold, emotionless. "Marlon Dunmore will face legal and appropriate consequences. *None* of which will be the death penalty." Before Mary could retort, Susan refocused on the rest of the group. "Anyone else?"

A few minutes later, the rest of us, save for Professor Plum—Mary Smith—gathered outside the police station. The snow had stopped the day before, and spring had sprung as the day had dawned. A warm breeze combined with the fluffy white clouds and soft light overhead; a few birds chirped. Across the street at Bond Park, a small herd of elk grazed on the grass. Watson strained at the end of his leash, sniffing in their direction.

What were we to say? How were we to part after this? It felt wrong to somehow simply go back to our shops and our lives.

Apparently, Delilah felt the same. "Anyone wanna grab lunch?"

"Yes!" Anna and I spoke at the same time, then shared a chuckle and a smile with each other.

"No. Um... thank you." Vivian cast a glance toward me, a very clear inquiry.

"Vivian." Delilah reached out a hand and gently touched the older woman's shoulder. "You won't find judgment from us."

Vivian's questioning glance became narrow-eyed accusal. She turned and walked away, patting her shoe-polish-black beehive as she headed toward her car.

We only watched her go for a moment, then Carla spoke up. "I'd like to. If that's okay."

"It will always be okay." Perhaps it was sappy, but I meant it.

From Carla's gentle smile, it appeared she appreciated the sentiment. "However, I'd like to get Maverick. I didn't want him to hear any of this, not that he's going to miss Ethel, she was grandmother in name only, but still. I'll pick him up from Donna's if you're okay with having a three-year-old at our—"

"Invite Donna, too." Delilah didn't hesitate. "She kept your baby safe when we weren't sure if we would get out. Donna has a seat at our table." She flashed a smile toward me. "Always."

It seemed sappy was what we were all going with.

"Okay, thanks." Carla nodded, headed toward her car, then paused. "Oh, where?"

There was a silent debate, then I filled in the void. "How about Habanero's? They let Watson eat inside."

"Yes." Delilah clasped her hands. "Queso and margaritas, yes, yes, yes."

I laughed, thought it was a pretty great combination myself, then had a horrible thought. "Oh no, I wasn't thinking. Marcus... he'll want the whole story. Probably take pictures of us to put on the wall."

Carla cringed.

"Oh—" Anna waved that away. "—so what? Let's let him, it'll make his day." She preened. "Plus, while he might not be as good of a scrapbooker as me, Marcus Gonzales is no schlump. Give him a week and our whole experience will be documented in cardstock, glitter, and stickers."

"The last thing I want to see is a scrapbook of that night." Carla looked horrified. "What is *wrong* with you people?" She headed back toward her car.

Delilah and I exchanged a glance, but it was Delilah who called out, "Are you still coming?"

"Well, *yeah*." Carla didn't turn around, just made a very Ethel Beaker-like commanding motion as she raised her hand in the air, and spoke over her shoulder. "And make mine a strawberry margarita, with lime salt on the rim."

THIRTY

The growing sunset deepened the pink hue over the giant copper apple gleaming at the top of an ostentatious granite pillar. One thing was certain, Colin Apple had never been subtle. The other headstones surrounding Colin's plot were a fifth of the size, and not a solitary one held the surname of Apple. Colin had been buried alone in one of the prettier spots at the graveyard. It would have been sad and rather lonely if not for the recent addition under his engraved name and years of life—which, considering he'd only passed a couple of months before was recent as well.

Granny Smith

The old cat's name didn't have birth or death dates, but below it an apple had been carved, with the inset of a paw print in its middle.

"Is that Granny Smith's actual paw print? Or a

generic stock option?" Leo leaned over the grave, running a finger across the apple.

"This is *Colin Apple* we're talking about." The mayor smirked. "Did he have anything that was a stock or generic option?"

"And he loved that cat." Dr. Sallee smiled at the headstone fondly. "Which he should. He had Granny Smith for the last eighteen years of his life. I dare say she was the closest relationship he'd ever had."

Again, that should have felt sad, but it didn't. She'd been the one creature in Colin's life who hadn't used him in one way or another for money. Okay... that *was* a little bit sad; however, Colin hadn't gone out of his way to try for anything different, as evidenced by the glistening apple atop the mausoleum-quality headstone.

"Well..." I sighed and kneeled on one knee, patting Watson, who was sniffing at a purple crocus at the edge of the grave. "We couldn't have asked for a prettier evening for her memorial. A gorgeous sunset, warm breeze, fresh flowers springing up all over the place."

"Yes, Granny Smith would have been miserable." Dr. Sallee chuckled again. "And *that*, she would have greatly enjoyed."

Only the four of us and Watson clustered grave-side to remember Granny Smith—even that seemed appropriate. The only one who really mattered in her life was gone, and she wouldn't have given a snit about anyone else remembering her or not. However, that wasn't true. Though the bond was unexpected and unexplained, one other soul had worked its way into her hissing and snarling heart.

Watson studied the vet with suspicion as Dr. Sallee opened the small plastic bag and sprinkled the little remains of ash and bone over Colin's grave like a blanket.

"You lived a long, regal life, Granny Smith." Dr. Sallee tucked the empty plastic bag into his pocket as he spoke. "Now that you've joined your master on the other side of the Rainbow Bridge, I hope you enjoy plenty of sunshine naps interrupted by rain clouds, have endless opportunities to snarl at all the other felines in pet heaven, and when you think of it, send a little rumble of thunder our way to let us know you care."

"Ah..." The mayor leaned into her husband, rubbing his arm. "She would have hated that."

"Thank you, my dear." He patted her hand. "I do what I can."

Watson moved past the purple flowers and onto

Colin's grave, sniffing at the ashes. He gave no sign of recognition, and after a moment, even his interest evaporated. He looked up to Leo and gave a whine.

"I think someone is ready for naptime or dinner." Leo bent and ruffled Watson's fur, his hand grazing mine with the motion.

"I almost forgot." Dr. Sallee's voice shot up as he addressed his wife. "Do you mind?"

"Oh, I did too." Jennifer cast a glance toward Watson, then opened her purse and pulled out a dirty oversized cream-colored sponge covered with lint and handed it to her husband.

Dr. Sallee took it, then offered the thing a little smile before looking up at Leo and me. "This was Granny Smith's favorite toy, she brought it with her to every fluid injection at the end. I'd originally planned on just leaving it on the grave, but I actually think she would have preferred something else." He kneeled and held it out toward Watson.

Even on closer inspection, it took me a moment to realize it wasn't a sponge but a stuffed animal—a cat, not identical, but a similar color to Granny Smith, and just as patchy and tattered as she'd been over the short time we'd known her.

Watson stretched his head out cautiously, sniffing Dr. Sallee's offering like it might be medicine or a ploy to administer a vaccination. The moment of recognition was evident, and all of us let out a group sigh when Watson's whole body trembled. He snatched the little cat out of Dr. Sallee's hand, plopped it on the ground next to the flowers and then lay down, resting his head over the little stuffed animal like a pillow.

"Ah... he knows. He can smell her." Jennifer clutched at her heart as if the scene was nearly too much to handle.

Dr. Sallee simply smiled and nodded. "Of course he does. He was Granny Smith's protector and comforter."

Watson didn't release the stuffed animal all the way home. He carried it from graveside to the car, then from the car into the house. I had a feeling I knew what he would do, but even so, Leo and I stood just inside the doorway, arms around each other, and watched.

Watson trotted over to his little tub of random toys and stuffed animals, all of which he rarely used. He gave a grunt, then waddled away, disappearing into the bedroom.

Leo and I followed, hand in hand. We arrived

just in time to see him approach his bed and place the tattered little cat next to the stuffed lion and duck —his two favorites that he carried back and forth between bed and hearth, depending on where he wanted to nap.

He took a few steps backward, inspecting. Then with a chuff, Watson returned to his bed, stepped in, gave a couple of obligatory spins, and then settled down with his lion, duck, and Granny Smith.

DASTARDLY DUCKS

SPRING 2023

Pre-Order Book 29

TWISTER SISTERS MYSTERIES

Twister Sisters Mysteries

Katie's Earl Grey Rolls Recipe provided by:

CLOUDY KITCHEN

Never miss a scrumptious recipe:
CloudyKitchen.com

Follow Cloudy Kitchen's creations
on social media:

Cloudy Kitchen Facebook
Cloudy Kitchen Instagram

KATIE'S EARL GREY ROLLS RECIPE

DESCRIPTION

Earl Grey Buns with Dark Chocolate and Cocoa Nib Filling. Fluffy brioche dough is filled with an earl grey dark chocolate custard, and a crunchy cacao nib filling, then rolled up and sliced into buns. Once baked, the rolls are brushed with butter and rolled in a cocoa nib earl grey sugar. These are a must for tea lovers!

INGREDIENTS

Brioche Dough

3g (1 tsp) active dried yeast
42g (3 Tbsp) Sugar

110g (½ cup) warm water

1 large egg

110g (½ cup) heavy cream

1 tsp vanilla bean paste

385g (2 ¾ cups) all-purpose flour

½ tsp salt

5g loose leaf earl grey tea, finely ground

3 Tbsp Unsalted butter, melted

Chocolate Earl Grey Custard

220g whole milk

10g loose leaf earl grey tea

115g chopped 70% chocolate

1 large egg

50g sugar

1 tsp vanilla bean paste

pinch of salt

Cocoa Nib Filling

110g (½ cup) light brown sugar

60g (½ cup) cocoa nibs

Earl Grey Sugar

200g Sugar

30g (¼ cup) cocoa nibs

pinch of salt

5g loose leaf tea

INSTRUCTIONS

BREAD DOUGH

1 Place the yeast, sugar, and warm water in a medium sized bowl, and stir to combine. Leave for 10-15 minutes, or until foamy.

2 In a small bowl, whisk together the egg, cream, and vanilla bean paste.

3 Place the flour, salt, and earl grey tea in a stand mixer fitted with the dough hook attachment. Add the yeast and water mixture, the cream and egg mixture, and the melted butter, and mix on low until the dough comes together.

4 Increase the mixer speed and mix on medium for 8-10 minutes, until the dough is smooth and pulling away from the edges of the bowl.

5 Remove the dough from the bowl, shape into a ball, and then lightly grease either the mixing bowl, or a large bowl, and place the ball of dough in it. Cover the bowl with plastic wrap and leave to rise overnight in the fridge.

CHOCOLATE EARL GREY CUSTARD

1 In a medium saucepan, heat the milk to just shy of a simmer. Add the loose leaf tea, cover, and steep for 20 minutes. Strain through a fine mesh strainer, pressing with a spoon to get as much flavour as possible from the tea. Clean the saucepan, then re-weigh the milk and top up to 150g if needed. Warm again to just shy of a simmer.

2 Melt the chocolate either in a double boiler, or in 30 second increments in the microwave. Set aside.. In a medium bowl, whisk together the egg, sugar, vanilla bean paste, and salt.

3 Add about half of the hot earl grey milk mixture to the egg mix, whisking constantly. Whisk until smooth, then return to the saucepan with the rest of the milk. Cook over medium heat, stirring constantly, until the mixture has thickened enough to coat the back of a spoon.

4 Remove the milk mixture from the heat and pour over the melted chocolate, whisking to combine, and finishing with an immersion blender if needed.

5 Place in an airtight container and press a piece of plastic wrap directly against the surface of the custard. Place in the fridge to chill overnight.

ASSEMBLY

1 Lightly grease a muffin pan with butter or non stick cooking spray. Combine the light brown sugar and cocoa nibs in a medium bowl. Turn the dough out onto a lightly floured surface, and roll into a rectangle 13"x18" (33x45cm).

2 Spread the cooled chocolate custard evenly over the surface of the custard using an offset spatula. Sprinkle with the sugar and cocoa nib mixture, and press down lightly to adhere.

3 Starting at a long end, roll the dough up into a tight spiral log. Cut into 2" pieces using a sharp knife. Place each piece into a cavity in the muffin pan.

4 Lightly cover the muffin pan with plastic wrap, and leave in a warm place to rise for 30 to 45 minutes. While the buns are rising, preheat the oven to 350°f / 180°c.

5 Once the buns are risen, bake for 20 to 25 minutes, rotating the pan once to ensure even browning.

6 While the buns are baking, place the cocoa nibs and loose leaf tea in a spice grinder or mortar and pestle. Sift through a strainer, and then combine the sifted mixture with the sugar and salt.

7 Remove the baked buns from the oven, and

allow to stand for 10 minutes, then remove from the muffin tin. Brush each all over with melted butter, then roll in the cocoa earl grey sugar.

8 Serve immediately. Store leftovers in an airtight container.

PATREON

Mildred Abbott's Patreon Page

Mildred Abbott is now on Patreon! By becoming a member, you gain access to exclusive Cozy Corgi merchandise, get a look behind the scenes of book creation, and receive real-life writing updates, plans, and puppy photos (becuase, of course there will be puppy photos!). You can also gain access to ebooks and recipes before publication, read future works *literally* as they are being written chapter by chapter, and can even choose to become a character in one of the novels!

Wether you choose to be a villager, busybody, police officer, super sleuth, or the fuzzy four-legged star of the show himself, please come check the

Mildred Abbott Patreon community and discover what fun awaits.

Personal Note: Being an indie writer means that some months bills are paid without much stress, while other months threaten the ability to continue the dream of writing. Becoming a member ensures that there will continue to be new Mildred Abbott books. Your support is unbelievably appreciated and invaluable.

*While there are many perks to becoming a patron, if you are a reader who can't afford to support (or simply don't feel led), rest assured you will *not* miss out on any writing. All books will continue to be published just as they always have been. None of the Mildred Abbott books will become exclusive to a select few. In fact, patrons help ensure that writing will continue to be published for everyone.

Mildred Abbott's Patreon Page

AUTHOR NOTE

Dear Reader:

Thank you so much for reading Salacious Socialites —this is one of the installments I've been dreaming of writing since book one, and I loved every second! If you enjoyed this love-letter-to-Clue mystery, I would greatly appreciate a review on Amazon and Goodreads—reviews make a huge difference in helping the Cozy Corgi series continue. Feel free to drop me a note on Facebook or on my website (MildredAbbott.com) whenever you'd like. I'd love to hear from you. If you're interested in receiving advanced reader copies of upcoming installments, please join Mildred Abbott's Cozy Mystery Club on

Facebook. You can also join the Mildred Abbott's Patreon Page, where you get early access to *everything*, help craft future Cozy Corgi characters, and help guide the new series.

I also wanted to mention the elephant in the room... or the over-sugared corgi, as it were. Watson's personality is based around one of my own corgis, Alastair. He was the sweetest little guy in the world, and like Watson, is a bit of a grump. Also, like Watson (and every other corgi to grace the world with their presence), he lived for food. In the Cozy Corgi series, I'm giving Alastair the life of his dreams through Watson. Just like I don't spend my weekends solving murders, neither did he spend his days snacking on scones and unending dog treats. But in the books? Well, we both get to live out our fantasies. If you are a corgi parent, you already know your little angel shouldn't truly have free rein of the pastry case, but you can read them snippets of Watson's life for a pleasant bedtime fantasy.

Much love, Mildred

PS: I'd also love it if you signed up for my newsletter. That way you'll never miss a new release. You won't hear from me more than once a month, nobody needs that many newsletters!

Newsletter link: Mildred Abbott Newsletter Signup

ACKNOWLEDGMENTS

A special thanks to Agatha Frost, who gave her blessing and her wisdom. If you haven't already, you simply MUST read Agatha's Peridale Cafe Cozy Mystery series. They are absolute perfection.

The biggest and most heartfelt gratitude to Katie Pizzolato and Donna Day, for their belief in my writing career and being the inspiration for the characters of the same name in this series. Thanks to you, Katie—our beloved baker—and Donna—our corig-catnip-pharmacist—have completely stolen both mine and Fred's heart!

Desi, I couldn't imagine an adventure without you by my side.

A.J. Corza, you have given me the corgi covers of my dreams.

A huge, huge thank you to all of the lovely souls who proofread the ARC versions and help me look somewhat literate (in completely random order): Melissa Brus, Bernadette Ould, Victoria Smiser,

Lucy Campbell, Laurie A. Fan, Polina Posner, Sue Paulsen, and Heather Dryer. Thank you all, so very, very much!

A further and special thanks to some of my dear readers and friends who support my passion on Patreon: Mike Martinez, Karin S. Kramer, Adrienne Singleton, Linda Brizendine, Melissa Brus, Jan Gillespie, Victoria Smiser, Heather Martin, Mary Liberty, Susan Wendt, Peggy Ryan-Wansley, Jaclyn Schrauger, Pamela Cummings, Lynn Morrison, Peggy Wansely, Nancy Smith, Ric Shaffran, Emily Lee, Debbie, Annette, Cathy Ramsey, Kel Kendall, Sylvia Rynerson, Connie Boyle, Debra Caldwell, Debra Schwendeman, Marianne Lawhead, Erin Kapp, Kathleen Niemi, Vanessa Hooper, Margie White, Kathleen Soncrant, Jane D Smith, Janie, Jenny Respress, Lee Sullivan, Pat L Hicks, Patricia Panagoulias, Eirlys Evans, Donna Day, Leslie B Mink, Kay Jones, Kathryn Stain, Lawren Kinsey, Karen Mesikapp, Marcia Jones, Mary Kirby, Gretchen, Amy Johannesen, Nancy Beeman, Carmen Taylor, Martha Bennett, Marypat Mulville Sampson, and Thessaly Angevine. You are helping to make sure there will continue to be new Mildred Abbott cozy mysteries. I've had so much fun planning Twister Sisters with you and getting your input on upcoming Cozy Corgi installments! I'm humbled and grateful beyond belief! So much love to you all! Thank you!!!

ALSO BY MILDRED ABBOTT

-the Cozy Corgi Cozy Mystery Series-

Cruel Candy

Traitorous Toys

Bickering Birds

Savage Sourdough

Scornful Scones

Chaotic Corgis

Quarrelsome Quartz

Wicked Wildlife

Malevolent Magic

Killer Keys

Perilous Pottery

Ghastly Gadgets

Meddlesome Money

Precarious Pasta

Evil Elves

Phony Photos

Despicable Desserts

Chattering Chipmunks

Vengeful Vellum

Wretched Wool

Jaded Jewels

Yowling Yetis

Lethal Lace

Pesky Puppies

Deceptive Designs

Antagonizing Antiques

Malicious Malts

Salacious Socialites

Dastardly Ducks-Early 2023

Stormy Stars-Spring 2023

(Books 1-10 are also available in audiobook format, read to
perfection by Angie Hickman.)

-the Twister Sisters Mystery Series-

Hippie Wagon Homicide

Casserole Casualty

Bandstand Bloodshed

-Cozy Corgi & Twister Sisters Merchandise-

now available at:

the Cozy Corgi store at Cafe Press

https://www.cafepress.com/mildredabbott

Made in the USA
Monee, IL
08 January 2023

24844235R00277